GUILTY – UNTIL PROVEN OTHERWISE

Guilty –
Until Proven Otherwise

GF Newman

A
Judge John Deed
Novel

ASHGROVE PUBLISHING
London

First published in Great Britain by:

Ashgrove Publishing

an imprint of:

Hollydata Publishers Ltd
21 Ewen House
London N1 0SH

© GF Newman, 2020

The right of GF Newman to be identified as the author of this work has been asserted by him in accordance with the Copyright, Designs and Patents Act 1988.

No part of this publication may be reproduced, stored in a retrieval system or transmitted, in any form or by any means, electronic, mechanical, photo-copying, recording or otherwise, without the prior permission of the publisher.

ISBN 978 185398 200 2

First Edition

Book design by Brad Thompson
Printed and bound in England

'I view with apprehension the attitude of judges who on a mere question of construction when face to face with claims involving the liberty of the subject show themselves more executive minded than the executive… In this country, amid the clash of arms, the laws are not silent. They may be changed, but they speak the same language in war as in peace.'

Lord Atkin, 1941

My thanks to:
DAVID ETHERINGTON QC,
without whom there would be less authenticity;
PROFESSOR GARY SLAPPER,
without whom there would be less accuracy;
LORD NEUBERGER, 1st President of the Supreme Court,
without whom there'd be less justice;
IAN BLOOM, my lawyer,
without whom there might've been no Judge John Deed;
REBECCA HUGHES HALL,
without whom there might be no GF Newman
and TOM HALL, for his diligent read.

PROLOGUE

WATCHING THE COUPLE FROM behind the two-way mirror on the front of the large built-in cupboard, arousal was fighting anger for a reason he couldn't fathom. Something was different today. No longer was this just an exciting watch as she made love to her casual pick-up; then suddenly it hit him and he tensed, trying not to shake and reveal his position. This man wasn't one of her pick-ups; she knew him and was enjoying their love-making. The realisation was shocking and sucked the air from his lungs as anger built to rage. He wanted to burst from the cupboard and throttle them both, but couldn't move. Never before had Mariana allowed this to happen.

It pained him listening to her laughter as her smooth, tanned flesh squelched on connecting with the young man's puny white body, all the while drawing him deeper into her. The blatant enjoyment she was displaying inflamed raw jealousy in him. Not a single murmur of protest did she utter as on previous occasions as if coerced; instead their urgent moaning confirmed their intimate familiarity. Blood was pounding in his ears like a noisy washing-machine as time seemed to stand still. Then he heard the urgency in Mariana's breathing and he knew what was about to happen.

Breath surged into his lungs, freeing him to slam open the cupboard.

'No, no. Don't do that…' was all he could say. In less threatening situations he had never been lost for words. The strange hypnotic spell Mariana Ortega cast caused him to accept the sort of behaviour from her that he wouldn't tolerate for a moment in anyone else.

Pushing her lover off, he saw how she slipped with ease into the role of the helpless, overpowered woman. He didn't need to hear the words in her quaint English. The 26-year-old was less than beautiful with her crooked nose and mouth too small for its crowd of teeth with their overbite, but her large, round eyes never failed to captivate him and just being near her caused his breath to quicken. The thought of another man possessing her was unbearable.

'Oh, you not do that me. You not do!' Mariana cried, springing away.

As if sensing the danger, the so-called pick-up jerked back in panic, reaching for something with which to defend himself. His hand seized an onyx Buddha on the night table and lashed out, screaming, 'Get away! Get away…'

The glancing blow catching him on the side of the head at once turned him from an enraged observer to a homicidal maniac, whose life was now being threatened. At 46 he kept fit using the rowing machine at the House of Commons' gym and believed he could handle himself if anyone got physical. Wrestling the statuette off this little squirm, he whacked him with it, then again. 'You weren't supposed to make love to him like that,' he shouted at his lover. 'Not like that –' swinging the Buddha once more with force.

'I not stop him, she too powerful.'

'You know him, you know him, you slimy little whore. You done him before,' he screamed, reverting to his working-class origins.

Seeing her stoop to the man on the floor, he wanted to hit her, too, and didn't at first register what she was saying, and then didn't believe what he heard.

'She dead! You killed him!'

'It's he's,' he corrected from habit before fear clawed at his intestines. 'Dead? Don't be stupid… He can't be. No…' his voice rising several octaves as he got on the floor and examined the man.

'Christ alive, he's not breathing,' was his idiotic response. 'I didn't mean… I didn't.' He fought tears that were at once pushing against his eyelids, knowing she would rip the piss out of him if he showed any weakness.

'You go to prison,' she was saying. 'Lose your position. They find out you employ no-legals for cleaning…'

'Illegals,' he shouted. 'How many times have I told you?'

'Legal no-legal, no care, you kill him…'

She showed so little emotion here he wondered if this man meant anything to her after all.

'Self-defence,' he heard himself saying. 'He attacked me. You saw him.' He repeated this several times as though she was the legal arbiter, then he began thinking about the possible awful consequences which would follow, his career in ruins, along with his marriage. He needed to act fast, but couldn't think beyond running.

Mariana was saying, 'They send me back Colombia.'

'What will we do?' – panic rising as he saw his job gone, his wife casting him out, him sinking into the social and political abyss. He would go to prison.

Concern for herself, as always, caused Mariana to offer a quick solution, which he found himself helpless to resist. Any action that avoided him being pulled off the ladder was worth a go, but losing his high position and the status that went with it was something he would risk rather than lose this woman. How utterly foolish was that…? something in his fogged brain was saying.

Wrapping the body in the duvet, he helped drag it through the flat.

In a semi-daze he drove his official car with Mariana directing him to Leith Hill in Surrey. It was 1.30 A.M. when with tense muscles and shaking hands, he heaved the duvet-wrapped body down the wooded escarpment off a narrow lane. No houses or other vehicles were in sight, and best of all, no CCTV cameras. He closed his eyes, not wanting to look as the bundle lodged against a sapling.

'She be seen,' Mariana said. 'Someone in morning see.'

Again he wanted to correct her ridiculous, idiosyncratic English while at the same time trying not to vomit; most of all he wanted to get back in the car and speed away.

'Let's go, please. Before anyone comes.'

Mariana pulled on his arm and then he felt that familiar electricity from her touch and bizarrely started to become aroused. 'Get duvet. They find. Trace to Rupert flat. You get.'

'I can't go back. I can't face seeing him again. Look, it's a bog-standard duvet from Peter Jones. No one will trace it. Please, Mariana, let's just go.'

'Buddha, she in duvet. They find. Trace fingerprints you,' she insisted.

Her iron nerve was admirable. She flinched at nothing, would stop at nothing to protect them. Not like his wife who would betray him in a blink in such circumstances; he had married her for her pedigree, not her loyalty. In his confusion he couldn't remember if his prints were on record but knew he must somehow go down the grassy bank and find the Buddha.

When she said, 'I get,' and disappeared into the darkness he felt relieved, then guilty that he wasn't up to the task.

As he waited for Mariana to return, tension made his wide neck rigid with pain. Trying to ease it, he bent forward against the steering wheel, staring the whole while at his large hands, wondering what was taking this woman so long, thinking maybe she'd run off and left him. There was only one way to guarantee her loyalty and silence, offer her something she couldn't resist. He peered into the darkness, seeing little through his thick glasses. Perfect conditions for such work: murky, damp and moonless, but the legacy of lockdown meant there were eyes everywhere attached to informers.

Without warning, the passenger door flew open. His heart jumped, imagining the police… Mariana shoved the blood-stained duvet in ahead of her.

'We get rid,' she said. 'We go now.'

'At last,' he sighed and started the car, but didn't engage the drive. 'Where's the Buddha?'

'I not find.'

'What d'you mean? You said we have to find it. They'll trace it.'

'I not find. We go.'

'What if they trace it to me?'

'How they do that? It at Rupert's flat. We go, or police come.'

He knew she meant the police could happen past. Without further argument he let the Jaguar XJF glide away, determined to put this night behind him. He loved this woman beyond distraction and knew what would bind her to him forever.

CHAPTER ONE

THE VICTORIAN GOTHIC STYLE OF the High Court building in The Strand was British architecture at its most imposing, but nothing about it comforted or reassured those attending there, whether litigants or lawyers. The great vaulted ceilings were intimidating, making those who came seeking justice feel humble and inadequate. Possibly this was the Victorians' intention, so that any who approached did so with seriousness of intent; now the high cost of actions in the High Court determined the seriousness of intent.

Having dealt with a case of a young black man who dared to come to this august institution and sue the police for damages, John Deed, a High Court Judge for the past three years, felt a great weight lift off him. On the bald facts alone he would have found for the claimant, the police having raided his grandmother's house in the early hours of the morning and shot first his dog and then him, leaving him with a permanent spine injury that confined him to a wheelchair. Deed knew the police wished to settle this case out of court, but the young man wanted public vindication, the charges of supplying drugs online having been dropped when a nearby neighbour was found to be piggy-backing on his wi-fi. The shame was that despite the defendent's success in court the case attracted little media interest. Perhaps the settlement he had approved equal to the *Set for Life* lottery of £10,000 a month but for life rather than 30 years would capture the attention of news editors in these times of constrained police budgets.

John Deed had a reputation for being no particular friend of the police from his days as a radical barrister, when again and again he found them wanting. This would put him further at odds with them. There was never a time that he recalled when the police were paragons, just occasionally more polite and less afraid of the public than they seemed to be now.

He was wearing a suit under his black robe with red tabs on the collar and no wig as he headed for his room along the tall, cream-painted corridor. This style of dress was designed to make High Court judges seem less remote. With a never-ending backlog of cases awaiting, he could have done without hearing this one, but hadn't dodged it, even though he knew it would be stressful. Money would help the young man, who was without a meaningful life as a result of the police action. How much money might compensate for being paralysed from the waist down at the age of nineteen and living with his grandmother, his parents having disappeared long ago into drugs, was unanswerable. In such cases one party was always hurt or left aggrieved and rarely did common sense and decency prevail, and only then when he managed to talk to each of the parties as someone who had experienced suffering in his own childhood. Empathy helped him pull clear of the emotional vortex which often threatened to engulf him. With some parties before him it was difficult to be empathetic.

As if by some mystical instinct Coop, his long-suffering clerk, stepped from her room to intercept him and take his papers.

'The Associate called through, Judge. Mr Daniels, the litigant, wants to thank you in person,' she said, her South London accent having lost most of its harsh edges. 'He's waiting in court.'

'I'm not sure that's a good idea, Coop.' He saw her look and knew she would make a case if he said 'no'. Meeting litigants, especially one in whose favour the case was settled, was to be discouraged, but the young man's determination had affected him. 'Very briefly,' he told her.

It transpired he wanted to give him a present as part of his thanks and produced a locking knife from under his seat. 'This is all I have, Sir John. My great-grandfather brought it back from France after the war.'

'I can't take that, Mr Daniels. It has obvious sentimental attachment.'

'That's why I want you to have it, sir. You gave me some sort of life.'

'How did you get it past security?' Deed asked.

'I sat on it, sir. Security's not that tight.'

'I'll remind them to tighten it up. Thank you for this,' Deed said, flipping open the blade. 'I might need it for security breaches.' It was a well-preserved weapon and he slipped it into his pocket, wondering if he could get it through security.

'That young barrister from your old chambers is waiting to see you, Judge,' Coop reminded him, as she led the way back to his room, opening doors for him.

At 50 she was still attractive in her black suit and white shirt, both of which were getting a little too tight. Despite her being married, he sometimes thought of making a move on her when they were working late out of town. To have done so would make life impossible and he relied on her too much to allow sex to complicate their relationship. One thing he could be sure of, in the event, there would be no complaint to the Ministry of Justice about his conduct. She wasn't that sort of woman. Alas, he was still the sort of man to cause such a response, regardless of his endeavours to straighten out his sexual waywardness.

'I'd forgotten about her,' Deed said.

'You won't when you see her, Judge. She's what you call eye-candy.'

'What does she want me to do, lower her profile?'

'I doubt it,' Coop replied in her familiar way. 'She's worried she might not be a barrister for much longer.' Coop filled him in on the details.

'She's probably chosen the wrong champion.' There were occasions when Deed came close to not being a judge, and a number of officials in the administration as well as fellow judges might have preferred that he wasn't. He arched his eyebrows with a suggestion of hopelessness and preceded Coop into his room.

The young woman who rose out of the armchair and introduced herself as Jessie Rogers was too good-looking for a barrister, and in too short a skirt to pass unnoticed with her long, well-sculpted legs in bright blue tights. 'Judge,' she said with a confident air as if she was about to interview him.

Captivated, he hesitated as she extended her hand, knowing his watchful clerk would be rolling her eyes behind him, but at that moment he didn't care.

'Coop tells me you're in trouble,' he said, taking half a step back – unsure whether to break this magnetic attraction or to get a better look at her. Her pale blue eyes wouldn't let him go, while her high cheekbones and pillow lips held out the sort of promise that at once found him in a drowning place. She was the sort of woman that other women might instinctively dislike without ever knowing her.

'A bit of an icky mess, as my Gran used to say.'

'Did she?' Deed said with forced stiffness, trying to retrieve ground. 'I can think of a more apt description. I heard that you got rat-arsed at a function and made a pass at a Minister in the Defence Department. He or she, I can't remember.'

Jessie Rogers stopped her laugh. 'Oh, he, and it wasn't a pass, Judge. He has man-boobs out here,' – gesturing with her long, elegant fingers. 'He Harvey Weinsteined me, so I prodded his boobs and said, "They're as ugly as your corrupt policies in the Middle East".'

Now Coop began to laugh and quickly squashed it to a snigger.

'He's a close friend of the Home Secretary. They champion the cause of personal morality in public office together…'

It was Deed's turn to try not to laugh. 'I'm glad someone does.'

'I've followed a number of your cases, Judge,' Jessie Rogers said, using the form of address like an old friend – more confidence. Deed preferred people he liked to address him as Judge rather than Sir John. He realised he would probably have allowed this woman anything, so was further convinced he wasn't the person to help her.

'You're fair and straightforward,' she continued. 'I'm daring to hope you might speak to the Bar Standards Board on my behalf. I need a fresh start.'

Who could fail to be impressed by this 28-year-old? he wondered, sensing his judgment slipping as he pulled some money from his pocket.

'Coop, would you get me a sandwich while I hear the case for the defence?' He stepped behind his desk as Coop went out. 'Let me hear your argument, Ms Rogers,' he said in a formal manner, struggling with himself.

Thinking about the beautiful young woman as he sat in court listening to the young male barrister with his sharp facial features and shock of blond hair protruding from under his wig, Deed liked to think he'd be as sympathetic to him if he knocked on his door appealing for help. But would he? Doubtful. Heathcote Machin was bright and arrogant and making a name for himself. He was arguing on appeal against the extradition of a well-dressed young Lebanese man who was sitting on the first bench in Court 62. Machin was able to think on his feet, reminding Deed of the late George Carman QC, and like him was capable of shredding the opposition's witnesses. Was that a reason not to like this man?

Deed was sitting as a winger with his ex-father-in-law, Sir Joseph Channing and a good-looking younger black judge, Sir Tom Witham, also a winger here.

'With the utmost respect,' Machin was saying from the second bench, 'Mr Salibi must not be extradited to Saudi Arabia. If I might refer your Lordships to HH and PH v Deputy Prosecutor of the Italian Republic and FK v Polish Judicial Authority, 2012, the European Arrest warrants case. FK was charged with dishonesty offences totalling £6,000. Her husband was physically impaired. FK's appeal was allowed as her extradition would have had a severe effect on her two youngest children.'

'What about the rights of Mr Salibi's alleged victims, Mr Machin?' Deed asked. 'Should we not consider those?'

'With the utmost respect, my Lord,' – the familiar expression in a tone suggesting none – 'these are not our concern, only those of Mr Salibi. Further, there is no extradition treaty with Saudi Arabia. We have only their word that he'll get a fair trial.'

Sir Joseph covered the microphone and turned to Deed. 'He's right, John. We're not to consider the victims here.'

The third Judge leant in. 'I'm with Sir Joseph.'

Deed was arguing contrary to his position, having no conviction as to the worthiness of Salibi's cause but resisting his extradition on principle. 'We'd better consider that,' he snapped, knowing his colleagues favoured extradition, and suspecting why. They were interrupted by the appellant who said, in impeccable English, 'I am not leaving. I will not, sir. I have a family here.'

Ignoring him, Sir Joseph Channing said, 'We will rise to consider the matter, Mr Machin.'

The Associate called, 'All rise,' as they started out of their seats.

In Sir Joseph's room, cluttered with legal memorabilia, Deed was as restless as Joe Channing, whom he knew was in need of a cigarette, while Deed was still thinking of that young female barrister. Only the newest addition to the High Court bench remained calm, displaying the familiar detachment of older judges.

'I'd tie this wretched man up and carry him to the plane myself,' Sir Tom said without emotion.

'There is doubt about his raping the two women in Saudi Arabia?'

'Not in my mind, John. I'd throw that smart-alecky barrister over there with him,' Joe Channing said.

Never having sat with this younger Judge, whose finely chiselled features seemed to glow like someone fresh from the gym, Deed momentarily warmed to him when he chipped in, 'I doubt even the Saudis would accept the smarmy little git, Joe.'

They argued for an hour with Tom Witham clearly influenced by his mentor and neither furthering nor weakening Joe Channing's position. Finally the need for a cigarette was getting to the senior judge, who began to fidget. 'I suggest a time constraint,' he said irritably. 'Fourteen days to find support for your argument or he gets put on the plane to Riyadh.'

Determined to persist, Deed argued, 'Our people being so keen for him to go suggests some backdoor deal has been done here.'

'I can't see that – John,' the new boy said.

'You'd lose on a vote,' Joe Channing warned.

'I won't lose, Joe, faith in the sanctity of law will. We'll all lose, especially those who look to the courts as the last refuge against corrupt government. We'd be turning this man over to a despotic state our Government loves being in bed with.'

'By the same token, John, Mr Salibi could offend against women here.'

'If I could make the world right, Tom, I would. Let me do some research.'

'What do you propose we do with him meanwhile?'

'You could have him locked in the Tower, Joe. That might please Riyadh.'

'Alas, I don't think the Tower is any longer secure. Fourteen days.' Joe Channing was ready to run outside for a smoke. 'Agreed, John?'

Deed gave a curt nod, and with a glance of acknowledgement to Sir Tom, he strode out, inexplicably feeling challenged by this younger Judge. Perhaps it was related to his thoughts about Jessie Rogers and whether he could measure up.

CHAPTER TWO

IN HIS ROOM DEED FOUND his clerk tidying and sorting bundles of legal papers. She never allowed herself to be idle.

'Coop, find out if there's anyone available on the Judicial Assistant Scheme who knows the European Convention regarding extradition?'

Coop gave a dismissive laugh. 'When do you want this, next Christmas? They're all half-asleep. Mrs Mills rang, Judge. She said it was urgent.'

'Did she say what was urgent?'

'Only that her chambers were being raided by the police.'

'Oh, is that all?' She got his sarcasm at once. 'Nothing surprises me anymore. Not even a barrister's room being searched.'

As Coop went out Joe Channing stepped in, rapping the door as a courtesy.

'Are you any calmer now?' he asked.

'You probably are for having smoked a cigarette, Joe.'

'It's so oppressive, not being allowed to smoke in one's own room. Now they want to stop us smoking out in the yard!'

'You could challenge it, all the way to the Supreme Court – loss of personal liberty, or possibly inhumane and degrading treatment?' He laughed. 'I'm not convinced by your new broom.'

'Witham's a useful addition. I daresay he'll bed down well enough. You could try adopting a more relaxed view – for your career, John, as well as your blood pressure. He's a handsome fellow. He'll turn the heads of our female bar.'

'Not being a girl I hadn't noticed,' Deed said, avoiding eye contact. The older judge didn't comment. 'I'm concerned that Mr Salibi's been labelled a dangerous sex offender. This position the Foreign Office is taking worries me.'

'I'm not sure you'll stop it. If you do manage to pull it off you wouldn't earn the gratitude of the right kind of people,' Joe Channing warned. 'I wouldn't like to see you further out of step with the Executive.'

'Isn't it the Executive who are out of step with the popular view?'

There was almost always another agenda with this foxy old judge and his apparent concern made Deed alert.

'There's a move to get you onto the Appellate Bench, John. The consensus is you'd make a useful contribution there.'

'Hah, you feel my acquiescence might help my elevation?' he said, deflecting the sudden surge of excitement he felt at the prospect of going up.

'It wouldn't harm your prospects. This regime wants new faces – younger judges, like Tom Witham. He took silk at 36, was a High Court judge just eleven years later. It took me twenty-two years.'

'Perhaps the Lord Chancellor's man fancies him, Joe.' What was the old boy telling him, that this younger man was better than him, not having taken silk himself until he was 42? Deed wasn't exactly laggard, but it then took him eight years to be appointed to the High Court. Now his mind was racing with thoughts of the Appellate Bench. In a year or two from there he could go up to the Supreme Court. If he was honest with himself it was his ambition, something a working-class boy could only have dreamt of. Joe Channing interrupted those thoughts of elevation. 'Are you suggesting Ian Rochester is homosexual?'

'Would it matter?'

'Nowadays we all have to take a different view of things that should have been left at one's public school.'

'I didn't have that distraction,' Deed said, 'too busy with my paper round.'

'I had no idea about Rochester.'

'I'm not suggesting Ian Rochester is homosexual.' Joe Channing was the only person Deed knew who referred to gay men that way. 'I'm not sure the Appellate Bench could be a runner while Haughton's still Home Secretary, Joe. He's not without influence. We'd need a game change there.'

'The appointment has nothing to do with him. It's for Justice and the Prime Minister advised by the Chief.'

'Haughton is unforgiving of past slights. I'm sure he'd make it his business to put in a bad word or two.'

'He's practically out of the door – according to George.'

'Not into prison where he belongs,' Deed observed.

Joe Channing laughed, having little time for the current Home Secretary, whom George, his daughter, was living with. 'The Chief would like some sort of early smoke signal from you on this, John.'

'Is it really a fresh start?' Deed was more excited than he dared show. 'You must stop rocking the boat – at least until any such appointment.'

'I would like to see Haughton gone.'

'Rest assured, he will be – not to prison, to the back benches. Excellent!' He clasped Deed's hand like this was a done deal. 'I'll give the Chief a nod.'

The Lord Chief Justice and Joe Channing were friends from the same chambers. It was likely the Chief would take his mind on such an appointment. Again Deed hesitated. 'Let's jump the first hurdle, Joe.'

That was sufficient for Joe Channing, who turned out with a spring to his step, leaving Deed slightly breathless and telling himself to ease back. Anything might happen to stop his elevation. He saw the message pad and remembered Jo Mills. He dialled her familiar number.

'John! An ambulance might have responded sooner,' she said, sounding exasperated. 'The police are still trawling through our papers.'

A sense of outrage flared in Deed. 'They'd better have a very good reason. Whatever you've got there is bound to contain privileged material.'

'They came at me with everything from the Terrorism Act 2000 to the Counter-Terrorism and Security Act 2015, and all the imperatives of national security in the 2020 Amendments.'

'Wait there,' he said, anger continuing to rise.

The offices Jo Mills occupied with her radical set were in three adjoining basements in Kings Cross. Not the obvious chambers for a prominent QC, but it reflected her commitment to getting justice for people who couldn't ordinarily afford it. Deed admired her for this, even though he believed her stand was both impetuous and foolhardy. He admired her for those qualities and much more besides. He should have married her as he loved her more than any woman he had known. He had known too many women, each of whom he had moved on from, accepting as he did the fault was his rather than theirs. That wasn't how it was with Jo, with whom he started an affair when she was his pupil and still married, yet he found himself up against some inexplicable barrier which stopped him making the final commitment. Capable of analysing most situations, he couldn't penetrate this emotional blockage which was an endless source of inner conflict. He relied on her friendship, and despite loving her he continually upset their relationship with transient affairs, which she seemed to dismiss as being part of his 'emotional immaturity'. That hurt.

When he reached her dingy, cramped chambers with their low ceilings, where fluorescent light seemed to drain the life out of everything, a dozen police officers were packing box files into red bags. The colour indicated this was something to be looked at by special counsel, who would decide what could be released for examination by the prosecution and what needed judicial determination. The floor and desk surfaces were awash with files and Deed couldn't tell which were there as part of this messy chambers' regular filing system and which was pulled out by the police. Jo Mills, the clerks and several younger barristers were challenging every item, arguing that each was needed for an ongoing case. Deed would have accepted their argument and stayed the hand of the police if this was before him. His anger increased as they searched without apparent care.

'I would hesitate before removing any of those,' Deed said with sufficient authority to make them all stop.

Officers stuffing the red bags glanced round to a young woman, who stepped in front of Deed. She was small in stature but spoke with great self-assurance. 'You are, sir?'

'I might ask that of you. Well?' he demanded.

'Unless you have business here, I advise you not to interfere.'

'You bet I have business here. Anyone who prizes liberty should be concerned about the police raiding barristers' chambers. I won't ask you again. Give me your name and rank.'

The young woman hesitated now, a tick in her cheek betraying slight uncertainty. 'I'm Superintendent Petra Hamblyn, sir – Counter Terrorism unit attached to the Home Office.' She pulled her warrant card from her boxy suit jacket pocket. 'You are, sir?' – a more conciliatory tone to her voice.

'Mr Justice Deed.'

'Ah, we've been expecting you,' – recovering her poise.

'At one time the presence of a High Court Judge would have policemen shaking,' Deed said. They made him quake when he was a junior barrister.

'We've got a warrant to seize and remove certain property here, signed by a High Court judge – Mr Justice Witham, sir.' She unfolded her trump card.

So much for coppers shaking in their boots.

At once Deed saw it was signed eleven days ago. 'Why has it taken you so long to execute?'

'Operational reasons, Sir John – collecting other evidence.'

'Privileged information, like that you're trying to gather here?'

'Not according to Mr Justice Witham, sir,' Superintendent Hamblyn said.

'If you execute this warrant you will cause a constitutional crisis. Is that what you want? Mr Justice Witham is new to the High Court bench – I'm sure he didn't realise its implications. It's easily remedied.' Removing his fat Mont Blanc pen, a present from George Channing during a less stormy period in their marriage, he scrawled, "Cancelled, by order of Mr Justice Deed" across the page. He was sure he carried no such authority and was relying on Supt Hamblyn not challenging him. 'Return to court, superintendent, and reapply and see how you get on.'

The policewoman waited, as if more unsure. Deed followed her glance to Jo Mills, who with her colleagues watched silently. The detective nodded Deed away.

'A word outside, sir,' – her confidence bordering on arrogance made Deed curious.

In the narrow hallway, with its worn carpet and walls in need of a coat of paint, Supt Hamblyn rounded on Deed.

'That might impress the lady, sir, but it doesn't me.' She was shaking – with anger or fear, Deed didn't know. 'We believe Ms Mills is aiding terrorists by handling certain documents, Sir John. A lawyer has a duty to disclose information about terrorist activity to the authorities under the Terrorism Act, which I'm sure you will remember even if Mrs Mills has forgotten.'

Deed felt even more angry with this cop. 'Not in your wildest imaginings, superintendent,' he said with restraint. 'Go. Get out.'

With a tense nod Hamblyn said, 'We'll be back.' She opened the door and angrily barked at her officers. 'Out! Leave it. Let's go.'

Policemen set down files and red bags and started out.

Jo looked drained, her dove-grey eyes sunk deep behind high cheekbones peppered with girlish freckles; her full mouth was tense, pinched at the corners. Deed steered her into her cell-like room, its one small barred window high up the wall let in little natural light. He needed answers from her fast.

'What was that about, Jo?'

'Nothing, nothing I know of.' Unlike her to avoid his look.

'The police wouldn't risk raiding a QC, not even in this set, for a frivolous reason. The rule of privilege is long established. If it didn't exist, people would be even more mistrustful of lawyers.'

'Oh, the police have their reasons. Are they valid?'

'Jo, even a brand new shiny High Court judge like Mr Justice Witham knows how important that rule is. He wouldn't undertake this without a lot of hand-wringing.'

'Or political pressure,' Jo Mills said with a scornful laugh. 'We're allowing this Government to be more repressive than the one in Egypt.'

It was his turn to laugh. 'It has its problems, but there are safeguards. People aren't disappearing off the street.'

'Mr Justice Deed isn't on the street. Nor has he been in a long while.'

'These weren't ordinary coppers,' he reminded her.

'They've been watching me and my clients for months. Their surveillance is intimidating, collecting information they've no right to hold.'

'What sort of information? What have your clients been doing, Jo?'

'That's not the point, is it?' – as if knowing she was on borrowed time.

Remembering Joe Channing's advice, thinking perhaps he shouldn't get involved here if he was to go up to the Appellate Bench, Deed at once felt guilty. 'What justifies that sort of surveillance? Are your clients radicalised Muslims?'

'Just ordinary citizens stupidly trying to bring an action against this Government over its corrupt dealings with Middle East oil cartels for arms.'

'Ah, and you've never given the Government a moment's concern.'

'Once people are labelled terrorists it seems to justify almost any action by the state.'

Exasperated Deed said, 'Jo, why don't you just learn to knit or bake bread?'

'It might surprise you to know I can do both.'

'You haven't knitted or baked for me.'

'Has anyone, John?' When he didn't answer, she said, 'They want papers that show how people in Government are directly connected with corruption – ministers as well as civil servants.'

'That's not why they were here, Jo. The warrant was eleven days old.'

Jo turned away. He knew her well enough to know there was more involved. 'Jo, you dragged me into this. What more is there?'

'I don't know what they imagine is involved. These are good people who think our Government should come clean.'

'That would be novel! Are these papers covered by the Official Secrets Act?'

'If they are, they shouldn't be.'

'Don't smart-lawyer me,' Deed said, sensing this was a situation that wasn't easy to resolve. 'I won't go in batting for someone who is doing something a silk of your standing shouldn't do.'

'John, I don't believe I'm doing anything wrong…'

This was like a code and Deed now knew where he stood. Regardless he said, 'In your eyes – I'm not asking if you have papers you shouldn't have. You don't. Good. But do you want to give me anything for safe keeping?'

Her hesitation concerned Deed, but before he could withdraw the offer Jo pulled a cardboard Amazon envelope out of the waste-paper bin. She slid it into a large manila envelope and sealed it before handing it to him.

'Who would ever think to search there for a live file?'

'A trick I learnt from you: hide things in plain sight – when you were still a radical barrister,' – an edge to her voice.

Deed tried to ignore her jibe, but wondered if this apparent loss of faith was a wedge between them. 'Was I ever such a barrister?' he said, fearing that little by little the system of patronage was chipping away his sharp edges: first by his taking silk, then by his appointment to the High Court, notwithstanding his acting as an effective gadfly to some of the sleazier aspects of Government. Perhaps a move to the Appellate Bench, if it happened, would temper him further. At least Jo still turned to him when she was in trouble, but for how much longer? He went out, knowing this drama was far from over.

CHAPTER THREE

NEIL HAUGHTON WAS NO FRIEND of Mr Justice Deed, nor was he ever likely to be, which suited Sir Ian Rochester, who would do all he could to deepen the fissure between them. In constitutional procedure the Home Secretary was not directly connected with the judiciary, but many of Deed's judgments seemed designed to thwart the Home Secretary, such as his move to stop the Salibi extradition. Haughton complained often to the Justice Secretary, hoping to have Deed removed from the bench. That wasn't going to happen unless he was caught breaking the rules. Rochester knew of many breaches, but Deed always somehow slid clear of any consequence. As the all-seeing senior civil servant at Justice he was sure the day would come and believed it could be soon with what he was setting in place, something Deed wouldn't be able to resist.

The excitement Haughton displayed as he strode along the narrow, pale green painted corridor in the Home Office building worried Rochester. The large, less than diligent Sir Percy Thrower was almost as animated. Rochester wished both would shut up, at least until inside the Minister's office, but it wasn't his place to advise another Permanent Secretary or his Minister how to conduct themselves. Not all civil servants here were on Haughton's team, any one of them might overhear some indiscretion and tell someone who might carry it to Deed.

'Can he really be so stupid, Percy?' Haughton asked, slapping his hands together and laughing. 'He actually took this file away with him?'

'That's what the camera secreted in Mrs Mills' office showed, Home Secretary.' Sir Percy chuckled. Rochester knew that Thrower held no particular loyalty to Haughton, so why he was rejoicing at the thought of Deed's possible fall? Deed hadn't shagged his wife, whereas Rochester was certain this wretched Judge had once seduced Lady Rochester.

'We don't actually know it was the file that Mrs Mills gave him, Home Secretary,' Rochester cautioned.

'Oh, come on, Ian, it doesn't need much imagination. If we catch him with that, it would be goodbye, Mr Justice Deed!'

'We would create a constitutional crisis were we to violate the sanctity of a High Court Judge's office and seize it.'

'Then find a way to "discover" it. Can't you get one of those miniaturised spy cameras into Deed's office?'

'Home Secretary?' Rochester questioned with incredulity.

'If he spots it you simply say it's for his protection. You have night-time security cameras in the Judges' building. Hasn't he been complaining about security lapses?'

'These operate only when Judges are not present.' Rochester felt his ire reigniting, remembering the night-time camera that caught Deed with Lady Rochester; worse was his failure to get the recording which a whole network of court staff, encouraged by Deed's clerk, conspired to keep from him – such disloyal people had no place in his department.

'This interfering judge is so close to self-destruct, I'm tingling,' Haughton said in a state of excitement. 'Give Ian whatever help you can on this, Percy,' – his tone peremptory as if giving instruction to some low-grade department employee. He stepped into his large, grey-painted room with its odd mix of modern and antique furnishings and shut the door.

The two senior civil servants exchanged a look. Ian Rochester glanced up and down the corridor to make sure it was clear, and lowered his voice anyway. 'Is he completely barking, Percy?'

A tight smile crossed Thrower's thick lips. 'Deed's become an obsession. His recent award against the police made it worse. I'm sure the PM will move him on before he ever gets one over that judge. Unless that girl you're putting with Deed can compromise him.'

Rochester winced with regret at ever mentioning his idea. 'We live in hope. One's not entirely sure of her. She needs more persuading. Deed's demise might more easily be achieved by encouraging Haughton to assassinate him.'

The day started for Deed around 6 A.M. most mornings. Even at his reading speed it was rare if he managed to clear everything. He wasn't a tenth of the way through the papers when Coop came in with a load more documents. These she set on the left-hand side of his desk.

When he raised his eyebrows at them, she said, 'This is only half of what we've downloaded on the European Convention, Judge. I don't know when you're going to do your list work. You've got the murder trial starting – and they've bumped us down to Southwark.' He knew from her voice she was chiding him about both what he looked at beyond his list, and Southwark. High Court Judges heard murder cases in a Class 1 Crown Court – in London, that was the Old Bailey. It irked Coop that they were assigned to Southwark where mostly fraud cases were heard. She was convinced the MoJ was somehow trying to outflank him.

'I'll have to stop moving my lips when I read, Coop. Any sign of a marshal to help me get through it?'

'The Department's response was that they are thinking about a judicial assistant for you. Anyway, they're usually not up to much.'

'They're supposed to be some of our brightest young barristers.'

'Most can't even tie their shoe-laces. You know they'll probably spy on you and report back.'

A sharp rap on the door startled Coop. The visitor was Mr Justice Witham, who was tall and carried himself with an erect bearing that gave him a strong presence. Despite Deed flapping his hand to casually usher him in, he didn't step across the threshold but waited, as if expecting Coop to leave. She showed no intention of leaving and ignored his frosty stare.

'We need to talk – in private.'

'I've got a lot of reading if I'm to stop Salibi's extradition, Tom.'

'This won't keep, Sir John.'

The use of his title grabbed Deed's attention and he invited Sir Tom to go with him while he walked his dog Baba – a "gift" from his daughter who was too busy to care for her at the start of her own legal career. Mostly Coop walked his much-admired Jack Russell-Chihuahua cross.

On reaching the courtyard, Sir Tom tensed and said, 'I might be a new boy, but I am a High Court judge. I gave a great deal of thought to matters surrounding the search-and-seize order relating to those King's Cross chambers.'

Deed said, 'I didn't hesitate about cancelling it.'

'You must know it can only be set aside by a judge having heard it in the Divisional Court on appeal.'

'Mrs Mills wouldn't do anything illegal,' Deed said. 'I know she does many things that make the Executive uncomfortable, but…'

'And the raggle-taggle bunch of crypto-communists and anarchists who inhabit her chambers, Sir John?'

'They're barristers, regardless of their politics. I'd sooner vouch for them than many of the back-passage crawlers in Government. Jo Mills was the object of your order. She assured me there is nothing related to it that she's hiding.'

'Then she's lost all sense of perspective.' His face was set rigid.

'Evidence?' Deed asked, keeping his cool even as doubt was creeping in.

'Superintendent Hamblyn knows Mrs Mills is in possession of documents that may pose a serious threat to this country. Now we may never know.'

'I know,' Deed said, sensing his ground becoming less stable.

'Of course, you're the nearest thing on the bench to God. This monumental arrogance is even greater than I was warned about.'

Deed laughed as the ground suddenly become solid again. This judge's emotional reaction suggested he was being influenced by political patronage. Judges losing their neutrality, along with objectivity and humanity, was a growing problem. Remembering how Joe Channing hinted at his move to the Appellate Bench, he wondered about stepping onto the same slippery slope.

'This whole enterprise is possibly little more than a gambit to save the Government from embarrassment,' he said.

Sir Tom Witham snapped back with, 'Evidence?' and when Deed offered none, 'That would make me a Government hack.'

Deed gave him a steady look, and then stooped with a bag to pick up a mess after Baba as Sir Tom strode off without another word.

Wading through the swamp of papers, trying to find something to prevent the undesirable Salibi from being kicked out, Deed saw Coop was at her table falling asleep over the references she was collating.

'Coop, perhaps we should stop.'

She started awake. 'I'm fine, Judge.'

'I still think we should stop.'

'You need proper help, Judge. All I've done is pulled what files I could find and copied them. Maybe you should approach Sir Ian Rochester in sackcloth and ashes and beg for a marshal.'

'What, someone who can't tie their shoe-laces?' He got up and stretched, then collected his phone and punched in Jo Mills' number. He was invited to leave a message. Deed hesitated, and seeing Jo's envelope on the desk, he decided to call his ex-father-in-law.

'Go home, Coop,' he said, pulling on his jacket. 'Tomorrow's a whole new day.'

In the near-empty wine bar Deed settled at the farthest table with Joe Channing, noticing stiffness in him that betrayed his 68 years, and as many cigarettes a day.

'You intrigued me, John. Why so cagey?' he asked, reaching cigarettes from his pocket and placing the packet on the table.

'You might get away with lighting one in here tonight.'

'No. There's always someone ready with their wretched phone to photograph and report one. You didn't answer me.'

'I was being cautious, Joe. Phones get tapped nowadays.'

'It helps the authorities catch these idiotic Muslim terrorists.'

'Then the terrorists have won.'

Joe Channing said, 'You still haven't told me what this is about.'

'Would you look after this envelope for me?'

'Should I know what's in it?'

'If you insist – better you don't.'

'Then I'll try not to leave it on a number 11 omnibus!'

Deed laughed, relieved the senior Judge didn't turn him down. 'Don't we still use horse-drawn trams, Joe?'

'You must get out there more often, John. Trams, that was a transport system the Government regretted scrapping. Ernest Marples thought he had a better idea – Macmillan's transport minister in '59.'

'Didn't he close all the train branch lines?'

'Yes. So utterly self-serving and corrupt.'

'Are they any less corrupt today?' Deed asked.

'Does dog poo stink less?' Joe tapped the envelope lying on the table. 'It's safe with me, John, rest assured.' He swallowed his drink, collected his cigarettes and started out, then turned back for the envelope, winking at Deed.

CHAPTER FOUR

SIR IAN ROCHESTER APPROACHED DEED as he arrived at 7.40 A.M. in the near-empty Royal Courts of Justice car park, the throb of buses heading along Fleet Street disturbing the tranquillity even here. Not many judges were in this early, and even fewer Civil Service department heads.

'Did you sleep in the car park, Ian?' Deed said, collecting papers from the passenger seat and letting Baba out to charge across the tarmac to pee.

'I've just packed away my sleeping bag, my Lord,' – he sometimes used Deed's first name. The use of his court title indicated he was here on business.

'Mrs Cooper has been requesting a marshal to help with the workload. Is she getting past her best? We could replace her with a clever young lawyer who'd be an excellent coping clerk.'

'But could whoever make white China tea at the right temperature, Ian?' Rochester waited, ignoring his rebuff. 'Am I getting a marshal?'

'I'm sure we can find you one.' He cleared his throat and glanced past Deed, settling his gaze on his dog. 'I believe Joe Channing spoke to you about the Chief wanting you on the Appellate Bench.'

Deed laughed. 'Isn't there a Judicial Appointments Commission to go past?'

Now it was Rochester's turn to chuckle. 'The JAC convenes the selection panel – you know how influential the Chief is.'

'Would Haughton be gone from the Home Office by then? Almost all the moves I make seem to somehow go across his desk for review.'

'The Chief has no influence there. The PM makes those decisions.'

'The Prime Minister could recommend his prosecution. I'd happily try the case.'

'Sir Percy Thrower tells me the Home Secretary is moving on. Can we take it you'll allow your name to go forward when it happens?'

'Are there strings?'

'You know as well as I, there are and always were. They would be for you to deal with as and when.'

'Yes, the Appellate Bench would suit very well, Ian.'

Rochester was satisfied that Deed had no sight of the pit he was falling into. 'The Lord Chief Justice will of course call you himself,' he said and smiled, feeling he was out-manoeuvring this judge at last.

Before any trial there were written submissions from the defence to clarify points or knock the case out. Not many criminal cases got knocked out before trial, but that didn't deter defence counsel. The murder trial at Southwark was no exception. When Jo Mills rang and suggested meeting at lunch-time Deed hoped it wasn't to further her submission as she was appearing for the second defendant.

Nor was the Middle Temple gardens chosen for romantic reasons. She was afraid of being overheard or spied on, and was angry about it.

'I can't speak freely anywhere anymore. I feel as though someone is watching my every move.'

'Perhaps you should join a more respectable set, Jo,' Deed suggested and saw her frosty look. 'Have you got any evidence of your being watched?'

'No, it's just an odd feeling.'

'That's hard to act on. If I ask questions in certain quarters on your behalf it might make whoever more cautious.'

'I need to get to judicial review with this case. Can you help speed up the process?'

'It involves terrorists.'

She rebuked him. 'I'm surprised at you, Judge. Suspects are not terrorists.'

'No. What's involved?'

'A woman tainted by her brother's alleged connection to a Muslim terror cell. She's been named by an informer. The police won't give any other information.'

Deed thought about this, then said, 'I'm not sure I can help.'

'Why?'

The force of her challenge caught him off guard. 'The police don't like to give out that sort of information.'

'That's my point. You could make them.'

Deed felt himself getting dragged to somewhere he didn't want to go. 'I can't bat for you on this, Jo – because of our relationship.'

'You mean, because you've slept with me? That rules out half the female bar ever appearing before you if you choose to let it.'

'Now you're being childish.'

'Or perhaps you've no longer got the stomach for that kind of fight.' She stopped and met his surprised look. 'The word around the Inns is that you're going to be an LJ.'

'That sounds like an accusation,' he said, trying to ignore the discomfort it brought. 'If only getting to the Appellate Bench was as fast as the rumours.'

'It might explain this sudden change in attitude.'

'It's not sudden, it's considered. Jo, do yourself a big favour, dump that set you're in.' He regretted that the moment he'd said it, and possibly deserved her response.

'You're not yet a Lord Justice but you're performing exactly as the Establishment would expect. How will you be on the Appellate Bench? Deluding yourself about the changes you can make as an insider?'

'Would it be a delusion?'

Jo didn't bother to answer, but said, 'People who come to our set for help aren't automatically guilty, as you now seem to think.'

'I think no such thing. Nor ever have.'

'You're sounding like you do.'

'What must I do, punch Superintendent Hamblyn in the face?'

'I wouldn't risk it, not while she's helping to make us so safe! I'd better have my file back; it might be safer.'

That shocked him. Recovering, he said, 'What? You can't. I don't have it.'

'I hope you're joking – I can see you're not,' – alarm in her voice.

'I gave it to someone I'm not sure I entirely trust – a higher authority.' Were she less angry she might have guessed who that was.

'No. How could you?'

'That's the risk you ran by trusting a craven Judge who's selling out for a bum on the Appellate Bench,' he said, provocatively.

'Yes, I'm so stupid. I must be losing it!'

Deed watched her stride away as Baba ran up as if to see what the fuss was about. He glanced around trying to spot if anyone was watching. No one seemed to be, but Jo Mills wasn't prone to fantasy. How would he win her back? Not with flowers, while dinner carried the expectation of going to bed. That now seemed a far-off prospect. Perhaps by declining the Appellate Bench? Turning down that opportunity, in the event, seemed an equally far off prospect.

An unsettling feeling of betrayal seeped through Jo, bringing in its wake a mixture of emotions: disappointment, anger, self-loathing, none of which were justified but none of which she could stop. She felt like a young girl who had just discovered her outpouring of love wasn't reciprocated by the object of her affection. Resorting to alcohol seemed the easy way to avoid the emotions trying to overwhelm her but it didn't blunt the edges of her acute longing for John.

Sitting on her own with a bottle of wine, she was aware of a smartly dressed man across the room taking more interest in her than she wanted. He was vaguely familiar but she had drunk too much to recall how she might have known him. In this Fleet Street bar he was certain to be legal, and guessed he was a barrister from his arrogant body language, or perhaps a policeman. Her thoughts kept returning to her earlier encounter with Deed, which made her angrier. Losing him to another woman was painful, even though she knew he would eventually return to her – but losing him to the Appellate Bench was unbearable. He might forever be out of reach, unless she joined the forces of reaction. Impossible.

She had stayed in love with Deed ever since their affair started when she was his pupil. At the time she was married to David Mills, who was paralysed from a hunting accident, and Deed was with the ambitious Georgiana Channing. With his bizarre attraction to country sports, her husband was more suited to George, who was always competing with Deed only wasn't as clever. Jo didn't know anyone as clever as Deed or as courageous in creating precedents or challenging bad ones. Now she felt he was lost to her and she wanted to cry, but knew she would be crying for herself. Instead, she tipped her glass back and saw the man with the arrogant body language standing at her table in his well-cut suit. She was puzzled that she hadn't run across him before.

'Is this a good idea?' he asked.

Jo decided he was a judge and wanted to tell him to get lost, but life at the bar was often difficult enough without her upsetting yet another judge.

'Is what a good idea? You approaching me, or me getting smashed?'

'May I join you?' His voice suggested Oxbridge and the right schools.

'Not if you plan to stop me finishing the bottle.'

He took the bottle and filled his own glass, then emptied the rest into hers.

'I'm Tom Witham,' he said offering his hand.

Jo closed her eyes, feeling stupid. She laughed to cover her embarrassment. 'This will definitely result in a negative report.'

'Happily the Minister of Justice no longer encourages judges to report on barristers. The senior Bar has had a number of outliers over the centuries, so you may not be quite dead in the water.'

'Beyond a liking for white wine, could we possibly have anything in common?'

'We could explore that possibility over dinner.'

Jo disliked his presumption and no longer cared if she did give offence. 'Hah, your former chambers make President Assad's regime seem liberal.'

Rather than causing offence, her remark made Sir Tom Witham laugh, which worried Jo. She wasn't intending to be funny.

'There's a long tradition of right-wing barristers becoming quite leftish leaning once they're judges, you know.'

'A yet longer tradition of them developing fascist tendencies.'

'We'll have to wait and see which way I go, Jo – may I call you Jo?'

'If I can call you Sir Tom,' she said.

Again he laughed and Jo wondered if this was for her benefit, or trying to appear cool. 'I can see I have a lot of convincing to do.'

'I really would prefer to drink on my own, Judge.'

'You know you shouldn't. It's not good for either of us.'

'Is that from friendly Sir Tom or nasty Mr Justice Witham?'

'They're both quite friendly, and quite concerned about you. I think you really should have dinner with me.'

'I will only if you give me an answer to my question.'

There was a blank look from him and Jo realised she hadn't asked her question which made her feel more foolish, and no longer competent to ask it. What the hell, he might make a report on her anyway. 'How do you get to be the youngest High Court Judge in the country? Did you win a beauty contest?' It was unkind and she expected him to leave.

'At least you didn't suggest it was the PC principle. Obviously, I was the most obsequious.'

Without warning laughter burst out of her. 'You are quite funny.'

'No, I'm very funny. I may be quite truthful, too.'

Jo gave him another steady look. In some ways he reminded her of Deed. Perhaps that was what got her out of the wine bar and to dinner, then back to her apartment.

At the street door he said, 'Should I let the taxi go?'

Jo was quite sober now, and surprised by the question. 'If you hadn't asked, I may not have resisted…'

'I'm too well brought up not to. But why stop now, Jo?'

'Maybe I'm not convinced of your lurch to the left.'

'Will the parts we both want to put together mind?'

Jo was startled by his clumsy, inept remark, but tried to avoid her instinct to flee. 'That doesn't sound like a well brought up boy.'

'I sensed the case going against me. I apologise. Sleeping with an attractive radical barrister would increase my street cred.'

'I'm not sure sleeping with a sexy right-wing judge would improve mine.'

She slipped into the building alone, leaving him frustrated. Despite herself she was more than a little pleased by the interest.

CHAPTER FIVE

THE LEGAL VISITS ROOM At Belmarsh Prison in Plumstead seemed drabber and more depressing than usual today with her hangover, and her 30-year-old instructing solicitor offering her paracetamol in spite of her repeated refusals didn't improve things. She tried to avoid pharmaceuticals and anyway, felt she deserved her thumping head for resorting to alcohol to escape her feelings. The client she was having a con with was helping neither her condition nor his own predicament and Jo couldn't decide whether he was mentally defective, plain stupid or being purposely obtuse. She didn't seem able to make him understand what the consequences would be if he were found guilty of murder. He seemed more concerned to protect his co-defendant Mariana Ortega. From what her instructing told her, Ms Ortega was quite something in her attitude, but Jo wasn't running her defence.

'Your best interest is not served by coupling your defence to Ms Ortega's. It won't help you,' Jo said.

'But we were both supposedly there,' Rupert Fish said.

Jo glanced at Simon Chester, the solicitor, who seemed equally exasperated.

'There's little evidence that you were there at all, other than the fact that Ms Ortega said she was with you the whole evening and you confirmed that. And the fact that it was your flat where the victim died.'

'We were together, it's true.' His delicate features carried a distant look, suggesting he wasn't connecting with any of this. He appeared quite vulnerable and Jo almost wanted to put her arm around him to reassure him while wanting to slap him to wake him up to the reality of his situation.

'The prosecution hasn't submitted concrete evidence that puts you there at the time of the murder,' Jo pointed out. 'There's your coerced confession to the police saying you did it. Clearly Ms Ortega knew the dead man intimately.'

'Why do you keep referring to her like that? Her name's Mariana.'

'I want as much distance as possible between you and her,' Jo told him. 'You didn't know the victim.'

'No. He was stalking Mariana; he was a sex pest.'

'Who said? Ms Ortega? It didn't happen, Rupert. According to the prosecution evidence she was having an affair with this man at the time of his death.'

'No, that's not true. It's a lie. She loves me,' Rupert Fish insisted. He was thirty-two yet seemed to have the emotional age of a love-struck teenager.

'If she was, the prosecution will argue you killed the victim in a jealous rage.'

'No, he was attacking him – me, I mean me.'

Jo made a mental note of his slip, suspecting 'him' was a third party who maybe did the killing with Ms Ortega.

'The risk is, Rupert,' Simon Chester warned, 'Mariana's barrister going cut-throat on you. He will blame you for the killing, and she'll let him.'

'No. She wouldn't do that. We're in this together.'

Here Jo knew that somehow, she had to drive a wedge between the two defendants. 'The only way you'll survive is with a clear separate defence.'

'No, absolutely not,' the young man said, panicking. He seemed to think their relationship would survive if he went to prison.

'Rupert, did Mariana dump the man's body?'

'Me, it was me,' he insisted.

'According to the medical report he was still alive when the duvet he was wrapped in was removed. The prosecution will dine out on that,' Jo warned. 'Did you notice if he was still breathing?'

Rupert Fish closed his eyes and shook his head, as if not wanting to go there. As a witness on his own behalf, Jo knew he'd prove a total liability.

'We should consider not putting him in the witness box,' she said as they were leaving the prison building for the car park and the tedious drive back through South East London to the Strand.

'I'm not sure he'll go along with that, Jo.'

'If he doesn't, he'll do the prosecution's work for them. You know, Simon, I've got a strong feeling this man wasn't even there that night.' His fingerprints being on everything at the murder scene, including inside the cupboard, didn't worry Jo as it was his flat. A fourth set of prints in the cupboard and on the night-stand belonged neither to Ms Ortega nor the victim. These intrigued her.

'Will you try to cross-examine him?'

Jo sighed. Could she get away with that? 'We have to get the truth from him somehow. If I don't, Heathcote Machin will slaughter him, and Mariana Ortega will walk.'

'Rupert's obviously madly in love with her.'

'Love? It's sex, Simon, obsessive sex.' Having witnessed it up close, Jo knew just how their client was caught in its snare.

'Sex causes some men to change the world.'

'How is it some women inspire that, while others can't even get men to wash up?' She glanced at her watch. 'Oh Lord, I'm late. I've got a High Court application. Can you drop me?' She assumed he would.

Arriving at the Royal Courts of Justice and finding Court 49 empty, Jo at once imagined the case was over until her instructing solicitor arrived with the client, 40-year-old Anita Plant. She was small and plump with an open face that seemed to register surprise at everything that came her way when her response was to laugh. It was hard to imagine her dealing with tricky situations she sometimes found herself up against in dangerous parts of the Middle East. Reports Jo had read about her suggested she ably confronted the Arab male on his home turf.

The prosecution barrister, Dick Royston, florid-faced with a large, disproportionate nose, sauntered in and dumped his papers on the second bench. Behind him was the over-confident Superintendent Hamblyn.

'Do you know who's hearing this?' Royston asked.

'I haven't a clue,' she said, 'It wasn't listed.'

When the Associate called, 'All rise,' to Jo's surprise Sir Tom Witham stepped in wearing black robes. He was tall and moved with the grace of a ballet dancer. He looked a wonderful specimen sitting up on the bench, but his expression was blank as he glanced at her and said, 'Ah, Mrs Mills, how nice to see you again.'

Half-rising, Jo couldn't stop herself saying, 'I hope the pleasure's going to be all mine on this occasion, my Lord.' She was aware of Dick Royston giving her a curious look.

The Judge responded briskly, 'You have an application?'

'Yes, for the return of the passport and property belonging to Ms Anita Plant. This we maintain was seized illegally, and deprives Ms Plant of earning her living. She's an international field worker for Oxfam and cannot travel without a valid passport, not even in a good cause.'

'Mr Royston? Is there a reason why this lady shouldn't have her passport?'

'We believe so, my Lord,' Dick Royston said, struggling up, clutching papers like a child's security blanket. 'Ms Plant was once married to a Libyan who belongs to the Muslim Brotherhood in Tripoli. She has travelled extensively throughout Libya, Syria, Iraq and other parts of the Middle East where she had contact with members of the Islamist coalition known as Libya Dawn, some of whom are part of the so-called Islamic State.'

'Has she been charged?'

'I don't believe she has, my Lord.'

'Then she's not a member of this proscribed organisation?'

'The police have reason to believe she is in contact with members of the terror group here known as Al-Muhajiroun,' the barrister ventured.

'This is a smear tactic contrived to arouse enough suspicion to persuade you to resist my application,' Jo protested forcefully.

'Doesn't contact with members of such an organisation render one liable to arrest, Mr Royston?' the Judge asked.

'I am given to understand the police are still gathering information, my Lord.'

'Is that a reason to deny Ms Plant freedom of movement?' The Judge sounded cross, and Jo felt encouraged. 'What is the police case, Mr Royston?'

'I can't say, at present, sir, for fear of undermining it.'

'We can't simply label people terrorists without evidence, especially not someone doing valuable work for NGOs. Mrs Mills?'

'Ms Plant has contact with all kinds of people in her essential work, none knowingly with terrorists. With an order from a judge, police removed property which prevents her functioning professionally and socially. Although not incarcerated, she remains a virtual prisoner.'

'Because the Crown doesn't reveal its evidence in open court that doesn't mean it doesn't exist.'

'With respect, that is a licence to remove anyone's property at any time,' Jo argued, feeling aggrieved as this judge she was before had himself signed an order for her property to be seized.

'Surely only where terrorist involvement is known or suspected?'

'I've seen no such evidence, my Lord, and I doubt you have. It seems all the police need do is say someone is suspected of terror connections for their life and livelihood to be severely restricted.' She knew permission to seize property or intercept emails frequently wasn't sought and where it was ninety-eight percent of applications were approved.'

'It's better the police err on the side of caution.'

'Then their actions are a form of state terrorism,' Jo said, ignoring his increasing impatience.

Turning to Dick Royston, the Judge said, 'You have seven days to return to court with reasonable grounds for continuing this action or return Mrs Plant's property.'

'My Lord, would you hear further argument?'

'I have ruled, Mrs Mills.'

Despite knowing the risk she was taking, Jo stood her ground and said, 'This is depriving Ms Plant of her civil liberties under Protocol No. 4 to the Convention for the Protection of Human Rights and Fundamental Freedoms as amended by Protocol No. 1...' she got no further.

'I will see you in my chambers. Now, Mrs Mills.'

He rose and strode out. The prosecutor offered her a sympathetic look.

When Jo was shown into the Judge's stark basement room, with nothing on the walls and no books on shelves, her eye was drawn to Sir Tom's bright red braces against his white shirt as he stepped from behind his desk and she wondered what statement he was trying for. He waited for his clerk to go out.

'You might conduct yourself in that way before other High Court judges, Mrs Mills. With me you risk a trip to your professional body,' he threatened.

'And if you had fucked me last night?' Jo asked, not enjoying the inelegance but hoping to rattle him. Instead his face froze and he returned behind his desk to recover himself, side-stepping the provocation.

'You must recognise your boundaries, Mrs Mills.'

Jo smiled. 'I'm aware of my boundaries.'

'No. You continued to argue after I'd ruled.'

Jo persisted. 'I will apply to have that decision urgently reviewed by another High Court judge.'

'Not even your friend Mr Justice Deed will grant such an application. Not now.' His confidence both irritated and alarmed her.

Suspecting something else was going on, Jo steadied herself and said, 'Is this because I turned you down?'

He ignored her question. 'You know the procedure for judicial review.' He opened the door for her. She left without another word.

Finding Deed with Coop's help was easy. Jo interrogated him as they strode along the corridor in the older part of the Law Courts with its elaborately detailed Victorian cornicing which she found oppressive.

'Why is he so damned sure you won't hear this case? Why is he presuming to speak for you?' She was slightly wary in view of their last exchange.

'Is this client the same woman you wanted a review for to get the informer's evidence?' Deed asked.

'She's not a terrorist, John.'

'We've had this conversation, Jo. I can't help you.'

'Isn't this setting a terrible precedent?'

'High Court judges know what's likely to set precedents.'

Jo wanted to scream, and might have done in a less public space. Instead she employed a tense whisper hoping it would be just as effective, 'If it's not struck down all lawyers in future will refer to Mr Justice Witham's ruling. It'll mean we're that much closer to a police state.'

'Oh, come on, Jo, that's an exaggeration.'

'Is it? Since 1997, over 30 pieces of legislation have torn away strips of British civil liberties, including the 2020 Amendments, chipping away our freedoms. The chips seem tiny compared to the perceived danger so most people aren't bothered. When we look back, we'll see a mountain of liberties gone. Then it will be too late.'

'The State has a duty to be cautious with the security of its citizens, Jo. Whether from a terrorist or a pandemic.'

Deed preceded her into his office. It was cavernous, with a high, over-elaborate ceiling and heavy brocade curtains – a world away from her cramped quarters. She understood why judges clung to office, to this rarefied atmosphere.

'We are all photographed everywhere by the State or private security. In London there are half a million CCTV cameras operating. Our citizen-protecting State wants to access and know everything about us down to the amount of coffee we drink. Security now means total surveillance.'

'Most of us prefer to be safe, Jo. That's the price, and there's nothing I or anyone else can do about it.'

'Time was when you'd have stormed the citadel.'

'There's a new order nowadays,' Deed argued. 'Things will get better.' There was a distance in his manner that made her uneasy. How could she be uneasy with the man she most admired and loved, despite his sexual waywardness? Perhaps it was she who was changing, not him. That worried her.

'Things won't get better,' she said. 'We won't even be made safer. Help me, John. Please.'

'I can't. Not on this.'

Now it seemed like she was headed for another judge-confrontation, but what the hell. 'Tell me it's not because you've sold out for the Appellate Bench?'

'There is nothing good, Jo, and there is nothing bad but perception.'

Again Jo wanted to scream at his evasion. She knew him too well to argue further. She gathered up her bags and left, heading for another bottle of wine and the inevitable headache which would follow.

Having resisted a whole bottle, she was getting drunk just the same, single glass by single glass. Turning to signal the waitress, she knocked over her empty glass, breaking it. The barman came across to clear up the pieces.

'I call you a taxi, Mrs Mills.' His heavy Spanish accent left Jo unsure if it was a question.

'No, call me Jo, and bring another glass of this.' Her words weren't slurred, but she knew she should stop now before they were.

She didn't see Simon Chester come through the bar until he was standing by the table, taking her arm. 'Jo, I'm taking you home.'

'Simon' – surprise cutting through the alcohol. 'I thought you were gay.'

'I am,' he said. 'We've got a heavy day tomorrow. Rupert Fish may be in luck. We've drawn Mr Justice Deed.'

'Huh, I'm glad you think so.'

CHAPTER SIX

❦

MARIANA ORTEGA AND RUPERT FISH sat in the dock of number 2 court at on the 2nd floor at Southwark holding hands and whispering to each other, although she seemed to be doing most of the whispering, Jo Mills noted as she glanced round from the front bench. Whatever was being said behind the heavy Perspex around the dock she was sure it would be for that lady's benefit rather than anything to benefit her client.

Jo was puffy-eyed and hung over and regretting her self-abuse, even though the wine had been a decent year. Next to her on the defence team was the smooth, sharp-looking Heathcote Machin, who was in his late thirties, still single and pursued women with the same enthusiasm as Deed. Perhaps that was why he always seemed to irk Deed. Their junior barristers were on the bench behind them. Simon Chester, who was on the third bench with the other instructing solicitor, was too polite to mention her pass at him last night. The prosecuting QC, Newman Mason Allen, whose parents were from Trinidad, wandered along the front bench with the standard gambit – a try on.

'It's not too late to enter a plea,' he said, a smile dropping over his large, round face. The QC often smiled, even when he was angry. This disconcerted witnesses, causing them to say things they might not otherwise have said.

'A plea to what, Newman?' Heathcote Machin wanted to know, his eyes flitting over to the dock. 'Has my client got a speeding ticket she kept from me?'

Mason Allen gave Jo a look. She tried to smile but couldn't, her head felt too fragile. 'My client's a funeral director, he's never speeded in his life,' she said, joining in the joke. 'Or is it sped?' She turned as the usher called, 'All rise.'

Deed stepped in at his familiar brisk pace wearing his black robe, and bowed before taking the central seat. Coop followed him and sat to his right.

'God enters stage left, with handmaiden,' Jo said loud enough for those in the immediate vicinity to hear. No one responded.

Deed glanced over at the defence bench. He waited, thinking he wouldn't acknowledge her remark, then decided to. 'Mrs Mills? Do you have an application?'

'I don't think so,' she replied, barely rising to do so.

Deed felt like asking her if she was all right; she looked as if she hadn't slept. Like most judges he was of concerned how barristers presented in court, but he tried to remain relaxed, provided they didn't overstep the mark, which might happen with Jo Mills in her current frame of mind.

He turned to the Clerk of the Court, who was awaiting his signal. Deed nodded and the clerk indicated to the usher that the jury should be brought in. For Deed a courtroom was a workplace and as long as the acoustics were adequate and the sightlines between jury and witnesses good, he didn't much mind which court he occupied. Coop, however, took a different position. She was satisfied that they had the biggest, most comfortable court, well-lit from its tall windows and pale oak panelling.

The clerk indicated for the two defendants to stand.

'Mariana Ortega and Rupert Aslan Fish, you are jointly charged with murder, that on the night of April 15th you did murder Peter Bartlett contrary to common law. Mariana Ortega, how do you plead, Guilty or Not guilty?'

Both defendants eagerly piped up, 'Not guilty.' This was going to be one of those trials, Deed could tell.

'I'm sure your respective barristers have told you that you must answer separately to the arraignment, on other occasions they do the talking for you, except when you're giving evidence,' he explained. 'Is that clear?'

'But I not guilty,' Mariana Ortega said.

'Nor am I,' the second defendant echoed.

'We understand, but that will be for the jury to decide. Perhaps, Mr Clerk, you'll put the indictment to Ms Ortega for her to answer formally?' Deed said, glancing at the raven-haired woman in the dock. Her dark eyes with thick black eyebrows held him as if to suggest she was offering all you ever wanted from a woman, the kind of sex you would never forget. Deed drew back mentally, unsure if that was what he saw in her or if this was his familiar jest. Either way he shouldn't have been having such thoughts here and knew he should seriously consider therapy again to try to help him deal with the problem. His hypersexuality was sometimes disruptive to his life, only when he tried therapy before he started an affair with his attractive therapist.

After the clerk finished reading the indictments Newman Mason Allen QC rose to introduce counsel, as was the tradition. 'M'Lord, I appear for the prosecution and the defendants are represented by m'learned friend Mr Machin for Ms Ortega and Mrs Mills for Mr Fish, the second defendant. I understand that Mr Machin has a preliminary application.'

'Thank you, Mr Mason Allen,' Deed said. 'Mr Machin?'

Rising, Heathcote Machin said, 'My Lord, could we ask the court's assistance in seeking a witness for the defence?'

'The normal procedure is for the defence to seek a witness summons, Mr Machin.'

'The witness refuses to acknowledge our existence, my Lord.'

'Is this witness in the country?'

'He is, my Lord. It's the Rt Honourable Neil Haughton MP the Home Secretary.'

That brought the two sleepy reporters in the press box wide awake. For a moment Deed was tempted to smile, intrigued to know what possible connection Haughton could have with the two in the dock. He would doubtless find out.

'I'm sure he has a lot of pressing affairs of state. However, none takes precedence over court business. The court will issue a witness summons. Tell the witness he has twenty-four hours to comply or very good reason not to. Mr Mason Allen, are you ready for the jury to be sworn then to open for the Crown?'

The QC got to his feet with a sheaf of papers, a familiar tool which he often used to great effect, implying this was the killer piece of evidence. 'I am, my Lord. But I too am having difficulty securing the attention of a witness.'

'Not the Prime Minister by any chance?' Deed quipped.

'That important person might prove easier to get here, my Lord.'

'Are you ready for the court to hear your case in the absence of this witness? Who is the witness you need?'

'Ms Channing, the Home Secretary's partner, my Lord. She is a fully bound witness.'

'It's going to be quite a family affair,' he said without irony. Deed cursed himself for having missed her name among the witness lists and wondered if he shouldn't recuse himself at this late stage in view of his having once been married to George Channing QC. He could have done so with Jo Mills appearing before him, but there was no codified rule prohibiting him hearing cases involving either. The Supreme Court guidelines were that a judge should step down if there was apparent bias on his part. He felt there was none in relation to Jo Mills, but guided by Lord Denning he had asked counsel if there were objections to his hearing the case so he couldn't later be reported to the MoJ. There were no objections and Deed would be at pains to remain impartial. He decided not to step down. 'Can either of you do without these witnesses?'

'Not if Ms Ortega is to have a fair trial, my Lord,' Machin said.

'Ditto for the prosecution's case, m'Lord.'

'Do you wish to call their dog, Mrs Mills?' Deed asked.

Rising, Jo Mills said, 'Any dog might be more reliable!'

'I will issue the summons to compel her attendance and see what we get,' Deed said. He could guess what their initial response would be.

Sir Ian Rochester got dragged to the Home Office so often he began to think that he should ask for his own desk there instead of standing as he was in Neil Haughton's strangely-appointed room, like a schoolboy on the head's carpet. He didn't enjoy this man's company, and couldn't care less that Sir John Deed had summoned him to answer questions as a witness. He minded even less if Deed one day managed to haul Haughton all the way into the dock as he threatened on occasions. Here he was yet again looking to him to thwart Deed. Rochester was beginning to feel almost as irritated with his Home Office counterpart, Sir Percy Thrower, for going along with it. Had procedure never been explained to this Secretary of State? Or perhaps he was too dim to take it in.

'There must be some sort of exemption you can offer, Ian,' Haughton was saying. 'It's bad enough being called to a criminal trial as Home Secretary. It would be even more embarrassing if by then I'm appointed Secretary of State for Justice and Lord Chancellor.'

The prospect of that filled Rochester with horror. 'Exactly so, Home Secretary,' he said and smiled, masking his true feelings. 'We are looking for an exemption. However, I'm not certain we would be able to do the same for Ms Channing as she's a fully bound witness. If she fails to turn up voluntarily her appearance could be forced under arrest.'

'I am aware of that, Ian,' Haughton snapped with apparent irritation, then turned on a sixpence and said without a qualm, 'George can look out for herself. She is a QC, after all, used to the rough and tumble of court.'

Rochester glanced at Sir Percy, who was smiling, perhaps at the prospect of this dolt being passed onto him at the Ministry of Justice.

Later that day George Channing emerged from his office like a freed tiger. Haughton could almost see her claws extended, ready to rip him to shreds as he chased her, feeling uncomfortable at their row having become public as they walked through his building. He'd be glad to get away from the Home Office and take a new portfolio at Justice. The belief was that he could use his experience to resolve some of the problems that were becoming extant with more and more people being forced through the criminal justice system while budgets were shrinking. The solutions were the same, whichever office he was in: they needed to build more prisons, or perhaps adopt his idea of adapting some of the navy's obsolete vessels as prison ships. Haughton was brought up sharply as George stopped at the car door and turned. She was tall and poised in her high heels, and displayed the confidence that came with having been to the right school and university and mixed with important persons from a tender age.

'I sacked the wretched Ortega woman and you know why, Neil,' she said. 'I'm not prepared to announce the reason in open court. Those worms told me when I made my witness statement that was it.'

Haughton gave a nervous glance to his driver waiting at a discreet distance but close enough to hear everything and so feed the gossip mill. 'That wouldn't help to secure the prosecution's case, darling,' he said a low voice.

George said, 'Don't *darling* me. Find a way to get me out of this or do I tell the jury all about your sordid affair with a wretched cleaning woman.'

'It wasn't an affair,' – remembering with breathless excitement still.

'Perhaps the jury will *believe* she was in the bedroom helping you find your cufflink!'

'This has nothing to do with the court case, George; I won't let it…'

'That tricky minx is trying to make it so,' George Channing said.

'I'll be laughed at throughout my entire department,' Haughton said, again glancing towards his driver and praying George would shut up and get in the car.

'You should have thought of that before you *lost* your cuff-link, *darling*. Get the case dropped. That will spare your blushes. What's the point in your going to Justice if you can't get Rochester to perform such a simple task?'

She wrenched open the car door and slid in, slamming it after her. The driver opened the other door for him, meeting his eyes with what he was sure was man-to-man pity. Haughton needed to come up with the answer and would catch Sir Ian in his office first thing in the morning and get this sorted.

'Can I offer you some coffee, Home Secretary?' Sir Ian Rochester said, standing at the coffee machine in his ante room. None of his assistants were in yet so he was enjoying the quiet of early morning before Haughton arrived making demands. 'It's a roast I have blended especially – superior to anything you get offered at the Home Office – I pay for it myself, of course.' Gone were the days when good coffee and biscuits were provided at meetings with bottled water. Barristers visiting the MoJ got tap water, in a posh jug.

'Half a cup, Ian, with milk and sugar,' Haughton said, distracted.

Why would he expect anything different – superb coffee made undrinkable by milk and sugar? He passed him the half-filled cup and took his own through to his office, where three original Hogarth drawings adorned one wall. Everything was of the Chippendale period. He wondered how much longer these creature comforts would survive.

'The easiest solution is to have the case stopped. Get the prosecution to withdraw, Home Secretary.'

'Could they do that?' Haughton asked, astonished.

'They could, it's whether they would.'

'Couldn't we make them?'

Rochester tried to imagine what it would be like with this man here at Justice.

'What legitimate grounds are there for letting the prosecution drop?' Haughton asked.

'Ah, possible embarrassment of the Home Secretary wouldn't suffice.'

'I suppose not.' Haughton waited, uncertain, as if expecting him to produce the solution.

Leaving Haughton hanging, Rochester sipped his coffee, enjoying the moment. 'Insufficient evidence is the most obvious route out,' he said finally. 'Better to have the defendants plead guilty to a lesser charge with the expectation of a light sentence. I'll speak to someone in the Crown Prosecution Service.'

The Home Secretary relaxed and swallowed his coffee, ready to run. If he did come here as the Secretary of State, Rochester knew he would be beholden and easy to handle.

CHAPTER SEVEN

ON THE OCCASIONS JO MILLS saw Mariana Ortega and Rupert Fish together at a joint con in the court cells, the less convinced she was of them as a couple with feelings for one another. She couldn't imagine Ortega feeling for anyone but herself, and thought how she deserved the self-serving Heathcote Machin representing her. Jo accepted this was a jaundiced view, for even the cold Machin was thawing under the Colombian's sexual charisma – as Simon Chester referred to it. The two male cell officers outside the door were all but panting from her flirtatious glance.

Both legal teams were in the court cell to discuss the prosecution's surprising 11th-hour offer of a guilty plea to manslaughter. The offer was puzzling to Jo and she wondered what might have happened to the Crown's case. Machin was convinced that the prosecution wasn't finding a case it could win and Mason Allen was trying to catch anything he could. Whatever Machin advised Mariana Ortega the guileless Rupert Fish would doubtless go along with it, regardless of Jo's advice.

'What sort of sentence would it be if we pleaded guilty?' Fish asked.

Before Jo Mills could respond Machin cut in with, 'Anything from a suspended sentence to twelve years in prison. Any conviction means Mariana would be deported' – adding a negative spin.

That didn't reassure the young man. 'What do you think, Miss Mills?'

'It's a good offer,' Jo said. 'You might even walk with a non-custodial – it's not guaranteed. They seem to be getting nervous and anxious to help us.'

'Because we're calling the Home Secretary,' Machin ventured. 'If we push hard enough, Mariana, you could walk away from this.'

'Yes, she scared. I walk off free,' Mariana Ortega said.

'It's he, Mariana,' Rupert Fish quietly corrected.

'I wouldn't advise pushing that, Heathcote. This is a good offer.'

'Not good enough. Mariana can do better,' Machin said to Jo as if only his client's opinion mattered. 'That's what I advise, Mariana.'

'Yes. They let me free.'

Rupert Fish changed tack. 'Yes, I'm with Mariana. What she thinks is best.'

– 49 –

'As long as you appreciate the risk,' Jo said.

'I'm not going to risk them throwing Mariana out of the country.' The young man smiled at his co-defendant but got no response.

'That might happen anyway, Rupert. She came here from Colombia as a student of English – eight years ago – !' Jo pointed out.

'I very slowly learner,' Mariana Ortega said.

'You're doing all right,' Rupert Fish assured her, clasping her hand.

Jo glanced at Heathcote Machin and said nothing. She turned and rang the bell for them to go back to court. The door flew open and each of the two overweight officers tried to get through first, as if wanting the honour of escorting Ortega back to court. There's one born every minute, Jo thought as she went out.

Deed stared across the court at Mason Allen QC, who got to his feet as if he'd grown weary during the adjournment.

'What have you got to tell me, Mr Mason Allen?'

The jury was out for these 'without prejudice' discussions.

'M'Lord, the prosecution has decided to offer no further evidence in this case.'

That surprised Deed. He expected something to have resulted from their discussions, but the QC's words didn't accord with his body language.

'What are you saying? You're calling no further evidence, or are discontinuing the prosecution altogether?'

'Yes, I suppose so – withdrawing, that is.'

'You don't seem sure. Has some startling information come to light that skews your opening argument?' Deed enquired. He glanced at the defence barristers but got no clue there.

'I'm not aware of any,' the QC said.

'From my reading of the pre-trial submissions, Mr Mason Allen, there was a case to answer, certainly against Ms Ortega.'

'No,' Rupert Fish said, leaping up in the dock.

'I not did,' Mariana Ortega said right alongside him.

Deed ignored them.

'These are my instructions, my Lord,' the prosecutor said like a confession.

'Then, Mr Mason Allen, I suggest you return to those who are instructing you and take further instructions.'

'No, my Lord…' Heathcote Machin was on his feet, 'You can't.'

'I can't, Mr Machin?' Deed said. 'You have the precedent that stops me proceeding in this way?'

Jo Mills was on her feet, book in hand. 'In R v Grafton, the Court of Appeal confirmed that the ultimate decision over whether to continue is for the prosecution, so a case can be ended by a prosecutor even when a judge takes the contrary view that there is a prima facie case. The Crown tried to withdraw the case for lack of evidence. The trial judge suggested this was due to "the crass incompetence" of the Crown Prosecution Service in making part of their case a witness they knew would support the defendant, and then seeking to discontinue when he did just that. The judge insisted on hearing the case; the Appeal Court judges were unanimous in their opinion that he was wrong.'

'I am familiar with that case, Mrs Mills. Discontinuance under section 23A of the Prosecution of Offences Act 1985 is not available at this stage of the proceedings. A judge can invite the CPS to consider another prosecution. In R v Swansea Justices, Lord Justice Mustill said, at 712, that "the public has an interest in ensuring that properly brought prosecutions are properly conducted in court just as much as the defendant has an obvious interest in being allowed to present his case to the fullest advantage".' He waited a moment, but got no further argument. He glanced at the clock. 'In view of the hour and Mr Mason Allen needing to take further instructions, until the morning,' he said, and rose.

In other circumstances he might have let this case fall, and wondered if he wasn't pursuing it because of Neil Haughton's curious involvement. So much for the impartiality of the High Court bench. May be there was a hidden, more sinister motive he wasn't recognising.

That was George Channing's view when she came to see him. This approach made him more curious as she strode along the corridor with Coop. Deed waited at the door to his room, having just walked Baba. George's anger was obvious as she let off a volley ten yards away from him.

'John! What the hell do you imagine you're playing at? Isn't it enough that Neil is losing the Home Office –? You're trying to humiliate him further by insisting that this sordid little murder trial goes ahead.'

'He's making a good fight-back, George, with you representing him.'

'He's hardly going to roll over to be a victim of your spite.'

'Your presence suggests there's something he doesn't want out.'

'There's nothing. How could there be?'

'To ignore a witness summons brings the law into disrepute. It's a bad example for the Home Secretary to set, even a soon-to-be ex-Home Secretary.'

'Don't be pompous, John.'

'Coop, would you mind getting us some tea?' Deed said, stepping through into his office. He knew Coop would have preferred to stay. He would have preferred her to stay in order to provide some check to George.

When she left, George said, 'The Home Secretary cannot appear in a murder case just because some woman throws up his name.'

'Is that what happened? You look very attractive, George. Haughton doesn't deserve you.'

'You'll make me a laughing stock around chambers.'

'Why are you so nice to him?' Deed asked, stroking her lapel with the back of his finger. He still found George attractive, even if impossible to live with.

'This is about negative publicity to try to aid her case. An agency sent her as a cleaner while ours was on holiday. How can Haughton possibly help by giving evidence?'

'That depends what he knows.'

'No, it's not-so-subtle pressure. The Home Secretary employing an illegal. You can see the headlines.'

'He wouldn't be the first in this Government to get caught out, George,' Deed said, feeling sorry for her. 'It's an easy mistake. Anyone who's ever employed a temporary cleaner is likely to have made it'.

'Have you?' George Channing enquired.

'Like Home Secretaries, High Court judges have to be extra careful,' Deed replied without irony.

'It's too much to hope that you would've slipped up.' She went to one of his cupboards and helped herself to a drink without offering him one. He followed her, touching her long, pale neck. 'Now she's putting pressure on Neil to help her out of her hole.'

'I can understand why,' Deed said. 'What I can't understand is why someone in high office thought it a good idea to press the prosecution to withdraw its case.' He waited, sensing she wanted to tell him something, but had changed her mind. 'Is there something, George?'

'No, of course there isn't.' The force with which she responded told Deed there was. Having lived with her, he could read her. Then he had it.

'Haughton had sex with this woman.'

George slammed her glass down, 'Don't be ridiculous. She's a cleaner!'

'A sexually inviting cleaner, who most men in court are thinking about in those terms, I'm sure.'

'You would notice that, of course.' She poured herself another drink.

'At least it makes your man human. I could dismiss that as a meaningless peccadillo, as I'm sure you have, but for his insisting on a go-ahead young barrister going before the sacking committee – she got drunk and made a pass of some sort at a Minister in the MoD.'

'She wasn't that drunk, and she called the Secretary for Defence a useless – I won't use the "c" word. Not how barristers should behave.'

'The same word could be used about most Government ministers – metaphorically. A word he would have heard many times on visits to servicemen,' Deed added. 'We shouldn't sacrifice this barrister for being honest. There are too few of those.'

George's face came alive. 'Is that what you want, a straight swap, Neil for this young woman?'

Deed laughed. 'Oh George, how did I ever let you go? Why are you so loyal to him?' He waited, as if expecting her to tell him. Instead, she glanced away, her mood changing. Deed stepped around her to look at her. Her eyes were wet.

George wasn't given to tears but now she seemed vulnerable. Perhaps she was changing, but then he suspected some ploy that he hadn't yet worked out. 'George,' he said, giving her the benefit of the doubt.

'Oh he's an attractive man, and he's clever, and wealthy. The truth is, John, I don't want to end up alone, bitter and broke and full of regrets.'

'Come on, George, you're still a beautiful, intelligent woman, and a clever barrister. I can't believe you haven't earned a lot of money.'

'Did I ever find time to be a mother to Charlie, or a wife? I barely had time to see Mummy in the hospice when she was dying. You know what they call me – the Ice Maiden. Will anyone be there for me at the end, apart from Neil?' Her mood changed again; suddenly the hard George was back saying, 'Do what you must, John. But remember what's at stake for you – the Appellate Bench.'

Deed stepped away as if shoved in the chest. 'For a moment there, George, I thought there was a thaw in the ice. If I'm subject to that sort of pressure, the Court of Appeal is not worth it,' but immediately his thoughts went to how he might retrieve the situation.

George gave him no opportunity. 'It's your funeral, chum,' she said as she strode out.

CHAPTER EIGHT

⤖

SEEING JESSIE RODGERS WAITING ON a brocade chair on the panelled corridor, wearing a skirt above her knees and a short narrow jacket, Rochester thought she looked good enough to eat. He glanced nervously at Sir Percy Thrower as they approached. It was clear why this 28-year-old might make some men breathless. He became aware of Percy melting at his side, ready to forget their purpose. Whether the disciplinary tribunal would prove forgiving with three older female barristers sitting was doubtful; there was little sisterhood among the female bar.

'Ms Rogers, how nice to see you again,' Rochester said, as though this were a casual encounter. Despite his Home Office counterpart having agreed how to conduct this, Percy pressed forward like an eager dog as the young woman rose on those long, shapely legs. How could Deed not be captivated by her?

'I heard your speech at the Law Society the other night, Sir Ian,' she purred. 'So daring and funny: Judges needing to observe the rule of law.'

At once Rochester felt unsteady and was ready to forgive her until Percy stepped forward to insinuate himself here. It had the desired effect and Rochester stepped back, irritated that he could be subject to such flattery. If he lost control of this and let Percy make an ass of himself, he might not achieve his objective.

'Sir Percy Thrower, Home Office,' he was saying. 'We're bringing out the really huge guns.' He laughed, and Ms Rogers responded.

'Oh, I must be in big, big trouble,' she said, like a young girl who knew she'd been naughty but didn't think it too serious.

'So you ought to be, considering who you attacked,' Percy said, moving in on her as if he was about the devour her.

Seeking to wrest back control, Rochester said, 'As I suggested before when we met there is a clear way forward.'

Jessie Rogers gave a confidential look. 'Is sex involved, Sir Ian?'

Rochester could see Percy was caught out, like him. What power this young woman had, if only she could be persuaded to use it against their target.

'We should go into the anteroom – it's more discreet there,' he said.

'I'm waiting to go before a disciplinary tribunal.'

'They will wait for us,' Percy assured her.

He pointed her along the corridor, his greedy eyes stumbling after her. He seemed like a man about to enter her boudoir rather than a private room to thrash out an arrangement which might save her and resolve the difficult situation Deed was fomenting.

'Is this meant to be a joke?' Deed asked. Coop had brought more references she'd found on the European Convention and told him who his marshal was to be. He was standing behind a stack of paper.

Both Coop and Baba looked at him as if wondering what the fuss was about.

'It seems the Conduct Committee of the Bar Standards Board thought you'd be a good influence,' she said.

Deed remembered his initial thoughts about the attractive young barrister. 'They're sending her to slow me down so Joe Channing and Tom Witham can extradite Salibi. We'll have a stream of judges at the door, licking the paintwork! Where is my new marshal?'

With some rancour, as if recognising she no longer stopped traffic, Coop said, 'Probably in the ladies, shortening the hem of her skirt. Why would you need her help, Judge, when you've got Baba to distract you?'

'Set her to work – our marshal.'

'I think she should start by scrubbing floors and washing up – so she realises life here isn't all breathless fun.'

'I thought you'd have approved of this young woman badmouthing a Government minister in public.'

'Oh I do, Judge, it's the fact that she gets away with it because of her long legs and tiny waist I resent.'

'She won't have got away with anything if you get her scrubbing,' Deed said.

He sat down to the huge pile of folders, wondering how useful this temporary judicial assistant would be. With a rap on the door five minutes later he sensed she wouldn't be any help as his heart rate suddenly quickened. This was ridiculous – at 54 he wasn't about to act the goat, but would tell her to turn down the volume. Wrenching open the door, he found Joe Channing there. Each seemed as surprised as the other. He stepped in unbidden and looked about, disappointment creeping over his sagging face.

'Ah, John,' he said as if unsure.

'Joe.' Deed gave nothing.

The older man hesitated. 'Now, what was it I wanted?'

'To lick the paintwork?' Deed suggested, getting a quizzical look, before adding, 'Long legs and wasp-like waist – the other parts good to look at too?'

'Oh, are they?' It might have been a point in evidence.

'You're the third judge to look in this morning,' Deed told him.

'Well, you're a font of wisdom, John – going on to the Appellate Bench.'

'The other two were Supremes, Joe.'

'Even so, even so.' He hesitated again. 'I came to see how you are marshalling your arguments against this deportation.'

'I daresay my new marshal will marshal them.'

'Oh, you've got a young barrister to help – good.' Joe glanced away. 'Tom Witham was asking. The clock's ticking.'

There was a soft rap at the door.

'Maybe here's the answer to our prayers, Joe.' Deed called, 'Yes.'

Jessie Rogers stepped around the door, as confident in her manner as her looks.

'Ah, Jessie,' Deed said, 'I forgot to ask. Can you scrub floors?'

'Does the floor need scrubbing, my Lord?'

The way she used his formal title seemed loaded.

'Joe, this is my new marshal.'

'I bet you can make tea too!' He shook her hand, not letting it go. 'That's about all marshals could do at one time.'

'Thank you for the Salibi reminder, Joe,' Deed said. 'We'll get working.'

Joe Channing gave him a sharp look, and went out with a quick glance back at the young woman.

'Do you want tea now, Judge?' she asked.

Deed slapped the pile of papers. 'What I want is every precedent and all the case law covering the extradition of alleged offenders, illegal immigrants and asylum seekers. Any that has run afoul of the European Convention. With this Government's record there could be plenty.'

'I shall scour the jurisprudence with a lynx-like eye.'

'Judgments anywhere could be useful. Coop has made a start. You might need to burn the midnight oil on this.'

'I've given up my social life as part of my penance.'

Deed glanced at her and she returned a frank look, giving nothing away. She would make a fine court advocate, he decided, and was about to say as much when Coop came in with a tea tray. 'Run!' he said.

'Is there a fire, Judge? Oh, I've forgotten the tea strainer. Jessie, could you run for that too?'

'Sorry, Coop,' she batted back. 'The coal-face awaits.' She hurried away.

'Have we heard when Mason Allen's coming back in the murder case?'

'Mr Machin's instructing solicitor said his client doesn't want any deal that involves prison,' Coop told him, pouring tea for him. 'She wants to walk.'

'I expect pigs would like to fly, too.' He collected his tea and glanced at the clock. They would know soon enough.

From the bench in court, Deed could see the prosecuting QC was not happy. No matter how hard you tried to avoid your thoughts, often they translated to the face and Mason Allen QC made no attempt to disguise his.

Even so, Deed was obliged to ask for the record. 'Mr Mason Allen?'

Climbing to his feet with apparent effort, he said, 'We haven't reached an agreement. In the light of your Lordship's observations and the kind opportunity to reconsider our position, the Crown would like to call Dr Derek Westbrook, the Home Office pathologist who examined Mr Bartlett's body.'

A round-looking man in his mid-30s stepped into the witness box wearing thick, round eye-glasses, heavy side whiskers and a tweed suit. He seemed out of place and out of time, but took the oath crisply like someone who had done this a hundred times.

'Dr Westbrook, were you able to tell from your examination of Mr Bartlett's body what gap, if any, there was between his death and the blows to his head?'

'Oh yes, we can pinpoint the gap between attack and death to within two and four hours,' the pathologist said, his light voice wrong for his size.

'Can you tell the court why you're so sure?' the QC asked, looking at the jury, watching their reactions.

'Because of how blood had coagulated around the wounds – work having been done by the body to heal the wounds made earlier.'

'Meaning what, that the victim was alive during this time and the killer blow came sometime later…?' still looking at the jury.

'Yes. Three earlier cuts to the head had started to heal. A final blow several hours later is certainly what killed him.'

Deed glanced over at Rupert Fish as he turned to his co-defendant, surprise on his face. Ortega gave an impatient shake of her head, which seemed to leave him more confused.

Heathcote Machin leaned forward to press his points in cross-examination. 'Doctor, can you tell how this supposed fatal blow to Mr Bartlett differs from the three previous blows?'

'It cracked his skull,' the doctor said.

'I'm sure the jury is ten yards ahead of you on that. Why didn't the other three blows do this?'

'Obviously the deceased had a thick skull,' the pathologist said with a degree of petulance. 'Plus, there was little resistance. The first three blows were in effect pushing him away.'

'And the fourth, doctor?' Machin glanced at the jury now.

'My opinion is that he was struck when he was on the ground, after he'd been dumped.'

'You mean it's possible that someone crept back and hit the victim much later?' He glanced round to the dock, focusing on Rupert Fish.

'Whatever the mechanism, his death certainly occurred sometime later.'

Deed could see where Machin was leading the jury, and it was clear some were shocked by this revelation. How Jo Mills would take this back and send it towards Machin's client he was curious to find out.

'Could you tell from your examination,' Jo Mills asked, leaning on her small lectern, 'if these blows were struck by a man or a woman?'

That might do it. A smile crept into a corner of Deed's mind.

'The police assumed from what they were told it was a man.'

'That wasn't what I asked you, Dr Westbrook. I too read the defendants' interviews. Is there forensic evidence to suggest it was a blow from a man?'

'No, of course there isn't.'

'So the blow could easily have been delivered by a young, fit woman?' She looked round at Mariana Ortega as the doctor conceded the point. 'Did you examine the murder weapon?'

'I was never shown it,' the witness said. 'I don't believe it was found.'

'Yes, it's not on the prosecution's exhibit list.' Again she glanced round at Mariana Ortega, causing her to react.

'Why you look me?' she demanded.

Jo Mills glanced at the jury, having sown enough doubt.

The next witness, Detective Sergeant Burrell, conducted the major part of the investigation.

'Did it strike you as at all odd that the murder weapon wasn't found?'

'It did. The second defendant said he couldn't remember what happened to it. We searched the whole area where the body lay.'

'It wasn't anywhere at the flat?'

'No. Somehow the weapon had been got rid of,' the detective said.

'In the circumstances would you have expected to find the murder weapon?'

'We would have, sir. Yes.'

'Did you draw any conclusions?' the prosecution asked.

'That one or other of them was trying to disguise what they'd done by disposing of the Buddha statuette that was said to have been used as the murder weapon.'

Heathcote Machin was having none of that. He leant back from his lectern and said, 'If you didn't find this Buddha, Sergeant, how do you know it was the murder weapon?'

'Mr Fish said he'd wrestled it off the victim when he tried to kill Mariana… I mean Ms Ortega…' he glanced at the Judge. Deed noted this woman's influence even here. 'He used it to defend her. We assume it was used to finish him off.'

'When he crept back to retrieve the duvet the body was wrapped in?'

Jo Mills gave Machin a sharp look – not pleased at his cut-throat line.

'That was our conclusion,' the sergeant said.

'I have no further questions of this witness.'

Jo Mills was writing a note and made no move to rise. The Judge waited. He was puzzled as to what she would manage to get for her client. 'Mrs Mills?'

'Might I have a short adjournment, my Lord, to consult my client?'

Deed glanced at the clock. 'It's 10-to-4, Mrs Mills. In view of the hour, you might have all evening with him if you wish. I suspect you'll only get until 4.30.'

The cramped court cell with its scarred walls wasn't high on her list of places Jo Mills wanted to spend time, but her client wasn't in a hurry to answer her questions and paced agitatedly. She doubted she'd get any sort of answer, much less the truth.

Again she said, 'The missing Buddha is hurting us, Rupert. Think carefully about what happened to it.'

'I don't know. I must have dropped it… Yes, I dropped it, like Mariana said – after I hit Mr Bartlett when he attacked her.'

'Like Mariana said?' Simon Chester made it a question.

'Yes,' he said. 'No, I mean, it's what happened.'

Jo Mills said nothing, more convinced that he didn't do what he claimed in his statement. It occurred to her that the police may have questioned them together, with the woman influencing him. She made a note to check that out.

'You realise Mr Machin is steering this murder your way?'

'That's understandable. He's defending Mariana.'

'You don't have to do so as well!' Jo was getting impatient. 'You're not letting us defend you, Rupert.' There was no reply but he avoided her look. 'Rupert, look at me. Were you actually present when this man was struck?'

'I hit him, Mrs Mills.' – without looking at her.

She said sceptically, 'But did you kill him? The pathologist suggested he was killed when someone went back for the duvet. That is premeditated murder. You could be looking at a 30-year prison sentence.'

Rupert Fish lowered his head and mumbled, 'I went back for the duvet.'

'Was Mr Bartlett alive at that point?' Jo asked.

'I don't think he could have been. No.'

'Then did Ms Ortega go back and kill him?'

'No, she wouldn't.'

'Rupert, do you love her?'

'Yes, of course.'

'Does she love you?'

'Yes, she said so.'

'Your loyalty could get you convicted. How do you think this love will endure when you're serving life in prison and she's free as a bird?'

'No she wouldn't… she won't. She'd… she'd…' He struggled to finish so Jo helped him out.

'She'd wait for you? I don't believe you killed Peter Bartlett. Someone went back long after he was dumped, found him alive and finished him off. I believe you know who that was.'

Rupert Fish rounded on her with such vehemence that for a moment Jo thought he was going to punch her.

'I won't let you blame Mariana. I won't allow that.'

This confused Jo, who now began to think perhaps this young man could have killed someone in defence of a woman with whom he was so besotted.

Outside the court building as she headed for the taxi rank with Simon Chester, she said, 'We've got two choices. Either we accept his instruction or I'm going to have to try to get consent to treat my own witness as hostile.'

'He won't thank you.'

'Not now, he might later.'

'Not ever if she goes to prison.'

'He might lose her anyway. She will walk if he continues like this.'

'He's convinced himself that she'll be waiting for him.'

'Ahh, men are so bloody stupid about sex!' Jo screamed, causing people to look round at her, one of them a circuit judge. Grimacing, she slipped into a cab ahead of the instructing solicitor.

CHAPTER NINE

DEED WAS AWARE HOW LITTLE time there was left for him to find the alternative to Salibi's extradition and wondered about abandoning his search. There was so much reading to do, the European Convention alone was a mountain of paper that didn't seem to diminish. Coop and Jessie Rogers had been reading for almost twelve hours. He should offer them dinner and a taxi home, but if they stopped, time would run out.

Frustration seeped through him and he glanced over at Jessie Rogers, who was making notes at a table opposite. Her close proximity stirred in him a yearning as dangerous and random as cancer he knew not how to eradicate. She gave off such heat, such exhilaration. He quickly glanced about, realising it was with a sense of what he was sure many defendants experienced: guilt. Her every movement seemed to stir something primal in him, the way she tilted her head, hair falling down her face to be unselfconsciously pushed aside, the way she leaned over the desk for a folder. He was entranced and barely aware of Coop at her desk on the far side of the room, upright in her chair, sound asleep. She got in each morning with the security people before 8.00 A.M. Some instinct caused Jessie to notice her and she glanced in Deed's direction.

'Coop, time you went home,' he said.

Jerking awake, Coop said, 'Yes, Judge, I'm fine. I'll get us some coffee.'

'I'm not finding what I want.'

'Might this be useful, Judge?' Jessie said, offering him a highlighted document. 'Denmark tried to throw out seven Pakistani men who'd groomed young girls for sex. They argued their right to a family life which they wouldn't have in Pakistan. They won.'

'I'd be amazed,' Deed said and took the papers, unsure if the excitement now energising him was at this possible route through or his fingers brushing hers. 'How long had they been living in Denmark?'

'Twenty years. Two were brothers. Five were from another family.'

Without looking up, Deed said, 'Denmark is a signatory to the Convention and has sound laws.' He continued reading, but his excitement was short-lived. 'Four of the men were subsequently killed by vigilantes.'

'Was it the court's business to know that might happen?' Jessie asked.

Deed liked her argument. 'There had been threats on their lives previously. It's poor law if we don't try to second-guess what might happen as a result of our actions.'

'Jersey and Collins Appeal case, the judges were emphatic it wasn't for the court to decide that – it was in my bar finals,' Jessie told him.

'If the law is divorced from the people it serves it becomes remote, a possible instrument of repression,' Deed pointed out.

'Can't it only act objectively?' Jessie asked argumentatively.

'I'm suggesting it shouldn't,' he said.

The young barrister wasn't done and he could sense Coop flagging. 'Then aren't you arguing against what you want to achieve, my Lord?'

'I am. I want to have my cake and eat it. That's the danger with acknowledging the human condition within the context of law. But somehow, we must. Let's go home. Can I give you a lift…?'

Coop cut in with, 'I go her way!'

'That's okay,' Jessie said. 'I'm not going home.'

'The judge likes to start early,' Coop told her like an admonishing aunt.

'Seven o'clock?' the younger woman challenged.

'Eight-forty-five will be fine,' Deed said.

'I'll be here, sir. Bye, Coop.' She flew, closing the door.

'Dressed like that,' Coop observed, 'I bet the poor mite has no social life at all.'

Coop could be both dry and caustic. Deed tried to meet her look, but she turned away. 'Is that all you've got to say, Coop?' – as she went on stacking a pile of papers on her desk. 'Coop?'

'It's probably not important.'

'You don't like her, Coop.'

'I don't trust her. Rumour is she has had affairs with several different QCs in her chambers.'

Deed laughed to hide the stab of jealousy he irrationally felt. 'None of them head of chambers, presumably?'

'It's not funny, Judge. They were all married.' She slammed her drawer shut.

'It's not for us to police the morals of others, Coop. We can only try to set an example,' he said with a straight face, wondering what Coop must have felt about his less than example-setting behaviour around women. Perhaps she felt as conflicted as he sometimes did.

Why the arrogant Deed should be blessed with a breath-stopping judicial assistant, Sir Tom Witham couldn't guess. He rather hoped the department was testing him, expecting him to disgrace himself. Many men with stronger resolve than Deed would fall victim to her beauty, touch her and fall. He watched her come along the deserted corridor as he stepped from Joe Channing's magnificent room. His own rather inadequate room in the basement made him feel a bit like a second-class judge, some might even have seen it as a racist sleight.

'Someone else who doesn't have a social life,' he said in a throwaway fashion.

'Excuse me?' Jessie Rogers said.

'Beautiful women who burn too much midnight oil use up their light,' – he felt foolish as soon as the words were out and tried to redeem the situation. 'Do you know who said that?'

She laughed and he immediately fell in love with her.

'It was you,' she said. 'I saw your lips move.'

Sir Tom laughed too. 'You're Mr Justice Deed's new marshal. I hear there's been a stream of judges in to look you over.'

'Not one of them under 65. So disappointing,' she said.

'We're not a young profession.'

'You didn't pay a visit, Judge. Why, because you're dangerously young?'

It was like an invitation, and despite the inherent risks he could feel himself drawn. Sir Tom waited, trying to psych her out, knowing he was losing this round, but thinking he may be able to glean some useful information from her about Deed.

The wine bar wasn't the most discreet place to take her, but he wanted to show her off, drawing looks as they crossed the room with a bottle of very expensive Pouilly-Fuissé.

'You know Deed has quite a reputation for bedding young barristers, Jessie?' he said as they settled at a table, realising he was making the man seem more attractive.

'I'm beginning to suspect you only invited me get information about him.'

'Oh my God,' he said, covering his embarrassment, 'a mind-reader as well as a *femme fatale*. Perhaps if I make a pass at you it'll crush that idea.'

– 64 –

'But I'm only attracted to men of a certain age,' she said.

He stopped pouring the wine and gave her an uncertain look, wondering if he should make his excuses and leave. Against his better judgement he filled her glass, then his own.

The invitation to the Home Office was like a summons and Witham went feeling peeved that Haughton couldn't have suggested a more convenient time. His irritation wasn't relieved by the affable Sir Percy Thrower who led him along the corridor, a smile a mile wide on his face, as if knowing something he didn't. The Home Office spied on all sorts of people, only he decided they would draw the line at a High Court judge.

'Why on earth does Government start so early, Percy?' It wasn't even eight o'clock and he was curious to know what time Haughton got to his desk.

'At Oxford I thought my career would take a more leisurely turn – I was a rowing Blue and I'd got involved with the acting set,' Sir Percy said. 'I was quite good, but regrettably I didn't stay with it.' He knocked on the Home Secretary's door and opened it without being invited to do so.

'Tom Witham, Home Secretary,' he announced.

'Ah, Tom.' Haughton sprang out of his chair and shook his hand with such vigour it irritated Witham more. 'How's the new job?'

'Which one?' Witham enquired. 'I'm holding my own in both roles, though I prefer being on the bench.'

'I'm sure you do, Tom.'

'Do you want me in?' Sir Percy asked.

'No, Percy,' – in a dismissive manner. 'Tell Alice we want more coffee.'

Witham saw the Permanent Secretary give a deprecating look as he went out, Neil Haughton being too full of himself to notice. Witham wondered if he'd treat him with the same distain. 'Some coffee would be most welcome,' he said. 'God, Neil, that girl can drink – and not cheap plonk.'

'Is she as fabulous as I hear?'

Witham sighed. 'Just let your imagination run riot.'

'Then you'd better be careful, Tom.'

Witham scoffed, not contemplating being such a dupe. 'I thought it was Deed you were hoping to catch out. I'm sure he'll be totally hooked.'

'I can't wait to see his face when the trap is sprung,' Haughton said in anticipation. 'It's a pity she's twenty-eight, not fourteen or even better, thirteen!'

The Home Secretary slapped his hands together, as though Deed were already compromised. The more Witham saw of this man close up, the less he liked him, he decided, and understood why Deed had no time for him. It occurred to him then that he may have backed the wrong side, even though he had had no choice.

CHAPTER TEN

In the witness box was a short, young Polish man with a ruddy complexion that ran all the way down his thick neck which sank into his shoulders like a melted candle. Over and again Rudi Kozlowski nervously washed his large hands with their short fingers as he faced Newman Mason Allen QC.

Deed wondered how he might respond when facing the defence barristers, neither of whom would be so friendly. The suit he was wearing immediately drew Deed's eye, its impeccable cut suggesting it cost a lot more than he imagined the income of a porter in a flat block to be. Or perhaps someone had gifted him it. Such a possibility made Deed curious about the man, who kept winking at the QC, a nervous tick rather than collusion.

'Mr Kozlowski, until what time were you on duty at Brunswick Mansions on April 15th?' the prosecution asked.

'Yes I was,' the witness replied in good English.

'Yes. What were your hours of duty?'

'All time.'

'Are you saying you were on duty all day and all night?' Deed enquired.

'I sleep at night sometime.'

'I'm pleased to hear it,' the judge said and made a note about the witness's reliability. 'Mr Mason Allen?'

'Were you asleep when the deceased man, Mr Bartlett, arrived?'

'He wake me up with lady, telling Mariana, I love, I love. He very drunk, sir.'

'You saw them come in?'

'I look out office.'

'Did you hear what she said?' prosecuting counsel asked.

'"You bloody drunk," she say. "Come upstairs. Be quiet."'

'She lured him up to his death…'

Heathcote Machin jumped up and the judge waved him down.

'I'm not asleep, Mr Machin,' he said, then to Mason Allen, 'You know better.'

'I do, m'Lord. I apologise.' He turned to the witness. 'Thank you,

Mr Kozlowski. Please stay there, as I'm sure my learned friends have some questions.'

In Jo Mills' absence her junior got to his feet out of turn, to the surprise of Heathcote Machin, who was expected to follow the prosecution. Stephen Vanner looked about 22 and behaved as if he had just been called to the Bar. Puffy bags under his eyes suggested he was sleep-deprived like so many junior barristers.

'Mr Vanner, I believe it's for Mr Machin to go first. But as you're here, would you mind telling me where your leader is?' Deed asked.

'She's in another court, my Lord.'

'In the middle of a murder trial?' Deed was not surprised but a little annoyed.

'It's in the High Court, my Lord,' the young barrister said as though that explained everything.

Deed wasn't about to let it go. 'I'm sure its importance outweighs this little Crown Court affair. I'm very pleased the death penalty is no longer in force. Ask her to see me in chambers at the end of the day.'

That seemed to make the barrister more nervous, and Deed regretted taking his irritation out on him. First the young man dropped his notes, then his glasses and when retrieving both, knocked over a carafe of water. Mopping the spillage with a tissue, he began, 'What sort of state was Ms Ortega in when she arrived at the flat block?'

'No, Mr Vanner – unless Mr Machin has no questions of this witness.'

'He does,' Machin said bobbing up, 'but I'm happy for my learned friend to go first as he's started.'

'Then continue, Mr Vanner,' Deed told him, fearing he might never get started again if he made him go in turn.

'What sort of state was Ms Ortega in when she arrived?'

'She had on clothes,' Kozlowski said and the jury laughed. Stephen Vanner looked around at them like he'd scored a point.

'Was she normally undressed?' Vanner asked.

'Mariana very sexy lady.'

'Was she encouraging the victim upstairs?'

'She say, "Come upstairs. Make love."'

'Had you ever seen Mr Bartlett visit the apartment prior to then?'

'Yes. He sometimes visit in day.'

'Did you see Mr Fish, the second defendant, there before?'

'Him sometime there, is his flat. Mariana she sometime not let him in.'

'Because she had other lovers there,' Stephen Vanner asked, 'is that what you're telling the jury?'

'Sometime yes; sometime no. She tell me he a big nuisance.'

That caused a stab of pain to cross Rupert Fish's face where he sat behind the security glass. Mariana Ortega took his hand and gave him a warm smile. Deed was thinking how that might do it for a lot of men, as he made his note.

On cross-examination Heathcote Machin was clear and incisive, left fist planted on his hip, barely referring to his notes. Not much older than Vanner but conducting himself with such elan he could have taught older QCs with his presentation.

'Mr Kozlowski, what are your duties at Brunswick Mansions?'

'I the porter, sir. Sometime service thing in flats.'

'Does that servicing sometimes include Ms Ortega?'

That brought a hush as the court awaited his answer. It wasn't forthcoming. 'Mr Kozlowski, do you understand my question? Did you occasionally have sex with Ms Ortega?'

'She a very pretty lady,' the porter said. 'Yes. Take me up to flat.'

'Was Mr Fish there in the cupboard, ready to spring out?'

'No, not in cupboard.'

'But you knew of this arrangement with the cupboard?'

Kozlowski said he did know about it.

'On the night Mr Fish allegedly killed Mr Bartlett, had he gone into the apartment earlier to await the arrival of Ms Ortega and Mr Bartlett?' Heathcote Machin wanted to know.

'No, I not see him go upstairs. Another man.'

'She not say that…' the first defendant interrupted.

That threw the barrister off his stride as he whipped round to the dock, then back at the witness box.

Recovering, he said, 'Mr Kozlowski was not the second defendant, in fact, waiting in the bedroom cupboard to catch Ms Ortega with her lover, which indeed led to his jealous rage, during which he attacked and killed Mr Bartlett?'

'No. He come much later when Mariana telephone.'

Again Mariana Ortega interrupted. 'She not say that.'

'Ms Ortega, please remain silent and let your barrister speak for you,' Deed told her, with not much expectation of that.

Heathcote Machin was further adrift, clearly having had a different story from his client. He turned towards her in the dock but she was staring at the man in the witness box. Machin grabbed a whispered conversation with his instructing solicitor, and then turned back.

'My Lord, might I have a short adjournment to consult with my client?'

'That would be sensible, Mr Machin. But first I'd like to ask some questions of this witness.' Deed turned to the witness-box. 'Mr Kozlowski, are you now saying there was another man who was in the apartment when Ms Ortega was there with Mr Bartlett?' He waited for an answer. None was immediately forthcoming.'

Rudi Kozlowski finally said, 'I no understand.'

'I think you do, Mr Kozlowski.' Deed saw him glance over at Mariana Ortega, who was pulling faces at him. 'The answer is not over there.'

Shaking his head, the witness said, 'I not know him. Maybe I see before.'

'Was this man you *maybe* saw before a visitor to the apartment where the first defendant was waiting?'

'I no sure.'

'During the adjournment you will return to the witness room and search your memory and come back with some clear answers. Is that understood? Good.'

Deed rose before the clerk could call, 'All rise.'

'Wow! I'd love to be a fly on the wall at Machin's con with Ms Ortega, Coop,' Deed said to his clerk as he came along the corridor with her.

'She seems a real piece of work, Judge,' Coop replied.

'She's a fool if she's keeping her barrister in the dark,' Deed said. 'He's a fool if he lets her tell him something that compromises her defence. But then he's just a mere man.' He was looking forward to going back after the adjournment to hear what the porter in the expensively-cut suit might have to say.

Emerging from the Law Courts in the Strand, searching for a cab to get back to Southwark following an alarmed call from her junior, Jo was aware of someone coming after her. She didn't want to be delayed, least of all by Detective Superintendent Petra Hamblyn who she saw approaching. She flagged a vacant cab that came down from the Aldwych.

'We have a car, Mrs Mills,' the young detective said. 'We can give you a lift.'

'Where to,' she snapped, 'Paddington Green Police Station?'

The copper laughed like someone who believed she was on top of her game. 'Well, sooner or later. Your Ms Plant is a go-between for Muslim extremists here and the so-called Islamic State.'

'Bollocks!' Jo said. 'There's not a single shred of evidence.'

'We know you received the list of terrorist contacts that your client had been given, Mrs Mills,' the detective said.

'You're not only being ridiculous; you're getting to be boring,' Jo replied.

'It's called persistence. It's what good police work is made up of.'

'Facts, evidence – it's what the courts of law respond to,' Jo pointed out.

'You gave the list to Sir John Deed.'

That shocked Jo and she stumbled, letting the taxi wait. 'What? Do you know what it is you're saying? What dangerous ground you're treading on?'

'Now that the judge here has refused to grant your application for the return of Ms Plant's property, we are prepared to approach Sir John for the list.'

'Do you need his address?' Jo said, and stepped quickly into the taxi before she lost control again.

'Thanks for holding the fort, Stephen,' Jo said, hurrying along the corridor with her junior, ready to face the music from Deed. She wasn't sure what was happening with him that he so wanted to exert his authority. Perhaps it was anxiety that he might not be appointed to the Appellate Bench. Now she worried about the file she'd given him and the fact that he said he no longer had it.

Heathcote Machin glanced up from the front row and averted his eyes. Perhaps she was being paranoid, but his reaction suggested something was amiss and Jo suspected it would be her client who would suffer as a consequence, not his.

'Anything you need to share with me, Heathcote?' she asked.

'I can't think of a thing,' Machin said. 'How's your other case, the one that's hacking off this Judge?'

Before Jo could answer the clerk called, 'All rise.' Deed entered, his glance speeding across her before taking in everyone else.

'Ah, Mrs Mills,' he said, adjusting his chair. 'Does your arrival indicate further cross-examination of the prosecution witness, or do you, like Mr Machin, need more time?'

In the court transcript there would be no stresses or inflections, but

Jo could hear his sarcasm. 'I believe my learned colleague was coping rather well, but with your leave I would like to ask about some additional matters.'

'Before you do, I would like to ask this witness some questions.'

'Is this a general interest enquiry, my Lord, or more in the way of cross-examination?' Jo asked with similar sarcasm.

Ignoring her, the Judge said, 'Mr Kozlowski, can you tell me where you got your suit?'

The question puzzled the lawyers as well as the man in the witness-box.

'I give,' he said.

'Yes, the name of your tailor?' the judge asked, further puzzling everyone.

'Yes. I give.'

'You mean it was a gift to you from someone?'

'Yes, I give,' Kozlowski said, his accent getting heavier.

'M'Lord,' Mason Allen QC said, rising, 'might I ask how this is relevant?'

'Well, if I wanted to get such a well-made suit, Mr Mason Allen, I'd need to know the tailor.'

'I'm sure Mr Kozlowski would oblige you with the name of his tailor.' He turned to the witness. 'Could you tell his Lordship who made the suit for you?'

'No, it give me.'

'Ah,' the judge intoned, 'we're making a little progress. Who gifted you the suit? Maybe he'd give me his tailor.'

'I no say,' the witness said.

'If it's a source of embarrassment, Mr Kozlowski, I can understand that,' Deed said in an even tone that Jo guessed was concealing some other purpose.

Getting to her feet, she said, 'Perhaps if the witness removed his jacket your Lordship might look inside and note the tailor's name.'

'Most helpful as usual, Mrs Mills. Is that agreeable, Mr Kozlowski?'

When the usher passed the suit jacket up to him Deed felt slight envy. He enjoyed good suits and had a couple of his own made in Savile Row, but neither of this quality, hand-stitched fine cashmere. Instead, he settled for tailored shirts with monogrammed buttons. Vanity. The tailor of this suit was Maurice Sedwell of Savile Row. Deed noted the details, and the customer's name, J. Pollock, with the order number on the inside pocket, before handing the garment back to the usher, who returned it to the witness.

'Was this a gift for a kindness you did for this person, Mr Kozlowski?' Deed asked. The witness blanched. 'Perhaps you'd rather not say? That's all right. Do proceed, Mrs Mills.'

Her cross-examination of the witness amounted to nothing special and Deed listened with only a fraction of his attention, considering instead J. Pollock and why he might have given a busy apartment block porter such a suit. Was there a homosexual relationship? Being a former criminal barrister this mystery would continue to exercise him until he found the answer.

The phone call from Superintendent Hamblyn worried Witham. Did his involvement now suggest that he was pursuing a vendetta against a brother Judge? Somehow, he knew he had to get out from under the Home Secretary's influence, but that might not make for a comfortable life on the bench. However, if there was in fact serious wrong-doing by Mr Justice Deed that proved instrumental in his removal, it would do his own career no harm at all.

'You're certain Deed has these papers?' he said as he brought the detective into his room.

'Our camera in Mrs Mills' chambers shows her putting the file into an envelope – she gave it to this judge when he rushed to her aid and cancelled your warrant.'

'I must be absolutely certain,' he said, hoping none of his unease was detectable in his voice.

'It's clear from the transcript he knew what he was being given, sir.'

'If we choose our moment to act, neither he nor Mrs Mills might survive.' He felt like beating a triumphant drum roll on his desk.

Haughton was elated by the development Sir Percy Thrower brought him about Deed. He wanted to ring George Channing, the Lord Chancellor and anyone else who'd be pleased to see Deed brought down, but this wasn't something he would reveal yet in case it became another failed attempt.

'Perhaps we won't need Deed's pants round his ankles with that young barrister Rochester has placed in his room, Percy.'

'This is Deed we're discussing, Home Secretary. It's likely you'd need his pants in the danger-zone and the document in his possession.'

'It is on camera being passed across?' Haughton was concerned in case it was no more than someone's idea of a wet dream.

'It was, but it's yet another matter to find it in Deed's actual possession.'

'Get his young judicial assistant to locate it. It's all in the timing, Percy. We'll be there to nab him – work out how we might contrive that. Perhaps Superintendent Hamblyn could get a camera in Deed's room at the Strand or in Southwark.' The thought of that happening exhilarated him.

Seeing Jo Mills across from him in an armchair in his room caused his anger to evaporate. Deed knew the reason for that feeling earlier was sexual frustration. Sex was like a drug when any port in a storm was needed, but no one quite did it for him like this woman. For sixteen years, from her being a junior barrister at his chambers, they had been on-off lovers and at one time came close to marriage.

He liked to think Jo was too smart to marry him, knowing he was addicted without being committed. He believed he could commit to her, so lived in hope.

'How's your judicial slave getting on?' Jo Mills asked as Coop moved around him to pour them tea.

'You'd better ask Coop.' Deed took his cup.

'She's very efficient, Mrs Mills – if we could only stop judges popping in for advice,' Coop said and sighed. 'Perhaps she should change her style of dress.'

'Perhaps you should suggest it, Mrs Cooper.'

'Oh, I suggested she came in a baggy full-length dress.'

'There are benefits,' Deed said. 'Wherever she goes for information, people fall over themselves to help.'

'Men do, you mean. How she gets it is what worries me, Judge,' his clerk said, and went out.

'How is your other case progressing?' Deed asked.

'You can't guess? My application was turned down in the interests of state security.'

'It's going to restrict us more and more, Jo. Lawyers included. It'll get far worse if the Human Rights Act is repealed.'

'We mustn't let the anti-terrorist legislation curtail our freedoms, John, or we might morph into the sort of repressive state that hundreds of thousands of British people died fighting against.'

'We'll try to keep whatever safeguards are necessary in place.'

'Whatever safeguards are necessary?' she questioned with dismay in her voice. 'That's a worrying statement from you.'

'What do you want me to do, stand alone on every single issue?'

'At one time that was the very air you breathed.'

'Perhaps I'm older, and wiser,' Deed argued, having had this conversation and now not wanting to repeat it.

'Sounds like you think the forces of reaction might be right, regardless.'

The edge to her voice hardened and pushed him further away. He wasn't sure how to draw her closer. At one time he would have reached out and kissed her. Why was he hesitating now?

'What was your great interest in that witness's suit? It got everyone puzzled,' Jo Mills said.

'Didn't it strike you as odd, a man earning what, £400 a week, wearing a £1700 suit? It did me.'

'Perhaps the person who gave it is his lover.'

'You can do better, Jo. The poor bloke is another one besotted with the first defendant. I don't think she gave it him, and he's not gay. It was more likely a gift to keep him quiet.'

'Then why didn't you get him to name his benefactor?'

'I thought that was your job. You've often complained about me asking too many questions,' Deed pointed out, and watched Jo dismiss his argument with a flick of her head. 'I got his giftor – or at least the name of the person the suit was made for, J. Pollock.'

That caused Jo to sit up, alarm in her eyes.

'Jo?' – puzzled by her change. 'What?'

'Something occurred to me – no, it could be anyone. There must be a thousand J. Pollocks…' as if trying to dismiss the notion.

'Go with your instinct,' Deed advised.

'There's a Jim Pollock in my other case – well, not in it. I think that's the source of the pressure we're getting. My client says the Secretary of State for Defence is at the heart of the bribery scandal involving arms sales to Saudi Arabia and Qatar.'

'Is this connected to the papers you gave me?' Deed asked and when he saw her glance away, he wondered what she had involved him in? At once his mind rephrased that, knowing he had involved himself. Another question jumped to mind: was the Defence Minister also involved in the murder case? He was the minister Jessie Rogers offended. Did Deed now drag him in and risk the Appellate Bench, or keep him out and risk losing Jo forever?

'Should I alert the prosecution to this possibility?' she asked.

From that Deed knew she too was concerned about the survival of their friendship. 'You know the answer, Jo. It won't aid the case against those in the dock, and I doubt he'd respond even if you called him. All we'd get is a media scrum.'

'If it is one and the same, my Lord,' Jo said using his formal and most distancing form of address – as a censure, he felt, 'and it was this politician in the cupboard, then almost certainly it's the wrong man on trial.'

'I could say it is up to you to find a way to bring him into your defence, Mrs Mills,' Deed said, playing her game.

'The prosecution would object and you'd have to uphold the objection.'

'We don't yet know if it's the same Jim Pollock at the MoD.'

'No. You can hardly ask.'

'Jo,' Deed cautioned, 'you know the rules. We didn't even have this conversation.'

'Then how do we go forward? Will you allow me to recall the prosecution witness and cross-examine him as to the identity of J. Pollock?'

'I will not. It's too dangerous. I will examine him without the jury present. If I'm satisfied it's not the man at the heart of your other case then you'll have to run whatever defence you've got for Mr Fish.'

'Thanks, John.'

The warmth in Jo's smile then suggested she was back, but still he hesitated to step up to her and kiss her as he so wanted. He told himself she was a barrister before him and that it was proper that they didn't have relations at this time, but in truth he knew he was growing more uncertain of her.

'I'll ask Coop to alert the prosecution that I want Mr Kozlowski back in the witness box first thing tomorrow.'

CHAPTER ELEVEN

WHEN HE WALKED INTO COURT Deed expected the prosecution witness to be in the witness box ready to reveal the possible mysterious giftor of his expensive suit, but Mr Kozlowski wasn't there and he looked to the prosecution. 'Mr Mason Allen,' he said evenly, 'is your witness not here?'

'He is available, m'Lord. He wasn't feeling well and had to go to the toilet.' He turned to his junior and asked him to get the witness. The younger barrister hurried out, forgetting to bow to the bench.

'Perhaps we should have the jury in and call your next witness,' Deed said after they'd waited several minutes.

'As you wish, m'Lord.' Mason Allen QC glanced towards the door. 'I can only assume Mr Kozlowski is not recovering quickly.'

That proved a huge understatement when the junior counsel finally came racing back in looking ashen, again forgetting to bow. He whispered with erratic gestures to his leader, who turned to the bench, his face crumpled with shock.

'M'Lord, my learned friend has just informed me that the witness is dead.'

'How is that, Mr Mason Allen? Was he far more ill than you suspected?' Deed said, keeping surprise off his face as he had learned to do long ago.

'He was found hanging – in the men's toilets.'

Now Deed struggled not to reveal his shock. 'Is there any history to this witness?' he asked. 'Mr Mason Allen, is your junior all right?'

The young man on the second bench looked as if he were about to pass out. The whole court was rigid with silence as if unable to comprehend this news; then a buzz of conversation started up.

'I'm going to adjourn. I want the full details of this man's death, his medical history. In fact, I want to see where this occurred.'

Deed rose and left the court. Coop quickly helped him to de-robe before following him, with the court recorder and security staff, to the public toilets. The facilities for barristers were bad when he last appeared here as a barrister; these were in poor state even without the body that was hanging by the neck with a piece of flex tied to the window fastener, its feet twisted to the side on the toilet seat lid. The police constable in charge said they were waiting for the medical team to arrive. There was no doubt about Mr Kozlowski being dead, but still Deed stepped into the cramped, smelly cubicle to check if there was any pulse. There was none.

'I shouldn't touch him, sir,' the old, court constable said.

'Has anyone touched him?' Deed asked.

'No, sir, that's the protocol unless there's a chance of reviving him – there was no chance, sir.'

'Quite right, constable. I'm sure you've done the right thing.'

He stepped back out of the confined space and turned to Coop, who was avoiding looking at the body. 'Coop, I want to take a picture of him. Can I use your phone? Mine doesn't have a camera.' He knew he ought to update his phone, but he didn't like the way modern phones tracked your every movement.

'Do you want me to do it, Judge?'

He spared her that ordeal and took two photos of Mr Kozlowski, who was no longer wearing his expensive, well-cut suit. There was something odd about the position of the body which disturbed Deed.

During the adjournment Jo came to see him in his room with Heathcote Machin and Newman Mason Allen. 'What does this mean, John?' she asked. 'Did you push him too hard, maybe?'

He shrugged. 'What he thought might happen in court this morning is anyone's guess. Coop, show counsel those photos of the late Mr Kozlowski.'

Coop scrolled to the pictures on her phone. Deed watched as the barristers studied them, puzzlement clouding their faces. 'I think you've got it.' he said.

'Is this how he was found?' Mason Allen asked.

'The police said no one touched him.'

'Then I think a post mortem might tell us a great deal,' Jo said. 'There's a good chance he choked to death hanging there like that.'

'If I remember right from the death sentence appeals we worked on in Jamaica, that takes three to seven minutes, if the neck doesn't break. This looks like his neck didn't break. Was he out of court that long, Newman?' Deed said, turning to the prosecuting barrister.

'I remember him going out. I didn't keep track of the time.'

'If he didn't choke himself to death with that flex,' Jo said, 'the alternative is someone putting him up on the toilet seat.'

'Why would anyone do that?' Coop asked, perplexed. 'It would be so obvious if he didn't choke – someone must have done it.'

'Maybe that someone, in the event, was careless or didn't care, Coop,' Deed said and caught Jo's eye. She nodded, ahead of him. More than ever he needed to identify the J. Pollock for whom the suit Kozlowski was wearing yesterday was made.

Before resuming in court Deed called his former fencing partner, Row Colemore, a deputy assistant commissioner at Scotland Yard. Despite the relationship having wobbled when Colemore used both him and Jo Mills in the furtherance of his own career, Deed felt he was the best option for the answers he needed. Row had risen beyond a warrant card-carrying investigator, but was still a policeman and responded as Deed hoped. When he told him of his unease about Kozlowski's death, he could hear the excitement the prospect of this investigation was provoking. Maybe what they had had wasn't lost after all and Row Colemore would at least make sure he saw a copy of the post mortem report without Deed having to summon a copy in court.

In an era with less financial pressure on the courts they would have adjourned for the day following the violent death of a witness. Perhaps it would have been better had they done so today despite the cost; Deed noticed the press bench was now packed for the prosecution's examination of its next witness. Like most people in court his thoughts were on the death of the previous witness, not the youngish Iranian man, Reza Jannatie, in the witness-box. Twice Mason Allen QC called him Mr Kozlowski by mistake.

Deed watched the usher unfold a duvet which the prosecution alleged Mr Bartlett, the murder victim, bled onto when wrapped up in it and carried away.

'Mr Jannatie, can you tell the jury what this stain is?'

'I believe it is traces of human blood, sir.'

'When Ms Ortega brought it to your dry-cleaning business did she say how it got there?'

'She said her friend had a big accident. Could I get it out?'

'Did she say who her careless friend was?'

'She said Mr Fish.'

Mason Allen turned to the jury to emphasise the point and said, 'The second defendant. Had you seen this man before?'

'He sometimes came into the shop with cleaning for Mariana.'

'Were you able to remove the blood stain?'

'Not all of it. I couldn't put it in the solvent like that. I had to clean it by hand. This was the best we do.'

Turning to the jury again, Mason Allen QC said, 'Enough blood was left behind to identify it as type AB with a DNA profile matching Mr Bartlett, who was rolled in the duvet and carried out of the apartment while he was still alive.'

In other circumstances Deed might have picked him up on that sort of statement as the QC directed him to the report in his bundle and sat down. Heathcote Machin stood to his lectern. He didn't look at all distracted.

'Have you had blood-stained items to clean from Ms Ortega before?' he asked.

'Yes, a man's dark suit.'

'Do you know how blood got on the suit?'

'I believe Mr Fish got angry and hit someone.'

'Over the attention being paid to Ms Ortega?' her defence barrister asked.

'Yes, I believe that is so.'

'Thank you, Mr Jannatie. I have no further questions.'

'I do, before you cross-examine, Mrs Mills,' Deed said without looking up from his note. 'Was it Mr Fish who told you that?'

'No, sir, Ms Ortega told me.'

'Mrs Mills,' the Judge directed.

'Mr Jannatie, did Ms Ortega say to whom this duvet belonged?'

'She said it was Mr Fish's.'

'Is either one of them more familiar to you?' Jo asked, glancing at her notes as if the question was unimportant.

'Mr Fish comes to the shop more often,' the witness replied.

'That wasn't what I asked you.' She waited, watching Mr Jannatie's confusion deepen. 'When was the last time you had sex with Ms Ortega?'

That sent a buzz of anticipation around the court as the witness stammered and looked towards the dock. Deed wondered how counsel got that; perhaps female intuition. The picture she was painting of the first defendant was making a clear impression on the jury.

'It was more than dry cleaning she was giving you,' Jo said and got a laugh. 'It was mostly Mr Fish who would bring you cleaning. But on the occasion in question it was Ms Ortega who brought in Mr Fish's heavy, blood-stained duvet, saying he had had some sort of accident?'

'Yes,' the witness managed to say.

'Your erstwhile lover gave all this information but didn't say what Mr Fish's accident was that he should bleed on this duvet from his bedroom?'

When the witness answered in the negative Jo Mills glanced round at the jury, who were with her in doubting the first defendant was capable of any decent or honest feeling for Rupert Fish. He was staring at the floor, close to tears. Observing him, Deed was thinking about J. Pollock and where and how he fitted into this, possibly the man in the cupboard? More important was his identity.

'Thank you, Mr Jannatie. I think in view of the time.' Deed glanced at the clock, then cautioned the jury not to discuss the case with anyone, before rising.

As he stepped through the door, which Coop held open for him, he said, 'Did Row Colemore call me?'

'No judge.'

He guessed she would have told him if he had. Perhaps he was attaching too much importance to J. Pollock. 'Despite her sex-with-everyone stunt, Mrs Mills seems to be letting Machin steer everything towards her client,' he said, as he often shared his thoughts with his clerk.

'How the poor chump's stays in love with his co-defendant, despite everything.'

'Half of London has been at some time by all accounts – the male half. Can you see if you can catch Mrs Mills before she leaves the building, Coop?'

'Just Mrs Mills, Judge?'

'Yes, this relates to one of her other cases.'

In these circumstances Mrs Cooper could move fast, knowing busy barristers fielding any number of cases didn't hang around after court.

She showed Jo Mills out into the courtyard where Deed was walking Baba.

'What was Tom Witham's reason for not granting the return of your client's property?' he asked as she approached.

That seemed to surprise her. 'I thought you brought me here to tell me something else.' She stooped and stroked the little dog. 'He based his argument on Protocol No. 4 to the Convention – no restrictions shall be placed on freedom of movement other than what is "in accordance with law and necessary in a democratic society in the interests of national security or public safety, for the maintenance of *ordre public*, and for the prevention of crime".'

'He didn't expand on that?'

'No.' There was irritation in her voice. 'I'm sure the Lord Chancellor only appointed him to spy on us.'

'Judges don't do that, Jo. It's not how the appointments process works.'

'Oh, isn't it? I seem to recall you once saying it was.'

'Perhaps you should take back your envelope and keep it safe elsewhere,' Deed said, avoiding her look.

'Hah, I thought you'd at least stay loyal.'

'With you I'm like that doe-eyed chump in the dock with the woman selling him down the Swanee,' he protested. 'But I won't support you being foolhardy. If anyone in your client's papers is remotely connected to terrorism, you're in trouble.'

'I'm not propounding a defence I know to be false.'

Deed didn't respond.

'Did you look at the list?' she asked.

'You know me better.'

'There's a big principle at stake here.'

'With you, Jo, how could I imagine otherwise?'

'There used to be with you,' she retorted.

'You can't change the law. Only Parliament can do that. Meanwhile, the risk is too great.'

'You could change the law by precedent. So could your spineless brother, Mr Justice Witham. Enough High Court judges have done so and later been vindicated. Denning said, "If we never do anything which has not been done before, we shall never get anywhere. The law will stand still whilst the rest of the world goes on: and that will be bad for both".'

'That was in 1953,' Deed argued. 'Much has changed since, and I'm not Denning.'

'You could be if you dared to be.'

Hearing the anger and hurt in her voice, he wanted to reach out and drag her back from the brink, but she cut the concern he was feeling by adding, 'Now you're too self-satisfied with your high office to dare to stand alone.' With that she strode away, to what he asked himself, to fight her hopeless battle alone?

He knew he should call her back and offer to join her at the coalface of radicalism, but couldn't bring himself to so and disliked himself more because of it.

Deed began to question if the mass of documents Jessie Rogers was pulling up for him wasn't some conspiracy to stop him finding the means of preventing the Lebanese man being shipped off. There were more papers than one person could read in a year. She was intelligently marking up all the relevant passages, which helped, and was possibly getting assistance elsewhere. He listened to Jo's phone ring unanswered and her voice came on delivered like a speeding train. It beeped. He hesitated about leaving her yet another message. After a brief silence he said, 'Jo, it's me again. Don't be childish, talk to me. No one's abandoning principle for a seat on the Appellate Bench. Why can't I have both?'

He switched his phone off as Jessie came in with more photocopied pages pressed to her breast. He imagined he could smell her on the pages long after she placed them on his desk.

'Not more reading, Jessie?' he protested.

'Afraid so, my Lord,' she said, again using his title like an invitation, one he was ready to accept. 'Adjuncts to the main cases. They all appear to have relevance, sir.'

Deed sighed. 'Make a start categorising them. Coop can help.'

'Mrs Cooper's gone home. She wasn't well. You work her far too hard.'

That got his attention, enjoying this young woman's self-assured manner, and the fact that they were alone. He nodded, as if agreeing about Coop, and sat at his desk, pulling the papers towards him, wondering what he'd taken on in arguing this case. He would rather be pursuing Jo Mills amorously, despite her being before him in court. Suddenly he became more aware of Jessie standing beside the desk, imagining he could feel the heat from her body.

'Do you want anything, Judge?' she asked.

From the way she posed the question she must have read his thoughts and this gave him pause: was he just another middle-aged fool recognising his own mortality and stumbling in fear after youth? At that moment he wanted to lose himself in her, and knew all he had to do was reach out. A stronger willed man might not have resisted. He realised she had spoken. 'What?'

'I can make tea.'

Meeting her look, he said, 'I'm sure you can, Jessie. I'm sure you can do any number of things,' – holding her look, his thoughts not straying from her exquisite body. Now he was sure she was reading him like a book as her clear blue eyes stared back at him, her lips parting slightly. She was about the same age as his daughter. Was their age difference any real barrier?

'It is available, my Lord.'

Deed breathed out, blood coursing through his veins and he started to get an erection, knowing at any moment he could lose control. 'Stop calling me my Lord,' he said, trying to divert what was happening. 'What will you be doing in ten years' time, Jessie?'

'What about the next ten minutes?' she suggested.

His breathing became heavier, blood hammering in his ears. 'Would you want to be hanging around a man who by then would be on his way to 70?'

'Older men are more reliable. What they may lack in passion they often make up for in control.'

Why not? What could be the harm? Struggling to get beyond the coaxing influence of his thoughts, he said in a sharp tone, 'Get me two fingers of whisky.'

He watched the sensual roll of her hips as she went across the room to the cupboard and poured equal amounts of scotch into two glasses. She turned and stepped back and put one in front of him, hovering there as if waiting to see what he might do. Finally she moved around the desk with the other glass and sat opposite him sifting through the pages. Deed continued to watch her, his thoughts still churning, before finally resuming reading with a great effort of will but little concentration.

Deed splashed water over his face and looked at himself in the mirror, not liking much what he saw. Having started and abandoned therapy a while back to deal with his addiction, he wondered if he shouldn't try again; none of it had helped him so far, still tormented as he was by demons which made him seek uncommitted sexual encounters. He knew he could go back into his room and take from the young woman all she was offering, satisfying a hunger which seemed to increase rather than diminish. Where was the harm, he again asked himself? There would be none. They were both consenting adults, despite the difference in age and rank. She was back waiting, wanting, and he was in great need. Snapping down a couple of paper towels, Deed dried his face and hands and pushed out of the washroom.

Along the corridor he glanced up at the security camera in the corner of the ceiling, and then stepped into his room where there was no immediate sign of Jessie. As he returned to his pile of papers the young woman stepped in and closed the door with her back to it. She glanced round as if looking for something.

'Jessie?' he said, puzzled.

She turned and met his look, then without saying anything, opened her arms which were across her chest, letting her blouse fall open, exposing her wonderful, round firm breasts. Deed waited, deciding whether to step across the Rubicon. He felt like Julius Caesar when uttering his phrase *alea iacta est*. Only for Deed the die was not yet cast – he knew he could still tell this young woman to close her shirt and go home. Instead, he found himself getting up and going over and standing in front of her, causing his heart to labour, his breath to quicken and his erection to get harder. With supreme effort he tried to move off this precipice to safety and almost succeeded until Jessie reached out to him.

'They won't break,' she said. 'You do want to touch, don't you?'

'Is there a man alive who wouldn't want to do that?' he managed.

'Then what is stopping you, my Lord?'

Once again that submissive use of his formal address was an invitation which found him adrift from his senses and scattered most of his common sense. In an instant he gained clear insight as to how the man who was before him in the murder trial could lose all reason to the woman being tried with him, and do any bidding she desired. We were helpless before them. The thought sobered him as he reached out and caught hold of Jessie, knowing what action must follow.

CHAPTER TWELVE

⁓⁂⁓

DRINKING ALONE WAS A BAD habit and one Jo Mills found herself doing more and more. She knew she was being bloody-minded in not answering Deed's phone calls, but felt angry and betrayed by him even though she knew she had no right to be. He was a career judge, not the polemicist she was turning into; he fought the causes he believed he could win whereas she seemed to take on any lost cause. It was madness. Soon there would be no fee-paying clients and she'd be kicked out of chambers. That might happen soon anyway if the case involving Anita Plant got any dodgier.

'I'm probably the last person you want to see.'

Jo looked up, startled by Sir Tom Witham standing at her table. She didn't see him come into the wine bar. 'There are a couple of judges a bit lower on my list,' she snapped back.

'That's something to build on. Do you mind?' he asked, pulling out a chair.

'At risk of ending my career, I think I'd rather fall under a bus.'

Either he had the skin of a rhinoceros or was desperate for her company.

'I simply do my job,' he said. 'You do yours.'

'Only it's not a democracy. I argue; you rule; I try to argue further; you throw me out of court.'

'Only when I believe you're wrong and you won't desist.'

'I am sometimes right.'

He conceded the point then, to her surprise, sat at her table. What could she do to get him to leave, short of ruining her career – if she hadn't already? 'What are you doing?' she wanted to know. That wasn't going to get rid of him as he took her glass with a cool peremptory air and sipped from it. This was just the sort of move Deed would make.

'See me as a legal social worker,' Witham said, 'saving a talented lawyer from self-harming.'

Jo gave a sardonic laugh, causing him to smile. He had a nice smile. 'How many have you saved so far?'

'I'm starting with you. The law is such a game, Mrs Mills. Sometimes you win; sometimes we win…'

'Who are we?' Jo asked.

'The moral majority representing probity, decency, justice.'

'Hah, I thought that was what I sought for the underdog.'

'The Left doesn't have all the best cards. Usually the Right is more reliable. You are a most attractive woman, but you know that,' Sir Tom said, changing tack. 'Would you have dinner with me?'

'Is this in furtherance of saving a talented lawyer?'

'More about feeding her. I know some excellent vegan restaurants.'

That surprised her. 'Are you vegan?'

'Occasionally. Tonight I'll be anything you want me to be.'

'Left-leaning, liberal and compassionate?' she suggested.

He smiled again and drank some more of her wine.

Making love, almost, with her clothes on inside the front door of her apartment both startled and excited and confused Jo. Getting from there to her bedroom further confused her as she was neither drunk nor drugged, but perhaps a little desperate to get back at Deed. Tom Witham kissed her with great urgency as they made love, his hands caressing her with more enthusiasm than skill. One High Court judge was much the same as another! She felt annoyed; her earlier protests had only been half-hearted as he went beyond where any man should go when the woman says no. His sudden energetic thrusting interrupted her thoughts, doing nothing for her, and when he fell off her, there was a sense of anti-climax. He was like so many men – all that mattered was what they got out of it. Sometimes Deed was like that, while at other times quite sensitive to her needs in his passion. Perhaps this High Court judge would improve were she to let him. She became aware of his hand stroking her, but the moment had passed. Now was the time for recrimination and regret.

'I'm sorry,' he was saying. 'I'm sorry, I couldn't stop myself. You are so absolutely wonderful.'

Was she now expected to compliment him? She couldn't and instead – 'What would you do now if I'd an application before you? Would you recuse yourself?'

That caused him to laugh. It was laughter she couldn't read.

'Your friend Deed never seems to suffer that dilemma.'

'He's had no cause to,' she lied. 'But he would never allow a trifling thing like sex to affect his judgement.'

Tom Witham craned round to kook at her. 'Was it trifling, Jo?'

'Men always seem to want to be judged in that area,' she said.

'We're such pathetic creatures.' He laughed again. This she could read, and it was clear he didn't believe this. 'You're not going to win for this client with terrorist connections, Jo. Off the record, the Government is bringing all the pressure it can to bear on the situation. Not even Deed will be able to help you. He's rather cooked his goose taking those papers from you.'

'What are you talking about?' She sat up, not bothering to cover her small breasts. 'What papers did he take from me?'

'Superintendent Hamblyn's not a fool. Be careful. I wouldn't want to see you get into serious trouble, especially not now. I can say no more.'

Nor would he say another word on the matter, despite Jo questioning him. Soon afterwards he departed, leaving her angry and frustrated. She wanted to call Deed to warn him, but was unsure how she would tell him she came to such a cryptic warning at this time of night.

Neil Haughton considered himself a fine singer and this morning as his car turned through the iron gates into the yard at the Law Courts he felt like singing. Then his letting go a couple of lines from a Gilbert and Sullivan operetta caused Sir Percy Thrower to glance at him askance.

'Are you familiar with Gilbert and Sullivan, Percy?' he asked.

'I believe it's from *The Yeoman of the Guard*, Home Secretary.'

'Ah, but do you know its original title – so apt for Deed?' He waited, then clapped his hands as if gonging him out. '*The Merryman and his Maid*, only life won't be so merry for Mr Justice Deed when we're done.'

Sir Ian Rochester was waiting for them, looking as bright as Haughton felt.

'Where is it, Ian?' he said straight away. 'Where? I can't wait to show George – or post it on the Internet. We'll put such a squib up the backside of the hypocrite.'

'Posting it on YouTube could bring the Bench into disrepute,' Rochester warned, leading them along the vaulted corridor and through a door that took them down the uncarpeted stone stairs to the lower floor where new judges were given rooms.

'Only Deed will get the blame,' Haughton said.

'You'd have to deal with the tedious flak that resulted, Home Secretary, if you take over Justice,' Sir Percy pointed out.

Haughton rounded on him. '*If*, Percy? Is there some doubt? We'll show the country what a firmer hand on the tiller can achieve,' – ignoring Rochester's presence. He expected the Prime Minister to confirm his new appointment any day. There was no response from his supercilious Permanent Secretary with his superior Oxbridge ways. Although he'd be well rid of him, would Rochester prove any different? Somewhat, as he was just as keen to see Deed ousted. In his ebullient state he smashed the heel of his hand so hard against the door as he pushed through that it stung and made his eyes water.

The cellar room they entered was vast and ill-lit, dusty and full of large, insulated pipes, all doubtless covered with asbestos. At once he was reassured to recognise Supt Hamblyn reaching behind one of the pipes for something.

'Can this be right, Ian, our sneaking around as if we're the guilty party?' Haughton felt affronted.

'We couldn't leave the monitor in the security room – for obvious reasons. Plus Deed's clerk has so many friends among the staff working there. They carry any little bit of information to her.'

'Then we'll have a clean sweep and get rid of her at the same time. I'll expect total loyalty from all my people.'

Supt Hamblyn brought down a tiny digital monitor and set it on a shelf and soon Deed was on the screen with his gorgeous young judicial assistant. At a steep angle Deed was shown standing in front of Jessie Rogers, who was back and sideways to the camera, masking what Deed was doing to her as his greedy fingers reached for the prize.

After a tedious moment watching Haughton said, 'It's not a useful angle. Even so, it's plain what he's up to with her – on Crown property.'

He watched as Jessie Rogers turned towards the camera, showing a glimpse of her small, well-formed breasts under her unbuttoned shirt before stepping beneath the camera. Deed was watching her with his tongue almost out, before sighing and turning back to his desk. Haughton glanced at the Permanent Secretary in astonishment, not at what he had seen, rather at what he wasn't seeing.

'Is that it?' He was incredulous, expecting an orgasmic feast only to get a peep show with the tiniest of peeps.

'It does indicate where his mind is,' Rochester said.

'I wanted *him* in the girl's crotch followed by him in the sewer.'

'There is this, sir,' Supt Hamblyn said tentatively. 'If we fast forward about half an hour...'

This she did to show Deed walking from under the camera in his Calvin Kline underwear, his shirt unbuttoned. He went the sofa and lay down, pulling a plaid rug over himself.

'What is this, a bed-time story?' Haughton demanded, getting more impatient, the prospect of entertaining George and everyone else with the recording evaporating. 'The woman, where's the wretched woman?'

'We don't know, sir. Short of bursting in on Sir John -' Hamblyn shrugged and glanced at the two senior civil servants. When they offered no assistance, she said, 'We think she's in this recess, here,' – indicating an area off camera. 'There's another sofa.'

'Is the young woman still there, naked with her legs up around her ears?' Haughton said. 'I thought she was actively working for us.'

'Oh she is, Home Secretary,' Sir Percy Thrower told him.

'Then why isn't she manoeuvring Deed onto camera. She is still in there?'

'Unless there's another door, sir.'

'Is there, Ian?'

'I don't recall. I'm not that familiar with their lordships' rooms.'

'You could walk in on them,' Sir Percy suggested, 'as the prospective Minister of Justice – inspecting his new domain.'

He warmed to that for it would establish his *bona fides*. He turned and strode out with no idea where Deed's room was or how to get to it. The two senior civil servants at his heels would soon direct him.

Haughton led the charge along the over decorated corridor, thinking about his rather stark surroundings at the Home Office. He didn't hesitate to throw the door wide as if entering his own room, Rochester and his Permanent Secretary close behind. Deed, fully clothed, was surprised but didn't miss a beat – which suggested guilt, Haughton decided.

'Neil?' Deed said, 'You're in the wrong building. The trial's at Southwark.'

'What?' Haughton said, feeling foolish; while responding with, 'Oh no, I think I'm exempt,' – made him feel stupid.

'If you're here seeking exemption as a witness, I'm going for coffee.'

'I barely knew the Ortega woman – a stand-in cleaner, I believe. No, I'm here inspecting the new ship.' He stepped further into Deed's room, trying to look into every corner where the young woman might be hiding. He became aware of Deed coming after him.

'What new ship?' he was saying.

'Who's around there?'

'A lady who won't be pleased if you disturb her.'

Haughton chuckled and said, 'Oh, John, it was only matter of time before you were caught out.' His chuckle turned to a throaty laugh and he stepped around the corner to find curled on the sofa a little black dog, who bared her teeth with a snarl. He never liked dogs.

Deed cornered him. 'What does this mean, Neil?'

Haughton tried to remain cool in the face of this set-back. 'I'll be leaving the Home Office to become the new Minister for Justice. Won't that be cosy?'

Deed spun round to Rochester, who shrugged. 'It hasn't been announced yet.'

'I can't be called as a witness in this murder trial, John, that's final.' Before Deed could give him an argument he slipped out.

Back in his own office with all the players assembled to work out a new strategy, Haughton said, 'I would have preferred Deed doing a dirty and not to have to rely on a constitutional crisis landing on my desk at Justice. If Deed is harbouring information on terrorists for his lover…' He glanced at Sir Tom Witham, who looked uncomfortable.

'Mr Justice Deed does have the envelope, sir,' Supt Hamblyn insisted, straightening off the chair she was leaning against.

Haughton turned his coldest gaze to the young counter terrorism detective, wondering if she was as competent as she was arrogant. 'Like the girl with her panties down? Even after I leave here my reach will be long. Do I make myself clear?'

'You do, sir.'

Haughton enjoyed seeing her blanch. He would make her suffer if she didn't succeed in this enterprise. 'Make this work a hell of a lot better than that non-sex scandal you dragged in here.'

He flapped his arm, dismissing them as though they were cleaners. He liked that sort of power and looked forward to the day he could exercise it over Deed and all judges.

CHAPTER THIRTEEN

※

DEED OPENED HIS PHONE SEVERAL times as he was helped into his robes for court by Coop, checking yet again to see if Deputy Assistant Commissioner Colemore had called him. He knew he hadn't or he would have heard the phone, but that didn't stop this anxious process.

'Still no word from Row Colemore, Coop?'

'No, Judge. I'll tell you when he calls.'

'Maybe he can't get the information I want. Maybe it doesn't exist.' He was further convinced something was wrong in this trial other than the Polish witness's apparent suicide. He didn't know what but was determined to find out.

Coop joined Deed on the bench where she dealt with correspondence. This she could have done in his room, but he suspected she preferred not to be with Jessie Rogers, who was not displaying her usual confidence this morning. Even so, he was pleased she was bold enough to show up.

Getting to his feet, Mason Allen QC said, 'My Lord, I have one further witness, but she doesn't seem to have answered her witness summons.'

'Do you wish me to send the bailiffs to arrest this witness?'

'I rather hoped that wouldn't be necessary as she's a member of the noble profession.'

'Some members are more noble than others,' Jo Mills whispered, loud enough for Deed to hear. He gave a sharp look, causing her to glance away. Both knew, along with those crowding the press benches, who the witness was.

'Can you close without this witness, Mr Mason Allen?' he asked.

Before prosecuting counsel could respond, a loud protest issued from George Channing, telling the usher not to manhandle her. She marched into court ahead of the robed usher, wearing a neat black suit with white lapels.

'How could I not respond to the court?' With a smile she went into the witness-box and picked up the Bible unbidden. 'I swear by Almighty God that the evidence I shall give shall be the truth, the whole truth, and nothing but the truth. George Channing, Her Majesty's

Counsel and learned in the law. I don't know what else I can help you with.'

'Just answer counsel's questions,' Deed told her, stopping her grandstanding.

'Ms Channing, do you know the defendant, Mariana Ortega?'

Impatience burst out of her. 'Isn't that the whole purpose of this ridiculous exercise?'

'Is that yes?' Deed asked.

'It is, of course.' Belligerence bordering on disrespect wouldn't be noticed if the transcript was later read back at a notional Bar Standards disciplinary panel. Never once during their marriage had Deed abused George, other than by his infidelity, but now he felt like slapping her.

'She was in your employ for three weeks in June last year?'

'Strictly speaking,' George Channing said, 'she wasn't. Our regular cleaner went home to Poland for family reasons. Ms Ortega came via a domestic agency.'

'Did you have any problems with her in the house?'

The witness was seen to think about that 'No, I don't think so.'

That surprised the prosecutor, who stepped back smiling. 'Was there a time during her employ when you noticed money missing from your handbag?'

Machin bobbed up to protest. 'Really, my Lord?'

'Yes, it was leading, Mr Mason Allen. But I can ask it,' Deed said glancing up from his note-taking. 'Did you notice money missing during this period?'

'Money did go missing from my bag,' George Channing said, then turned to Deed. 'Is this relevant, my Lord?'

'You're not representing her, Ms Channing. You're here as a witness. Answer the question please.' He waved her back to Mason Allen, who raised his eyebrows and waited.

'This was a misunderstanding. Nothing went missing. I subsequently discovered my partner had borrowed the cash.'

Mason Allen allowed his impatience to surface even though he continued to smile. 'Were you equally mistaken about your partner's affair with Ms Ortega?'

This was what the reporters were gathered for – it grabbed the attention of everyone in court.

George Channing gave a derisive laugh. 'An affair with a cleaner is highly unlikely – in view of Neil's position.'

'Some of the jury might not know Neil's position,' Deed said, causing his former wife to glower at him. He laboured the point, 'I'm not even sure I do now.'

The witness waited a long while, as if considering whether to answer. 'The Secretary for Home…' she stopped abruptly as if realising what she was about to say, then added, 'He's the Home Secretary.'

'Did you or the Home Secretary know Ms Ortega was working in this country illegally?' Mason Allen asked, making Deed wonder if he'd get any more prosecution work from Haughton at Justice.

'How could we? She came from an agency.'

Trying to excavate this area with delicacy, Mason Allen got nowhere and despite his pleasant demeanour he was becoming impatient with the witness stone-walling his legitimate questions. He then turned to the bench in frustration. 'M'Lord, I have an application to make in the absence of the jury.'

'No need to disturb them,' Deed said, 'as they look so comfortable. You doubtless wish to treat this witness as hostile. Carry on.'

'What else would I expect?' George Channing said *sotto voce*.

'Ms Channing, didn't Ms Ortega tell you she was in fact illegal when you challenged her over the affair with your partner, when she said your partner would be in trouble for employing her?'

'If that were the case Neil would have marched her off to the police station, regardless of any consequences.'

That did it for Mason Allen. He let his notes slide from his hands and sat down.

On cross-examining the witness, Heathcote Machin was politeness itself, as if wanting to keep her on side. 'I believe Ms Ortega was truthful, honest, hard-working…?'

Half-rising to object, Mason Allen said, 'My Lord…'

'It is cross-examination, Mr Mason Allen. Mr Machin can lead her.'

'Oh yes,' the prosecutor said sarcastically. 'I'd forgotten she's my witness.'

'Ms Channing?' Machin prompted.

'She had all those qualities.'

'Thank you.' Machin sat, and Jo Mills made no move to cross-examine. Both Deed and George Channing glanced over at her and saw her shake her head.

'Can I go?' George Channing said.

'No,' Deed told her. 'Would the jury go out please?'

He waited for them to leave, and then turned to the witness box. 'That is perhaps the worst fabrication I've heard from a witness in a long while. I'm considering reporting you to your professional body.' He put up his hand to stop her replying. 'Another word and I will hold you in contempt. Now go.' She fled.

Mason Allen QC got to his feet. 'That is the case for the Prosecution, m'Lord,'

'Thank you, Mr Mason Allen. Are you ready with your defence, Mr Machin?'

'I am, my Lord. But might I have briefest adjournment to consult with my client?'

'Fifteen minutes – before we have the jury back.' Deed was keen to try and reach Row Colemore before the trial progressed further.

Working alone in Mr Justice Deed's office at the Law Courts, Jessie Rogers hesitated at the sound of someone stopping in the corridor. She froze as the door-handle turned, experiencing a prickling sensation on the back of her neck. The door crept open and Mr Justice Witham looked in, appearing startled at finding her there.

'Oh, is Sir John not here?' – recovering himself.

'He's down at Southwark, Judge.'

Straightaway she could see what was happening to him; so many men became utter wets when alone with her. Sometimes she wished it were different, and could have hoped the response from someone who sat on the High Court bench might have been more elevated. Why she bothered to treat them like demi-gods she didn't know. This one seemed momentarily mesmerized and when he opened his mouth, she could have spoken the words for him.

'You do know the extraordinary effect you have on people?'

'On men, you mean? Why is that?' she asked.

'Are you teasing me? I can't believe you don't know, Jessie.'

That caused her to step back a little and become hesitant. 'Men seem to like what they see,' she told him. 'They always think it's available.'

'That single chance they're afraid might never come their way again; the missed opportunity to which the mind returns with regret, saying over and over, if only.'

He was talking too much; the poor bloke couldn't seem to help himself.

'Oh, I'm sorry to have caused anyone such regret.'

Anger flashed across his handsome face as he said, 'Don't tease me,' – the atmosphere around him changing in an instant.

'I do have a lot of work to get through, Judge.'

Leaning across her with more purpose than was necessary, Sir Tom picked up a file from in front of her and glanced over it. 'Sir John's rebuttal to our argument for extraditing the rapist to Saudi Arabia – is it making any headway?'

'I'm only a very junior counsel,' she replied.

'If you were before me, Jessie, I'd give way to you.'

The smile she offered was intended politeness, but he read something else and without warning seized her, kissing her on the mouth. Her lips softened and any resistance was lost in the face of his raw lust. The truth was she enjoyed the power she had over men, even if she couldn't quite control their responses. Fleetingly she thought about the tiny camera planted here and wondered what Supt Hamblyn would make of it, if she would care that it captured the wrong judge.

In his room at Southwark Deed got a cryptic message from Row Colemore, who refused to say anything on the phone. He could be with him in 20 minutes. Deed asked Coop to advise counsel and the jury that the adjournment would be longer than planned.

'Shall I tell them to take an early lunch, Judge?' she suggested.

'Yes, that might be best, Coop.'

By the time the DAC arrived Deed was tense with expectation. 'For Chrissake, Row, did you get something from this Savile Row tailor?'

'Not from his records – the premises were burgled last night.'

'Let me guess what was stolen?'

'Whoever it was wasn't after a suit. The computer and all the records of customer details are missing,' Colemore informed him.

'First the apartment block porter with the sharp suit kills himself – maybe; then the record of who the suit was made for is stolen. What does your instinct as a detective tell you, Row?'

'It's a long while since I've been a detective, but I'd venture someone's moving in behind you. That's why I wouldn't say anything on the phone. It's looking like the porter didn't hang himself.'

'The evidence suggests he didn't,' Deed said. 'When can we expect the autopsy report?'

'The post mortem's being conducted now. When I get sight of the report, I'll let you have the findings.' Row Colemore hesitated. There was more he had to say, so Deed waited. 'I think the tailor knows who the suit was made for. Those instincts as a policeman aren't all lost. He was being evasive.'

'He's a gentleman's tailor, Row. Perhaps he was being discreet.'

'Is it likely to end up in *Private Eye*? I doubt it.'

'Did he deny knowing J. Pollock?' Deed asked.

'He said he has lots of clients. It was hard to keep track of them all.'

'Was there evidence of a break-in at the premises?'

'The break-in was reported this morning. Whoever did it got through the locks without damaging them.'

'Perhaps I'd better ask the prosecution to call the tailor so I can examine him under oath.'

'I rather hoped you might. He's likely to be more concerned about your sending him to gaol for contempt than anything we could do by way of sanction.'

The murder trial was delayed further because the tailor, Ralph Blanxart, was brought to the court only with great reluctance. Deed saw no point in proceeding with the defence as he suspected that one of the defendants shouldn't be in this trial.

The tailor was an elegant figure in the witness box wearing an immaculate suit of the same high quality as the one the porter had been wearing, his being cut to disguise a slight hump in his back.

'Mr Blanxart, thank you for attending here at such short notice,' Deed said courteously, 'but we need some information about a suit you made that an earlier witness wore. I'd like you to tell the court for whom the suit was made.'

'For Mr Kozlowski,' the witness said without hesitation.

'How much do your suits cost as a rule, Mr Blanxart?'

'This varies according to the cloth, sir.'

'A particularly fine cashmere. The suit must have been at least £250,' Deed said, like he didn't know better.

The tailor laughed. 'Perhaps if you added another thousand or more,' he said with a sense of pride.

'How do you know it was made for Mr Kozlowski?'

'I do remember some of my customers, sir.'

Deed glanced across the court to Row Colemore sitting at the back. The tailor followed his glance.

'Tell me, Mr Blanxart – and I want you to think carefully before you answer,' Deed cautioned, 'because if I suspect you're mocking this court I will have you taken to the cells – why was the name J. Pollock inside this particular suit?'

Without hesitation, the tailor said he didn't know. 'Oh, I think you do, sir,' Deed told him. 'Please identify J. Pollock.'

'I'm afraid I don't remember him, sir.'

'Let's see what time in the cells does for you memory. Usher, will you summon a police officer to take Mr Blanxart to the cells?' He hoped there was one on hand.

Anxiety building in the witness caused him to say in a waspish tone, 'I cannot be expected to remember all of my customers.'

'Mr Blanxart, we ask about a suit worn to court bearing the name J. Pollock. The witness wearing this suit died in strange circumstances. Next your premises are broken into and your records stolen. Now you can't remember J. Pollock, a fairly short client because the suit you *didn't* make for Mr Kozlowski fitted him quite well. Are you being threatened?'

The tailor remained silent. Deed nodded to the police officer who stepped up to the witness box. 'Take him away.'

'James Pollock,' the tailor said as he was brought out of the box, 'The MP, sir.' That sent some of the reporters running out to record this to camera.

'It not him!' Mariana Ortega blurted out from the dock.

'Thank you, Ms Ortega,' Deed said, and gave her a warm smile. 'Please remain in court, Mr Blanxart. I'll see counsel in chambers.'

'Interesting developments, don't you think?' he said when counsel had settled in his room with bottled water. Some of them he knew would have preferred Coke, but Coop wouldn't have the stuff in the fridge.

'I'm at a loss to see how, Judge,' Heathcote Machin said.

'Undeniably it affects your client less than Mrs Mills' client. I question whether he should be in the dock – other than for perverting the course of justice. I'm going to suspend the trial and ask you to call James Pollock MP to give evidence, Newman.'

'Am I calling him for the prosecution or as your witness, Judge?' Mason Allen QC asked.

'The prosecution has closed its case, my Lord,' Machin pointed out.

'I'm sure we'd let them re-open it in the interests of justice,' Deed said. 'Jo, any objections?'

Jo Mills shook her head. 'Do we have any idea if this Government minister will answer his summons? Or how long that will take?'

'Oh, he'll answer it and fast, or spend time in a cell instead of his tailor.'

'That I would like to see,' she said with feeling.

Neil Haughton and Percy Thrower crashed through the MoJ and pulled Rochester out of a meeting. Behind the thick door of his incongruously circa 18th-century office in this brutal 70s building overlooking St James's Park, Haughton said, 'Has Deed completely wigged out, Ian?'

'Oh, I do hope so, Home Secretary,' Rochester replied.

'I was summoned to Downing Street. The Prime Minister is livid. Deed's ordered Jim Pollock to this murder trial he's conducting. It's all over the news. Is there no end to his madness? Jim's leading the negotiations for our biggest arms sale ever to the Saudis. In total it'll be worth some thirty-six billion pounds – small compared to our deficit, but very necessary to our survival.'

'Presumably he's not going to question him about that,' Rochester said.

'There's no telling what he'll do if he gets him under his jurisdiction.'

'I'm afraid he's already under his jurisdiction if the judge has summoned him.'

'No, Ian, he most certainly isn't. The Prime Minister made that oh so clear. My coming to Justice might depend on it. Deed has to be stopped now. I don't care if you have to assassinate the fucking lunatic. I'll do it if no one else in this department has the balls. The Defence Minister's appearance in court must not happen. Do I make myself clear, Ian?'

'Oh, perfectly, Home Secretary,' Rochester said.

Haughton saw that superior little smile in the corners of Rochester's mouth and wanted to rip it off his face, and then do the same to Deed. He would get the same treatment from the PM in the event of Rochester failing. The prospect didn't bear thinking about.

CHAPTER FOURTEEN

THE DOORBELL WAS LIKE AN alarm and any moment Deed expected the door to be hit and lifted off its hinges by a police battering ram, though why he couldn't imagine – he wasn't gunning for the police in any current case. Whoever's finger it was didn't let up on the bell. Wrenching open the door, he found Jo Mills standing there.

'I began to think you were out, in spite of the porter not seeing you leave.' She stepped in past him.

'I sometimes climb out of the window to avoid him. Why didn't you ring to find out?' Deed closed the door.

'Do you have anyone here, John?'

'No. Luck doesn't seem to be with me just now. Do you want to look? What's so urgent, Jo?'

'I didn't want to risk using the phone in case it's being listened into.'

'We're not so-called celebrities. I'm a High Court judge. Would anyone dare?'

'Spooky security people might,' Jo said. 'Superintendent Hamblyn, perhaps?'

'If that were the case my flat could be bugged. Shall we turn on the taps or the television, or whatever it is they do in the circumstances?'

'Where are the papers I gave you to keep? Are they safe?' The urgency in her tone was tinged with fear and this worried Deed. 'Are they, John?'

Deed poured her a drink. 'Do you want to give me a hint at what this is about, or should I try to guess?'

'I told you before, but perhaps you don't listen. The witness you summoned to court is named in those papers,' Jo said and swallowed her drink. 'Jim Pollock, the Defence Minister, is implicated in a bribery scandal involving the sale of arms to Saudi Arabia that's being negotiated. There's chapter and verse as to amounts and who got paid and who handed over the money from where.'

'Are you saying that's why the Counter Terrorism unit's coming after you?' He didn't want to believe it. If true it would amount to gross abuse of power by the Executive, one that could undermine the rule of law and even bring the Government down. As much as he disliked some members of this Government, he preferred not to have the chaos that would follow such an ignominious end.

'Why do you think they would hesitate?' Jo asked. 'They're a branch of the Home Office. This could gut the Government.'

'An interesting choice of verb, Jo, as I always thought this Government was gutless,' Deed said.

'Now isn't the time for semantics. Where are the papers?'

'Joe Channing has them.'

'Oh, shit,' Jo said. 'Does he have any idea what they are?'

'Well, I suppose there's always the possibility that he opened the envelope and checked its contents,' Deed ventured. 'Knowing Joe Channing, I doubt he has.'

'I need to get those papers back.'

'To do what with them? If they have the potential to do as much damage as you suggest, do you think you can keep them any safer?'

'I'd feel more comfortable if they were in my possession.'

'So you might, but safer? What if officers from the Counter Terrorism unit come knocking on the door as they did before?' When she offered no answer, Deed said, 'How do you plan to use the papers?'

'I don't know. Yes, any way I can to maximum effect in protecting my client. She doesn't have terrorist connections, other than people from the Middle East who gave her this information.'

'If Jim Pollock proves to be involved with Mariana Ortega this might all come out. The corrupt ethos of this Government could be exposed, its sleazy palism brought down,' Deed said. 'I'd have to be convinced there's substance to what you claim. As of this moment I'm not.'

Jo challenged him with, 'In case it interferes with your elevation?'

'If that's what you think, Jo, what's the point in continuing this?'

After a moment she stepped back from her position. 'First you have to get this Minister in court to examine him. I doubt if even you can bring that off.'

Deed saw what she was doing, pushing him into a corner to get him to act. 'If what you say is true your client could be in danger. We've already had one witness show up dead. Perhaps she should be looked after by the witness protection people.'

'Oh, yes,' Jo Mills said with heavy sarcasm. 'I think she would find that very reassuring. More police, under the control of the Home Office.'

'Jo,' Deed cautioned, being fully prepared to trust her safety to the protection police.

'No, John, it's not going to happen. She wouldn't feel safe at all. You should look to your own safety. If you manage to achieve what you suggest, with what's at stake even a High Court judge might not be safe.' The finality to her words chilled the air.

'Are you absolutely certain Lord Justice Channing has these missing papers?' Witham asked Supt Hamblyn yet again as he hesitated with her outside the house in West Halkin Street, Belgravia. He was nervous about the whole enterprise, even though Haughton, soon to be the Justice Secretary, had sanctioned it. Sir Joseph was his principal sponsor to the High Court and this somehow felt like a betrayal. Haughton wouldn't care about that, or him.

'Tom, what is the mystery?' Sir Joseph said when he opened the door. He glanced past him to Hamblyn. 'Do we need your protection officer in with us?'

'She's more than just that, Joe – Supt Hamblyn from Counter Terrorism.'

'How do you counter it?' Sir Joseph asked as he led the way through to the sitting room where *The Big Bang Theory* was playing on the television. He turned it off, saying, 'It is so very clever.'

'The only way we can counter terrorism, Sir Joseph, is by staying ever vigilant,' Hamblyn said and glanced round at Witham.

'Joe, an enormous threat to the country has been uncovered by these detectives.' Witham shuffled, becoming more uneasy. 'The people concerned are listed in a document they believe Deed gave you.'

The belief that the senior judge would be at pains to co-operate didn't bear out. Instead he asked, 'Is there evidence of this?'

'Of what, sir,' Hamblyn enquired, 'the existence of the document?'

'Are you being obtuse, madam?' Joe Channing asked. 'I'll spell it out: evidence of its existence, its contents and the belief that I have it.'

'We know it was passed to you, Sir Joseph,' Witham heard the young police officer say, and knew it was the wrong approach.

'I don't like the sound of this, Tom.' Sir Joseph turned to Hamblyn. 'Just how do you know? I don't recall your ever being present at any meeting I may have had with Mr Justice Deed.'

'We have a strong suspicion, Joe only a suspicion,' Witham said, trying to retrieve the situation, knowing they'd all end up in the Tower if it came out that anyone had bugged a High Court judge's room. He felt himself slipping in over his head and wished more than anything that he hadn't gone along with this, even if sanctioned by the Prime Minister.

'Supt Hamblyn was quite emphatic. She said, we *know*. Again, I ask how you know if you weren't present?'

'The fact is, those papers are of vital importance to our security, Sir Joseph.'

Hamblyn was trying to deflect him. Another mistake.

'We've yet to establish the existence of any papers,' Sir Joseph said.

'I can't answer that, sir, and I wouldn't, even under threat of imprisonment. I love this country and try to keep it safe.'

'You imagine I'm any less attached to it? I will give you one more opportunity – answer or there will be consequences,' Sir Joseph warned.

Supt Hamblyn remained silent and tried to catch Witham's eye, but he refused to glance her way in case he became further implicated. Why did she dress in a suit and tie? Such attire on a woman would always cause the likes of Joe Channing to be less gentle with her.

He said, 'I suggest you step outside while I speak with Mr Justice Witham.'

After the policewoman left Sir Joseph turned his gaze on Witham, who smarted and wished he were elsewhere and wasn't indebted to Haughton.

'I can only apologise, Joe. I should have interrogated her further.'

'Something is wrong here. I will find out what. There seem to be too many speculative adventures by the anti-terrorism police.'

'Aren't some very necessary to keep us safe, Joe?'

'It's a sorry state of affairs that they are allowed to encroach upon the bar. It would be even sorrier if we let them have their way here.'

Witham felt comforted by the senior judge's inclusive 'we'.

'They do have a thankless task. By and large they acquit themselves well but there is a line they must not be permitted to cross. We allow that at the peril of becoming a police state. Make that abundantly clear to your over-enthusiastic policewoman.'

Witham felt relieved to have escaped with his skin intact, and vowed to be more circumspect in these matters.

Knowing the senior Appeal Court judge liked to start his day early, Neil Haughton decided to pay a surprise visit to him in his room. However, he didn't look forward to it, even though Channing might soon be his father-in-law – he doubted that would make the old boy any more agreeable towards him.

'I've a lot of reading to do,' was Sir Joseph's response when his clerk showed him in.

'When haven't you, Joe?' he said, attempting to be winsome. 'I'll look to relieve judges of some of that burden, but I fear it might get heavier for you at the Supreme Court.'

That caught his attention and caused him to stop ordering his papers.

'Is that why you're here, to give me prior warning?' Sir Joseph asked, his tone telling Haughton he was hooked and might be steered in the direction he chose.

'I'm not quite at the MoJ yet, Joe, and of course it's not in my gift. I should warn you, there's a move afoot to appoint Mohammed Khan.'

'Does he have sufficient experience?'

'His track record on the Bench hardly qualifies him,' Haughton said, dangling the carrot a little closer. 'But Whitehall is so painfully PC these days. The thinking is it would be good to have a Muslim Supreme. I won't have it.'

'The civil servants who manage the Department can be quite tricky, Neil.'

'I can be very bloody-minded, Joe. You're the right man for the vacancy when it comes due later this year.'

'If it happens, it happens. I do still have a lot of reading.'

'Of course, I'm just spying out the lie of the land,' Haughton said and made to leave, but turned back. 'There's a potential constitutional crisis looming. Your former son-in-law was given some papers by his erstwhile lover, Mrs Mills,' Haughton said, putting a negative spin on this while seeming casual. 'She may still be his lover for all I know, despite her being before him.'

'Ah, for a moment I thought you were going to ask me to persuade him to desist from bringing a Government minister to court.'

Haughton noticed his relief. 'You'd heard about that, Joe?'

'The High Court bench does watch the news. My brethren await the outcome.'

'I wouldn't dream of stopping it. I'm sure Jim Pollock can take care of himself in or out of court.'

'He must appear, Neil – now Deed has summoned him. If he refuses and your colleagues support him that has the potential to bring about a constitutional crisis: the judiciary pitted against the Executive wouldn't be pretty.'

'I'm sure it won't happen. The papers Mrs Mills gave him relate to a bunch of terrorists, one of whom gave them to her client. The Counter Terrorism people had a court order to seize the papers. Deed strong-armed them, and now we fear there'll be mayhem.'

'Have you asked Mr Justice Deed for their return?' Sir Joseph glanced at a large manila envelope on his desk.

Seeing the glance but resisting the urge to grab the envelope and run, Haughton smiled. 'You know John. Is he likely to hand over the papers to the appropriate authorities?'

'He's no more amenable to my influence than yours. We saw that with the Salibi extradition,' Sir Joseph said. 'He thinks no more of the Libyan than we do, yet now he's spending hours trying to find law to support the man's staying.'

'I was hoping to have a somewhat more relaxed time at Justice. Now I wonder.' He opened the door. 'We'll just have to hold our breath and hope to catch these Muslim fanatics in the act. I'll keep you posted about the Supreme Court opening, Joe.'

'I'm not ready with my argument, Joe,' Deed said, meeting Channing in the corridor, 'if that's what you're after.'

'As vigorous as your mind is, I somehow doubt you'll find one, John.' Channing stepped into his room and looked around. 'Where's that pretty young marshal of yours?'

'Ah, you too are tempted to chance your luck, are you?' Deed asked.

'If I were fool enough. I'm old enough and I hope wise enough not to prove such a fool. I don't want her or your clerk to hear what I have to say.'

'You look serious, Joe.'

'This is a serious matter.' Channing shifted as if uncomfortable in his suit. 'That envelope you gave me. Do you know what it contains?'

Deed hesitated, not liking where this might be going. 'It sounds as if you do.'

'I haven't looked inside the envelope, nor would I in the circumstances it was given to my care. You didn't answer the question.'

'You won't like the answer, Joe,' Deed told him.

'Is it something that could embarrass the Government?' the older judge asked.

'If what's in it is true, it wouldn't give them much comfort.'

'Is Mrs Mills somehow involved?' Channing said.

'Rather than interrogate me in this fashion,' Deed said, feeling irritated, 'why not tell me what you know?'

'Not a lot, and from the little I do know, I'm not sure I want to be drawn in further.' Channing waited, avoiding looking at him. That was always a bad sign. 'Neil Haughton came to see me a short while ago.'

'Ah,' – allowing the air to slide out past his lips. He could barely stop himself smiling as he imagined that conversation.

'He seems to think the contents of the envelope could be the means of preventing widespread acts of terrorism.'

'Rather than being the means of securing the liberty of an innocent party as well as possibly embarrassing the Government?'

'I'm in no position to judge, not having seen the contents of the envelope, or knowing the case involving the owner of the document,' Channing said. 'Nor do I want to,' he added with a sharper note. 'The safest course might be to hand it to the Counter Terrorist unit. They'll soon tell if it's likely to prevent mayhem.'

'I'd like to trust them to be objective, Joe but I'm not sure I can. I'd need to speak to Mrs Mills. It's her client's property. Do you still have the papers safe?'

'Of course, I gave my word. The fact is, John, I don't want to be embroiled in the sort of political scandal you seem to thrive on. I hope to reach the Supreme Court quite soon.'

'Is that what Haughton promised you?'

'I hardly think it's in the gift of the Home Secretary.'

Deed laughed now, seeing right through his avoidance, wondering if the offer was any more substantial than Rochester's to him about getting the Appellate Bench if he were good. The problem was that judges were only flesh and blood so clung to the most tenuous of promises that might fulfil their cherished desires.

Soon after Joe Channing departed Rochester was at Deed's door, smiling like a man with too many teeth.

'I hope I'm not disturbing you, Sir John.'

Deed knew this man was most dangerous when being his most obsequious.

'I can guess why you're here, Ian,' Deed said, teasing him. 'To tell me the Lord Chancellor is endorsing my elevation to the Appellate Bench.'

'It has been discussed on several occasions. Would it be impertinent of me to tell you that at this juncture you're still thought to be a loose cannon?'

'Would revoking the summons to bring the Government minister to court make me more reliable?' Deed asked.

'There is no denying it would spare the Government embarrassment.'

'But would justice be served? My reading of the case is that it wouldn't.'

'My reading of the case, Judge, is that the two people in the dock are the clear perpetrators, while the Minister can add nothing.'

'It's encouraging, Ian, having the Permanent Secretary at the MoJ take such a cavalier view of trial by jury. It makes me more determined.'

'The only way Government can function is by accommodation and compromise, however unpleasant and unacceptable that may be to you.'

'Were I to compromise and accommodate certain members of the Government, it's tantamount to saying the Executive is above the law – a recipe for disaster.'

'Surely you're overstating the case? Ministers are honourable men and women who know just where to draw the line.'

Deed laughed again but with neither mirth nor malice, just surprise. Having dedicated his working life to proving that no one is above the law, he wasn't about to step back. 'What planet are you from, Ian? How long have you worked among these people not to know that to remain in office most politicians would crawl up the back passage of the devil.'

Rochester stiffened and said, 'I'd hoped to appeal to your sense of propriety. Some things about Government business cannot be open to public scrutiny.'

'You're making me more interested in seeing this man in the witness-box. He'll not be questioned on Government business, rather what he knows about the murder case before me.'

'Nothing, how could he?' Rochester said with force, like he thought he was sole guardian of the truth.

'That's something we'll only know from him. If my elevation to the Appellate Bench is dependent on my slithering around in political stench, as you seem to imply, I'd rather remain a lowly legal scribe in any backroom in the world.'

That made Sir Ian Rochester defensive. 'I really implied no such thing.'

'Then I apologise, and assume my name remains on the list of the Judicial Appointments Commission.'

'My Lord,' – in his ultra-polite manner.

This was a morning of surprises and the biggest for Deed was Row Colemore at his door looking shame-faced. Deed didn't think a policeman of his experience would ever feel shame, much less show it.

'What's the problem, Row? Are you being forced to retire without a pension?'

'Mind-reading is now one of your many talents.'

'Is that a question or a statement?'

The Deputy Assistant Commissioner hesitated, and then laughed, as if embarrassed. 'I'm afraid I've not been able to get a copy of the post mortem report on the Kozlowski death.' Deed waited. 'When I tried to retrieve it, I got summoned to the Home Office. An Under Secretary told me it wasn't available for my consumption and to pursue it I might risk being charged with perverting the course of justice and find myself out of a job with no pension.'

'Bollocks! Does he have any fucking knowledge of the law?' Deed was furious but laughed with great enjoyment. 'It's that imbecile who's perverting the course of justice. I'll haul him right into my current trial and tell him so. These fucking people are not above the law and I won't allow them to behave as if they are.'

'Things could get rough for you, John. From the little bits I'm privy to I get a real impression that the Establishment intends to clip your wings.'

'I will have that post mortem report or I'll have Haughton in court with it, along with his fellow conspirator, James Pollock.' He saw Row Colemore's questioning look. The man couldn't stop being a curious policeman, despite threats to his livelihood. 'Pollock is named in papers Jo Mills has in another case. He's implicated with the Government in bribing the Saudis to make arms purchases.'

'Oh, Lord,' Colemore said. 'This could get heavy.'

'First he needs to be questioned in my murder trial. Now I know a PM report exists I will have a copy of it. Perhaps you should stay clear.' Deed hoped he wouldn't distance himself and would think less of him if he did. But doubts crept over him as the senior policeman departed looking like a man who had been reprieved. That left Deed feeling more alone, and more determined to see this through.

CHAPTER FIFTEEN

'THIS SITUATION IS LUDICROUS, IAN.' Haughton stormed into his office, followed by his current Permanent Secretary and Sir Ian Rochester – his soon-to-be Permanent Secretary. 'I gave my word to the Prime Minister that I would resolve this matter with no embarrassment to the Government. Now what have we got, a bloody mess with me looking a complete fool? It won't do. I want action, a satisfactory outcome.'

'What do you propose, Home Secretary?' Sir Ian Rochester asked.

'I thought that was what senior civil servants did: propose solutions for Ministers to approve. You've not even found a way of stopping Jim Pollock having to appear at Deed's behest, much less offered the means of obtaining those documents that might spare us a great deal of mayhem.'

'Short of forcefully taking them from Joe Channing, we're at a loss.'

'Are we indeed?' he said with arch sarcasm. 'Someone might have to take them by force. I'm sure he wouldn't want the deaths of someone's loved ones on his conscience. I certainly don't when it could be so easily avoided.'

The two civil servants waited, as if waiting for him to find the solution. He knew what it would be, Supt Hamblyn having someone slip into Joe Channing's office, lifting the file and copying it. He would be better off talking directly to the young policewoman rather than relying on these ineffectual mandarins doing so. Hamblyn was ambitious and keen to re-establish her usefulness after the strip he had torn off her previously. First, he needed to talk with Jim Pollock to find out how damaging those documents could be for Government before deciding how big a risk to take.

The Commons Tea Room was probably the safest place to talk. Unless the portraits above the wood panels were capable of eavesdropping. Two ministers together at a corner table was a perfectly natural sight. 'The general public being unsophisticated,' Jim Pollock said, 'would never appreciate the expediency of what we're doing in the Middle East, how much it goes to providing funds for the NHS and all their other fucking benefits.'

'The papers can't be exposed to public scrutiny?' Haughton speculated.

'Fuck, no, all sorts of terrorists could slip through the net.'

Haughton stared at this short politician with his square head and squashed facial features, wondering if he'd missed something. He wanted frank answers about the envelope's contents and was being told about potential terrorists. Was this *Alice in Wonderland*, with really no Government threat? That wasn't the impression the PM gave him. He decided that Pollock was being circumspect because of where they were.

'If your people can't retrieve those papers, Neil,' Pollock was saying, 'there's someone who could – in the Saudi security service. It might be a better option; it would distance us if anything went wrong.'

The idea at once both excited and alarmed Haughton. If something were to go wrong, how would the Foreign Office field something that could result in a diplomatic row with the very people the Government least wanted to offend?

'I'd need to be confident of the success of such action, Jim.'

'Oh, you could be,' Pollock assured him. 'We'd wish these people in and wish them out.'

'What about your summons to appear at Southwark Crown Court?' The question startled the Defence Secretary.

'Why the fuck hasn't that gone away?'

'I'm afraid Deed isn't easily silenced.'

'I can't add anything to this trial. I don't know the defendants or anyone else involved.'

'Would there be a problem going into the witness-box and saying that?'

Jim Pollock gave a high-pitched laugh. 'Are you being quite fucking serious? Yes, you are.'

'It might be the only way to shut Deed up, Jim.'

'Can't anyone control this cunt?' Pollock said in a heated whisper. 'The PM was complaining about him before the Saudi dinner last night. I thought you had a girl who was going to fuck him on camera?'

Haughton cringed. 'She hasn't managed it yet. Short of pushing him under a bus, the bods at the MoJ have not the foggiest idea how to find a solution.'

'We might easily arrange for the bus.'

There was dead-pan seriousness from this Minister and at any moment Haughton hoped he would laugh, or at least smile. Finally he said, 'When would I have to appear?' Immediately Haughton felt a surge of relief; conspiring to kill a High Court judge, even in jest, scared him.

'Answer your summons. Offer a time convenient to you. I'm sure Deed will be accommodating for not finding himself embroiled in a constitutional crisis.'

'You're sure Lord Justice Channing has the papers Mrs Mills got from her client?' Pollock asked.

'They were on his table in a manila envelope.'

'Good.' Pollock said no more, and Haughton felt further relieved. This was something he would deal with through his Arab contacts, wishing them in and wishing them out. He would try to remember that phrase.

Without any real belief that Rupert Fish needed a defence, believing in her gut that he shouldn't even be in this trial, Jo called him as the opening and only witness in his defence. He was a slight man, thin-limbed and with a prominent Adam's apple that bobbed up and down when he swallowed. Nervousness. He seemed even less confident now, separated by a matter of twenty-five feet from Mariana Ortega. Still Jo was having difficulty getting her head around the possibility that obsessive love compelled him to stand accused with this woman. Men often lost their heads over women and respond in stupid, irrational ways, but Fish had been on remand away from the object of his desire, yet still clung to this stupid, irrational position. In order to bring that out she would have to try to cross-examine him and risk the judge objecting. Heathcote Machin would certainly prove ruthless in defence of his own client, regardless of whether or not Fish was involved.

'Mr Fish, can you tell the jury about your feelings for Ms Ortega?'

'I was with her that night,' he said at once and glanced over at the woman in the dock, who gave him a sweet smile. Jo considered asking the judge to clear the dock so Ms Ortega couldn't manipulate the witness.

'We'll come to that later,' Jo said. 'First tell us how you feel about her.'

'I love her. I love her very much.'

'Would you do anything for her?'

'Of course, I want to marry her, so she can stay here legally – no, I want to marry her anyway,' Fish said.

'Even though she is still married to a man in Colombia?' The question shocked him and his Adam's apple rattled semaphore.

'She's not. No, she is not,' – again glancing to the dock for reassurance.

Jo read her note. 'Unless I have the wrong person: Mariana Pia Ortega, married to Jesus Miguel Ortega.' There was no response, only members of the jury making notes. 'Can you tell the court what happened the night Mr Bartlett was brought to your flat?'

'I don't remember it clearly,' Fish said, his attention going across to the dock again. 'It's a bit of a blur.'

'Was that because you weren't there?' Jo asked.

'Mrs Mills,' the Judge interrupted, 'are you intending to cross-examine your own witness?'

'Oh, is that what I was doing, my Lord?' – innocence itself.

'I'll try to keep you on the straight and narrow,' Deed said.

Jo smiled. 'I'm obliged, my Lord.' She turned back to her client. 'Who brought Mr Bartlett to the flat?'

'Mariana did, I think.'

'You don't remember such a detail?' Jo challenged.

'No. I'd been worrying about my business and wasn't sleeping. So Mariana suggested we played a game – picking up a man and bringing him back and me springing out like an irate husband.'

'That helped you to sleep?'

'No, it distracted me so I didn't worry.'

'Remind the court what business you're in, Mr Fish?' Deed said without looking up from his note.

'I'm an undertaker, sir.'

'Did this distract you, the pick-up, and the jumping out?' Jo asked.

Fish lowered his head. 'Yes. It was our game.'

'How often did this happen?'

'I don't know. Once a month, I suppose, perhaps more.'

'Did you choose the victim or Ms Ortega?'

'I'm not sure really.'

'On this last occasion, who chose Mr Bartlett?'

The witness didn't respond, and Jo didn't push the point, having something more surprising for him. 'Did you know Ms Ortega had been having an affair with the man you say you killed?'

A shocked Fish said, 'She couldn't have been. She loves me.'

'Mrs Mills,' Deed cautioned again and waved Heathcote Machin back to his seat. Jo half-bowed to the bench.

'Mr Fish,' she said regardless, 'did you know Ms Ortega was having sexual relations with Peter Bartlett, the estate agent she was purported to have picked up in the pub that fateful night and brought to your flat?'

Anger and confusion were clashing with disbelief in the undertaker and he couldn't speak for a moment; when at last he managed to it was with a level of calm. 'She wouldn't, not Mari she is the most kind and loyal person. She'd had a difficult life in Colombia, always having to rely on powerful men for protection, men who took advantage of her. She needs protecting, but they all try to possess her. She said I'm the only one who didn't try to do that.'

'The truth is, Mr Fish, the estate agent wasn't powerful enough for her and was becoming possessive. She wanted to be rid of him because he was making too many sexual demands without worthwhile results ...'

Fish lost it and screamed, 'She wouldn't ... She wouldn't hurt anyone.'

'Did she hurt you, Mr Fish?' Jo asked gently. When nothing was forthcoming – 'Prior to the night of the killing, had she ever told you to get lost?'

Fish shook his head violently as if dealing with some internal conflict and Jo's impatience turned to pity for him.

'Yes, no,' he said. 'I don't know. I'm too clingy – I have to learn to give her space. I don't give her the freedom she needs...'

'Do you trust her not to sleep with anyone who might serve her purpose?'

'I love her. I'll do anything for her...'

'Would that include going to prison for a murder someone else committed?' Jo became aware of the silence in the courtroom. It was as if no one was breathing as they waited for his reply. There wasn't one.

'Was orgasm ever achieved between Ms Ortega and the casual pickups?'

'No, of course it wasn't,' – his reply on a sharp intake of breath.

'Then were you surprised when she achieved orgasm with Mr Bartlett?'

'She didn't. She didn't,' Fish insisted.

'How long were Ms Ortega and Mr Bartlett making love before you burst out of the cupboard to surprise them?'

'I don't remember. Usually it was no time at all.'

'Was this time one of those usual occasions? Or was it long enough for Mr Bartlett to orgasm, possibly Ms Ortega also – the post mortem report in your bundle marked 'F', my Lord.' She waited for the judge to find it and remind himself.

'Ms Ortega may well be the archetypal red-hot Latin lover, but underneath she coldly calculates her own best interests. She planned to use her estate agent lover, who she was finished with, to dump not only him, but the man waiting to spring out of the wardrobe. But realising she had a much tighter grip on the man in the cupboard who suddenly made her an offer she couldn't refuse, she calculatingly drew you into the frame to help get rid of the body, nor caring that you might go to prison. When Peter Bartlett was found to be alive after you claim you dumped him, Ms Ortega went back and finished him off, did she not?'

'My Lord,' Heathcote Machin said, rising. 'My learned friend is clearly calling for unfounded speculation.'

'And some, Mr Machin,' Deed quipped, 'while making her closing argument too. Well, Mrs Mills, the whole court is waiting.'

Jo looked over at her client, hoping he would say something about how he got drawn into this web. He just shook his head. She thought she heard a sob from him.

'I have no further questions at this stage,' she said.

'Hah, a question would have been novel, Mrs Mills.' Deed turned to Machin. 'Do you wish to examine this witness, should the prosecution choose to defend him?'

For Deed the courts represented the very embodiment of truth. It was why he first became a barrister, then accepted a better than half paycut to become a judge. The process could be incisive, slicing away the web of lies and half-truths, penetrating to the heart: truth. When it happened it was majestic, inspirational, while the lies and obfuscation he sometimes encountered left him feeling soiled. Some witnesses told blatant lies, but they were rare in criminal trials. More often they were being human with all the familiar foibles and inadequacies, or were plain nervous when encountering the august court room. Deed tried hard to give due process a human face and help people through this stressful time – to leave behind their anxieties and fears.

He would like to have helped this witness to reveal more of the truth, but it would have meant going further than he even allowed Jo Mills to go. He thought she was on the money about this man's lesser involvement, if he was involved at all. It was clear he didn't wish to help himself, but clung to his misplaced loyalty to a woman who seemed to be selling him short. He understood all too readily why he was doing so as he stole a glance to Mariana Ortega.

Now it was the turn of her barrister to finish the job. It wasn't incumbent upon the first barrister in the defence to cross-examine this witness, but Mrs Mills had given him little choice. Machin would seek to do the prosecution's job by sticking it to Rupert Fish, making him appear both instigator and perpetrator. Heathcote Machin wasn't a barrister who sought truth; rather the reverse. While Deed didn't believe he would lie, anything possible would be pressed into service in order to win.

With a few easy strokes he painted the co-defendant as an obsessive, desperate to possess his client body and soul, who wouldn't let anyone come between them. All this Mr Fish accepted like it was a clear display of his love, and short of Deed dismissing the case against him – a move the prosecution might appeal – this jury was certain to convict.

After Machin had done his worst, Mason Allen QC got up and attempted to anticipate Deed by looking at the clock. 'Might this be a convenient moment, my Lord?'

At ten-to-four Deed was confident the prosecution could not only get started on this witness but finish also. He was hoping James Pollock MP had answered his summons to appear. 'I'm sure you can skate through this, Mr Mason Allen – as Mr Machin has done most of the work for you.'

'My Lord,' Mason Allen conceded, and then to disprove Deed's point went through his cross-examination at a snail's pace, with frequent glances at the clock. Perhaps he needed to be elsewhere, but there had been no request to Coop for an early finish.

At ten-past-four things picked up pace when he said, 'Mr Fish, you have a very short temper and seeing a man between the legs of the woman you love having a full orgasm was way beyond anything you could cope with emotionally. You saw red and lost all control, did you not, and smashed the stone Buddha on Mr Bartlett's head?'

'No. I think he attacked me...'

'You were so consumed with jealous rage that you went back on Ms Ortega's instruction and finished the job after you had already dumped the body...' Mr Fish looked across the courtroom at Ms Ortega with a thousand-yard stare, tears in his eyes. Deed wondered if the truth was just dawning in him.

Heading for the rear of Southwark Court Centre with Coop, Deed sharing the weight of papers from the current case, he saw Jessie Rogers waiting near the exit and remembered the earlier phone call from her. She was dressed in her usual eye-catching fashion.

'She hasn't joined the Amish!' Coop observed.

In other circumstances Deed might have laughed, instead, he handed her his papers. 'I'll see you back in The Strand,' he said, avoiding the look he knew his clerk would be giving him. Holding her in high regard, he would hate her to think him a simpering fool, but knew he could easily wear the mantle. He caught Jessie's arm and steered her beyond his clerk's hearing.

'What is it, Jessie? Your phone call sounded like it was a confession.'

'It is, I'm afraid, Judge,' she said.

'Perhaps you'd be better off with a priest. He might feel safer. Well, you've got my attention.' He headed out with her, not noticing Jo Mills approach Coop.

'Coop, I wanted a word with the judge,' she said.

'You'll have to get in line, Mrs Mills. Madam needed an urgent word. I suspect we won't get him back quickly, if at all.' Coop tensed and looked round at her, checking herself. 'Can I make you an appointment?'

'Perhaps I should just wear a shorter skirt.'

'It seems to do it for most men.'

'Ah. It does need his undivided attention.' She turned back the way she came.

The meeting Deed called with Witham would be difficult, especially as his own thoughts about his judicial assistant had not been far behind Witham's actions. He would rather Coop had caught up with Jo Mills and got her in to talk about the problem she seemed to be having. Somehow the two might be related.

There was a sharp rap at the door. Coop pulled it open it and announced Mr Justice Witham, allowing the tense, younger judge to push past her.

'Thank you, Coop. Perhaps you'd be kind enough to take Baba for a walk.' It wasn't part of her job description, and he tried not to take his clerk for granted. He waited for her to go out with his dog and close the door.

Witham got off the first volley, as if trying to cut the ground from under Deed.

'I know you have seniority, but I don't enjoy being summoned by your clerk.'

'I'm sure she was polite in her mission.'

'What is this about, Sir John?'

'It's called revisiting the scene of the crime,' Deed said, shocking him.

'What crime? What are you talking about?'

'First, I want the papers in the Anita Plant case you're hearing.'

A sneer appeared on Witham's lip. 'Do you intend to give her a free ride as a favour to Jo Mills?' – his confidence coming back.

'I'm taking over the case…'

'You can go to hell. I've never heard anything so outrageous.'

'Then let's lower the tone a bit and talk about your visit to my room earlier today, shall we?' Deed said.

This brought a sudden chastening as Witham swallowed hard and avoided his eyes. 'What visit?' he tried.

'It doesn't become a High Court judge to molest young women of lower rank. They find it difficult to refuse – she calls it Weinsteining.'

'Hah! You do it all the time, sir.'

'I'm older!' Deed joked, but doubted Witham appreciated the humour. 'Jessie Rogers is my marshal, under my protection.'

'Would anyone believe her – with the sort of reputation she has?'

'Every man on the jury would, and all the women would know it was true.'

Changing tack, Witham said, 'Look here, John, she welcomed my advances.'

'Yes, I could *just* believe that from what I saw – but on government property.' Deed shook his head as a stricken cry emerged from Witham.

'No, you weren't there…'

'That's not my turn-on. There was a hidden camera…'

The younger judge seized on this with righteous indignation. 'Why did you put it there? To spy on this unfortunate young woman?'

Deed laughed. 'You might know who put it there and why.'

He went to his computer where the footage had been uploaded and turned the screen towards Witham. 'Perhaps you'd like me to send you this as a souvenir. You should destroy it before it finds its way onto YouTube.'

Witham lowered his head and gave a simple nod. Deed watched him start out, then stop and turn back.

'My position on the Salibi extradition doesn't change,' he said.

Deed laughed again. 'I'd think less of you if it did.'
'Yes. I'll send my clerk with the Anita Plant papers.'

In the corridor Jo Mills met a crestfallen Mr Justice Witham and was curious to know what might have happened in Deed's room. She wasn't about to ask him as she came along with Coop and Baba. Witham gave her the briefest of glances.

'I suppose you'll have a good laugh now,' he said.

'I will, Tom?' she said, her curiosity deepening. Using his first name seemed appropriate here. 'I was about to apologise for last night.'

He was surprised. 'Oh, it's for me ... I'm sorry.'

'Then we're both sorry.' Recovering, he said, 'Yes. Yes, excellent.' He strode now. Jo was amazed how the tiniest of gestures could so change a powerful man.

'He's come down a peg or two,' Coop observed. She knocked on the door to Deed's room and went in. 'Mrs Mills, Judge.' She unclipped Baba and put her in an armchair, then went out.

'What did you say to Tom Witham?' Jo asked, deliberately using the familiar.

Deed gave her a sharp look, but didn't respond. 'Not important.'

'Was it about me?' Jo said. 'We had dinner.'

Deed said brusquely, 'You have a peculiar taste in High Court judges.'

'Perhaps I'm a sucker for punishment.'

'I sometimes wonder if you're not too like me for us ever to marry and succeed.'

Jo felt as if she'd been slapped and before she could gather a response, Deed hit her with another surprise. 'Are you ready to argue the Anita Plant case?'

'After last night I thought it was a lost cause.'

'I won't hold it against you,' Deed said. 'I've taken the case. How relevant is that envelope you gave me?'

Reeling a little, Jo managed, 'You still haven't looked in it?'

'Of course not, it might have compromised me.'

'Thank God for an honest bench.' Jo kissed him hard on the mouth. Before he could respond in his time-honoured fashion, she was gone. There was work to do.

CHAPTER SIXTEEN

LYING IN WAIT FOR DEED at Southwark Court Centre to attempt somehow to wrest the Anita Plant case back was absurd, yet Rochester felt it incumbent upon him to try. More time was spent manoeuvring to manage this judge than the entire High Court Bench. An Act of Parliament to simply enable the sacking of High Court judges was much needed. Short of that he'd have to employ an assassin, and to be there to make sure they got the right judge. He had no expectation of Neil Haughton, if he came to the MoJ, ever proving any match for Deed. Perhaps he should bow to the inevitable and recommend that Deed be elevated to the Appellate Bench. Although that might have more far-reaching consequences for Government, his ability to meddle with justice on a daily basis would be less. Rochester himself might even have retired himself before havoc rained down from the Appellate Bench.

Deed strode across the wide forecourt like a pyromaniac with a can of petrol and a box of matches. Rochester almost ran to keep up.

'John, why on earth do you *want* this vexatious case…?'

'Tom Witham can't manage it after all. We do like to help fellow judges when the lists bunch up.'

'You'll have Mrs Mills before you again. Is that wise, in view of past gossip?'

'We're appointed for our objectivity, Ian, as well as our breadth of legal knowledge.'

'But you're going to be a Lord Justice of Appeal, John,' Rochester pointed out, stopping Deed at the security door.

'Am I? Excellent. Have the JAC and the PM signed off on that yet?'

'Only a matter of time, I assure you,' he lied, looking him directly in the eye.

'I'll await the call with anticipation. If we don't deal with Ms Plant in the High Court, we'll eventually have it on appeal. Think how many resources that will occupy.'

Deed disappeared through the security gate, the familiar guards merely waving him through. Despite having the appropriate app on his phone to get him in unchallenged, Rochester wasn't going to risk following and having to submit to the indignity of emptying his pockets and being scanned. Last time the app didn't work and they even made him remove his shoes and braces. He would rather take a bawling out from the Minister of Justice designate – at least Haughton was toothless, and might even lose his seat next time round.

'How the fuck did you let Deed take this case?' Haughton demanded pacing around his office, angry flecks of spit spraying from his mouth. 'No, no, no, Deed cannot have this case, I'll strangle him first. It'll unpick whole strands of our anti-terrorist legislation if he lets Mrs Mills win.'

'That isn't how the courts work, Home Secretary,' Rochester pointed out, knowing his clever response was risky.

Haughton didn't notice. 'Isn't that why we appointed this dickhead, Witham – because he was reliable?'

'Deed might not find in Mrs Mills' favour.'

'Yes,' Haughton said, going red in the face, 'and we might win another term. Or somehow lower the deficit! Where's Superintendent Hamblyn? She must go into Deed's office and nail him with those papers, so prejudice his hearing the case.'

'That's a serious violation of judicial privilege, sir.'

'Oh, I suppose planting the camera wasn't? Go with her, Ian. For God's sake get those papers.'

The door was rapped and opened by Sir Percy Thrower. 'Excuse me, Minister. Two police officers are here demanding your presence at court.'

'I'm in no mood for games, Percy. So unless they want to police sheep-fucking on the Falklands, they'd better buzz off.'

Percy had alerted Rochester to this and now if he caught his eye, he would corpse.

'They're here to take you, Minister.' There was a slight tremor to Percy's voice, which might have been mistaken for fear, only Rochester knew it wasn't.

Deed had had three calls from George Channing and taken none of them. He quite expected her to storm into his room, or even his court, demanding to know what he was doing hauling Haughton before him. If it happened, he really would throw her into a cell for contempt. He did once before, but he doubted George had learned anything by it. A child born to privilege, wanting for nothing, believing everything was accessible; through her well-placed chancery set and living with the wealthy Neil Haughton, most things were.

Despite the legal imperative placed upon him with Heathcote Machin calling him as a witness, Deed was surprised the Home Secretary didn't throw up some serious roadblocks to his route to court. He wasn't sure who was being the most mischievous, Machin for calling him or himself for allowing it, but here he was in the witness box, being examined. He needed to be careful not let the young barrister overstep the bounds of propriety.

Even more journalists now jammed the press benches; possibly someone on the court staff alerted them.

'Mr Haughton, I believe you know Ms Ortega, the first defendant, do you not, sir?' Machin was saying.

'Not really,' Haughton said, like a man in a cleft stick: admission drawing him into something; distancing himself making him seem haughty. 'I think she cleaned our house for a brief period some time last year.'

Deed looked round at him, keeping surprise off his face. The Minister was going to risk being thought haughty, but even if the jury judged him so, it wouldn't be him they might send to prison.

'You're not sure?' Machin glanced at the jury with a "Really?" look.

'I don't arrange domestic details.'

'Yes, we never trifle with such details,' – again glancing at the jury. 'Did you get to know this lady rather well?'

Haughton turned to Deed with the fearful eyes of a trapped rat.

Without looking up from his note, Deed said, 'Where is this going, Mr Machin?'

'I'm trying to establish the nature of the relationship, my Lord.'

'Yes, but to what end? If it's to embarrass a Government minister, move on.'

'It's the defence's contention that Ms Ortega had a sexual relationship with this witness, a fact which is conveniently being swept under the carpet,' Machin argued. 'She has been cruelly and unfairly used…'

'Cleaning houses? Just get to the point,' Deed warned him.

'Would you say she was reliable, diligent, hardworking, honest and decent?'

Growing more impatient, Deed said, 'Mr Machin, did you call this witness for political embarrassment, or are you implying he entered into the alleged sex games?' He turned to Haughton. 'Did you have sex with the defendant? Be very careful about this, Minister; remember you are under oath.'

Hesitating for a long moment, Haughton responded like a politician, turning to the jury with a frank, 'No, we did not have sex.'

Deed wrote his note, not believing him and was sure the jury didn't either. 'Mr Machin?'

It was clear that Machin had different information when he said, 'Are you quite sure you didn't have sex?'

'Mr Machin, this is a Minister of State. We must accept he wouldn't lie,' Deed said in a way that wouldn't show up in the court transcript when read back.

With as clear an edge to his voice Machin said, 'Of course not, my Lord.' He threw up his hands and sat.

Deed glanced at Jo Mills, then Newman Mason Allen. Both shook their heads, so Deed waved a relieved Neil Haughton out of the witness box. That was too much for Mariana Ortega.

'She promise me proper work permit for sex,' she blurted out.

This caused a great buzz of interest around the court as Haughton shrank in stature. Deed almost felt sorry for him, having been here many times, if not with the same corrupt promise.

'Whatever he may or may not have promised, Ms Ortega,' Deed told her, 'that is not for this trial.'

'The other one promise,' she persisted as the Home Secretary tried to slide away. 'Me Government minister say stay.'

'To which Government minister are you referring?' Deed wanted to know, the tension in the court becoming electric, petrifying Haughton. 'Are you speaking about James Pollock?'

'*Si*. She promises me get a work permit. Stay.'

'Would the jury go out please? I know this is deeply frustrating, but we have to be seen to be fair as well as being fair.' He waited until the usher closed the door behind the last juror before giving the press a severe warning not to tweet anything about counsels' exchanges.

'It seems the prosecution may have to re-open its case and question the minister. If Mr Pollock doesn't answer his summons, he'll be arrested for contempt.' He turned to an ashen-looking Haughton. 'If you have any influence here, Mr Haughton, please urge your colleague to report to the witness room by 09.45 tomorrow. Let's have the jury back.'

When the jurors were settled, Heathcote Machin got to his feet and Deed knew at once what he was going to ask.

'With your leave, my Lord, might I call my client after all? In the circumstances it's right to do so.'

The moment the whole court had been awaiting, Ms Ortega in the witness box. Even in the light of Haughton's denying having had sex with her Deed was surprised Machin decided to run her. He wouldn't have done so had he been her defence barrister, but there was a risk in that strategy. Juries wanted to hear from the defendant and often inferred guilt when they didn't speak for themselves.

'Ms Ortega, anything you don't understand during this examination, please don't hesitate to stop me and I'll explain,' Machin said in a way which signalled to the jury that his client was disadvantaged.

'Why you not tell I no kill this man?'

'This we will seek to establish, and by the end of it I'm sure we will have convinced this jury of your innocence. On the evening of the 15th of April when you returned to the flat with your lover, did you know Mr Fish would be hiding in the bedroom cupboard?'

'I love Rupert so very much.' She smiled across at the man in the dock.

'Yes, this is established beyond doubt and that he loves you and was very jealous of other men you knew,' – laying bricks with a heavy trowel. 'Did you expect him to be hiding in the bedroom cupboard?'

'No. I not even know she in the flat.'

'The flat belongs to Mr Fish, does it not?'

'Him mother buy he this flat.'

'So was it unusual for him to be at his own flat?'

'She lend me to it.'

'Was this so you could bring your lovers there?' Machin said.

'She lend me to it for tonight,' Ms Ortega explained.

'Did he know you brought lovers to his flat?'

'She very jealous, but I love.'

'Was it at this point that Mr Fish jumped out of the cupboard and struck the victim, Mr Bartlett?'

'She not a proper lover.'

Having got as much out of his witness without leading her, Machin gave the floor to Jo Mills, who wasn't easy on this witness, pitching in at her as though prosecuting her rather than defending the second person in the dock.

'Isn't it true that you not only knew someone would be in the bedroom cupboard, you planned this sex game in advance with your lover?'

'I not know this lover there.'

'Because this lover, Mr Fish, wasn't there, was he? Someone else was in hiding, ready to play the game.'

'Rupert, she play the game all while.'

'This particular evening it wasn't Rupert watching you with your current lover, was it, but another man?'

'I don't do that with other man.'

'Then was the porter, Rudi Kozlowski, lying when he said he sometimes took part in your games?' Jo asked.

'She fantasy after me.'

Opening a folder, Jo took out several statements. 'Does fantasist also apply to the Virgin cable man, the Ocado delivery man, the dry cleaner? All fantasists?'

'*Si*. Have big fantasy on me.'

'I'd like to offer these sworn statements in evidence. They can all be called.'

Machin gave a low groan as the usher carried the statements across to the judge, and glanced at the jury, knowing he had lost them.

'Would you tell the jury who it was hiding in the bedroom cupboard?' Jo invited. 'Or would you like me to tell them?'

'I not know she in the cupboard.' the witness spat the words at her angrily.

'This person in the cupboard was James Pollock MP, was it not…?'

'She not my lover…'

'Mrs Mills, are you bringing evidence to support this contention?'

'I would like the opportunity to question Mr Pollock.'

'Unless you have evidence indicating he was present I cannot permit this speculative hunt,' Deed told her. 'We must wait to see if the gentleman answers his witness summons.'

Even accepting that desperate situations sometimes called for extreme measures, Rochester found himself holding his breath as he entered Deed's room in the Strand with Supt Hamblyn; there he found the marshal sorting legal papers as if she had a real rather than a made-up purpose for being here. Hamblyn produced her ID to remind her who she was, as if the presence of the head of the Justice Department's civil service alone wasn't enough.

'You are?' Hamblyn challenged in a rather clumsy fashion. Rochester might have hoped for a more sophisticated approach.

'Mr Justice Deed's judicial assistant,' she replied, while looking at Rochester, making him feel uncomfortable.

'Good. Sir John has documents relating to the Anita Plant case he shouldn't have in his possession…' she hesitated and glanced at Rochester again. They assumed having taken over the case he had taken back the papers from Joe Channing.

Sighing under his breath, Rochester took control. 'It might accidentally be perverting the course of justice. That never looks good on a judge's CV. I'm sure you wouldn't want this.'

'I'm sure he wouldn't want that either,' the young woman said coolly. How did she manage that, he wondered? 'Sir John won't be here till after court rises in Southwark.'

'Then we'll find and remove them.' Hamblyn tried a smile. 'You can help.'

'Don't be a dork,' Jessie Rogers said, rounding on her. 'A High Court judge can have in his possession all that relates to a case whether it's treasonous, pornographic or anything else.'

Laughter almost escaped from Rochester at her audacity, never suspecting she would be so knowledgeable. With her refusal to budge he now envisaged the distinct possibility of the situation spiralling further out of control with what happened next. She said, 'I'll ring Mrs Cooper,' – reaching for the phone.

'We'd prefer you didn't,' Supt Hamblyn said and grabbed her wrists. Rochester wished she hadn't as the young woman looked at him with pleading eyes.

Hamblyn pulled her behind the desk and began searching for the papers.

'You stupid plod,' Jessie told her. 'You've got about three seconds before I start screaming.'

'There's really no need for that,' Rochester said as the situation slipped further towards chaos. He was at a loss to know why this wretched judge inspired such loyalty in people, even his own plant.

'The corridor's full of policemen,' the detective told her. 'None of them'll believe you're being harmed. Tell us where the papers are.'

At that point Jessie Rogers broke free of the policewoman's grip and raced out. In the corridor she would soon discover there were no other police officers around. All the while Hamblyn went on searching.

'Give this up as a bad job, superintendent,' Rochester advised, his concern deepening.

'You heard the Home Secretary, sir, he requires those papers.'

'Then he should have come for them himself.'

What an invidious position he was in, caught between the demands of the Executive, whom he served well, and the judiciary which he facilitated. How he wished he had followed his instinct and pulled out when the girl bolted, now he heard Sir Joseph Channing thundering along the corridor. The Appellate Judge threw open Deed's door expecting to catch burglars, which indeed is what Rochester felt like. Jessie Rogers was right behind, holding Joe's arm.

'What in God's name are you doing, violating the sanctity of a High Court judge's office?' he demanded. 'I'm minded to have you both summarily carted off to gaol, only to be released at his pleasure. There's not a judge in the land who wouldn't support him.'

'It's a simple matter, Joe, an urgent one,' Rochester lied. 'The Counter Terrorism unit has learned of an imminent threat from Islamist extremists. Papers relating to their identities are in Sir John's possession.'

'I had such an exchange with this policewoman and Tom Witham the other evening. Even if there were such papers here and these wretched people were to act with immediate consequences, it doesn't justify this violation,' Channing said. 'Further, it in no way permits an assault upon a member of the bar. I will report this to both the Commissioner of Police and the Lord Chancellor.'

Rochester almost smiled at that. 'I do apologise, Joe – the situation is grave.'

'Mr Justice Deed doesn't have the papers anyway. I have them…'

'No,' Petra Hamblyn said.

Channing turned and gave her a crushing look. 'Are you contradicting me, madam?'

'She's not, Joe, she wouldn't dare,' he said, accepting the papers were not now back in Deed's hands. Clearly, Hamblyn was proving less than reliable. 'Perhaps you'd wait outside, superintendent? You too, Ms Rogers.'

'Joe?' Jessie Rogers appealed in her familiar manner.

'In the circumstances she stays.' Then following the detective's departure, Channing said, 'Deed gave me the papers in question.'

'The situation is no less urgent, Joe.'

'Before I hand them over to the State, I'll take the mind of another judge. If he sees fit, then I'll hand them over. That still leaves you to face Mr Justice Deed over this gross violation.'

The judge who was invited to Channing's room could not have better been chosen, only when Sir Tom Witham arrived, he seemed to be on the horns of a dilemma; so Rochester began to think whatever the Home Secretary had over him couldn't be that effective. Someone more decisive who could elect according to the needs of Government was required here.

'I'm afraid I'm too much the new boy, Joe, to be taking a position here.' He glanced between them, uncertainty increasing.

'The question is the sanctity of a High Court judge's office,' Channing explained. 'We breach it at our peril.'

This caused Witham more problems. 'This is on the face of it... It's ... Look, it's a matter of grave importance and some delicacy ...' The wretch was falling to pieces before his eyes, and might even cry. Then without warning the younger judge stiffened to an erect stance and said, 'Our actions cannot be subject to police scrutiny. You must forego these papers, Ian – no matter how vital you feel they are to the State. Here the State is represented by Sir John Deed. I would suggest you leave with your policewoman or risk contempt.'

Et tu, Brute? Rochester's jaw dropped in astonishment. Was Haughton's amanuensis going to become one of the Gang of Three? Glancing back as he started out of the office, he saw the young marshal grab Channing's hand in excitement with, 'Oh, Joe,' employing the sort of familiarity only she could get away with. It was time for another private conversation with her about her future at the bar. If she imagined Deed or Channing could guarantee that she was mistaken.

CHAPTER SEVENTEEN

SIR PERCY THROWER, DESPITE HIS size, had the disconcerting knack of approaching without a sound, perhaps the result of his former athletic prowess at Oxford or possibly he had been an American Indian in a previous life. So often this man caught Haughton having thoughts he shouldn't be thinking and he was thankful that Percy wasn't a mind-reader. Or was he? Haughton was thinking about Jim Pollock and those butcher's hands of his when Percy startled him with, 'Mr Pollock is here, Minister.'

'He is?' Haughton stared at his Permanent Secretary as though a stranger.

'Do you need me in for this?'

'No,' he shouted in a voice almost breaking into a scream. Would this man think he was an emotional wet? 'No, Percy,' he managed in a calmer fashion. 'Tell Margaret we're not to be disturbed.'

He got up as the Defence Minister came in, shutting the door. His eyes went at once to Pollock's hands, almost if expecting to see a cleaver there.

'What fucking bollocks is this now, Neil?' Pollock asked. 'That cunt Deed's threatening me with clink if I don't show up tomorrow.'

'I was in court today – being totally humiliated by him,' Haughton said. 'It's obvious he has some political agenda.'

'That's reason enough to hoik him from office.'

'Possibly, Jim, but not before your appearance tomorrow.'

'Then the interfering bastard leaves me no option,' Pollock said. 'I'll cut his fucking balls off and choke him with them.'

Having qualified as a solicitor before going into business and making his fortune, Haughton was accustomed to this sort of aggression and ought not to be shocked, but he was and wasn't sure if he managed to keep it off his face. 'What?' he said, hoping his Cabinet colleague was joking. There was no humour in either his voice or his body language 'You can't. No, you can't.' Even though he had no idea what Pollock might be planning he was disturbed by this naked threat to a judge and knew he should take him to task.

'What, Neil? What the fuck is it you think I can't do?'
'We've tried everything possible to stop him legally.'
'And failed abysmally. The prick's still in office trying to trash Government policy. One man can't be allowed to threaten not only good governance, but our whole way of life. That's what he's doing. The PM thinks so too.' There was a note of finality in his tone.
'Did the PM say that?' Haughton was suddenly gripped by anxiety.
Pollock said, 'I have no qualms about going into the witness box and answering a few silly questions. That's not the point, Neil.'
'It's just the point. He made me appear a complete fool, one who poked our cleaner.'
'No one thinks worse of you for that.' Pollock grinned. 'She's a real hotty.'
This gave him no reassurance. As a lawyer he always observed the principle of never asking a question unless he knew the answer. Despite Pollock having met Ortega through him he didn't know if they'd had sex as was implied in court. Now he needed to know and surprised himself when the question emerged.
'Don't be daft, Neil. Would I contemplate going to court if I had partaken of carnal knowledge of this lady, as they say? If she's saying I did then someone ought to go and talk to her.'
'How? She's remanded in Holloway Prison.'
'You're the Home Secretary, prisons are your bag. You could organise access.'
'That's highly improper, Jim.'
'So is her naming Cabinet ministers and Deed having them called. You don't imagine this judge will stop at asking pointless questions about this case? Make the arrangements and we'll get someone to talk to her,' Pollock said. 'There's too much at risk to let this run out of control.'
Inside Haughton was quaking and wanted to divert his colleague. 'We didn't actually bribe these Arabs for the arms contracts, Jim?' he asked unthinkingly.
The look of amazement Pollock gave him was fringed with contempt. 'Are you being naïve? You don't sit down with the ragheads unless you can stuff their mouths full of gold. Two things they want to know: how big's their "facilitation payment" and what off-shore tax haven it's going into. Why do you think we've been so easy on HSBC? If those slimy gits ever started spilling the beans the shit really would hit, to mix my

metaphors.' Pollock paused considering whether to go on, then nodded, as if agreeing with some unspoken request. 'Making facilitation payments to the Saudis is but the tip of the iceberg, Neil. If any of this breaks loose, it'll make covering up historic paedophile rings seem about as harmless as a Roger Whittaker song.'

Haughton couldn't help staring at those butcher's hands at the end of Pollock's short arms. George had called them that after she first met him. Had those hands killed anyone? They looked capable. Had they in fact bludgeoned Mariana Ortega's lover to death in that apartment? Even thinking about the possibility terrified him. In the event what possible action could he take to stop this particular train? The real question was, should he try?

'Neil! Neil…!' He heard Pollock calling him, and knew he had to get a grip and try to divert whatever was going to happen; after all, he was still Home Secretary. But what could he do, have this valued colleague arrested? Was that really going to happen? He doubted it. He couldn't accuse a fellow Cabinet minister of things that might only be figments of his imagination. If he did, colleagues would assume he'd wigged out under the strain of high office and eject him from the most exclusive club ever. He would sooner not.

'There's been talk in Cabinet about you not being on top of your game, Neil.' The Defence Minister said as though a matter of no importance.

'Who, who says that?' Haughton demanded. 'Not the Prime Minister?'

'I don't want to dwell on the point, but the consensus is this is why you're being moved to Justice – a chance to wrench these fucking judges into line.'

Haughton felt both mortified and sick, having got no sense of this from the PM. He wanted to challenge Pollock, but was afraid to. Instead, the Defence Secretary could go straight to Deed's court to suffer his due humiliation. That wouldn't help his own cause in Cabinet, quite the reverse, it would be more evidence of him not being on top of his game.

'The judges will be brought in line, Jim,' he said. 'Our Cabinet colleagues can be assured. That still leaves the vexatious question of your appearance in court. My advice is to answer your summons, meanwhile I'll front Deed down.'

'I'll think about it overnight. Meanwhile, let me know about access to that prison so someone can talk to this woman.'

None of his anxiety departed along with his colleague, but still he wasn't sure how he might achieve what he was asking, but would try in order to secure his Cabinet position.

'Judge, Judge!' Coop said hurrying into his room, 'I've just heard from the usher in the witness room. The Prison Service has informed him this morning that Ms Ortega is dead. She committed suicide in her cell at Holloway.'

'What?' Deed rose from his desk, shocked. 'Don't tell me she hanged herself.'

'Yes, Judge, with a piece of cord from the safety grille over the window.'

'How can that be?' – thinking aloud, knowing Coop, usually a mine of information, wouldn't have an answer. 'First, we have a witness supposedly hangs himself, now a defendant? I don't think so, unless suicide has become a transmittable disease.'

'Will you suspend the trial?'

'There's no alternative in the circumstances,' he said, then changed his mind. 'No, have everyone in as usual, Coop. There's something here that needs exploring.'

'You're telling me,' Coop responded, excited at the prospect of his confronting whoever. Injustice was as much an anathema to his clerk as it was him, only her responses were often more emotional.

'What we must look for is any connection between these two incidents,' Deed said.

'That's obvious, Judge – the politician, James Pollock.'

'That might be wishful thinking, Coop,' he said, not wanting to encourage her along this prejudicial path, even though his gut feeling told him Pollock might somehow be connected. 'I doubt if politicians bump people off.'

'No, they get others to do their dirty work.'

'We'll keep this to ourselves, in case we're thought biased and the whole investigation gets kicked aside with a cosy enquiry conducted elsewhere. Has Mr Pollock answered his witness summons?'

'I don't think so, Judge.'

'If he doesn't, we'll ask the police to get him. I want the governor of Holloway brought here along with whoever was in charge of the wing where Ms Ortega was. Let's get the security camera recordings for last night as well.'

'Yes, sir!'

'And, Coop, ask counsel to join me here for coffee.'

For the first time ever Deed found Heathcote Machin at a loss for words. He sat in an armchair in a daze, not even noticing Baba climb onto his lap.

'Did you get any hint Ms Ortega might be suicidal, Heathcote?'

Machin shook his head, sipped some of his too-hot coffee and said, 'If ever a woman loved life it was her.'

'That was my impression. Might being locked down, with the possibility of going to prison,' he speculated, 'have caused her problems?'

'She was convinced she wouldn't be convicted.'

'It might have been more of a problem for the next witness up,' Jo suggested.

'Would we be less puzzled if he committed suicide?' Mason Allen said.

'I would. We never get that lucky with politicians,' was Jo's response.

Deed gave her a look and didn't comment further. 'Is there any sort of psychiatric report?'

'Not one that helps much, Judge. An assessment the prison authority did when she was remanded,' Machine said.

'I saw it in the bundles. It tells us nothing. I hoped you might have had one towards her defence.'

'You are still calling James Pollock?' Jo asked.

'I haven't revoked the summons. It won't have the same effect without your client in court,' he said to Machin. 'I still want to know why the dead porter was wearing a suit with J. Pollock stitched inside. With the tailor's premises broken into and his computer stolen, too many co-incidences are stacking up.'

'It's a pretty crude way of covering a trail,' Jo observed.

'Time might not have been on the side of whoever with Ms Ortega about to be cross-examined.'

'If this was foul play here,' Jo Mills said, 'perhaps there ought to be a close watch on Rupert Fish. Even if he wasn't at the scene of the murder, he may well know who was.'

'Coop, can you alert the security to be extra vigilant? Then contact DAC Colemore and ask him to come here.' When his clerk went out, he said to Jo, 'Do you want to run your client again? You may get more from him now the object of his veneration is no longer with us?'

'Depends what sort of state he's in, Judge. He was totally besotted. I'll try – if he's even capable of speaking.'

'I'd like to see the post mortem report on her death when it's done. I assume there must be one.' That caused him to remember the post mortem report on the death of Mr Kozlowski which he still hadn't received. There could be no question about it not being available to him. He would again summon the report.

When Coop returned, she said, 'Mr Pollock has answered his summons, Judge. He's in the witness room.'

That surprised Deed. He rose and set his coffee cup down. 'Let's see what he has to say.' He grabbed his wig, before turning back to the barristers. 'I'll order a news blackout on Ms Ortega's death without the jury in. Continue with the trial, Mr Machin, until I accept formal proof of the death.'

There was standing room only in court with James Pollock in the witness-box. He looked calm and confident, like a man who had nothing in his past to fly out and sting him.

'I'm most obliged to you, Mr Pollock,' Deed said, 'for interrupting your busy ministerial schedule.'

'Happy to help in any way I can, my Lord,' Pollock responded. 'Nothing takes precedence over the law, sir.'

Deed almost smiled. 'I will ask you some questions. Then possibly counsel for both defence and prosecution may wish to question you. Remember you are under oath. Will you tell the court what, if any, your relationship is with Ms Ortega?'

The response of the witness was to look across at the press box, jammed with news-hungry scribes, as if on the hustings. 'I have no relationship with her. I didn't know the poor lady, and as far as I'm aware I have never met her.'

Deed made a note. 'You didn't visit her at Mr Fish's flat?'

'I most certainly did not,' Pollock said, following Deed's glance across to the dock. His look was almost daring the subdued Rupert Fish to contradict him. The defendant was in no state to contradict anyone, staring at the floor in a daze.

'Then did you know one Rudi Kozlowski?' he asked, feeling certain of that.

'Again I have to disappoint you, Judge.'

'You don't disappoint me, Mr Pollock. I'm trying to establish the facts for the jury.'

'I don't see how I can assist here. I've never heard of the man.'

'You didn't see his death reported in the news?'

'Oh, I may have, but then I take in so much reported news. Most goes right past me, of course – unless my Permanent Secretary flags it.'

'Yes, I understand. Mr Kozlowski had a suit that may have been yours,' he said. 'Can you explain how he came by it?'

'Oh, was it established that it was my suit?'

He wasn't expecting this challenge, but it was clear that Pollock knew about both the suit and the porter.

'The tailor at Maurice Sedwell's of Savile Row seemed to think it was yours.'

The witnessed laughed. 'When you were about to put the poor bloke in gaol! On my salary, sir, even with the enhanced remuneration as the Secretary of State for Defence, I hardly run to bespoke Savile Row suits. No, modest Marks and Spencer is where I get my suits.' He opened his jacket and flashed their label like a badge of honour.

Deed wondered why he assumed he was talking about a bespoke suit. Perhaps it wasn't unreasonable to believe all of Savile Row was tailor-made, even though the majority were now manufactured in the Far East. Pollock's confidence was beginning to grate on him, and he knew he mustn't let it. The reason for this confidence puzzled him. Was it because the two witnesses who might otherwise have identified him no longer could, and the tailor's records that might have told a different story were gone? Deed stopped right there, recognising it was extreme prejudice on his part. Short of asking the Minister to subject himself to a DNA test in the hope that some match might be found on the suit Kozlowski was wearing, he had nowhere to go, having broken the cardinal rule: never ask a witness a question unless you know the answer.

Leaning round to Coop, Deed whispered instructions to bring the tailor into court. Perhaps he would more easily recall the faces of his clients than their records. As Coop hurried out, he invited counsel to question the witness, hoping his clerk would get back before they finished examining James Pollock. It was unlikely as the prosecution had no questions him, nor did Machin, whose interest in the case disappeared with his client.

Jo took him over ground Deed had covered, but went further by accusing him of being in the cupboard when Mr Bartlett was killed.

'This is outrageous,' the Minister protested. 'Judge, do I have to submit myself to this sort of slander?'

'It does seem rather unfair, Mr Pollock,' he told him, 'but counsel is defending a man accused of murder. In defending their clients barristers sometimes do manage to reveal the real culprit. I don't know if Mrs Mills is bringing forward evidence to support this potentially outlandish assertion, but I do have to allow her to proceed. You might get to the point here, Mrs Mills, and indicate any possible evidence you think relevant.'

'Can you tell the court,' Jo said, with a bold thrust which he suspected was covering the paucity of her evidence, 'where you were on the night of April 15th this year?'

'Oh golly,' the Minister said with great affectation. 'Off-hand you've got me. I'd have to check my diary. I believe I was in Riyadh discussing electronics contracts with Saudi Government ministers. I'm sure my PPS will confirm that.'

'Weren't you in fact at Leith Hill Place Wood in Dorking, Surrey?'

'If you were other than in court with these sorts of statements, Mrs Mills, you would find yourself being sued.'

'The fact is, Mr Pollock,' Deed said, 'counsel in a court of law, like politicians in the House, have the freedom from sanction to ask what they like at my discretion; that is based on relevance. Are you in a position to produce evidence in support of this line of questioning, Mrs Mills?'

'Not at this point, my Lord,' Jo said. 'But I do reserve the right to re-examine this witness in defence of my client.'

'This is outrageous. You've no shred of evidence against me.'

'I think you can step down, Mr Pollock,' Deed said, noticing Coop at the door of the court. He gave an almost imperceptible nod and she opened the door wider and let the tailor through as James Pollock stepped out of the witness box. There was a slight tensing of recognition on Blanxart's face, but nothing showed in the politician's expression. Either he didn't know this tailor or he was very good at hiding the truth. Deed suspected the latter. Again this was prejudice seeping through to distort his judgement.

'Mr Blanxart, thank you for coming back. Would you go into the witness box? Remember you are still under oath.' He waited for the witness to get into position. 'Can you tell the court if your client called J. Pollock for whom you made an excellent suit is present in court?'

The witness waited a long while before answering – whether struggling with conscience or trying to find enough saliva in his mouth to speak, Deed wasn't sure. One thing he was certain, this man who was so reluctant to name the client did in fact know Pollock. He glanced at the jury and could see they believed he knew this politician as well.

'No,' he replied in a dry-throated whisper.

'I'm sure the jury didn't hear that, Mr Blanxart.'

'No. I don't see him, sir.'

He wished he could enter the tailor's mind to discover what he might be hiding or who might be threatening him. 'Do you know what the penalty is for perjury? I could hold the perjurer in contempt and send him to the cells at my pleasure. That means he or she stays there until I see fit to release that person for a trial by jury. I ask you again to search your memory and your conscience for the true identity of your client, J. Pollock.' Silence followed. 'Have you seen your client in court today?'

More silence before the tailor said, 'No, I haven't, sir.'

'Did you not tell this court on an earlier appearance that the suit was made for James Pollock MP?'

'I was entirely mistaken, sir.'

'Very well, you may step away.'

Without glancing in his direction Deed was aware that James Pollock was closely following this. Extreme prejudice was creeping up on him again as he tried to exclude the possibility that the Defence Minister and the J. Pollock printed inside the suit jacket the porter had been wearing were one and the same. Whatever hold this politician might have over the tailor there was no apparent lever that would prise free the information. Deed felt frustrated as he went off to his room, like he was entering a tight box of his own making,

CHAPTER EIGHTEEN

'HAVE YOU GOT ANYTHING that might help me penetrate to the truth of this case?' he asked on finding Row Colemore waiting for him.

'You were right in your suspicion about Mariana Ortega's death. I haven't seen the post mortem report, I had an off-the-record conversation with the pathologist. Her hyoid bone was broken – before she was hanged.'

'The bone covering the windpipe doesn't break from hanging.'

'It can happen, but not in the same way, according to the pathologist.'

'This is getting sinister, Row. Can you get the pathologist's report?'

'He was ordered to direct the only copy to the Home Office. I've had one threat from that quarter. I don't want another,' the senior policeman said.

'There has to be an inquest into both deaths.'

'I'm sure there will be – how independent Coroners are these days?' Colemore left the question hanging. 'If this gets back it won't help my career or pension.'

'Is it usual for the Home Office to request post mortem reports?'

'It happens if the case is politically sensitive, such as an unarmed black man being killed by the police, say. If the incident could trigger a public disturbance, they like to be forewarned.'

'That's not the case here,' Deed said. 'How was her neck broken?'

'Forward pressure from someone who knew what he was doing. Its conical projections orientate upwards, and the bone was crushed inwards – not the result of dropping on a cord.'

'Was "he" assumed, or is there evidence ?'

'An assumption based on the force needed.'

'Has the dead woman's cell has been secured as a crime scene?'

'I will make sure it is.'

'Despite the risk to your pension?' he asked.

Colemore laughed. 'Hopefully the Association of Chief Police Officers would have something to say about that.'

'I'd like to see the crime scene before I question the prison staff.' He paused, wondering how far he could get his old fencing partner to go along the road he wished to travel. 'Row, can I ask something else of you? Could you find someone reliable to get the CCTV recordings from the building where the porter Rudi Kozlowski worked? Not just for the night of the murder, we know they've disappeared, but as far back as they have them.'

'Do you know what we're looking for?' Colemore sounded uncertain.

'I want to see if Pollock lied under oath. I'm looking for any image of him going into the building, or one with Ms Ortega or the porter.'

'Shit, John,' the senior policeman exclaimed. 'I could be drawing heavy fire. Why not make it official to be on the safe side?'

'I'm on unsteady ground here. It might look as if I'm prejudiced. If you find someone reliable get him or her to check Mr Kozlowski's bank statements? I'd like to know what money went into his account and when.'

'You think the Defence Minister gave him money to shut him up?' Colemore asked.

'I'm fishing in the absence of the police doing so.'

'That's hardly fair. Nothing about this has dropped into our in tray. Where it has, the death of the porter, we got pushed away by the highest authority. It would be a brave policeman who went there regardless.'

'The police should have more regard for truth and justice,' he said with an edge to his voice, 'instead of ploughing a furrow towards conviction. I always believed there should be as much effort in gathering evidence to support the defence as you put into collecting for the prosecution.'

'You sound like the old defence barrister you were. Talk to the Home Office about it,' Colemore challenged. 'Who would pay for all this work with police budgets being cut?'

'Justice is what suffers under a system which favours the prosecution. With Legal Aid budgets disappearing some defendants barely get a recognisable defence, or are simply given incentives to plead guilty.'

'Some aren't worth spending sixpence on. If you think so, get your brethren to support such a cause. I bet you'd struggle.'

This conversation was making Deed angry, not at the stance of this senior policeman, which was held by a lot of police officers, rather because he knew his fellow judges wouldn't support such a cause. He made no response, and the DAC took that as his exit point.

'I'll see what we can dig up.'

When he had gone Coop said, 'You were a bit hard on him, Judge. He's right about some defendants. They're so wicked they don't deserve a defence.'

'Who decides that, Coop, the police? It's a slippery slope.'

His clerk didn't argue the point.

'Coop, can you get the parties in the Anita Plant case to the Strand for this afternoon?'

'It might be a bit short notice, Judge.'

'Try. The notice does say the case may be called at any time.'

A thought occurred to him as to how he might draw Pollock out, but he knew he was acting in a similar way to the police, with bias.

Entering court number 62 at the Strand, Deed glanced at the woman standing behind Jo Mills at the third bench and assumed she was Anita Plant. A less evident terrorist he couldn't imagine as she appeared more like some's favourite cake-making aunt, and possibly was. Looks could be deceptive, as on occasion he had defended the most benign-looking people who had been something else.

'Thank you all for appearing at short notice,' Deed said when he settled on the bench. 'I am now hearing the case instead of Mr Justice Witham, who is engaged elsewhere. Mrs Mills, I understand there are some papers that detectives from the Counter Terrorism unit at the Home Office are keen to see, papers your client assembled. Do these relate to the charges Ms Plant faces?'

'Directly, my Lord. We believe the charges under the Anti-Terrorism Act arose solely because of their existence in Ms Plant's possession. Ms Plant is, and has been for some years, a senior caseworker for Oxfam working mainly in the Middle East. A lot of time was spent in Lebanon.'

'Why is the Counter Terrorism unit so concerned about these papers?'

'They claim, without supporting evidence, that the papers contain contacts in the so-called Islamic State terror groups operating both here and in the Middle East,' Jo said. 'They argue that the papers contain not only names but imminent targets for attack.'

'Do they have grounds for this belief?'

'Ms Plant has been in touch with suspected terrorists both in Lebanon, Syria and Iraq. These people had insinuated themselves into the Oxfam organisation in order to move freely in frontline areas.' She turned for a brief whispered conversation with her client, and turning back, said, 'We believe the true reason for their wanting these papers is that information contained in them could embarrass members of the Government both here and in Riyadh.'

'If that's proves to be the case both Governments might be more embarrassed for attempting to use anti-terrorism legislation and the Counter Terrorism unit as a means of silencing potential critics.' He was aware of the Attorney General, who was here for the Government, bristling at this. 'However, if your submission is erroneous, Mrs Mills, I'd have no alternative but to order you to hand this document to the appropriate authority, when it's likely that Ms Plant would be arrested and charged under the Terrorism Act 2005. You might also lay yourself open to similar charges if you knowingly withheld a list believed to contain information about intended acts of terror against the State.' Seeing the Attorney half rise to stress the importance of this matter, he said, 'Sir Alan.'

This was a lawyer who was more politician than astute legal mind, and one more interested in his public persona than the law. Alan Peasmarsh was in his mid-50s with silver grey hair which he wore long, angular cheekbones and a thin, pointed nose. Deed had encountered him several times in court, a clubbable sort of bloke when he got his own way, but often vindictive in defeat.

'My Lord, might we know the whereabouts of this list? And having established that, request it is not read in open court because of the dangers aforementioned?'

'That's eminently sensible, Sir Alan,' he conceded. 'Mrs Mills, do you have this list?'

There was a long pause from Jo, as if trying to work out his thinking. 'The list is in the envelope which I gave to you for safe keeping, my Lord.'

'Then it couldn't be safer, and the State need not concern itself further.'

'It's the names the envelope contains the State is concerned about,' the Attorney General said.

'Then we'd better establish what this envelope does in fact contain. Mrs Mills, are you agreeable to the court examining the contents of the envelope?'

'My client's wish is that this information, when it proves other than a list of terror suspects, is made public, my Lord.'

'To what end?' he asked. 'Is this other than to embarrass the Government?'

'While working in the field for Oxfam Ms Plant gathered evidence of people in Saudi Arabia being persecuted and imprisoned without trial, and in some cases executed, with the knowledge of the British Government, who choose to do nothing because of our business interests in the region. When investigating further she discovered those 'business interests' involved huge bribes being signed off by our Government to facilitate arms sales to the Saudis with Ministers here being directly involved.'

'Thank you, Mrs Mills. Perhaps we'd better open the envelope.'

'Again I would urge that this be done *in camera*, my Lord,' the Attorney said.

'First we'd better find the envelope, which is no longer in my charge,' Deed said and turned to speak to Coop, covering the microphone. 'Would you see if Sir Joseph Channing is free? If he is, ask him if he'd come to court with the envelope I gave him.'

As his clerk hurried out, he noticed Rochester and his cuddly friend Supt Hamblyn slip out, too. Perhaps they planned on mugging Joe Channing for the envelope. He smiled at the thought

'We must await Sir Joseph's arrival,' he told the court.

Sir Joseph was a large man but still quick on his feet, despite the vast number of cigarettes Rochester knew he smoked, notwithstanding all the restrictions here and almost everywhere.

'Joe!' Rochester called, hurrying to catch him up as he sped with Mrs Cooper towards Deed's court. 'Could we have a brief word?'

'It will have to be brief,' Sir Joseph said, 'Mr Justice Deed is sitting, waiting to have sight of this...' indicating the manila envelope in his hand. 'I suppose Mrs Cooper might hurry on ahead in with it,' he suggested to Rochester's alarm.

'That's what I need to speak with you about urgently, Joe. Perhaps Mrs Cooper could go on ahead and inform his Lordship you're on your way.'

The look he gave this clerk offered her no alternative but open defiance. She tensed before going. Rochester waited until she was out of earshot, then speaking fast, 'This is a matter of the utmost importance to the good governance of the country, Joe. We'd rather not see that envelope opened in court, regardless of its being a closed court. If we surmise correctly as to its contents then the proper place for it is with the Counter Terrorism unit. They can take immediate and appropriate action on it.'

'I understood there's some doubt as to its contents, which is why Mr Justice Deed has summoned me with it.'

'You cannot be summoned, Joe – a Lord Justice of Appeal, soon to be a Supreme…' he saw the old boy's eyes widen, so added, 'Just as soon as Neil Haughton is confirmed as Lord Chancellor.' A deceitful stratagem, but this was a desperate situation. He was sure Haughton would agree to his recommendation for Channing's elevation if the Government was spared unnecessary embarrassment; the Judicial Appointments Committee would concur.

'Well, Mrs Cooper did ask nicely.' Sir Joseph chuckled, only Rochester wasn't clear if it was at his expense or in anticipation of his bum on the Supreme Court bench. 'Perhaps we should take a peep at the contents, Ian.'

'I'd rather not, Joe. Not here. I'll convey it forthwith to the Counter Terrorism unit at the Home Office and let them deal with it – if you're agreeable.'

Sir Joseph hesitated, and Rochester held his breath, as if all their futures depended upon this course, fearing this senior Judge might finally decline.

'That does seem sensible, Ian. We might suffer another of Deed's tantrums when he hears you've taken it.' Sir Joseph smiled conspiratorially.

'We can live with it, Joe.' Rochester plucked the envelope from his grasp before he could change his mind. 'He'll take the disappointment better coming from someone as high ranking as you.' Relief flooded through him and he made off down the corridor, missing what Sir Joseph said as he turned towards the court.

'I no longer have the envelope,' Channing announced, causing consternation to ripple through the court room. 'The one you took back from me and then later gave to me yet again for safe keeping I recently passed to Sir Ian Rochester to convey to the Home Office.'

Jo Mills started up out of her seat to protest but Deed waved her down, noticing how the Attorney General was now smiling. 'There's some confusion as to what envelope the Government is keen to obtain. Now that it has your envelope, Sir Joseph, I'm sure the correct use will be made of it.'

Again Jo rose from her seat with, 'My Lord…'

'No, Mrs Mills. I'm aware of your argument, you have rehearsed it often.' Deed turned to Coop, again covering the microphone in front of him with his hand. 'Did we keep our envelopes straight?'

'Yes, Judge.' She offered him the manila envelope containing the Amazon envelope from among her papers.

'It seems we had mixed up our envelopes, Sir Joseph. We believe this is the one Mrs Mills passed to me. As the Attorney was so concerned it shouldn't be opened in other than in a closed court, let's clear the court of anyone other than the parties directly involved.'

There was dismay from the media people as they were ejected along with half a dozen spectators, some of whom Deed suspected were police officers. Afterwards the doors were locked.

'Mr Associate,' he said to the Clerk of the Court, 'would you hand this to Sir Joseph Channing and invite him to join me on the bench.'

The black-robed clerk took the envelope as though fearing it might explode and carried it across to Joe Channing, who entered into the spirit of the game, looking around the court as if for either encouragement or objections before taking a seat on the bench. He ripped open the manila envelope, then the cardboard Amazon envelope, and pulled out several sheets of A4 paper with close printing on them and began to read. He got through the first page and about halfway down the second page, then glanced over at the Attorney.

'These contain accusations against named Government ministers, both here and in foreign parts. I won't at this stage show them to you, Sir Alan, or as Attorney General you would have to take immediate action against colleagues, which might place you in certain difficulty.'

Knowing how a corrupt or self-serving Government impoverished the whole nation, Deed took no pleasure in seeing the Attorney General turn ashen. He preferred honest Government regardless of its ideology, but wondered if that wasn't a contradiction in terms.

'With Lord Justice Channing's permission,' Deed said, 'the papers should be retained by the court for safe-keeping pending a judicial decision as to whether or not they should be made public.' He waited for Joe Channing to get the papers back into the Amazon envelope and pass them to him. 'Meanwhile, the police should stop harassing Mrs Mills and her client.' He glanced across at Jo, who sat eyes fixed on the bench before her and wondered if she was crying. 'I want Ms Plant to remain in court. I'll see Mrs Mills in chambers...' He saw the Attorney General rise, 'Yes, you too, Sir Alan. In case I'm thought to be acting prejudicially, I'm inviting Lord Justice Channing also.'

He rose and went out with the envelope, Coop opening the door.

In his room he read the document with a mixture of alarm, anger and disappointment, passing each of the papers to Joe Channing. After a short while Coop arrived with Jo and the Attorney and got them all some tea. From time to time he glanced up at Jo Mills, realising she had been crying, unsure if from relief or disappointment. Perhaps she expected him to start lobbing hand grenades at Government ministers. He had no such plan. A careful strategy was needed to achieve success, only he didn't have one currently.

Flapping the last sheet of paper as if trying to shake free of its contaminating influence, Channing said, 'I never had great expectations of elected politicians, but if an eighth of this is true it brings them way below that expectation,' – fixing the Attorney with a belligerent stare. Alan Peasmarsh avoided his look and flicked his comb through his hair with, 'No comment, Joe.'

'I'm not holding you responsible for the actions of colleagues, Alan,' Channing replied.

'Assuming any of this is true, Joe,' Deed said.

'Quite, John,' the Attorney said in appreciation.

The remarks by this senior judge amused Deed. Hitherto he had given no indication of holding ministers in such low esteem and wondered what had brought about this change. 'The question now, Joe, is what action do we take?'

'I'm inclined to Wellington's dictum, publish and damn the lot of them.'

'A bit harsh, Joe,' Alan Peasmarsh argued. 'Some of my colleagues are thoroughly decent.'

'What difference would publishing it make, Joe? We'd get a twenty-four-hour headline-grabbing scandal, a few heads would roll, then business as usual. There seems no depth to which we won't stoop for business in this present climate.' He paused and met Jo's look. 'What we can't ignore, Alan, is the fact that some of your colleagues were prepared to prosecute Ms Plant and persecute Mrs Mills to stop any of this getting out.'

'Yes, if that is the case it's unforgiveable.'

'We should do nothing until we've spoken with the Chief,' Joe Channing said. 'He might want to see some in Government prosecuted.'

'And if the buck stops with the Prime Minister? It may not just be the MoD that is mired here.'

That left senior judge thoughtful, possibly considering his elevation to the Supreme Court, just as Deed thought about his own elevation to the Court of Appeal. Setting this hare running might prove popular with certain sections of the public, but he wouldn't be thanked by those tasked to oversee the efficient management of the country.

'Jo, what arrangements have been made for Ms Plant's security?'

'She won't go into police protection,' Jo replied. 'She wouldn't feel safe there.'

'That's ridiculous,' the Attorney said. 'If we can't trust the police there can be no security for anyone. Why do you believe this lady might be in danger, John?'

'It's no more than a sense of unease.' He turned to Jo. 'Has she got somewhere safe to stay?'

'She's staying with my son, Tom, in Balham. He shares a flat with friends from university.'

'Novel, but safe? I'm going to order her to go into Witness Protection.'

'You'd have to order her arrest. She won't go otherwise.'

'There could be a threat to her life,' Deed said.

'Just what is it you suspect, John?' asked Joe Channing.

'Please don't push me on this, Joe. It's not that I don't value your wise counsel, rather I don't wish to be seen to be acting with prejudice. There are connections here that I find disturbing. I wouldn't want Ms Plant to become another suicide victim.'

'I think I know where you're going,' Jo said. 'It's not reassuring that two witnesses in another case before you were able to commit suicide, one within the court precincts and one while in prison.'

'The police will be thoroughly investigating those deaths,' the Attorney said.

Ignoring his platitudes, Deed said, 'Perhaps there is no protection when the adversary is either determined or desperate enough.'

'Then she may as well stay where she is,' Jo argued.

'Let's see what transpires in court tomorrow when we bring the prison governor to explain how Ms Ortega managed to kill herself.'

'What will you do with this document, meanwhile?' Joe Channing asked. 'I am concerned about its being left with either one of us.'

'I'll get Mrs Cooper to make photocopies and distribute them into safe hands. Yours, Joe, with a copy to the Chief, one to Mr Justice Witham, a couple in the mail, none to be opened unless something happens to any one of us or I so instruct. Is there another copy of this, Jo?' he asked, surprised that he hadn't done so before now.

'The person who assembled it and gave it to Anita Plant would be a fool not to have copied it. The little she's told me about him suggests he's not a fool.'

'Good. Then we might all sleep easier.'

'What about my having a copy, John?' the Attorney said.

'What…? No – !' burst out of Jo Mills.

'Yes, as a courtesy to Alan and his office,' Joe Channing insisted.

Alan Peasmarsh waited, giving him an expectant look. 'You are a member of the Government, Alan; inevitably partial.'

'I can't pretend otherwise,' Sir Alan Peasmarsh said.

'He is a Law Officer, John. You could bind him as an officer of the court not to open it until you so instruct,' Jo Channing said.

That was the way forward and ignoring further anxious looks from Jo Mills, Deed said, 'Is this acceptable, Alan?' It was.

After the Appellate Judge departed with the very glum Attorney General, Jo Mills hung back. Deed hoped this might indicate something other than business. It didn't.

'You're putting a lot of trust in the Attorney.'

He nodded, not wanting to give voice to doubts. Despite the evident corruption in Government, some of its apparatchiks would still allow themselves to be bound by honour.

'Things might be more complicated for you in the Anita Plant case,' Jo said.

Deed waited, feeling apprehensive.

'The person who gave her the list of corrupt Ministers in the bribery allegations was the man whose appeal against extradition you're hearing.'

'Mansour Salibi?' he was shocked, and suspected why the Government was so keen to kick him out, and why to Saudi Arabia. 'Is she sure?'

'I didn't want to mention it in front of Sir Joseph.'

'No,' he said, his apprehension increasing, torn over whether to push the document out into the public domain, and again asking himself for what purpose. What would it achieve? He should inform his brothers on the Salibi appeal, but it might seem he was manipulating them. He preferred to win with legal argument. 'I'm not going to give a copy to anyone after all. I'll inform the Attorney.'

Later that day Deed walked over to the Attorney, who was located in the Lord Chancellor's elegant offices. Peasmarsh seemed relieved at his decision.

'Some members of the Cabinet would have put a lot of pressure on me to reveal what's in the document if they knew I had a copy, John.'

'Yes, I didn't think it fair to burden you or anyone else,' – holding his eye.

The Attorney glanced away and pulled his comb through his silver hair. 'You're expecting the governor of Holloway Prison in court tomorrow – I understand she's in the US on a fact-finding jaunt.'

'When did she leave?'

'This morning, it seems. The trip has been scheduled for a while.' Smoothing his sleek hair, he delivered the statement in such an off-hand way the matter may have been of little importance. However, being an ex-barrister he hadn't lost the self-deprecating camaraderie that often existed between opponents and rolled his eyes as if to say, "Those are my instructions."

Deed felt thwarted but not defeated. This added to his belief that something more sinister was happening.

CHAPTER NINETEEN

THERE WAS STILL NO SIGN of the CCTV footage from the flat block that Row Colemore told Coop he'd biked over to the court, and in view of the strange and dangerous things happening around this trial, Deed knew this wasn't casual mis-delivery. There was a directing mind at work here and the recordings were almost certainly intercepted en route. Why weren't they sent via the Internet? Too long to upload? Intercepting something intended for a High Court judge meant whoever was responsible was either very powerful or certain of their position. This worried him. His mind chased various possibilities which got him nowhere, but he would go on pursuing them. For a moment he considered whether Colemore had actually sent the footage, then dismissed the notion. Although worried about his pension or going against his masters in the Home Office, Deed didn't want to believe the DAC would deceive him. This was possible evidence that might trip up the Defence Minister. Deed rang Row Colemore and asked him to present himself at court. Was that reluctance he heard in his voice? Apart from wishing to locate the missing evidence, Deed wanted to know if the murder investigation of the porter's death was now under way. This wasn't something he wanted to question him about on the phone.

'Have we got the Defence Minister back in court?' he asked when Coop brought him tea before he sat.

'Mr Pollock's in the witness room. The usher said he's furious and phoned the Prime Minister to ask what could be done about you.'

'What was the Prime Minister's reply, did the usher say?'

'It's not repeatable, Judge,' Coop said with a smile. 'You can't move in court for journalists.'

'We'll see if Mr Pollock is sounding any more truthful today.'

'A politician? You must be joking.'

'It can't be easy, Coop, forever trying to square the circle,' he said, stepping into his robes. 'Everyone wants something different from his or her elected representative. If he lies to the electorate Mr Pollock can only be kicked out of Parliament – assuming we have long enough memories. If he lies in court under oath, that's a far more serious.'

Deed took a mouthful of tea and was then ready. Coop handed him his wig and held the mirror so he could set it straight.

Mr Justice Deed had had many good moments in court, and some great moments. These he remembered for having helped penetrate a web of lies to reveal the truth that either set a defendant free or saw him or her go to prison, or a corrupt party receive his or her just due. At such times he felt exhilarated, experienced a tingle of electricity along his spine. There were such moments for John Deed QC in his earlier incarnation when he destroyed liars in the witness-box, but he suspected few were as base as the man he was expecting in court this morning. His egregious behaviour was made worse by the power and authority of his office, and Deed wished only to reveal his lies. He stopped himself, again fearing he was allowing extreme prejudice into his court.

'Good morning, Mr Pollock,' he said pleasantly to the Minister, who stood in the well of the court, as if trying not to be part of this. 'I know your ministerial duties are pressing so we will try not to detain you unnecessarily.'

'I'd appreciate that, sir. I am supposed to be in a meeting with the head of the Saudi air force,' James Pollock said, 'the outcome of which could mean a lot of jobs for Britain,' – the consummate politician first addressing the press corps then the jury.

'Please,' – waving him to the witness box. 'More questions. Remember you are still under oath.'

He glanced over at Jo as he waited for Pollock. She was looking like her old self this morning, and he wondered if she'd spent the night with someone. The thought took him straight to Jessie Rogers who was at his room at the High Court. Again, he knew he shouldn't be having such thoughts here, if at all.

'I want to ask you again, Mr Pollock, about your relationship with Rudi Kozlowski, the porter at Brunswick Mansions,' he said as if it was of minor interest.

The Minister was ready for this. 'I told you before, I don't know this person. Never met him, don't know Brunswick Mansions or where it is.'

'Mr Pollock, I have to warn you that evidence has come to light suggesting you did know this man, and met him on at least three separate occasions when you visited Mariana Ortega in the second defendant's flat.'

'This is ludicrous. I won't be subjected to this persecution.'

'I ask you to think carefully before going further in case you perjure yourself. The penalty for perjury is usually imprisonment.'

'This is persecution, sir, and for a political purpose. Either you stop this now, or bring forward your non-existent evidence and send me to prison, as it's clearly part of your agenda.'

There was no clear indication if this was confidence from the witness or bluster from a politician caught out on a lie. Deed hoped it was the latter, for confidence would mean for certain CCTV footage showing the Kozlowski connection wouldn't be found. This would push him further out on a limb, nearer to a point where he might be obliged to resign.

'Not political persecution, Mr Pollock, nor any other kind, but an exploration of the truth, such as a barrister might make in cross-examination.'

'No, this is your own particular brand of truth.' There was real vehemence in Pollock's tone. It was a long while since Deed had been spoken to like this in his court by anyone whom he didn't send to prison. Packing this man off to prison for contempt was something he might have enjoyed doing, but if he did, it would look like persecution.

'Step down from the witness box, Mr Pollock, so that any evidence can be produced to support your knowing the deceased porter. Then we'll have to take a view as to what we do with you if it's found you have committed perjury.'

'Am I free to leave? I have Government business,' – glancing at the press corps that was ready to run and file.

'You will stay within the precincts of the court building as you're likely to be called again at short notice.' Often, he made hardened criminals quake when he dismissed them thus, but Pollock didn't blink. Deed suspected he would ring the PM again, or the Lord Chancellor or even Neil Haughton, perhaps all three. More pressure. It was essential he got this right without resorting to political chicanery.

'Have you started your murder investigation into the death of Rudi Kozlowski?' he asked the DAC when he came to his room at Southwark during the adjournment.

'Is there a reason we should?'

Deed waited, uncertain what to make of this response. Colemore was like a different man, a stranger with a feeling of remoteness, offering him no bridge where they could meet. 'His hyoid bone was broken before he hanged himself in the toilets here. Quite some trick to pull off.'

Colemore looked away and said, 'Is that what happened? If it is there should be a murder investigation. It's not my decision these days.'

'Most probably Mariana Ortega was killed in the same way, which makes it urgent that both post mortem reports are made available.'

'They're not public records, Sir John. I can't get them.'

The use of his title caused Deed to step back. 'Then I'll make it official by summoning the Coroner's Office to deliver them to the court. This way you're not involved, and your pension won't be at risk.'

'I feel embarrassed that I made you aware of that.'

'We're friends, Row. Unlike me you don't have a bullet-proof job and pension. Although I'm not sure how safe either will be if I get this wrong.' He leant back in his chair and stared out of the window, feeling the world closing in on him. There was no view, except for a brick wall; sometimes he found counting the bricks meditative. Without turning to the tall policeman with his familiar stoop, he said, 'Is there any word on the CCTV footage?'

'Nothing I've been able to find out.'

It was what he expected. There was one last gambit, and he was unsure if this stranger would agree to it, yet he had to try. 'Would you go into the witness box and let me ask you a few questions, Row?'

After a long hesitation he agreed, but Deed was surprised he didn't ask him what questions. Having this conversation then calling Colemore as a witness meant he was skating close to the edge; to have told him the questions would have meant him doing something a judge never should.

DAC Colemore had a strong, resonant voice that was authoritative and reassuring, even though Deed suspected it was a while since this policeman had given evidence from the witness box. After the mandatory questions he asked if he had been requested by him to secure the CCTV images from Brunswick Mansions. He wanted this information on the record; the court reporter's fingers dancing over the keys of her stenograph machine recording responses in the affirmative until the Home Office mandarin along with Sir Ian Rochester slipped into court and sat at the back of the legal benches opposite Colemore. Both his attitude and body language suddenly changed.

'Did you take the opportunity to look at these images, Mr Colemore?'

'I looked at some, not all.'

'Can you tell the court if you identified anyone familiar to you or who is in any way connected with this trial?'

Thinking about that, the DAC then said, 'I saw the dead porter, Mr Kozlowski. I caught a glimpse of the defendant in the dock, Mr Fish. I also saw the defendant who is now deceased, Ms Ortega. I saw a few other people who I assumed were residents of the block.' He waited, his glance darting to the two senior civil servants at the back.

'Was there no one else familiar to you?' Deed asked.

There followed a longer pause when the witness glanced at him, then away and said, 'No, I don't think there was.'

'Are you sure you never identified another person on the tape, Deputy Assistant Commissioner, perhaps a public figure?' This was as far as he dared go and he felt like a prosecutor wrong-footed by his own witness. There was a hum of anticipation as those in court awaited his answer. Deed began to feel more unsettled.

'I don't think so,' the witness finally said. 'If I suggested that earlier I must have made a mistake. I'm sorry.'

Deed looked over at the jury to see what they were making of this. Confusion seemed uppermost on their faces. There was nothing of the kind on the faces of the two senior civil servants in their familiar grey suits. 'This may sound an odd question to such a high-ranking policeman, Mr Colemore, but is anyone threatening you or putting pressure on you in any way?'

Colemore gave a nervous laugh. 'No, no, of course not, sir.'

'Then step down with the court's thanks. We're finished with you,' he said in a tone conveying his deep disappointment with his former friend. Anger was clouding his mind and he realised he hadn't invited counsel to question the witness. He apologised to them and the witness. Only Jo Mills rose to examine him. She got what the jury missed.

'Did you not in fact identify James Pollock MP on the tape visiting Brunswick Mansions?'

When the witness failed to answer, Deed said, 'Is this so? Did you previously identify the Secretary of State for Defence?'

Row Colemore hesitated for another long moment and Deed hoped he'd find the courage to name him, but his hopes were dashed when he said, 'No.'

This was the end of their relationship and it saddened him, leaving him feeling more alone. Perhaps the two suits at the back of the court looking so pleased could be instrumental in taking Colemore's job, even his pension, and who was he to judge whether that should be more important to him than friendship? It was now clear to Deed how invidious was his position.

Seeing the hole Deed was digging for himself by going after the Secretary of State for Defence, Jo wanted to try to help him, but didn't know if he would allow himself to be helped. This judge seemed to have forgotten the basic rule of cross-examination. It was clear he hadn't got answers for the questions he'd asked. She was determined to try persuading him to stop this despite him possibly seeing her quest as impertinent. Had their relationship slipped that far?

By the time she got around to his room at the back of the Southwark Crown Court building Mrs Cooper told her the judge had left for his room at the Strand and invited her to leave a message. She declined and decided to go and find him.

The last person she wanted to meet was Mr Justice Witham, who was striding across the lobby and couldn't be avoided. She hoped he had an urgent appointment elsewhere.

'Ah, Mrs Mills,' he said in an openly friendly fashion, as if he'd had a good day. 'I hope it's me you've come to see.'

Jo didn't know why he assumed she'd come to see anyone. Perhaps the fact that she was coming into the building rather than heading out at the end of the day caused that impression.

'It's always nice to see you, my Lord,' she said with unnecessary formality.

He seemed crestfallen. 'That says you didn't come to see me.'

'Would a woman want to admit that?' Jo said, foolishly boxing herself in with her slight deception.

'One as frank and forthright as you might, Mrs Mills.'

'Perhaps in certain circumstances.'

'Let me guess, it's Deed you're here to see?'

'It's a possibility, but then it's equally possible that I saw enough of Mr Justice Deed in court today.'

A smile fell across his face. 'Then is it equally possible that there's hope for me? Perhaps we could have dinner?'

'It's a little early, Judge,' – another wrong response.

'I know a very nice hotel nearby where they serve excellent tea,' he pressed. 'You can continue to beat me up for my extreme right-wing views,' – his smile remained in place.

Jo was finding it difficult to extricate herself from this entanglement and smiled, which Witham took for acceptance. Deed was becoming a victim of his own authority, she thought, as she allowed herself to be steered away.

'Resigning is an option, John,' Joe Channing advised when Deed went to see him in his room, 'but quite unnecessary, in my opinion. No one can force you to resign, of course. It's a matter of honour. However, you will need to apologise to Pollock.'

'I think resignation would be infinitely preferable, Joe.'

'You have a fine career. As a result of the position you've adopted you may never be considered reliable enough to sit on the Appellate Bench now, but you can still do a lot of good work.'

When he married the highly regarded Georgina Channing his relationship with his conservative father-in-law had been difficult. Channing thought it utter folly for his daughter to get involved with a radical barrister who contrived to defend rather than accede to the cab-rank principle that most barristers accepted, and take cases as they arrived, prosecuting or defending.

Radical barrister? How had he ever become such an advocate? It got him undue attention, which he enjoyed, and that in turn pushed him further to seek justice for the underdog. He loathed injustice and any system that was prepared to tolerate its being perpetrated against its citizens, whatever their standing. Where that had started he knew precisely. It was when he was ten years old; he knew the exact day in early September before the return to school, and even the moment. He had been given a shirtful of windfall apples on a country lane not far from where he was living with his adoptive parents in Buckinghamshire. Further on down the lane he stopped outside an orchard when a police car had suddenly appeared and stopped in front of him, the huge, uniformed driver getting out to ask what was in his shirt. Deed remembered saying 'Nothing,' meaning nothing the police should be concerned about. The cop called him a lying bastard, whacked him hard around the ear, took all the apples and drove off, leaving him seeing stars rather like in cartoons with his ear hurting. Further injustice was to follow when he told his parents and his father didn't initially believe him, and worse was to come after his father was persuaded by his mother to go to the police station to complain. The police denied having a car on the lane that day and said he was lying, when his father simply accepted their untruth. The whole episode left him feeling betrayed by those he should most trust.

Following an acrimonious divorce when he got custody of their only daughter, partly because George, as she was known, was more interested in her career, his relationship with his ex-father-in-law got even worse. Although it had much improved of late to one of mutual respect, he never thought he'd get such praise from the old boy and wondered if there was some hidden agenda. He wasn't about to step back.

'It's my sincere belief that Pollock is somehow caught up in this murder, Joe – is possibly even the murderer. I made a grave error of judgment thinking I had sufficient evidence to bounce him into the witness box in order to test it. Not so. If I tried to apologise the words might choke me.'

'Of course he's a murderer, in the rhetorical sense,' Channing argued, turning his much-needed unlit cigarette over and over in his fingers, waiting to escape the building. 'He lives in the murky world of Defence. He sends young men and women off to almost certain death. He sells arms to oleaginous potentates who rain death onto hundreds of civilians, thousands even, but I doubt he'd ever be brave enough to do a killing personally.'

'There's something else, Joe. The document the State wants, that was in Ms Plant's possession, was compiled by Mansour Salibi, the man the Saudis want extradited.'

'Can that be so?' Channing seemed shocked. 'I wouldn't for a moment think you were using this to further your argument.'

'If only that were the case,' he said. 'It's deeply troubling, there are wheels within wheels and the courts are being used to do the Government's dirty work.'

'You'd be most unwise to ever consider resigning in these circumstances, but unless you can prove any of this you may have to. Do sleep on any decision in that direction, John.' He left in a hurry to light his cigarette.

The mood that settled over him was affecting Coop, he could tell from the way she moved around him. 'You've been in worse situations, Judge.'

'I have, Coop? Do you keep score?'

'You'll find a way through this; I know you will.'

'If only your faith in me could move mountains – a mountain of stupidity.'

'Jessie left these for you.' She placed a small pile of papers on the corner of his desk. 'She thinks there might be a way to stop the Government kicking Mr Salibi off to Saudi Arabia.'

'Oh, I'd forgotten our marshal was still with us,' he lied, seeing her lurking in his waking thoughts throughout the day.

Coop laughed. 'You're about the only man in the building who has. I think she's been avoiding you after you rumbled her little ploy. I would have thrown her out, but now the girl done good,' she said, using the voice and vernacular of one of the ushers.

'I might not nail our Defence Minister for murder, but we might still expose some of the sleazy deals he's been running with the Arabs.'

'That's the spirit, Judge.'

Such a prospect settled on Deed like a lump of concrete. He knew he was trying to justify going after the Minister as he had by exposing to public scrutiny what he felt should be exposed. Instead, he was boxing himself in and could no longer pretend he was taking such a course for the right reasons. He carried Jessie Rogers' file to the sofa and began to read while Coop went to get him some tea. When she came back, he was half way through the annotations on case law which he might use to further Mansour Salibi's argument for staying here.

'Judge, what is it that Mr Colemore let you down on? I mean, is it something my friend Sergeant Bridges could get?' She set the tea tray in front of him.

'If the forces of reaction scare a deputy assistant commissioner into lying to a friend, what sort of pressure might they put on a sergeant?'

'Unlike Mr Colemore the police have already done the dirty on Jake – Sergeant Bridges. Denying the electronic smog from Tetra communication equipment in the police station affected his health. Maybe he could find the police officer who got the CCTV footage for Mr Colemore in the first place. I could have a word.'

He felt his pulse quicken at the possibility. Perhaps it was better to rely on the comfort of strangers in dangerous situations than the convenience of friends. He had counted Row a friend, despite having come up short in his expectations of him once before. 'Sergeant Bridges would have to be so careful,' he warned. 'There are things going on here that we've yet to identify. It could be risky, and not just for his job and pension.'

'Then I'd better not ring him. I'll catch him at the police station.'

'Thanks, Coop.' He gave her a warm smile. 'If our "forgettable" judicial assistant is still around ask her to come and see me.'

Jessie remained as breath-taking in her physical manifestation as she was in his imagination. Apart from her looks and atmosphere which were like a siren attracting helpless souls onto the rocks of despair, it was clear from her work for him here that she possessed a good, organised mind,

Guilty – Until Proven Otherwise

and he was glad he'd made the decision to support her. He just wished he was 30 again and not so foolish as to be contemplating pursuing a woman almost half his age.

'This is excellent work, Jessie. I'm impressed with the way you've assembled the jurisprudence from the Strasbourg cases.'

'Oh, I can't take all the credit. I stumbled on most of it by accident, Judge, after Joe Channing pointed me there.'

This startled him, first that the Appellate Judge might help her in his cause to stop the extradition, then at her apparent familiarity. An irrational surge of jealousy followed, as if believing Joe Channing was succeeding in some kind of move on her. That was foolish as he was forty-plus years her senior, but then Deed knew how idiotic men could be around women.

'Digging it all out must be your work, and how it's organised. Well done. I haven't finished reading the Iraqi's case. What happened, was there a happy ending for him, Jessie?'

'Not exactly, Judge,' she said. 'The Home Office gave him leave to remain – reluctantly, – soon after he was murdered by Islamic extremists.'

He was disappointed as he preferred happy endings. Perhaps Islamic extremism was a convenient label for some other sort of murder; possibly this would be his fate if he kept on with his tack involving the Defence Secretary. What nonsense, he told himself.

'Are you all right, Judge? You look quite upset.'

'Perhaps I should learn to detach more from my emotions.'

'Oh no, sir, that's what makes you such a good Judge.' He met her look, trying to decide if she was coming onto him again, and whether this was another possible entrapment. 'Everyone says so, even those who have lost cases before you.' She was almost glowing with sincerity.

Allowing his guard to drop, he found himself thinking fatuous thoughts once more. He stood up, intending to dismiss her and send her back to his old set with his thanks, job done, only found he couldn't. Instead, he smiled and said, 'See if you can find any other references – if you can spare the time. I suspect there might not be any, but you seem to have done such a thorough job they probably won't be necessary anyway.' With time gained here, maybe he could get control of random emotions that were causing him to entertain his wild thoughts.

But without warning she scrambled both his emotions and thoughts when she announced, 'I'm staying at the Pestana Hotel by Chelsea

Bridge all this week.' It was a clear invitation and for once in his many approaches to women he was uncertain what to do.

'Are we getting Mr Salibi back for a decision about his deportation, John?' Tom Witham asked, stepping into Deed's room with Joe Channing. This change in the younger judge's demeanour puzzled him and irrationally he suspected it had something to do with Jo Mills. There was a bounce about him, like the proverbial hitching of pants and he felt those familiar claws of jealousy snatching at his genitals. His thoughts went straight to Jessie Rogers at the Pestana Hotel, the location of which he'd already checked.

'Is tomorrow too soon for you?' he challenged, forcing his mind back to the matter in hand.

Tom Witham stepped back in surprise. 'Oh, yes, I suppose that would be all right. Joe?'

'Tomorrow will be fine if we can get the parties here that quickly.'

'Do we need to go into court with this decision?' Witham glanced at Channing as if it was a done deal.

'If we're to kick him out, Tom, we might show him the courtesy of telling him why we've decided on that course.'

'Well, Mr Machin is in a case before me at Southwark but not doing much now his client is dead,' Deed said. 'I'm sure the Attorney could get someone along here. I expect the appellant will show up.'

'Do we know that?' Witham said. 'There was concern about that at the MoJ. The Counter Terrorism unit picked up something about him being in touch with Islamist terrorists here.'

'They always seem to have an opinion about things that they should have no opinion about,' Channing cut in with. 'You'll get the drift of these civil servants. If ever there was a case of the tail trying to wag the dog. Mind you, some of our brethren are apt to let that happen, hoping for preferential placement on the ladder, I dare say.'

Deed suspected the senior judge had been let down by Sir Ian Rochester not endorsing his elevation to the Supreme Court. Although Joe could still get elevated, it would be difficult without the Lord Chancellor's recommendation following that from his Permanent Secretary. If he was reading this correctly, Rochester might come to regret withholding his approval, for Joe Channing could prove troublesome on the Appellate Bench and they'd have difficulty shifting him from there.

'How do we stand at present?' Witham wanted to know.

'I'm more of the opinion Salibi should stay,' Deed said.

'Is there law to support it, John?' Channing asked with no hint of collusion on his part in steering Jessie Rogers.

'There is a strong human rights argument which Strasbourg upheld,' Deed said and handed them a draft summary. Channing glanced at it and looked away as if uninterested in this argument, taking an occasional glance in his direction as Witham read the four pages in less than three minutes. His expression was troubled at the end of it.

'It's a well-couched argument, John. I'm not entirely convinced. I'd have to read the whole of the ruling overnight. Joe?' he said, turning to his mentor.

'Oh yes,' Channing responded as if not on the page. 'It'll want thinking about overnight, Tom, I agree.'

Deed almost smiled.

CHAPTER TWENTY

❦

NEIL HAUGHTON DREADED THE MEETING that Jim Pollock ungently requested and the moment Sir Percy Thrower told him about it he felt a cold shroud drop over him and couldn't shake it loose. He knew what the tenor of the meeting would be and how powerless he was to deliver what the Defence Minister wanted. He could have written his script.

In his room at the Home Office from one of the four windows overlooking the quad gardens he watched a number of civil servants smoking, or eating sandwiches from cellophane packets and wished he were there, not here. On turning back into the room, he had Pollock thrusting his large head in his face, his angry breath washing over him as he spoke. It carried the taint of last night's undigested, over-rich dinner and red wine. Haughton was fearful that more than this man's breath would come up over him as he tried to avoid the spittle spray which flew out with his words. He was furious that Deed was going back into court later this morning with Salibi extradition. How he had learned of this so fast, Haughton didn't know, but assumed he must have spies at the Strand. Sir Percy had only informed him five minutes before this meeting.

'What in God's name do you expect me to do, Jim?' he asked, trying to get away to safety behind his desk. 'This is the Home Office.'

'You're supposed to be on top of this. You're supposed to be able to control these fucking judges, that's why the PM's moving you to Justice. Are you telling us they can't be controlled? In that case we should just piss over the Saudis' sandals and tell them to fuck off?'

'I'm not yet at the MoJ, and judges have been a law unto themselves from the word go. It's called separation of powers, our system of checks and balances.'

'This is bollocks, Neil. This fucking judge broke all kinds of rules naming me in court like he did. It'll cost this country a great deal of money if he fucks-up my negotiation with the Saudis. It makes me look a complete prick in their eyes.

They respect the strong man, not someone who can't get the right decision from the judiciary.' More spittle sprayed him as Pollock leaned across the desk to make his point. 'Salibi should be in custody until he's deported. We want to know when it's going to happen.'

Unsure who the 'we' were that Pollock referred to, Haughton feared it was the PM included in this demand to neuter Deed and send Salibi packing. 'Is Salibi's crime back in Saudi so great? They abuse women there every which way.'

'That's hardly the point. They expect us to act.'

'Again I remind you, Jim, I'm still at the Home Office.'

'Your people should have seized him and got him on a plane to Saudi and let Deed and whoever else stew,' Pollock said. 'What could anyone do once they'd chopped off his head?'

'It would be me stewing in gaol if I tried that.'

'This gets more ludicrous – a bloody judge thinking he can put a Cabinet minister in clink. Who would let him? This Government won't.'

'Well, if you want to chance it, Jim, have *your* security people pick Salibi up and put him on the plane. Or better still, have the Saudi secret police do it. We know they operate here.'

'I know nothing about their secret police,' Pollock said sharply. 'I expect they have security people here protecting the Saudi Royal negotiators.' He then became more agitated. 'I can't believe we're having this conversation, Neil. The PM still thinks you're the man to cut these judges down.'

'We need an Act of Parliament to give us the right to sack them. At this moment we can't stop them acting as they choose to within the law. We certainly can't do anything about Salibi going back to court – unless you kill all the parties, Jim.'

That caused the Defence Minister to bear down on him again like he was about to mount a physical attack. 'What the fuck is that meant to mean?' he demanded, his tone deep with offence. 'Are you trying to tell me something, Neil? Come on, out with it. Let's not have these snippy little remarks. Well?'

'Death or retirement is all that can stop judges. Deed is fit and I've no reason to think he's about to retire,' Haughton said on a weary sigh. 'By all means bump him off, be my guest.'

Pollock's look froze Haughton's blood – as if he was taking his joke seriously. 'We don't give a fuck what it is you do to him, Neil, just make it effective. I'm still being dragged through the mire in Deed's other case as he tries to implicate me. He's acting in a blatantly prejudicial fashion. It's political. That's a reason for sacking him. Just do it before he pulls half the Cabinet into some deranged conspiracy theory.'

With that he slammed out, leaving Haughton feeling like an upbraided schoolboy. At times like this, he wished he were a drinking man, but alcohol was as disagreeable to him as tobacco. There was a cursory rap at the door and Sir Percy came in.

'Did you hear any of that?' he asked in an inviting fashion, being in need of a friend from any quarter, even his rather superior Permanent Secretary.

'I try not to listen at doors, Home Secretary,' Sir Percy said. 'The Defence Minister does have a particularly grating voice.'

Those words, as indiscreet as they were, soothed him a little. 'I suppose I already know the answer, but is there anything we can do that we haven't already tried, Percy?'

'You summarised the situation for your Cabinet colleague most succinctly, Home Secretary. I did take the liberty of calling Sir Ian Rochester for his mind on this. You have a free slot to confer here at 11.45.'

Rochester came with no new ideas about how to circumscribe the troublesome Deed. They went around in circles and got nowhere before he said, 'According to Sir Joseph Channing, Deed is threatening to resign if his gambit with the Defence Minister doesn't play out.'

'Is this a real glimmer of light, Ian?' Haughton asked, hope getting airborne a little, but fearing it would come crashing down if he got too excited.

'He may prove honourable and do the decent thing, Home Secretary.'

'He's sufficiently disgraced himself going after the Defence Minister as he did,' Sir Percy said, adding to hope, which he then trashed. 'If he intended to go his letter of resignation would be on the Lord Chancellor's desk by now.'

'Perhaps if we gave him a little more rope, Percy, he may yet hang himself,' Rochester suggested. 'If we pulled Deed further into the ring with the Defence Secretary with the expectation of having evidence on him only to find it is unsubstantiated…'

'Well, I shall leave the details for you and Percy to work out, Ian. If we could be rid of Deed finally, a number of Cabinet colleagues would prove most grateful, including the PM.'

Haughton was pleased to get shot of the two Permanent Secretaries, for as much as he wanted Deed gone, he couldn't be seen to enter into any sort of conspiracy. Information had the nasty habit of leaking out as if with a will of its own and, if it did, showing him connected, other Judges would make life impossible for him at the MoJ.

'Judge,' Coop said, coming into his room, 'I have Mr Colemore on the telephone wondering if he could have a word.'

That surprised him, not expecting to hear from the DAC again. Perhaps that was why he had rung Coop, to test the water.

'I told him you were about to sit in the extradition case.'

He was curious and decided Mr Salibi could wait a few moments longer. 'Put him through, Coop, and apologise to Sir Joseph and Sir Tom. I'll be a few minutes late.'

When the phone on his crowded desk rang and he picked up there was a longish silence. For a moment he imagined Colemore had hung up.

'I wasn't sure you'd take a call from me now, Judge,' he said using the more familiar of his titles.

'Then why did you call?' – giving him no comfort.

'Look, it may be too late for you to do much, but I do have some evidence from the Defence Minister's bank statements, and from Mariana Ortega's.'

'Why didn't you come forward with this before, Row?'

Another long silence, then he said, 'Part cowardice, part bad timing. I'm forever being challenged in my current office to state whose team I'm on. It's not enough to say I'm on the side of truth or justice. You know the police have never operated on that principle, and when you get to my level where you no longer hold a warrant card, it's all politics. You choose your side. Perhaps I chose the wrong side. The truth is I've only just set eyes on Pollock's bank statements. Large amounts going out of his account correspond to money going into her account.'

'What does that prove?' he asked, more wary of this man now.

'Nothing of itself, Judge. My gut tells me it's the same money going between them. She was blackmailing him.'

He thought about this situation for a long moment, aware that he was meant to be elsewhere. Was this enough to bring Pollock back to court and question him further without his appearing to persecute him? Could Colemore be trusted in such matters any longer? Something was telling him there was a misstep here, but he couldn't get to what it was. Instead, he wanted to believe this old friend. Binding Pollock to the murder case might prevent a miscarriage of justice against Rupert Fish, and free himself of any obligation to resign. This wasn't a consideration he should be weighing in this equation, but he was.

'Bring this evidence to me in the Strand. Row, bring it personally, don't courier it.'

The senior policeman gave an embarrassed laugh, and well he might. Deed rang off and hurried to join his two colleagues waiting to go into court.

'Mr Salibi,' he said from the bench in Court 62 where he sat to the right of Joe Channing, 'this court has reached a conclusion about your extradition to Saudi Arabia to await trial on charges of rape, having listened to all the arguments. Before the court gives its decision, I would like to ask you some questions under oath. These aren't directly related to your case but they may bear upon it.'

He noticed the court was quite crowded for such a procedural case. Some of the faces he recognised, others were less familiar. There were journalists along with members of the Counter Terrorism unit among them, and people from the Ministry of Defence. This interest may have been signalled by the presence of the Attorney General himself and four barristers on his team. Perhaps he was expecting some heavy legal argument that would require devilling.

'Earlier I gave your barrister a document which I assume he's shown to you. I want to question you about its contents.'

The Attorney started to rise but Heathcote Machin got up first. Deed knew at once what he was about to ask. 'Is this to be without prejudice, my Lord, or is my client likely to face charges as a result of this questioning?'

'I'm sure you know the common law of privilege against self-incrimination, Mr Machin,' he said, appearing to keep a neutral position, but hoping Mr Salibi would understand he wasn't seeking to entrap him. 'Do you recognise this document or anything about it, Mr Salibi? You can answer from where you are, but remember you are still under oath from your previous appearance here.'

'Yes, sir, I recognise this document. I helped prepare it for a lady who works for Oxfam in the Middle East,' Salibi said.

'Why was it of concern to Oxfam that you would take such risks?'

'I wanted someone neutral who knew the region. People are dying there for all sorts of reasons, many of them to do with weapons supplied by western armaments companies.'

'Are you saying western governments supply terrorists with weapons?'

'Not directly, sir, but terrorists receive many of these weapons, sometimes through agents acting for weapons manufacturers here.'

'You're suggesting these go directly to the so-called Islamic State and the like?' Sir Tom Witham asked.

Salibi hesitated and glanced at his barrister. 'Sometimes. More often the so-called terrorists are the governments of the region who are sold the weapons which they use to suppress their own citizens. Many weapons supplied to Colonel Gaddafi are now being used against Libyans.'

'Isn't that more to do with the fortunes of war than any criminal activity?' Sir Joseph Channing asked with a glance towards Deed.

'You can never tell who fortune will smile upon, sir.'

'Often the side with the most weapons,' Deed commented. 'What was your object in compiling this document, Mr Salibi?'

'Hoping to restrict the flow of weapons in the region by showing criminal activity in their supply,' Salibi said.

'Criminal activity on whose part?' Deed asked, aware of the uncomfortable body language the Attorney was displaying, shifting around in his seat and turning to make casual conversation with his colleagues.

'Your Government was making facility payments.'

Deed felt he was onto something here that might take down corrupt ministers and possibly the Government, so knew he needed to proceed carefully. 'Were British Government ministers or their civil servants present at meetings with knowledge of what was being transacted?' he asked.

'With respect, sir,' Salibi said like a man proceeding with care, 'representatives of your Government were present and it would be naïve to think they didn't know into whose hands some of the money was going.'

'You have evidence to support this?' Sir Joseph said as though he hadn't read the document.

'What I supplied to Ms Plant, from Oxfam.'

'A list of names, impressive in the personnel it cites, but nonetheless an unsubstantiated list,' Deed said.

'All the dates and times of the meetings and the money in bribes that passed from Government ministers of one country to their opposite numbers in Saudi Arabia are documented.'

'Where is this documentation?' Tom Witham wanted to know.

'My Lord,' the Attorney General protested, getting to his feet, 'this is perhaps unwise to discuss in open court. Hitherto unimpeachable reputations might be damaged.'

The three judges conferred in whispers with their hands over their microphones. 'Apart from my argument as to why Salibi should not be extradited, if what he says is substantiated then he should certainly not be sent anywhere near to Saudi Arabia!' Deed insisted.

'There does seem an unconscionable haste on the part of certain Government departments to get rid of him,' Joe Channing said. 'If any part of this is to be substantiated it should be tested here in court.'

'In open court, Joe?' Tom Witham questioned. 'The Attorney is reasonable in his argument. This could damage reputations.'

'Equally it could damage the reputation of the court were we to go into closed session and find Salibi has nothing,' Deed argued.

'I'm with John,' Joe Channing said. 'We should proceed in open court with caution.'

The Attorney wasn't happy with this and, after a short discussion with one of his barristers, a young woman in a suit sitting behind them went out in a hurry – to phone someone in Government, Deed surmised.

'Mr Salibi,' he said, as Jo Mills entered with her client and sat two benches back from Machin. 'You were about to inform Mr Justice Witham of the whereabouts of this evidence.'

'I don't wish to appear coy, sir,' Salibi said with his impeccable accent, 'but the whereabouts of this evidence is what has kept me alive and caused the move to extradite me. The Saudis have no scruples about using torture to obtain the information.'

'We can be pretty gruesome, too,' Joe Channing joked. Few in court laughed.

'Then let us examine the content of this list and see whether we must resort to thumbscrews or the molten lead boot,' Deed said.

The Attorney popped up again. 'My Lord, I would again urge you to proceed with the utmost care.'

'Care over the use of thumbscrews or the molten lead boot, Mr Attorney?' Deed asked, more people getting the joke and laughing this time. 'Sir Joseph has given that reassurance.' He waved him down and turned to Salibi, his glance taking in Jo Mills. Was she here for him, Tom Witham or another purpose? 'How did you have contact with the arms agents on your list?'

Salibi hesitated. 'I worked for one of the biggest in Lebanon. We have contacts with all the main armaments suppliers both here and in France and the US. We entertained them in all three countries.'

'Who were you buying arms for?' Deed asked.

'One of our most profitable clients was the Saudi Government. They are still one of the major purchasers in the Middle East. Another is Qatar.'

'Did you deal directly with people from the Saudi Government?'

'We deal with members of the Royal Family there and their agents. It was their agents with whom we negotiated extra payments for contracts.'

'Are you referring to payments as bribes?'

'We refer to them as facilitation payments, sir,' Salibi said.

'English law refers to those as bribes, Mr Salibi. Who made these payments?'

'Sometimes the arms manufacturers, but if the contract was large enough, such as involving the purchase of Typhoon fighter aircraft, it would be the British Government paying.'

'When you say the British Government,' Joe Channing said, 'were these payments made by civil servants or members of the Government?'

'Both. The payments were cleared by Government ministers here.'

'Have you got evidence of this?' Tom Witham asked, glancing in Jo Mills' direction. Deed decided she was here for Witham, to see if he was robust enough in pressing for the truth. He felt disappointment, even though he knew he had no right to such feeling.

'I was at several meetings where British Government Ministers agreed the price that would be paid into bank accounts off-shore,' Salibi told the court evenly.

'Presumably this wasn't money going into their personal accounts?' Tom Witham asked, as if to exonerate them.

'There was no personal gain,' Salibi said, giving the younger Judge short-lived relief. 'The British ministers were paid by the arms manufacturers in the form of donations to party coffers.'

There was near total silence in the court, the scratch of pens having stopped along with clacking of computer keys. No one coughed or rustled papers; only the breathing of the building was heard. If blood draining from faces could be made audible that too would have been heard, which confirmed to Deed that most present were some branch of Government.

'Who were the ministers negotiating these payments going into offshore accounts?' Deed asked.

'My Lord,' the Attorney said, springing out of his seat, 'these are unsubstantiated allegations and again I urge the greatest caution.'

'Yes, Mr Attorney,' he said growing impatient with his interventions. Besides being a member of the Government, he was an officer of the court and should have been more concerned with truth than protecting reputations. 'We cannot go forward and test the evidence unless we ask these questions.'

'Wouldn't it be more prudent if your Lordships were to do this *in camera*?'

'The President of the court has given clear reasons why we should conduct this in open court.' Deed turned back to Salibi as the Attorney resumed his seat. 'Mr Salibi?'

'Your Defence Minister was there on two occasions. He argued that these payments were too high on one occasion, but agreed to increase the bribe when his opposite number in the Saudi Government agreed to take additional weaponry. The details of the extra tanks and gunships that were agreed are listed in the main document I have.'

'You minuted these meetings, Mr Salibi?' Tom Witham asked.

'Without a minute there would be disagreement later,' Salibi pointed out. 'The civil servant present from the Ministry of Defence also took a minute which was signed by both sides.'

'Where was the money taken from for these illegal payments, Mr Salibi?' Deed wanted to know.

'I believe from the British Treasury. A Minister from the Treasury was present also, along with her civil servant. The Saudi Prince conducting the negotiations wanted the money to go to the accounts in Luxembourg.'

'The money was sent as agreed?'

'The civil servant executed the order for the first half at the conclusion of the negotiations. A receipt was emailed from the account manager at the HSBC private bank on Boulevard d'Avranches, Luxembourg.'

'Tell me, Mr Salibi, were these alleged bribes signed off on in the minutes?' Joe Channing said.

'Everything agreed was signed off on, sir.' Again Salibi hesitated, before adding, 'In addition I recorded the meetings.'

'Was this with the consent of each of the parties?' Witham asked.

'I doubt they would have consented. My employer, Ali bin Talib, asked me to do this so there could be no mistakes afterwards about his commission.'

With shock and anger visible in his fleshy features, Joe Channing covered his bench microphone and leant first to Deed, who covered his microphone, then to Tom Witham. 'We should have a short adjournment to examine Mr Salibi's evidence to see if any of this corresponds and, if it does, to discuss calling this minister and requesting the minutes.'

'My concern now, Joe, is how we protect Salibi,' Deed said, with his head turned away from the court as some reporters would be able to lip-read. With the extent of the information the young Lebanese man seemed to have and all that had happened around him he feared for his safety. 'Perhaps we can best protect him by getting the ministers and their civil servants here and questioning them. The more of this that's out the safer he'll be.'

'Any thoughts, Tom?' Joe Channing asked.

'I don't like the idea of calling Government ministers without seeing this minuted documentation, and hearing his tape recordings. I don't imagine we'll get either unless we go further into this.'

Joe Channing took his hand away from the microphone to go back on the record. 'We're going to adjourn and ask you, Sir Alan, to use your good offices to secure the attendance of the Defence Minister, James Pollock, and the Treasury Minister named in Mr Salibi's document, Ms Alison Franc.'

The Attorney General was on his feet again saying he would speak to the relevant ministers and request their attendance along with the civil servants.

That still didn't guarantee Mansour Salibi's safety in between times. Deed considered asking him to go into protective custody, but imagined he'd feel the same about that as Anita Plant. Possibly he was better able to protect himself, remembering the recent deaths of Ms Ortega and Mr Kozlowski. Still Deed remained uneasy.

'More of Deed's fucking politicking?' Pollock shouted as he stomped about his office on Horse Guards Avenue where Rochester approached him about appearing in court. 'What the fuck could I have done to this judge that he's persecuting me like this? My pillorying has got to end, Ian. I won't have it. Deed can take a flying fuck – I hear he's good at that.'

'All three of their Lordships endorsed the request for you to appear, Minister,' Rochester said, staying calm and deferential, and resenting being the messenger. 'The Attorney General, it seems, guaranteed your attendance.'

That made Pollock angrier. 'Did he, by fuck? Witham went along with this? I thought Haughton had him by the balls. Now the black bastard's gone over to the dark side?' He laughed – 'No pun intended.'

Refusing to be drawn into the minister's racism, Rochester said, 'If you decline to appear it may cause both a legal and political difficulty. I suspect the President of the court, Sir Joseph Channing, would be reluctant to have you summoned, but then again he might under Deed's influence.'

'Of course they'll try a stroke like that. Deed'll go for maximum embarrassment both to me and the Government. Someone should bump him off. If he keeps this up, I'll fucking well do it before I have no job or reputation left.'

Nor should you, was Rochester's immediate thought from what was reported to him. His expression betrayed nothing. 'Only a law curtailing the power of the judges will stop them examining what Government involvement there might be in bribery.'

Pollock said, 'It has been discussed in Cabinet; this might do it.'

'Not in time to prevent your appearance, with the civil servant who was present, plus his minute of the meetings with the Saudis.'

'Bollocks. There was no civil servant present, and no record, certainly not one that could be delivered to court, Ian. Anyway, it's governed by the Official Secrets Act. Deed would have to wait thirty years. Yes, that would suit us fine.'

'Of course, Minister,' Rochester said, 'but I would advise you submit to the court, even if only to say there is no information not covered by the Act.'

'Even that could embarrass the Saudis. There is talk of them walking away from this deal that's worth many billions of pounds to Britain over the next five years. Do you know how many lost jobs that represents, Ian?'

'I understand the importance to the British economy, Minister,' Rochester said, being most placatory. 'I will convey as much to the Presiding judge. I'm sure Sir Joseph will prove responsive.'

'He'd better be or we'll chop off all their balls.'

The meeting was over.

There was a prickly edge to Sir Joseph Channing when Rochester called on him. The Appellate Judge could be quite sharp at times, but his responses were mostly amicable, even accommodating. On this occasion he was neither.

'You know the consequences of their not attending the High Court, Ian,' Sir Joseph said brusquely, as he pulled a law report from the shelf. He was of a generation of judges who preferred physical reports rather than those published online. To Rochester paper seemed an anachronism, with the electronic medium in such a relatively short time having captured everything and almost everyone. 'I did warn Deed of the dangers of seeking out a battle with the Executive. There'll be no clear winners.'

'So it's Mr Justice Deed who's bent on this course, Joe?'

'The three judges were unanimous. The ministers and their amanuenses must be examined on the substance of that which Mr Salibi alleges.'

Rochester was surprised and disappointed, but shouldn't have been. Often after High Court judges were appointed and given tenure, they found their own voice and made it heard. The selection process may as well have been via names from a hat; the careful selection of candidates who appeared to share your values then made a volte-face was galling. Even the once-compliant Joe Channing was now proving difficult. 'Tom Witham was of this view?'

'Unless Witham was a fourth judge who I hadn't noticed, Ian?' – his tone cutting. 'Unanimous does mean all of us.'

'Dare I ask if you would send them to gaol if they don't appear?'

'We may well if they are so wantonly reckless as to defy the court.'

'You know there is still a vacancy coming up in the Supreme Court, Joe,' Rochester slipped in, hoping that by placing the carrot back on the stick he might turn this Judge into a rabbit. 'The President did ask me if you had been sounded out for the post and whether you'd be interested.'

'We dined together at the Athenaeum two nights ago. David didn't mention the possibility,' Sir Joseph said, his back straight, his chest thrust out.

'I did say it had been spoken of and that the subject was moot. I'm sure we'll be having other conversations about this, Joe, which might prove far more agreeable than the current one. I will report back to the relevant Permanent Secretaries and inform them their masters had better appear or be ready to face the Tower.'

He left the senior judge to ponder his renewed position. Although he didn't expect him to go against what was set in train, Rochester was sure he would prove a lot more amenable as and when the two ministers got to court.

CHAPTER TWENTY-ONE

DAC COLEMORE STOOD BEFORE DEED in his room at the Law Courts like a schoolboy on the carpet before the head, even though the rug beneath his feet was a Persian Kashan. This uncomfortable atmosphere wasn't Deed's doing, but was reflected in the body language the senior policeman adopted, and he wondered if it was genuine. Was he merely acting contrite, or genuinely determined to make amends and right the situation between them?

Deed wasn't convinced it could be made right. Trust was like virginity: once let go it couldn't be restored.

'This isn't something you could rely on me for in court, John,' Colemore was saying. 'But the bank statements speak for themselves. A large wodge of cash comes out of Pollock's account, two thousand pounds on three separate occasions, then a day later the exact amount of cash is put into Ms Ortega's account.'

'That in itself isn't proof they knew each other, Row.'

'It's enough to suggest further investigation – perhaps examining the apartment she used for her sex games to check for Pollock's fingerprints or DNA. If he had been in the cupboard behind the two-way mirror there'd be evidence of it.'

'Mr Pollock already believes I'm persecuting him. How do you imagine he'd react if I started along that particular track?' he asked. 'I'm close to having to resign as a result of dragging him into court. Either I find a smoking gun, or I will have to resign. We've got him coming to the Law Courts in another case. It is beginning to look like a vendetta I'm running.' He paused, trying to see a way ahead; there was no clear or easy route. 'How are the investigations going into the deaths of Ms Ortega and Mr Kozlowski?'

'Murder files have been opened. It looks like they were possibly killed by the same person,' Colemore said.

'How can that be?' He was puzzled and alarmed. 'How does the same person have access to the court toilets – we assume a man – and a women's prison?'

'It gets more sinister. The hard drive for the CCTV cameras in the main parts of the court building was hacked. The period covering Kozlowski's death was erased.'

Deed was incredulous. He had a hundred questions, but when the DAC suggested someone in high office giving access, he knew he would have no means of knowing if the answers to any of his questions were the truth or a version spun for his benefit. Much better to have Coop ask one of her poles – people of low esteem – as she called her kind with self-effacing good humour. More information was obtained by her at the back-corridor level than frontal assault at department level.

After Colemore departed, Deed studied copies of the bank statements he'd been given. They showed just what the senior policeman stated: money out of one account followed by the same amount going into the other. What was the money for? Sexual services? Blackmail? He was getting ahead of himself assuming these were transactions involving blackmail when there may have been a logical explanation with no connection between the two parties. He was too keen for any connection that might remove his need to resign. His thoughts moved on to Kozlowski being a part of some blackmail scheme and getting an expensive suit as his reward. Did he receive any money? He needed the dead porter's bank statements to check if they revealed anything. He buzzed Coop through and asked her to try to find out from her sources what happened to the court building security hard drive for the day Kozlowski died.

'Do we have a phone number for Mr Salibi?' he asked.

'The Clerk's office will have. Do you want me to get it for you, Judge?'

'I'd like you to call him, Coop and ask him to meet me this evening, whatever time suits him. Perhaps you'd suggest the place to meet, Coop, and let me know.' She was used to his eccentricities and didn't question him, understanding the cryptic nature of his instruction would be for a reason. Perhaps she realised he didn't want unexpected visitors showing up.

Coop chose his Knightsbridge apartment for the meeting and Salibi arrived around seven o'clock as he was making himself some dinner. He invited the young Lebanese man to eat with him, still unsure whether he was a sex offender who should go off to Saudi or if it was an elaborate plot to get him under their jurisdiction to silence him. Not being an assiduous shopper there was little in the store cupboard.

'Can I add something to it, sir?' Salibi asked, looking at the rice pasta, tinned tomatoes, garlic and olives.

'Looking a bit bland, is it?'

The visitor found a jar of eggplant and some tahini in the cupboard, cayenne pepper and some dried basil which, along with a squeezed lemon, improved the meal. As they ate at the kitchen table Salibi said, 'I thought I wasn't supposed to have any contact with you outside court, sir.'

'Ordinarily you're not. These are not ordinary circumstances. What I'm about to ask is in confidence,' he said, giving the young man sitting at the worn, marble-topped table a frank look. 'If you don't want the confidence, Mr Salibi, then I won't go any further.'

'I was invited here, sir, for a purpose. If I wasn't prepared to consider that purpose might be valid, I wouldn't have come. If I'm tortured, I can't guarantee not to reveal your confidence.'

Deed watched him, attempting to read him, and felt relieved when he smiled. Clearly, he wasn't expecting to be tortured. 'I have another case before me in which I suspect the minister you've named in bribery allegations is involved.'

'The murder case with the woman from Wimbledon,' Salibi said, surprising him. Why was he surprised? The case had been front-page of every tabloid and broadsheet plus the lead story on news broadcasts? Perhaps he didn't expect someone from the Lebanon caught up in international politics to have even a passing interest in a domestic murder.

'A defendant who is now dead herself,' Deed said.

'You wonder if James Pollock could be involved in the woman's murder.'

'You're ahead of me, and any police investigation. It hasn't been established that she was murdered. Why do you assume she was?'

'Both the circumstances of her death, plus the fact that we're here and you're asking about it.' His mind was logical, his tone calm and matter-of-fact. It impressed Deed, who thought he might have made an effective barrister in another incarnation.

'The post mortem report suggests her hyoid bone was crushed before she was hanged in her cell, as was that of a witness in her trial, one Rudi Kozlowski. This was someone who may possibly have implicated Pollock in the murder. There are too many strange things happening: potential evidence going missing, the witness and defendant dying as they did.'

'You want to know, sir, could anyone be orchestrating these events?'

'I feel I'm stepping into rushing water and I'm about to lose my footing,' Deed said. 'I don't wish to be enmeshed in some paranoid fantasy about a Government minister that results in harm to us both. I can't ask the police to investigate Mr Pollock as he's not on trial.'

'I can tell you a little, having done business with him.' Salibi said, meeting Deed's eyes. That was something he always found reassuring, believing only people speaking the truth could look you in the eye – or psychopaths who lie. He couldn't rule out the possibility of Salibi being the latter. 'He has a marriage of convenience, without sexual relations.'

'How do you know this?' Deed asked.

'The Saudis look to know all they can about the people they do business with, especially sexual weaknesses. These they either exploit or accommodate,' Salibi said. 'This they shared with my employer.'

'Were sexual services provided for the Defence Minister?'

'Not that I am aware of, sir. I wish it could be otherwise for you.'

'At the risk of sounding pompous, I want only to arrive at the truth,' he said. Knowing his own sexual proclivities could be thrown into question, he didn't wish to judge anyone else's, unless they had a bearing on the case he was hearing. It was still possible that Pollock had been hidden in the wardrobe behind the two-way mirror while Ms Ortega had sex with another man, but Deed was getting no nearer to discovering that. 'I'm not someone who subscribes to outlandish or intricate conspiracy theories, but I'm led to believe there might be a directing mind behind all that has been happening around this trial.'

'The nature of conspiracy, sir, never knowing what's real or unreal.'

'Could there be a directing mind here?'

'Your justice system is inefficient and subject to error, but this is not the cause of what is happening. Almost certainly someone is arranging for evidence to go missing and key people to die.'

'Then the next question is: could it be the Defence Minister?'

'A question must come before your question, sir,' Salibi said. 'Does this man have enough to lose that would cause him to take such drastic action?'

'There's no simple answer. My experience on the bench, and indeed as a criminal barrister, tells me all manner of triggers, large and small, when distorted by an anxious or deranged mind can cause people to act in surprising and irrational ways. Is James Pollock one such? I can't tell.'

'From my dealings with him he's a man who enjoys his position, and the power it gives him. He would take seriously any threat to that position and possibly act upon it.'

'In direct action or as the organising mind?' he asked.

'Most certainly he would speak to the Saudis who this could also expose. Their secret police would undertake such things on his behalf.' Salibi paused as if waiting for Deed to respond.

'Would the Saudi secret police be able to get into Holloway Prison and murder a prisoner, and subvert elements of the police here?' he asked.

'All manner of things can be done most efficiently with money – with the approval of a British Government Minister they could be done with impunity.'

If giving a clearer picture of James Pollock it brought him no closer to understanding whether he was involved. Prejudice, he knew, was still his driver. He thought about Neil Haughton defending every twist in Pollock's possible misfortune. Was the Home Secretary being loyal to a fellow Cabinet minister, or somehow involved? Access to the gaol and the police required only a nod from him, along with roadblocks thrown in the path to uncovering the truth. The conspiracy was getting bigger – also the nature of conspiracy theories – and despite telling himself he should stop this, he couldn't. How compromised would he be if he produced no hard evidence? There was a way to get the evidence if it existed. In court tomorrow he could order a microscopic examination of the apartment where Peter Bartlett was murdered for any indication of prints or DNA which might implicate James Pollock. If ordering Pollock to give a DNA sample, and he was wrong, Deed would be so far beyond the pale he might never be able to get back.

In the Cabinet Room at Downing Street, while ministers were discussing the increasing welfare costs of the ageing population with no clear ideas on how to square the circle, Jim Pollock kept glancing his way, then at the PM as if trying to signal something. Haughton guessed what it was and refused to meet his eye. There was little for him at this meeting as the police and prison budgets had been notionally increased without either the police, prison officers or public noticing any beneficial effect. The battles were to come when he got to Justice and tried to make further savings there.

Pollock would want to buttonhole him about Deed's latest announcement in court surrounding the death of Peter Bartlett. He was behaving more like a High Court judge running a public enquiry than a murder trial and several Cabinet members were concerned this might set a precedent for others.

As soon as the meeting was over Haughton tried to slip away, but James Pollock was on him as he was getting into his car.

'Come on, Neil,' he said in a restrained manner, no doubt because of where they were. 'I've asked again and again for Deed to be stopped, but nothing is forthcoming.'

'We haven't given up trying, Jim. Most of the lawyers in the Home Office and half of those at the MoJ are looking for some legal means to oust him,' Haughton said, trying to open the car door with Pollock's knee against it. The driver was of no use, having stepped back to a discreet distance.

'Then hire a fucking assassin,' Pollock said in an angry whisper, 'or I will.'

Haughton gave a nervous laugh. 'We don't even joke about such things these days, too dangerous.'

'Who says I'm joking? Nothing else will stop this cunt's vendetta against me. The PM's sick to the back teeth hearing about him. There'll be hell to pay if it costs us the Saudi contracts. Crown Prince Ayad keeps asking why we don't stop him. I know why, because we're useless impotent gits.' Pollock glanced about, and then leant in closer, more angry, sour breath washing over him. 'I didn't know this woman, I didn't fuck her, my DNA will not be found at that flat.'

Uncertain what he was hearing, Haughton blinked, part of this declaration not according with what he knew. 'I'm relieved to hear it, Jim – not that I believed for a moment…'

'That's not the point. Deed continues to inflict damage on me, and by association on you, the PM, and the entire Government. The PM said I should urge you to use any means necessary to end this.'

Haughton watched him turn and walk away like a man without a care, greeting policemen in the street like old friends, again having shoved the problem his way. A partial solution to curb Deed was taking shape, but thinking about it made him feel sick.

Neil Haughton was shaking when he came to see him and Deed assumed anger was the cause when he turned down a drink. Being unaccompanied he suspected this man had something to say that he didn't want witnessed, misconstrued or repeated. After showing him in Coop made no move to leave. 'Perhaps you'd get the Home Secretary some tea, Coop,' he suggested.

'I didn't come here for tea.' Haughton was red in the face with impatience.

'I'll have tea. Thank you, Coop.'

Haughton waited for her to step out then closed the heavy door. He turned, no calmer. 'Are you completely mad, sir?' he said, and without waiting for a response, 'You seem to have lost all reason in pursuing this vendetta against Jim Pollock, a man you know nothing about, nothing of substance at least. He's a good and conscientious constituency MP, and a hard-working Secretary of State, who through skilful negotiations has brought many overseas contracts to this country. These contribute billions to our balance of payments, and here you are undermining his efforts by trying to draw him into not one but two sordid legal scandals, despite being asked again and again not to do so.'

'I would remind you, Home Secretary, I am a High Court judge. I was appointed by the Queen and swore an oath to act fairly and impartially at all times, to do right to all manner of people after the laws and usages of this realm,' he replied in an even voice. 'I do not work for HM Government PLC. I am not pursuing a vendetta against Mr Pollock. I'm seeking to uncover the truth of these cases, one involving three deaths to date, the other involving allegations of massive bribes that cannot go un-investigated.'

'This is not for you. No one appointed you judge-inquisitor.'

'Then who do you suppose will get at the truth?'

'Your rather coloured truth, Sir John. You will pursue this in your own arrogant way to the detriment of both yourself, a good and effective negotiator for Britain, and the British way of life, with a great many people losing their jobs.' Haughton spoke with the urgency and passion of a politician hoping the electorate would vote for him again. It wasn't a side of him Deed had seen before and could almost buy into his nonsense. 'Don't you realise how naïve you're being? Do you have the foggiest notion of how Government works? It works the only way it can work in these rather compromised times. We have to help companies do business with foreign governments any way we can.'

'By bribing their officials,' Deed pointed out.

'You might call it that from your privileged position. We prefer to say Britain is open for business.'

'The sort of business that is prepared to see a possibly innocent man extradited to a despotic regime in order to cover up wrongdoing.' As he expanded his rhetoric about the corrosive corruption which was tainting governments of all hues Deed got angrier, naming aspects of sleaze he knew about, stopping short of regurgitating the matter of the bribe he was convinced Haughton had taken when he was President of the Board of Trade: £700,000 for signing off on defence contracts that were over budget. He knew he should rein back as anger wasn't the way to beat this man, and he welcomed the knock at the door when Coop arrived with his tea. She set it on the table by the sofa as if they were about to sit for a polite *tête-è-tête*. With an uneasy glance between them, she departed. There were two Meissen porcelain cups so again he offered the Home Secretary tea, which was declined.

'You live in an ivory tower, John,' Haughton said in a calmer tone. 'Fine china; servants to fetch and carry; high ideals to which others can only aspire. Such a rarefied existence allows you to have abstract thoughts about justice and truth; politics are somewhat different. Often nasty and vicious, and even what you call corrupt. This is how the world turns and the money we generate helps pay for your ideals. If you want it to be different you should give up your comfortable, tenured position, get down on the dirty streets and enter politics and see how things really work.'

'No, I don't think I'll do that,' he said as he poured himself white Pai Mu Tan tea and watched a smug smile slide across Haughton's face.

'No, I didn't think you would.'

'When are you going to the Ministry of Justice, Neil?' he asked, changing tack and his tone.

A surprised Haughton took a step back. 'Well, it hasn't been confirmed, but the PM intimated that the sooner I bear down on the cost of the criminal justice system the better.'

'It's threadbare justice as it is. We'll all look forward to your cutting court budgets further.' It sounded sarcastic but he was intending to be conciliatory at this point and hoped the minister would believe him. There was immediate disbelief from Haughton when Deed said that instead of resigning, he would accept elevation to the Supreme Court in exchange for his silence and compliance in the matter under discussion. This was the sort of proposition that Haughton understood, yet it took him a while to get over his surprise before his smile suggested his mind had begun engaging the possibility.

'The price is rather high, John, and might be beyond our arranging it.'

'All the evidence I've so far gathered suggests the Government is biddable, why not in this? The price is reasonable considering what might otherwise come out.'

After a long moment, Haughton said, 'Then I'm sure if this is a true change of heart it's something that might be accomplished.'

'No,' he was emphatic, 'not, *might* be, Neil. What I'm asking for in return for my cooperation must be cast-iron clad.'

'There are several judges ahead in seniority, Joe Channing included.'

'I know, but do they have what I have, Neil?' He paused before adding: 'ruthlessness'. In this calmer atmosphere he now noticed the Home Secretary's suit, an immaculate cut without a wrinkle or pucker. None of his own suits looked as good or expensive and he was reminded of another suit of a similar cut, and realised what suit he was remembering.

'I always knew you to be bloody-minded.' Haughton gave a pleasurable laugh. 'I've never seen this side of you, John. I will talk to the current Justice Secretary and to the PM. I'm sure we can set this in motion. Yes, I'm certain of it. Perhaps I'll have tea after all.'

Deed filled the second cup and handed it to the Home Secretary. 'That is a wonderful suit, Neil. Who is your tailor? Could I afford one like it?'

'Is that to be part of the deal?' The smile on Haughton's face deepened. In this sudden, cooperative mood he said, 'I'll introduce you if you like. Ralph Blanxart at Maurice Sedwell – Savile Row, of course.'

The same tailor who made the suit Rudi Kozlowski was wearing in the murder trial. 'May I?' He opened Haughton's jacket to glance at the inside, noticing his name stitched onto the tailor's label: N. Haughton, just as J. Pollock had been stitched into the jacket Kozlowski had been wearing. Now Deed smiled, too.

With a feeling of elation Haughton carried the news of his success to the Defence Minister, who was less than impressed. What did this man want, Deed's balls on toast? He'd all but achieved that, having neutered him with a promise of elevation. 'I can assure you, Jim, we won't hear another peep out of Deed. I even gave him the name of my tailor.'

'Why did you do that?'

'He has human weaknesses like us all. I might even pay for a suit for him to cement the deal.' Haughton laughed, pleased that Deed was proving malleable.

There was a stone-cold glaze in the eyes of the man on the other side of his empty desk as he squeezed a tennis ball almost flat in his large hand. 'I wish I were as convinced as you, Neil. I'm scheduled to appear in court before him and his cohorts tomorrow, with Ali Franc from the Treasury. We won't worry as we'll be rid of this meddlesome judge in the proper fashion.'

Haughton laughed nervously. He'd prefer Deed wasn't on the Supreme Court bench. 'Have you found some infallible alternative way to compromise him?'

Now a smile fell over Pollock's squashed face as if it belonged to someone else and this discomforted Haughton. 'I think you made a shrewd move, Neil. I'll support you all I can.'

It was what Pollock wasn't saying that worried Haughton, fearing the hostility and ill-will he felt towards Deed might result in something reckless. He didn't much care what happened to Deed just so long as he wasn't dragged into it.

Rumours of Deed's forthcoming elevation to the Supreme Court went round the Inns of Court in a short time via George Channing. Haughton would doubtless have told her about her ex's desire to rise by revealing his human frailty. Not something that pleased Joe Channing, which he made plain when he came to see Deed in his room. He was furious and needed more than tea, instead pouring himself two malts and drinking them straight off, then lighting a cigarette, disregarding the building regulations, the law and Deed's dislike of tobacco smoke. 'What does Haughton think he's playing at?' he demanded. 'The Supreme Court is most certainly not in his gift. Rochester more or less promised me the next vacancy.'

Deed listened to his rant, then said, 'But are you ruthless enough, Joe?'

'I'm not ruthless, is that what the reptile said?'

'You had both the means and opportunity to blackmail this Government to get what you wanted. You didn't make the necessary move.'

'Is that what's required to get elevated nowadays?' He slammed down his glass and turned out with his bitter disappointment, muttering how he'd show Haughton and Rochester what ruthlessness was.

CHAPTER TWENTY-TWO

THE COURT ROOM WAS OVERFLOWING with the increasingly familiar faces of journalists and others. Both Rochester and the Home Office Permanent Secretary were also present – perhaps to support the Defence Minister and his Treasury colleague. Or possibly it was to witness his own shaming following his volte face. What he was sure of was their not expecting Joe Channing's change of tack. This morning the President of the court was in no mood to be accommodating.

'Are Mr Pollock and Ms Franc, the two ministers named in this action, present in court?' he asked.

The Attorney General rose to his feet and looked around as if for a signal before speaking. All he got from one of his team was a tense shake of the head. 'It seems Ms Franc is present, my Lord, but not Mr Pollock.'

Joe Channing glanced first at Deed, who shrugged, and then Tom Witham, before saying, 'This man is defying the court. This cannot be. I will ask the police to take whatever action they deem necessary to bring Mr Pollock to court.'

'But, my Lord,' the Attorney protested, 'the Minister may be engaged in important affairs of State.'

'I don't care if he has an audience with the Queen, the court is supreme. I want him brought here and thence quite possibly to the cells for contempt. Let it be understood for anyone who may be in doubt, a Minister of State is not above the law. No one is above the law. We will rise and await his arrival.'

Deed wanted to cheer as shock reverberated through the court.

'Did you see Rochester's face when you demanded the presence of the Minister?' he said. 'It was as if he'd been pole-axed.'

'That's nothing to what Mr Pollock will get if he doesn't show up.' Joe Channing marched off to his own room.

'What's happened, John?' Witham said. 'I've never seen him like this.'

'Perhaps he got out of bed on the wrong side.' He smiled and headed to his room where he could flirt with Jessie Rogers and fantasize about her open invitation to the Pestana Hotel.

It wasn't to be. Joe Channing's summons produced the desired effect and the Defence Minister presented himself in court almost at once with yet more spectators crowding in. What their expectations were Deed could only guess.

'Mr Pollock, are you the Minister of State named in the document supplied by the Oxfam worker, Ms Plant?' Joe Channing asked.

'I believe I am, but should not be,' Pollock said from the floor.

'Then step into the witness box and take the oath. We will see whether you should be here or not.'

'My Lord,' the Attorney said, getting to his feet, 'the Minister hasn't been charged with anything as far as I'm aware. He isn't on trial.'

'True, Sir Alan, but first we will examine him to establish the facts, then explore whether the State should be removing Ms Plant's property with a view to withholding information that might better be exposed to public scrutiny. It's an inviolable principle in English law that in certain circumstances public interest may override any duty of confidence or political convenience,' Joe Channing responded. Then rising to his theme, he nailed the point. 'We must take a broad view of this. The idea of the "public interest" is an organic one that changes with social expectations. As Lord Hailsham noted in 1978, in D v The National Society for the Prevention of Cruelty to Children, [1978] AC 171 at page 230, "the categories of public interest are not closed." This open-mindedness is a critical point for us today.'

'With respect, my Lord, this might give a great deal of comfort to the enemies of our country.'

'Then we will be careful to ensure that it doesn't, Sir Alan.'

In the witness box James Pollock was a picture of calm arrogance, batting answers back to the court President like a competent tennis player, neither scoring a point until Joe Channing said, 'What is your relationship with Ali bin Talib of Lebanon?' That caused the Minister to pause and glance across at the Attorney General as if expecting to be rescued.

'Do I have a relationship with him?' Pollock asked, his jaw tensing.

'According to the documents the State wishes to confiscate from Ms Plant, Mr bin Talib is an arms dealer, who works for the Saudis,' Deed reminded him.

'He'd be one of many who we employed while selling British goods to Saudi Arabia and the United Arab Emirates.'

'By goods, you mean arms?'

'They are still British-made goods that earn us much-needed foreign currency, my Lord,' Pollock said.

'According to Ms Plant's document he earned a great deal of money for himself, and for Crown Prince Ayad of Saudi Arabia,' Deed batted right back.

'This Government has never been shy about people making a profit, provided it's earned fairly through goods and services provided.'

'Can you tell the court why $35,000,000 was paid into an off-shore account in Luxembourg in the name of Mr bin Talib's wife?' he asked, glancing at the notes Mansour Salibi had made. The question caught the witness off guard along with the Attorney, who jumped up.

'My Lord, no such statement appears in Ms Plant's papers.'

'Indeed it does, Mr Attorney,' he told him. 'If you turn to page twenty-seven of the document, line eight reads money in the form of facilitation payments was paid via the agent bin Talib to an off-shore account.'

'There is no evidence to support this, Sir John.'

'That's what I'm bringing forth and questioning the witness about.'

There was a brief hiatus while the Attorney conferred with men in suits behind him to no satisfactory conclusion.

'Would you be so kind as to answer Mr Justice Deed's question?' Joe Channing asked the witness.

'I can't, Sir Joseph. To do so might compromise a sovereign state.'

'Then step down for a moment, sir, but don't leave the court. We will question your colleague in the Treasury. If you please, Ms Franc – the witness box, so the usher can administer the oath.'

Once there the tall, narrow-hipped lady from the Treasury was no more helpful, stating she didn't know where the money had gone. 'Are you telling us, Ms Franc, that you signed off on a payment of thirty-five million US dollars and you don't know what it was for or to whom it went?' Deed challenged.

'I don't know that I did sign off on it, my Lord.' She remained coolly remote.

'Then look at this minute of a meeting you attended with Mr Pollock and the Saudis back in March this year and tell me if that's your signature agreeing to the sum of $35 million?' He passed the document to the usher who took it to the witness. She remained cool but was a long time answering.

The Attorney got to his feet again. 'Might I ask how you came by this document, my Lord, and what its provenance is?'

'It was adduced by defence counsel in another case I'm hearing but had little significance at the time. Perhaps the witness will answer the question.'

Still she waited. Everything about her told him she recognised the signature, if not the document. She glanced at the Attorney, and then at Pollock, whose face was stone-like. 'It's similar to my signature,' Alison Franc finally allowed reluctantly, 'but I don't accept that it is as I don't recognise the document.'

'It will be a simple matter to examine the Treasury's audit trail to check if the payment went to the account of Mr bin Talib's wife at the HSBC private bank in Luxembourg,' he said.

'The Treasury makes thousands of payments daily,' the Minister said. 'It would be no easy matter to check this one as some of them are subject to the twenty-year rule, my Lord.'

'Not if the court rules differently, madam,' Joe Channing told her. He wasn't about to brook refusal by anyone in Government, and Deed felt honoured to be sitting on the bench with him proving just what an independent judiciary was worth. 'I suppose you do trouble to keep records of such,' he hesitated as if stuck for a description, 'odd payments at the Treasury?'

'We keep meticulous records of all payments, my Lord.'

'I daresay all computerised and available by pressing a few keys. So we will identify this payment, where it went, what it was for and who authorised it.'

'It may take a little time,' the Treasury Minister said.

'I think not, madam,' Joe Channing said. 'There are a number of your officials in court today. You will step out of the witness box, instruct one of them to retrieve the record in question and bring it to court forthwith, while we continue our examination of you and Mr Pollock.'

The Treasury civil servant ran from the court when the questioning of the two Ministers continued, one answering questions from the judges, having been reminded that he was still under oath. Very soon the civil servant quickly returned with a slim, manila folder and handed it to Ms Franc, whose already pale complexion grew paler as she read the document before passing it to Joe Channing. He read it and passed it to Deed, before it went across to Witham, who hadn't uttered a word throughout.

'It's clear from this, Ms Franc, that you did sign off on both the payment to Mr bin Talib's wife and the minute of the March 18th meeting which Mr Justice Deed so helpfully provided. The minute says the payment to the off-shore account is for professional fees and costs to facilitate the sale. In other words a bribe.'

'No sir,' Ms Franc argued defiantly, 'we make payments for goods or services and it's a matter for the recipient where those payments go.'

'But the recipient is an agent for the Saudi Government,' Deed pointed out. 'Why would the British Government be paying him to purchase our weaponry if not as a bribe?'

'I can answer that,' Pollock piped up, turning back to his civil servant who was whispering to him, just about lifting his backside off the bench to address the court. 'Mr bin Talib is a twin-hatted gentleman, who also works for the Ministry of Defence on occasions, helping facilitate the sale of arms.'

'In other words a bribe, as the President indicated.'

'You might call it that. We make a variety of payments in international trade – percentage payments for services rendered to cover the costs of the time and professionalism of those enabling transactions to take place.'

'And the minute of the meeting when Ms Franc signed off on the agreed payment?' Deed asked, now feeling that the ground was slipping.

'I suggest it's a forgery to try to discredit the deal,' Pollock said, a faint smile crossing his face. 'My aide informs me there was no meeting on March 18th.'

'Ms Franc wasn't convinced her signature was a forgery,' Witham obliged, coming to his aid.

'I said I wasn't sure if it was mine. Now I'm quite sure it wasn't my signature on that document,' the Treasury Minister said. 'I don't recall being at any such meeting with the Defence Minister and the Saudis.'

'We could ask for your diaries and records of meetings to be brought to court,' Joe Channing said, the edge now gone from his tone.

'My Lord, that is to imply the two ministers who are here of their own volition answering your Lordships' questions are on trial,' the Attorney said forcefully.

After a long moment and another glance at Deed, Joe Channing conceded. 'You're right, Sir Alan. We won't do that, but retire to reflect on the situation.'

'In the meanwhile, might the two ministers be excused to resume their important Government work?' the Attorney asked.

Joe Channing was too discreet to criticise a brother judge, much less from the bench, but the look he shot in Deed's direction was like a blow from a stave and he felt himself reeling. The same heavy atmosphere followed them into Joe Channing's room where his two fellow judges hammered him some more. Every question, every statement seemed to push him nearer to resignation. Joe Channing, who before was urging him to think long and hard about doing that, was now suggesting there was no other direction open to him. Maybe he was ruthless after all and was seeing this opportunity to better his chance of reaching the Supreme Court bench. Deed doubted he was so craven. Rather he himself had allowed prejudice get the upper hand in his pursuit of Pollock, both here and in his murder trial. The possibility that Salibi had used him for some political gain which he had yet to work out now occurred to him, when prejudice simply stopped him seeing anything else with Pollock in his sights.

'I still believe Mr Pollock and the Treasury woman are caught up in a massive bribery operation,' he said. 'I further believe that Government officers have been acting beyond the legal requirement placed upon them in trying to suppress evidence.'

'I daresay, John,' Joe Channing conceded, 'but the only way we could proceed is with evidence which you failed to produce. Were we to push harder in court we run the risk of turning this into some sort of Stasi commission. As a result we might destroy the judiciary's precious reputation for neutrality. We'd have judges descending into the well of the court with swords of truth on investigative missions of their own.'

'I'm with Joe on this,' Witham said. 'I'm afraid it has to stop now before more reputations are damaged, especially yours.'

'Unless I'm able to see Pollock convicted my reputation is ruined,' Deed said. 'I'll have no option but to resign.'

Both judges remained silent, which spoke reams. Deed walked the short distance to his own room like a man walking to the gallows, his mind searching for a way around the inevitable outcome just as the condemned man looked in vain for that eleventh-hour reprieve.

Coop saw at once there was a problem and when he told her his conclusion tears clouded her eyes. He had often seen Coop upset over tragedies and injustices that passed through his court and admired her for both being in touch with her feelings and showing them.

'You mustn't resign, Judge,' she said through her tears. 'You can't. It'll be a poor day for justice if you do.'

'It'll be an even poorer day for justice if I don't. I appreciate your support, Coop, but my mind is made up on this.'

Coop left his room to recover her emotions and even Baba seemed downcast where she sat on the sofa looking at him. Domestic animals often picked up on human emotions and this little rescue seemed most responsive to his moods.

'There's nothing else to be done, Baba,' he said. Sitting down to write to the Lord Chancellor, he thought about calling Jo and telling her first, but decided against it. Like everyone else around the Temple she would know soon enough. To his surprise his resignation was easy to write, and short, expressing regret and thanking him for his past considerations. He called Coop and asked her to deliver the letter by hand to the Lord Chancellor rather than trusting it in the internal post. Then, determined to leave everything in his office for someone to pick up and deal with in the most straightforward fashion, he spent several hours ordering his papers and indexing them, giving an opinion on pending cases. Whether those opinions would be acted upon was a matter for the Judge who followed him. He suspected they would be eschewed on principle, but on the points of law he directed his successor to, he was sound.

When finished he left his room at the Law Courts for his apartment. It was then he slipped into a deep depression and couldn't climb out, despite telling himself he would now have time to do the many things he never got to do. What things? He wasn't able to recall one thing he liked doing more than law, any place he liked being more than on the bench – unless it was on occasions in the arms or in the bed of an exciting woman. He had no garden to garden in, no book he wished to write. Perhaps he'd take up Neil Haughton's challenge and try entering politics. That thought made him more depressed.

CHAPTER TWENTY-THREE

※

Pushing into his apartment in Knightsbridge, Deed unclipped Baba. Her entry into his life was something he never regretted, despite his initial protests that a dog would interrupt his social life. Instead, she seemed to help it as many women paused to admire her when Deed admired any number of them right back. As he went through to the kitchen Baba raced into the sitting room and began her furious, high-pitched barking. Often the reason was a dog she heard outside so Deed ignored her and unloaded some shopping he'd picked up on his way home. He was thinking about Jo and felt he should call her. More than anything he wanted to be with her tonight and now the notional restriction of her being before him in two cases no longer applied, had it ever existed. He wanted to make love to her and realised more and more how much he missed being with her. She had been looking strained and he had had no opportunity to comfort her. All he did was try to bully her into getting protection for her client – for no real reason now. His bullying, he knew from past experience, only pushed her away – to Tom Witham? Was that possible or reasonable? His mind didn't want to go there, but it did nonetheless, and he was becoming more paranoid about the man. His depression would find no bottom were he to lose Jo as well.

His thoughts went to Jessie Rogers at the hotel near Chelsea Bridge. Perhaps she would be less interested in him now he was no longer a powerful, near unassailable High Court judge. Baba's continued barking broke his train.

'Shut up, Baba,' he called through the flat. 'It's just another dog. You can't get out to him.' In all the time she'd been with him she had never stopped being the noisiest little dog imaginable. His daughter had told him she came from Spain, as if that explained everything about her.

His mind jumped back to Jo. She might have a peculiar liking for judges – she and Witham were about as far apart as could be. Opposites attract, according to what he remembered of Newton, but he still couldn't believe her and Tom Witham, or know what he could do about it. Knocking him down and marrying her was perhaps his best option.

He was amused that despite his legal training and the veneers of sophisticated, civilised behaviour laid down over the years he could still think in terms of the crudest responses.

Not feeling like cooking for himself, he wished he'd gone to his daughter's favourite restaurant in North End Road, Fulham. They even tolerated Baba, provided she didn't eat off the table. He should try Jessie at the hotel, but made no move for his phone. This was a night of regrets. Stirring some shallots, mushrooms, broccoli and almonds in a pan with a little oil and soy sauce, his meal was ready in minutes and he carried it on a plate through to the dark sitting room with a bottle of beer, planning to watch mindless junk on television. Baba was still making a fuss over near the window.

'You just don't give up,' he said, reaching for the television remote control without switching on the light.

A strange, yet familiar voice startled him. 'I wouldn't do that, sir.'

He whipped around, trying to see who was in the corner by one of the full-length windows with their heavy swagged curtains. The lamp clicked on, revealing Mansour Salibi – not, he assumed, paying an impromptu visit to see if he'd still be able to prevent his extradition to Saudi Arabia. Baba stopped barking and looked round Deed.

'What the hell are you doing, Mr Salibi?' was all he could think to say, anger blotting out clear thought process as he tried to reason why he was burgling his apartment. 'How did you get in here?'

'The same way Al Mukhabarat Al A'amah did – the Saudi secret police, sir,' the Lebanese man replied in his even tone. 'Give me the remote, sir.'

'Why, do you want to catch up with *Coronation Street*?'

Stepping forward, Salibi plucked the device from his hand and opened the back and stripped out the battery.

'Why would the Al Muk – the Saudi secret police break into my apartment? You'd better start making some sense or you're in trouble.'

'Your television is wired with explosives to the frequency of the remote – enough Semtex to kill both you and your little dog, along with a number of neighbours.'

While Salibi had the calmness of a man in complete control of the situation, Deed could feel his heart pounding, first at the invasion of his space, then at the possibility of his world violently falling farther apart. His immediate response was to not believe this could happen, but Salibi had got in without forcing an entry, so why not others?

'Why didn't you simply remove the explosive or the remote?' he said, trying to stop the trembling in his voice. 'We might have been killed. You might have been killed for waiting.'

'Would you have been convinced if I had removed it, sir?'

'You could have taken the battery from the remote. Show me this explosive. How is this possible?' – his brain beginning to engage despite his fear and he remembered Semtex carried a detection taggant these days. 'Why can't I smell it?'

'The detection tag, p-mononitrotoluene, has been removed. You should call your policeman friend and ask him to get your bomb disposal people here,' Salibi said. 'Your enemies may have wired a trap for those trying to dismantle it.'

Curiosity about his enemies was overtaken by his surprise at this man knowing about his friendships. How many other people might have a similar information, more dangerous people?

He felt inclined to call the local police, but then thought this would give Row Colemore the opportunity to recover some of the lost ground between them. The DAC was at dinner when Deed reached him, with a new woman from his reaction, but said he would come right away. While they waited Deed plied the Lebanese man with questions, wanting to know more about his enemies, as Salibi described them. 'Why would the Saudi secret police be interested in me?'

'You are proving to be a persistent obstacle to a big deal that will earn their employer a huge amount of money in bribes.'

'Who would that be – someone in the Saudi Government?'

'One of Crown Prince Ayad's brothers-in-law, Sheik Muhammed bin Faisel. He runs these people. You will know from the documents I gave to Ms Plant that resulted in the case before you, he is due to receive the second payment of $35 million from the British Government to an offshore company, this one in Malta, again via Ali bin Talib – a bribe for the purchase of arms.'

'I'm no longer such a threat, Mr Salibi. I resigned from the bench this evening, having over-reached my remit.'

Surprise showed on the young man's unlined face – good-looking despite his strikingly billed nose. 'This is bad, sir. Bad news for British justice.'

'You're the second person to take that view.'

'Then you won't be hearing my extradition appeal, sir?'

'The other two judges are reliable and fair. They'll find an equally reliable third.' Deed twisted the cap off the beer he was still holding and took a long drink, uncertain if his answer was accurate now. 'Why would they try to kill me?' he asked, anger was driving him forward as he began to recover.

Salibi took a considerable while to respond and Deed began to wonder if he was going to get an answer. 'These things take time to set in train – you showed no sign of backing away from this. Had they known your intention to resign they may have proceeded with the death sentence anyway as a punishment.' A weather report might have had more inflection.

A new shock wave hit him as he realised the terrible mistake he'd made. To have continued after Pollock and his corrupt cronies might have made him safer. Somehow, he knew he had to stop the Foreign Office extraditing this man, but he no longer had the authority, having thrown it away. He now felt less than powerless. The realisation brought on a kind of nausea. His boast to Haughton about being ruthless seemed pathetic; he couldn't measure up to the likes of Pollock. This minister might have written a new definition of ruthless without regard for Salibi's life and liberty, and possibly none for his. At that moment Deed realised Pollock would have been quite capable of killing Peter Bartlett at the flat and letting another go to prison for it, and he could do nothing about it.

No longer constrained by being a judge in the case, Deed allowed himself to hear more from this man. Even if he hadn't resigned, stopping himself would have been impossible with such terror edging into his life.

Salibi told him about his nefarious work as a fixer in Lebanon. This included arranging bribes on the deals with his boss Ali bin Talib, with whom he had since fallen out over young British girls he was supposed to procure for the Saudis. He told how some of the arms being purchased from Britain were knowingly going to a middleman who was supplying terrorists.

'This can't be true,' Deed protested, further shock assaulting him. Ever since his student days he knew just how sleazy and immoral the arms trade was, but what he heard was something else. Could Pollock or anyone in Government be involved in this? He didn't want to speculate. That was for detectives who tended to operate with prejudice, not for a judge – only he was no longer a judge, so could speculate and explore whatever avenues he chose. But to what end with no power to order any kind of investigation? Would the police embark on such a course unbidden? It was doubtful.

'My God, John!' DAC Colemore said when he looked in the back of the television. 'What the hell are you doing sitting here like it's no more than a box of matches we're dealing with?'

'Mr Salibi disconnected the battery that would have detonated it.'

'Did he? Where is he now?' Colemore asked.

'He was in no mood to meet another British cop.'

'I bet he wasn't.'

There was something in Colemore's tone that worried Deed, it was mistrusting rather than someone relieved a friend had narrowly escaped death. He decided not to reveal what the young man from Lebanon had told him, but was anxious to get away and meet up with him as arranged.

'I have called the Counter Terrorism unit and the bomb disposal people, John. Whatever you think about this Salibi character, I'd say there's a good chance it was him who planted those explosives.'

This gave Deed pause and he questioned whether he was daft for trusting him. What possible motive could he have had for planting the explosives and then defusing them?

As if reading his mind, Colemore said, 'He could be trying to impress you to encourage you not to boot him out to Saudi Arabia.'

'It's a thought,' Deed said, without telling the policeman he had resigned and wouldn't now be involved in the extradition appeal.

'Did you get any further in discovering what happened to the CCTV footage from the block where Rudi Kozlowski worked?' he asked.

'The investigating detectives are making it part of their murder inquiry, and to look at who hacked into the security system at the women's prison the night Ms Ortega died. They're also looking into those deposits going into her account. Each was paid in cash at various ATMS so I'm not sure they'll learn much.'

'Isn't there CCTV at the ATM nowadays?' Deed knew there was.

'Of course. We'll try to locate what was recorded, assuming it has been retained.'

Leaving Colemore talking to the head of the Counter Terrorism unit, Deed exited his apartment on the advice of Supt Hamblyn, taking Baba with him. At a clear distance, sitting in his car, anxiety crept over him. Plainly Supt Hamblyn had no liking for him, so what if her unit took this opportunity to plant sophisticated listening or watching devices at his flat as someone had done at his office? This was paranoia, he told himself. Why wouldn't he be paranoid after what had happened? No,

Row Colemore was there and wouldn't allow Hamblyn to plant bugs, he argued, but remembering how the DAC was prepared to sacrifice friendship to survival, anxiety returned. If such a device was put there what could they learn, that he was no longer pursuing Pollock or the Saudis since he ceased being a High Court judge? He didn't know that he could stop now, which was why he was meeting up with Salibi.

'They may have planned a similar surprise for Mrs Mills, sir,' Salibi explained when he joined him in a pub opposite Harrods.

'Are you serious?' Deed said, more alarmed by this than anything so far tonight. 'Why the hell didn't you spell that out before?'

'First you needed to be convinced, sir.'

'A television packed with explosives is pretty convincing, Mr Salibi.' Pulling out his phone, he dialled Jo's number and got her a voicemail. He didn't want to leave a message, wanting instead to hold her, to make sure she was safe. The only solution was to go to her apartment and break in if she wasn't there.

'We must await her return,' Salibi said as Deed stood at the street door, his finger jammed to the buzzer.

Sitting in his car, waiting for Jo, he got Salibi's life story, or as much of it as he was prepared to tell. A tale of intrigue and corruption from the time he worked in his father's rug business and met the fixer who worked for Crown Prince Ayad. A lot of what he did was illegal under international law and indictable in most countries where bribes were taken. He was puzzled by Salibi's changed allegiance; procuring girls for clients seemed minor compared to some of the things he'd done.

'They weren't just girls, sir,' Salibi explained. 'These were children the Saudis wanted – some very young children, four and five years of age.'

'Where were you supposed to find these children?'

That caused him to laugh without mirth. 'In this materialistic world, some parents sell their children into bondage to satisfy their needs. Some in charge of care homes also are willing to sell the services of children.'

'Are you prepared to identify these people?'

'Does anyone in your Government wish to do anything about them? I think they do not, otherwise something more would have been done about historic sexual abuse of children.'

'There are other authorities that will certainly take action. You give me the evidence and I will issue arrest warrants,' he said, again forgetting he didn't now have that authority.

'Then your life would be even more threatened, sir.'

Deed gave him a long look, trying to read some kind of emotion in his blank face. 'We have to make some attempt to stop them, by whatever means,' he said. How far he would go if the threats got beyond his ability to take effective action he didn't know. Telling himself that life wasn't worth living without core values which drew red lines of acceptability was an intellectual response, and like most human animals he was emotional. Only by employing the ability to reason, developed via the educational regime he went through, did he manage not to respond emotionally. Too frequently he saw people up before him who had been incapable of finding the path of reason through their emotions.

The car that came along the quay and turned onto a parking space was Jo's Volkswagen and he felt relieved; then seeing someone in the car with her, he felt a familiar stab of jealousy on recognising Tom Witham. Jealousy reared its head and he knew he was being irrational, but couldn't change gear to function in his intellect – perhaps the result of all that had happened this evening. Trying to deny he was caught up in the undertow of base emotions like many defendants he had seen in the dock seemed impossible.

He got out of the car and strode across to Jo as she reached the door of the building, startling her and Tom Witham. Deed assumed this man was about to be invited inside to make love to her.

'John?' Recovering herself, she was immediately angry. 'Are you spying on me?'

'We just had dinner, that's all,' Witham began like he was explaining to an irate father why he'd kept his daughter out late.

'It could have been your last supper…'

'What are you doing here?'

'I'll explain inside. Let's go inside, Jo.'

'No. Not until you tell me what's going on.'

Deed glanced round at Salibi, who joined them from the car.

'This is Mr Salibi – we'll find out if anything is going on inside.'

'Mr Salibi,' Witham said with slight alarm. 'You shouldn't have any contact with Mr Justice Deed outside the court room, or me for that matter.'

Salibi ignored him and took Jo's keys from her hand and opened the door like he was used to taking charge of dangerous situations. Deed was happy for another authoritative figure to take over. 'Someone may have planted explosives in your flat, Mrs Mills.'

'Hardly likely,' Jo said.

'I thought the same an hour or so ago,' Deed told her, throwing a glance at Witham, who seemed to be viewing the whole enterprise with scepticism. 'We found explosives in my television linked to the remote. The Counter Terrorism people are there now.'

Alarm snatched Jo's breath as she managed to say, 'Oh, John – who?'

'You say the police were informed?' the younger judge asked.

'Let's go inside and have Mr Salibi check around.'

'Wouldn't it be better to let the police?' Witham suggested.

'Not if nothing's here.' He followed Salibi through the door and up the stairs, where he approached Jo's flat. Here Deed felt something was wrong and assumed it to be the danger they might be walking into, so dismissed his feeling.

Wired to the back of the television was enough explosive to destroy the entire flat. Jo dropped to the sofa, the colour draining from her face. 'Who did this, John? You know, don't you? Is it connected to the Anita Plant case?'

He was about to tell her, but stopped when Witham came into the flat putting his phone away.

'I called Counter Terrorism unit detectives,' he said. 'They'll be here shortly with the bomb disposal people.'

'They should be careful about trip traps, sir,' Salibi said, preparing to make his departure.

'I think they'll be conversant with such dangers.' Witham was stiff in his response, as if trying to distance himself from Salibi. 'They'll have done this many times. I'm not sure you should leave.'

Salibi looked over at Deed, framing a question in his face. 'I think he should,' Deed said. 'He's certainly earned his right to stay in this country with our protection, if that's what he wants.'

'We must decide that with Joe Channing, John.'

'Meanwhile, go, Mr Salibi – with my blessing.'

He didn't need to be told twice, and Witham did nothing to stop him.

'Where is the perpetrator, Sir Tom?' Supt Hamblyn asked when she arrived soon after his bomb disposal people.

'Gone, superintendent,' Witham said. 'About fifteen minutes ago. There was little one could have done to stop him.'

'It was wise not to try, sir, with his background.'

This incensed Deed and he felt like slapping the detective, along with this idiotic judge. Or was he the foolish judge? Despite himself Deed said in a tone that made both of them step back, 'He was never here, not as a perpetrator. It was he who alerted us to bombs which might otherwise have killed me, and later Mrs Mills. The public might just have shrugged off my murder, and even that of a barrister, but killing my dog Baba they would never have tolerated.' Both Hamblyn and Witham gave him an uncomprehending look. Neither of them had a sense of humour.

'We can't rule out that Salibi planted these bombs, Sir John.'

'Bollocks!' he said, staring at Supt Hamblyn's dour countenance, wondering what her reasoning powers were. Like many police officers he'd encountered as a defence barrister, she just jumped on the most convenient suspect regardless of evidence – that could come later. From what Salibi told him, and at this point he had no reason to disbelieve him, the young Lebanese man as a suspect in attempted murder would suit the political agenda. Without bothering to argue the case, he started out, pushing Jo ahead of him.

Outside and at a safe distance, along with most of her neighbours, he said, 'I'd invite you to stay at my flat, but like here it's crawling with police officers, and will be most of the night. I suppose you could stay at Tom Witham's place.'

'Would that matter to you?' Jo asked, her voice fragile; she looked ghost-like.

'It would, Jo,' Deed said sincerely. 'I realised how much when I came this close to losing you. I don't want to lose you. I've lost enough tonight already. I've resigned.'

Jo was a long time silent, which increased his anxiety, suspecting it might already be too late. Without warning she turned away and vomited into the canal, before collapsing against the protective railing. At once two paramedics from the ambulance crews standing by were at her side, pushing Deed away.

'I'm fine now,' Jo was saying as they tried to persuade her to sit in the ambulance. She still didn't look fine.

'Come on, Jo,' Deed said, taking her arm to support her. 'We're going to get a drink, then a hotel.'

'What about Tom?' It sounded half-hearted as he steered her to his car, where Baba greeted her. She clung to the over-familiar dog for comfort as he drove about a mile to a smart, canal-side hotel. There he got them two rooms and two glasses of brandy before calling Row Colemore to ask him to collect some clothes for him and have a policewoman do the same for Jo.

'Have you really resigned, John?' Jo asked at last. 'I hope you haven't.'
'I acted in an unacceptable way towards Pollock – with extreme prejudice.' This made Jo laugh. 'I see such extreme prejudicial responses from the bench every day towards defendants less able to take care of themselves than Pollock. Why should you be any different just because it's an MP?' She was angry and didn't let him answer. 'You are different, that's what makes you special and much needed in our judicial system. Why are you always so bloody well decent?'

'Maybe I overreacted in my response to Pollock. It seems he may be involved with levels of corruption even I find hard to comprehend.'

'Can't you un-resign?'

He laughed. 'Jo, the Executive has been trying to dump me off the bench almost since the day I got there. Do you think they'll let this opportunity slide past?' He swallowed his drink. 'There is nothing to be done tonight. You look shattered.'

He wanted so much to go to her room with her, to reassure her that everything was fine, despite the potential mayhem swirling around them. He tried to reassure himself that everything was all right, but wasn't convinced. Now he faced the threats without the protection of his unassailable office. Instead of accepting his offer, Jo took Baba and closed the door, thanking him for all he'd saved her from. Part of his brain hoped it was for saving her from Tom Witham, for the rest he'd have done for anyone. Willingly he'd walk through fire for her, but the opportunity to tell her was gone and he couldn't sleep. Thoughts moved unbidden to Jessie Rogers and again he contemplated calling her. This was insane; here he was convinced Jo was the love of his life and he was thinking about sex with a much younger woman. He got himself another brandy from the mini-bar and swallowed it and lay down on the bed.

Having drifted off to sleep, he woke after a short while with a feeling of unease about Jo and assumed the external threat was the reason. That didn't disappear with their diffusing the bomb, for the people who perpetrated this outrage were still walking around, possibly believing he and Jo were a threat and willing to try again just to punish him. James Pollock came to the forefront of his mind. Could a Cabinet Minister in the British Government be behind this? Or involved in the murder of Peter Bartlett and the subsequent murders of Mariana Ortega and Rudi Kozlowski? Random thoughts cannoned about in his head as he grasped at ever wilder possibilities. How wild with so much at stake?

It was a little after 11 o'clock and sleep felt like an absent lover. Picking up his phone, his finger found Jessie's number. As it started ringing, he lost his nerve and ended the call, his intention being both stupid and impertinent. The phone rang almost at once, startling him. It was her.

'You want me, Sir John,' – her meaning unmistakable. He certainly did want her, every sensation in his body was telling him so and all he could do was nod. Somehow, he must have answered in the affirmative for twenty minutes later he was in her room on the third floor of the modern hotel, in her arms, kissing her like nothing else mattered. He wanted to be slow and gentle, a lover of great expertise who could make every sensation last; instead he was as clumsy as a hungry youth grabbing at everything and fumbling with her buttons. It was too much for her to bear and she wrenched open his expensive shirt, causing two of the buttons to come off, and she began biting his chest. Then an alarm bell went off in his head and he almost looked around to see where it was coming from.

'What? What is it?' she said.

'I'm sorry, Jessie. I can't do this.'

Mistaking what he was saying, she said, 'You can, of course you can, I can feel how much you want me.'

'I know, but it's not right. I'm taking advantage and I can't allow that. I'm sorry.' He grabbed his jacket and left before she furthered her argument and he lost.

Collecting his car from the underground carpark adjacent to the hotel, he couldn't exit because he hadn't paid the parking charge. Finding a credit card and exiting, he turned the wrong way on Queenstown Road, south instead of north and across the bridge for his own hotel. Jessie wouldn't leave his mind and he was in no fit state to drive, so pulled onto the filling station forecourt on the roundabout and stopped to calm down. Slowly he was finding calm when his phone rang. When he saw who was calling his pulse started to race again. He hesitated, sensing he could easily be drawn back so put the phone to message and listened. 'I do understand how you feel,' she was saying. 'You are such a decent human being, as well as an attractive one…' There was a knock at the door of the hotel room and Jessie said, 'Ah, I suspect this is you returning, Judge.' The phone call ended abruptly. At once he thought about going back, but knew what would happen if he did. After a long, long struggle with himself he finally found the will to resist.

Following a period of entrenched indecision, the other events of this evening flooded back: was Jo safe? Was Anita Plant, and who might secure her safety? He considered ringing Jo to ask where Anita Plant was, but instead was ringing Salibi's phone. This was ironic, his eschewing his own security people in favour of someone who had been involved in all sorts of dangerous intrigue.

'Do you know who this is?' Deed asked without identifying himself.

'Of course, sir.'

'I'm concerned about the safety of the person you gave that list to.'

'Me too. I'm outside the apartment.'

'Is she all right?' he asked.

'I haven't attempted to enter. There are several young people living there. They don't seem to sleep.'

'What about the television being wired?'

'Unlikely, sir. People of this age group tend not to have television.'

'Give me the address. I'll come over there and talk to her.'

South London wasn't familiar and he got lost, not having a sat-nav or Google maps on his phone. When he eventually arrived at the address in Balham in South West London the local police were there, but no Salibi and no Anita Plant. 'Where is Ms Plant?' he asked the detective chief inspector in charge. Others were searching the flat that Jo's son, Tom, shared with four other ex-students.

'You are, sir?' the detective wanted to know.

'How did you get here so fast?' Deed demanded. 'How was it you were alerted, as if I can't guess?'

'You didn't tell me who you are.'

Standing up close he looked hard into the youngish, acne-scarred face before him, wondering what games he was playing, if he was in on it or had simply been sent there by the Counter Terrorism unit?

'I'm Mr Justice Deed,' guessing word of his resignation wasn't yet broadcast. The detective stiffened, which told him all he needed to know about his involvement here. 'Where is Anita Plant?'

'She's been taken to a place of safety, sir.'

'That wasn't what I asked you.'

'Tooting police station, sir.'

'I'll get to her in a moment. Where is Mansour Salibi who was here?'

The detective avoided his eye. 'There was no one here when we arrived, sir.'

'I don't believe you. So unless you want to be prosecuted for attempting to pervert the course of justice and find yourself sharing a cell with some deeply unpleasant suspects, I suggest you try again.'

Hesitating for as long as he dared, the detective said, 'He got taken away by the Counter Terrorism unit.'

'So, how did you get here so fast?'

Again the young detective hesitated for a fraction of a second before informing Deed that the Counter Terrorism unit had called the local nick and asked them to secure the flat. This confirmed to Deed that someone from the unit was tapping his phone for he was certain that Salibi, in the world he inhabited, would not allow his phone to be hacked.

Before going to check on Anita Plant, he went and talked to Tom and his flat-mates. They weren't delirious about cops trudging through their messy, poster-hung space, having no interest in the cannabis a couple of them had been using. If anything at all could be found among the chaos of their untidy possessions he would have been surprised. He gave Tom his phone number and told him to call if they got any unwarranted problems from the police. Tom said, cool. He wondered if this connection was really cool, or how much longer it might even be useful.

CHAPTER TWENTY-FOUR

TOOTING POLICE STATION, A FORMIDABLE five-storey brick building with an Art Deco look, was in the process of being closed, police officers taking over High Street shops where they could be more easily accessed by the public. Many of its rooms were empty and locked. The ground-floor interview suite where Deed found Anita Plant had old worn furniture, helping create an atmosphere which said a lot about police thinking for the metropolis.

'I don't want to be here, Sir John,' Anita Plant said when he eventually got the suite unlocked.

'Nor are you going to be. We're getting you out of here right now.'

'I don't think you should do that, Sir John,' said the superintendent, a neat, tight-faced woman who had been called back on duty.

'You don't? Unless Ms Plant says she wants to stay here, that's what I'm going to do.' He was directing his anger at the police when it should have been at the people trying to harm him and Jo, and possibly, Anita Plant. 'Is she under arrest for some offence?'

'No, sir, she is being held for her own protection.'

'Then who is it you're protecting her from, superintendent?'

There was no answer and all the police woman did was revert to the stock answer, following orders. When questioned about who gave that order, she said someone in the Home Office, with no name. 'I understand you feel under some pressure here, superintendent, but I'm countermanding your order. Let's ask Ms Plant if she wishes to stay here so there is no mistake.'

'No, I want to leave,' she said emphatically.

No one attempted to stop them walking out of the police station. Deed drove her to Jo's son's flat to collect her few things, watched by other policemen who were still present. Afterwards he took a circuitous route to his hotel – why he wasn't sure, as the watchers would soon find him if they wanted him. Nor did he know how to protect this woman, but thought Salibi might have a good idea, if he could find him. He gave Anita Plant his room at the hotel then went to his room at the Law Courts in the Strand.

The security guard seemed alarmed when approached and it wasn't because he was startled out of his slumbers. How safe would any of them be relying on such people employed at not much above minimum wage? At once he felt there was something wrong as the guard grew nervous and tried to delay him, looking for the book to make him sign in, all the while his eyes darting along the corridor. Then he understood why, or thought he did, and started to run. As he reached his corridor a short, thick-set man emerged from his room carrying a bag of some kind and ran. Deed shouted and instinctively hurtled after him, catching him at the corner and wished he hadn't. The man turned on him, hitting him with his hard body, his arms locking around him and bringing him down before he could get off a single blow to defend himself. Something was wrestled over his head, and then he knew what it was the man was carrying: a plastic bag which started to tighten around his neck, shutting off his air. He flayed and struggled but couldn't dislodge the man who was sitting across his back, knees anchored on either side of him. Breath was getting shorter and panic was increasing. He remembered the knife the young, disabled litigant had gifted him and struggled get it from his pocket before he passed out. Calm down, use less air, he told himself, as he got the knife out. Releasing the blade by hooking the end of the handle in his pocket, he then dropped it in his flailing. Pressure on his neck increased; his lungs ready to burst. Bringing his hand up, he managed to tear at the plastic. The assailant saw what he was doing and slackened his grip to stop him, but some air seeped in. Deed found the knife and thrust it hard into the man's thigh but couldn't pull it out to take another stab; then the pressure disappeared as the man hobbled away along the corridor. Deed pulled the bag off his head and gulped in air, feeling sick and dizzy. He staggered to his feet but was in no state to give chase, even though he had the inclination to do so. He hit the nearest alarm bell. No one responded to the alarm, the sound of which filled the deserted building.

Deed found his door unlocked with the light on in his room and felt uneasy, looking around for any kind of disturbance. Whoever had been here would have left little obvious trace if he hadn't been disturbed in whatever he was doing. What was the intruder doing? Another bomb came to mind as his eyes traversed the room. The prospect of getting a couple of hours sleep of on the sofa and a shower sped from him as he called Row Colemore. 'Shite, John,' the DAC said when Deed told him of his concerns, 'this is becoming a habit almost.'

'I hope not, Row. Get someone here to check the place and talk to the security people. I'm sure the guard knows something. Have them check the CCTV cameras for an image of the attacker.'

'We have done this before.' It was clear Colemore hadn't been home since he called him earlier and he was grateful for his swift response.

His people found nothing alarming in his room, nothing on the CCTV hard drive other than the unidentified man limping at speed and disappearing along the corridor, while the security guard said he had been startled by Deed's arrival at that time of morning. Deed didn't believe him, but let his explanation stand for now. The senior policeman simply thought he was spooked after what had happened earlier. None of this reassured him. He was just back from taking a shower when Rochester arrived with the inevitability of summer rain.

'My Lord,' Rochester began, being his most solicitous, 'are you all right? You've had a very upsetting few hours.'

The Permanent Secretary's use of his formal title made Deed alert: was it just habit, or had he not seen the letter of resignation? He would have opened it for the Lord Chancellor. 'Hopefully it's at an end now.'

'Let us hope so, my Lord. Yet despite everything you seem to be endeavouring to alienate yourself from every police officer in this country. Not a good idea when it's clear you rely on them so much in these circumstances,' Rochester said.

'I'm prepared to go on alienating them in the interests of justice.'

'No one had arrested Ms Plant. The police were protecting her, as they will you, regardless of what you think of them.'

'I'm entirely grateful for their prompt response,' Deed said sincerely. 'I'm less sure that locking this woman inside an interview suite against her will is the right sort of protection. She's a vital witness in a case that may spill into another case, if not into a third. I'd hate for anything to happen to her as it has to two other witnesses, both under the protection of the civil authority.'

'Weren't they suicides, my Lord?'

'You can't believe that, having seen the post mortem reports,' he said. 'I can't imagine you wouldn't have seen them, Ian, as you have overall responsibility for the courts and their precincts, where one witness died.'

'These are matters for the police and coroner, surely?'

'Both died in unusual circumstances during a case I am hearing.' He waited, thinking Rochester might challenge that statement by telling him he no longer was hearing the murder case. When he didn't, 'Was there anything else you wanted with me this morning, Ian?' – expecting him to get to the real purpose of his visit. Still he didn't and Deed suspected he was playing games.

'These were truly shocking incidents for both you and Mrs Mills, John. I hope she was not too disturbed by this threat. I understand the Counter Terrorism unit is putting every resource into finding the perpetrators. I'll make sure my minister discusses the matter at the highest level to ensure increased police protection for judges, and barristers as well, when involved in sensitive cases. In your case that will be 24/7.'

'We'll be greatly reassured by that,' Deed said. 'I'd be further encouraged if the police released the man who saved us both from almost certain death.'

'I understand Mr Salibi is being held pending his extradition to Saudi Arabia,' Rochester informed him like he was delivering a trump card.

'That has yet to be decided, Ian.' This man was irritating him and he began to think it intentional in view of their sudden inversion of power. Deed tried another stroke to test the matter of his resignation. 'I'd like him returned to court to hear our thoughts.'

'I'm not sure that's possible in the circumstances, my Lord. Salibi is helping the police identify terror cells both here and abroad. Further, it would be for the presiding justice and Mr Justice Witham to decide whether you can continue to sit in view of your letter of resignation.'

So, now the die was cast. 'I presume it's for the Lord Chancellor whether he accepts it or not.'

'Indeed it is,' Rochester said with a smug smile. 'Were he to do so I'm sure it would be with great reluctance. I'll see it goes before him as a matter of urgency as soon as it comes into the office.'

That left Deed unsure. Rochester knew about his resignation, but it would seem he hadn't seen the letter.

The senior civil servant started to leave without the usual courtesies and turned at the door. 'Perhaps it's no longer of interest to you, but I have news of the governor of Holloway Prison. The Home Office informs us that she's further delayed abroad on her fact-finding trip.'

Deed remained calm, but he felt weak and helpless after Rochester's departure. He dialled Coop's number to find out what had happened to his resignation letter but she wasn't answering her phone. Anxiety and frustration buffeted him and there wasn't a thing he could do. His thoughts tried to move on.

It was inconceivable that Rochester could be involved in hiding facts concerning the deaths of those two participants in the current murder trial, but Deed was sure he was somehow a party to obfuscation of truth. Obfuscation seemed to be the by-word of the civil service and nowhere more so than the Justice Department. Again he tried Coop's number and got no answer. A moment later she walked into his room as though nothing was amiss. 'Coop?' – greeting her like a long-lost friend.

'Judge,' she said in her familiar concerned fashion, 'are you all right?'

He stared at her, expecting her to tell him what was happening. Instead she said, 'Would you like coffee now, or perhaps some of your white tea?'

'Coop,' he almost shouted, 'what did you do with my resignation letter?'

'Oh that,' she said with a dismissive gesture. 'I went to the Lord Chancellor's office and told his secretary why I was there. Do you know what she said, Judge? How sorry she was you were resigning, you made life more interesting than any other judge. She told me to leave the letter; she'd see the Lord Chancellor got it.'

With difficulty Deed asked, 'Did you – leave it?'

'You said deliver it to the Lord Chancellor. It's here – shall I take it now, Judge?'

He closed his eyes and shook his head. 'Something that possibly involves the Defence Secretary caused me to think again about resigning.'

'Oh I hoped you'd change your mind,' Coop said, 'that's why I didn't leave it.'

He wanted to kiss her. 'What would I do without you, Coop?'

'Well, you might have to get your own coffee.'

He told her what happened last night and Coop went white and sank into her chair. 'I'd better get *you* some coffee,' he said.

'No, I'm all right, Judge. He is involved, you know – Mr Pollock.'

'That's my feeling – I have no concrete evidence.'

'No, in the murder you're hearing – oh, I'm sure he's involved in all sorts of shenanigans with the Government as well. You know I asked Sergeant Bridges if he could find out anything about the CCTV recordings from the building where the man was murdered, when Mr Colemore couldn't. He's got a friend at Wimbledon nick who's about to retire. It was only the recordings from the building during the time of the murder that went missing. There were earlier ones Mr Kozlowski kept from months before the murder took place. On two occasions they show Pollock entering and leaving the building with Ms Ortega.'

Why would he have those, Deed wondered? It looked like he was blackmailing Mariana Ortega or Pollock, or both, which might have explained the two-thousand-pound withdrawals from Pollock's account and the deposits in Ms Ortega's. Perhaps he was paying her to pay Kozlowski. This was pure speculation, but he was now certain about what had occurred during Pollock's earlier court appearance.

'Pollock lied in the witness box. I could bounce him into gaol for contempt and leave him there until the police get fingerprint and DNA samples to check against any at the Wimbledon flat. Brilliant, Coop, you're totally brilliant.'

'It's Jake Bridges who's brilliant,' she said. 'What he and his friend from Wimbledon nick found at Mr Kozlowski's bedsitter was an onyx Buddha with blood on it.'

'The missing murder weapon! Keeping it to blackmail Ms Ortega or the real murderer?' More speculation on Deed's part.

'I bet she was involved in blackmail,' Coop said, giving her nothing, not even in death; then she turned even paler. 'You must be careful, Judge. If someone dared that with you and Mrs Mills last night, they'll try anything.'

'No, we will stop them, Coop.' A thought occurred to him about the security of his room, whether his unwanted visitor had left another bug. He scribbled a note to Coop asking the whereabouts of the recordings found among Kozlowski's possessions.

She gave him a puzzled look, before catching on. She scribbled a note back. He nodded, encouraging her to speak now.

'Sergeant Bridges said the *only* copy is in the evidence store at Wimbledon Police Station for safe keeping,' she said with exaggerated emphasis.

'Brilliant, Coop. If you weren't already married, I'd ask you to marry me!' he said, feeling buoyant about what she'd achieved.

'If I was free, I'd marry Jake Bridges. He's asked me often enough since his wife died.' Deed met her look, surprised. 'Perhaps it's catching, Judge.'

He laughed. This was going to be a good day after all.

At times like this he realised just how much he enjoyed being a High Court judge. How foolish it was his attempting to resign – even if for a principled reason. As corrupt as he believed Pollock was it didn't justify him behaving in other than a proper fashion. That's something Deed tried to do, notwithstanding his relations with the female bar, but never allowed those relations to influence his judgments on the bench.

When Coop returned with their coffee she said, 'What's happened to our traffic-stopping marshal? Is she less keen now, d'you think?'

'What do you mean?' Deed responded guiltily.

'She usually beats me in,' Coop said.

'Perhaps she had a late night,' he said, deflecting her, before asking her to contact Mansour Salibi's barrister to have him come to chambers at his earliest convenience.

'Just Mr Machin, Judge?'

Because of the nature of their relationship it was obvious that Heathcote Machin assumed he was in trouble when he came to his room at Southwark Crown Court.

'It's your client who may be in trouble, Mr Machin. I think there's a move afoot to dump him out of the country before we give our ruling.'

'Would anyone dare, Judge?' the young barrister asked.

'The consequences might not be sufficient to worry the parties who may try. Draw up a writ of habeas corpus for me to sign and for you to present to Supt Hamblyn of the Counter Terrorism unit at the Home Office.'

The prospect appealed to Machin who went right to it, his role in the current murder trial being reduced to that of an observer.

After he departed, Deed picked up Baba's lead when Coop stepped forward.

'Do you want me to take her, Judge?' she said.

'Yes, Coop, that's exactly what I want.' She gave him a quizzical look as he nodded her out and followed her all the way past the security desk to the inner courtyard. Even Baba looked puzzled. Outside he said, 'I didn't want to speak inside. Someone might have bugged this room.'

'No one would dare, Judge.'

Deed found it ironic that the authority of his writ was deemed so high. 'Someone possibly murdered those witnesses and tried to kill me and Jo Mills; a bug here might seem a minor peccadillo.' Coop became subdued. He didn't want to involve her further, but there was no one he trusted more. 'Contact Sergeant Bridges and get the CCTV recordings Kozlowski kept, and the onyx Buddha. I don't want them disappearing. Don't call your friend. Go and see him.'

Coop was breathless with anxiety when she went off, and at once Deed wondered if he shouldn't have gone instead. He too was anxious as he awaited her return. Return she did within the hour with the willowy, lugubrious Sergeant Bridges, the CCTV recordings and a forensic report on the Buddha, along with the statuette itself in an evidence bag.

'Has this been for forensic examination officially?' Deed asked.

'No, sir, my friend at Wimbledon nick got it done. It's in the forensics bag to prevent contamination,' Sergeant Bridges said. 'This was found hidden at Mr Kozlowski's flat along with the CCTV recordings. If you want my guess, sir, I'd say he was blackmailing someone with them.'

'We'd better avoid guessing at this stage, sergeant.' He saw the look of disappointment on the policeman's face. 'For what it's worth, that's my guess too, but it won't run if the right set of prints isn't present for identification purposes.'

'Mr Kozlowski would have had a good idea about that, sir, or why would he keep the Buddha?'

'What we have to do is try to tease out some facts. Thank you for all you've done so far. The tape might help me order the taking of prints and DNA tests from the person identified with Ms Ortega.'

'If you can get a clear set of prints from the suspect,' Bridges said, 'then they could easily be checked against the prints on the Buddha, even though some aren't very clear.'

He gave the policeman a long look and nodded his appreciation. 'Why have you only reached the rank of sergeant, Mr Bridges? You seem to have a talent for investigative work.'

'I got lumped in with the awkward squad, sir,' Bridges said. 'I didn't quite fit in, if you follow me.'

'Ahead of you. Welcome to the club.'

This caused the policeman to become about six inches taller, and he deserved his stature-raising. Deed was pleased to be associated with him.

Soon after showing Bridges out Coop came running back in a state of great agitation, 'Judge, Judge,' – barely able to get her words out, 'it's Jessie,' – at which point she broke down in tears.

'What? What about her…?' suddenly feeling his chest tighten, at once sensing something was seriously wrong. Recovering a little, Coop told him his young marshal had been found dead in her hotel room this morning and the police suspected she had been murdered. Deed felt as though he'd been punched, his mind going momentarily blank as he tried to shut out this terrible truth, not wanting to believe it yet knowing he had to somehow deal with it; after a few moments when paralysis made everything frigid, 'what if' thoughts began to assail him. What if he'd stayed the night with her? Why hadn't he? What if he hadn't requested her help? Or had sacked her when he learned of Rochester's plan? Who and how then followed, but there were no ready answers. His instinct was to call the police and ask for some information on her death, but he hesitated. Finally he rang DAC Colemore.

'This must be a terrible shock to you, John, knowing how you felt about her.'

The policeman's remark caused him to mentally step back. What did he mean? He tried to recall if he had ever discussed his almost overwhelming feelings about Jessie with him. He was sure he hadn't.

Uneasy with himself and looking for space, he said, 'Yes, she was a highly efficient marshal. Both Coop and I are deeply shocked. Are there any more details that might help us to come to terms with this?'

He assumed there were none that Colemore was prepared to give at this point rather than there being none. Why had he made such an assumption? The DAC said he would find out what he could and let him know, but Deed doubted he would. Again he questioned why – was he being paranoid? Why hadn't he mentioned to the senior policeman that he'd seen Jessie at the hotel, that if he'd stayed with her she would still be alive? He knew he would have to tell someone.

Resuming the murder trial in these circumstances was difficult for both him and Coop; there were emotional road-blocks which seemed almost physical. He was distracted watching the CCTV tape showing James Pollock accompanying Ms Ortega into the building; Coop was equally distracted and displayed none of her usual outrage knowing the Defence Minister had lied to the court.

With his mind trying momentarily to escape the tragedy, Deed's thoughts turned to Pollock. He was convinced that what he was planning was the right course, but knew he still needed to carefully choose his moment for summoning the politician back to court.

He barely noticed the woman who stepped into the witness-box without the jury present and swore to tell the truth. She was the prison officer on duty the night Mariana Ortega died. Rose Brickett was about 45 and as much in uniform in her neat dark blue two-piece suit as if she had come in her prison outfit.

'Ms Brickett,' he asked, hearing the words in his head like an echo, 'where were you stationed when the remanded person in your charge died?'

'I was in the observation room, sir, situated at the end of the wing.'

'Do you have any idea how this…?' He couldn't remember her name and thought about adjourning so he could step away and wail for Jessie. The name suddenly returned and he forced himself to continue. '… Ms Ortega, how she might have acquired the cord with which she hanged herself?'

'No, sir. Prisoners hide all sorts on them, sir. She wasn't "high risk" so weren't body searched.'

'How often do you check on prisoners throughout the night?'

'We do it about every two hours.'

'What does that involve?'

'A prison officer walking along the landings to check everything. The log shows we done it around 2 A.M. She was found about 4 A.M.'

'Who does this check involve?' he wanted to know, curious that the prison officer wasn't saying.

'It would be either me or the other officer on duty. I done the 2 A.M. check. My colleague done the 4 A.M. while I was watching the screens.'

'There was no camera in Ms Ortega's room?'

'No, only in the rooms of prisoners at risk of self-harming.'

'Then what do the cameras cover if not the prisoners?'

'The corridors and the entrances to the wing, and the cell doors.'

'Did the CCTV cameras pick up anything untoward, Ms Brickett, such as anyone who shouldn't have been entering or leaving the cell?'

The woman in the witness box hesitated. Before she answered he knew what it would be. 'There was nothing on the security hard-drive for that period, sir.'

'Yes, the copy I requested hasn't materialised. What happened, do you know?'

'No, sir. I know when we checked the recorders later that day they was all working proper.'

'Then possibly a third party could have entered Ms Ortega's room without anyone observing this?'

'It would have been on the camera facing along the wing.'

'We would only know had it been recorded on the hard drive and we had a copy for the period. What is the routine for checking the hard drive? Is there someone who is responsible for doing this?'

'It's only looked at if there's an incident what requires it,' Rose Brickett said.

'Such as someone dying in a cell,' he pointed out. 'Who checked the hard drive subsequent to discovering Ms Ortega was dead?'

'I done that, sir. That's when I discovered there was nothing there.'

'Is it possible the hard drive wasn't functioning and the prison authority was saving money by not getting it fixed?'

'No, sir, if it weren't working a red light comes on. There weren't no red light flashing, sir.'

Another momentary lapse as he thought of Jessie, then brought his mind back to bear on the issue, deciding he believed this woman. Slack she may have been, but not lying. 'Did you leave your station at all during this period of duty?'

Now she hesitated. 'Only to a call of nature,' she said, 'and when I was summoned to admin to check my overtime sheet.'

'During that 2 A.M. to 4 A.M. period, when you believed the camera was recording any incident you'd have needed to know about. Who called you away from your station?'

'The principal officer in charge of the wings.'

The principal officer he discovered was away on annual leave – abroad. At the conclusion of this examination, he was further convinced there had been a mind directing Ms Ortega's murder and the subsequent cover up, the same mind organising the Rudi Kozlowski murder. All that was left to him was to call Pollock and ask him to agree to his fingerprints being taken and to giving a DNA sample. Not for a moment did he think he was wrong about his involvement, but even if he were, he'd no longer feel obliged to resign having caught the minister out lying under oath. He suspected it might mean the end of Pollock's career, but even that wasn't guaranteed.

When he was done with Ms Brickett, Jo Mills declined to question her. She seemed withdrawn and stared into the middle distance as if none of this was connected to her, or her client, who seemed equally out of things. After what Jo had experienced last night it was a wonder she functioned at all, and he suspected that what she saw him doing now from the bench might endanger them further. Perhaps she read the death of Jessie Rogers as another warning. Jo was a barrister who always gave too much of herself, often getting involved in her clients' personal lives, and was possibly suffering burn-out. In the most fraught situations she refused to step back but would push on regardless of danger. Maybe he should adjourn this trial to give him more time to investigate some of the matters swirling around which seemed to be sucking him into a dark hole. He resisted, feeling this and the other case were becoming too urgent.

Heathcote Machin returned to court and Deed could see by his expression he hadn't succeeded in springing Salibi. He called a brief recess to see the barrister in his room.

'The Home Office denied knowing where Mr Salibi was, Judge,' Machin said. 'Then when I presented the writ, Supt Hamblyn said what they were doing was more important. It would save lives.'

'Coop, would you get two of the court police officers,' he said. 'I want them to take a summons for Supt Hamblyn to attend the court forthwith, along with the Home Secretary. Is Neil Haughton still in that office?'

'I haven't heard that he's come across to Justice yet, Judge.'

'If they refuse then they are to be arrested and brought here.'

Coop struggled out of her lassitude and became quite animated, hurrying away to get this actioned. As she went a smile creased the corners of Machin's mouth. Deed wished he felt as positive about what he'd just ordered.

Word of what he'd done sped around the courts and soon brought Joe Channing down from the Strand, first to express his shock at the tragic loss of Jessie Rogers. 'Word around the Strand is she was murdered. Have you heard differently, John? If she was, I'd like to be the judge trying the culprit.'

The weight of her death still oppressed Deed and he shook his head as if it were too heavy for his body. 'I have no more information than you, Joe. I'm trying not to let my mind go there, being so close.'

'It is difficult to put one's mind elsewhere,' the old judge said before moving on. 'This most recent action of yours is precipitous; it could pitch the judiciary headlong against the Executive – something we have been at pains to avoid.'

At once Deed decided to tell him all he knew and all he suspected. When he was done Channing said, 'Evidence, John. Do you have any, apart from the CCTV recording showing Pollock with the dead woman? This may amount to no more than his lying in court, as serious as that is. You could well understand why he might lie in the circumstances.'

'My gut tells me the wretch should be in prison, and not just for contempt – along with those who are doing his bidding,' Deed said.

'I'm not sure that will do. If you fail and fall as a result, it won't be a minor mishap that we all soon forget. Haughton will never forgive you, especially if he gets Justice. Perhaps it's as well you've tendered your resignation.'

That almost caused Deed to smile. It was clear Rochester had fed the rumour mill without hard evidence. Now Deed was out on a limb without hard evidence.

'If I'm proved wrong, Joe,' he said, 'I'll have to live with the consequences.'

CHAPTER TWENTY-FIVE

Having answered the summons, Superintendent Hamblyn stood in the well of the near-empty court and faced Deed with a defiant set to her body, canted forward, feet apart, ready to attack. She hadn't come with any apology for not producing Salibi, rather believing, like so many, that Deed was on his way out.

'I ask you again, Superintendent, where is Mr Salibi?'

'He is a suspect under the Prevention of Terrorism Act, my Lord,' the detective said, a slight smile brushing her cheeks. The first Deed had seen. 'He is helping us with inquiries that will prevent many acts of terrorism that would result in great loss of life.'

'Fortune-telling is now added to your list of talents, is it?' Deed said, giving her a scalding look. 'You were handed by Mr Machin a writ of habeas corpus, signed by me. This isn't an object for discussion. It means produce the body.'

'There is a grave risk in producing him. He could signal his co-conspirators.'

'Yes, he might even communicate with such people by telepathy! Defying the summons is contempt of court. You will be taken from here to the cells and then to prison and held there until I'm satisfied you've sufficient respect for the court. Officers, remove her.' He signalled the two officers who had brought her.

'This is utterly ridiculous.'

'Do you have a phone on you? – of course you do. Show me.'

He waited as the detective, flanked by the police officers, retrieved her phone from her inside jacket pocket. 'Call your office and get your people to bring Mr Salibi here and fast or each one of them will join you in a cell.'

The call was made, but whether it would bring forth Mansour Salibi was another matter. Time would tell, but now Deed had set his course, he would send more policemen to gaol for contempt until Salibi was produced. After making the call Hamblyn clearly expected to walk away as if nothing were amiss.

'They are on their way here with him, sir,' she said.

'It doesn't change the contempt. Give up your phone to the Associate.'

'It has a lot of sensitive information on it.'

'He is an officer of the court; he can be trusted with sensitive information. You will surrender it or it'll be removed.'

Supt Hamblyn tensed as if about to fight them and, despite her small stature she looked capable, but finally she passed over her phone and was escorted away. Throughout this Machin was smiling, like it was an entertaining game of 'dare'. Catching Deed's eye, he dropped the smile and rose. 'Should my client be produced, my Lord, will we be resuming the extradition hearing in this court, or the murder trial?'

'Your client will be produced, Mr Machin,' Deed said with certainty. Soon after he rose he was sure he'd get a visit from Rochester telling him what a rotter he was to put a policewoman so vital to the security of the country in gaol for no good purpose, and that his suggested move up to the Appellate Bench would be just a bit further away. At times Deed was tempted under the Freedom of Information Act to request his file from the Justice Department, but he knew whatever they sent him would be so redacted there would be nothing to read.

Noticing Jo on a seat near Machin, Deed wondered why she was still here. She looked done in, with heavy grey hollows below her eyes and pale skin stretched across her tense face. Perhaps like him she was awaiting news about Jessie's death. Every time his thoughts went there he felt sick as his mind reeled off alternative possibilities had he stayed the night or returned after her last phone call. There was no point regretting what he didn't do. It changed nothing. Although he didn't like delays in his court, and would often stretch the day beyond the hour when barristers needed to scoot back to chambers or check their phones and tablets, he decided for Jo's sake not to push on.

'I'm awaiting more information in this case, Mr Machin. My clerk hasn't signalled its arrival, so I'm going to adjourn for today. I hope these delays don't inconvenience you.' He rose and bowed to the crowded court, suspecting the news hounds present would speculate now in the absence of facts.

'Did we ever hear another word from DAC Colemore about what happened to those CCTV tapes that were supposed to have been biked here, Coop?' he asked, coming into his room and removing his robes.

'No, Judge. I checked with security several times. They would have had to come through security for scanning.'

He rang Colemore's number and got him out of a meeting. 'Is there any progress on identifying who put the explosives in my flat or Jo Mills' place, Row? Or anything on Jessie Rogers' death?' After events of the past 24 hours paranoia refused to budge and he now convinced himself there was a too long silence and an edge to the DAC's voice. He didn't doubt this man's sincerity when he assured him the police were working flat out on both investigations, but what he didn't say worried Deed. Something was wrong. 'What is it, Row? What are you not saying?'

'Nothing, nothing at all.' Another long pause, then, 'Was it absolutely necessary to send Superintendent Hamblyn to prison?'

'I didn't undertake it lightly.' He was surprised this had reached him so fast. 'Do you have my court room bugged?'

'It doesn't help anyone here do their job,' the DAC said.

'A different case, Row, a different issue, the two shouldn't be confused. It shouldn't cause the police to soft-pedal on any of this.'

'The police were under the impression they had the right person in custody for planting the bombs – but you insisted he be released.'

'I hope I'm right about my impression of Salibi, and your people are wrong. The death of my marshal can't in anyway be connected?'

After another silence Colemore made his apologies to go back to his meeting, leaving Deed wondering if this senior policeman knew he'd seen Jessie at the hotel before her death, and how many others might. Doubt slid through him. Was he behaving suspiciously? As a barrister he would repeatedly caution defendants to offer the police any information they had rather than risk it coming out later in a detrimental way. He was behaving like someone with something to hide. He should have told Colemore about having seen Jessie. Was he wrong about Salibi? Could he have been involved with Jessie's death? He couldn't see how. His mind leapt to Pollock and the possibility of his involvement.

That was nonsense, he told himself, hoping he may yet be proven right. Both he and Salibi needed further investigation. He needed to find a way to test Salibi's statement about the Defence Minister's involvement with the Saudis, and their secret police operating here; Pollock's possible relationship with Ms Ortega and whether it was him in that flat in the wardrobe behind that two-way mirror. The question most troubling him: who could he now trust to do this?

With Salibi still not making an appearance before Deed left for the Strand, he was beginning to feel frustrated and contemplated putting the Home Secretary in a cell for contempt. Joe Channing's warning echoed in his head about the judiciary clashing big-time with the Executive. Although he might be wrong in this and not survive as a result, the idea of the Home Secretary in one of his own prisons amused him. At least Haughton would experience first-hand what the problems were with drugs and violence, over-crowding and under-staffing, rather than pretending everything was fine and that he could go on stuffing prisons with more and more offenders.

It wasn't Rochester who came to see him when he arrived back at the Law Courts, but Haughton. Deed might have anticipated this, after all it was one of his foot-soldiers whom he'd committed to prison and was in no hurry to let out.

'With respect, John,' Haughton launched right in, 'you're making a fool of yourself, especially in view of your intended resignation.'

'Oh, you heard about that?' Deed said, playing along.

'The whole of Whitehall's abuzz with it.'

'Can it be that significant?'

'Regardless, you won't find a single police officer who'll have any respect for you, not one. You'll need them after you leave.'

'My prime concern is that they have respect for the law,' he said. 'I'm determined they do wherever I fetch up. Flagrantly disregarding a writ of habeas corpus doesn't indicate any kind of respect.'

'They do respect the rule of law, that's why these brave men and women go out every day in the fight against terrorism. They will find those who tried to kill you and Mrs Mills despite what you do.'

Incensed now, Deed demanded, 'Despite *what*, my insisting the court should be held above all else?' He got no answer. 'Habeas corpus is older than Magna Carta; it's been a bulwark against illegal imprisonment and state tyranny for over 800 years.' Side-stepping, Haughton responded like the politician he was.

'You must let this police officer out right away.'

'The remedy is simple. But if Salibi isn't delivered to the court and in short order, it'll be you next who goes to prison,' he told him in an even tone which he saw worried the Home Secretary.

'Don't be ridiculous.' Haughton gave a nervous laugh. 'You can't put me in prison. I'm the Home Secretary.'

'Just so, Neil, but not above the law. The law says, by the power vested in me as a High Court judge, Salibi must be delivered to court. You being the ultimate boss of those holding him, you're accountable. No one is above the law.'

This time Haughton managed a scornful laugh. 'You seem to think you are. You act the whole time as though you are.'

'I'm sure if you could bring evidence to support that it would be sufficient to get my decisions overturned. Until you do, produce the body as required or face the consequences.'

'Any such decision would get struck down by a more senior judge in nanoseconds, especially as it seems likely you'll be gone.'

Notwithstanding the uncertainty he detected in the Home Secretary's voice, he was sure he was right. There would be other judges who would do this rather than risk that confrontation with the Executive. Few were like that one dissenting voice of Lord Justice Atkin in war-torn England arguing against the subjective ministerial power to imprison; any number when faced with claims involving the liberty of the subject showed themselves to be as Executive-minded as the Executive. They may speak the same language, but Deed doubted if they would support him as he crawled farther out on this limb with no easy way back? Perhaps he had already over-reached as Joe Channing warned he might.

Haughton's anxiety was apparent when the door was rapped, he barked, 'Yes,' as though it were his office without so much as a glance at Deed. Sir Percy Thrower opened the door and slithered in with silent, mock deference and whispered to the Home Secretary. Deed wanted to have him bounced into gaol along with his minister, but that would be an abuse of power.

'Excellent, Percy,' Haughton said and turned to Deed. 'I'm sure you'll be pleased to learn that I'm to be spared the indignity of having to slop out, John. Your body awaits you in court here.'

Deed slipped on his jacket rather than robes and went with Coop to Court No 62 where he found Salibi on the front bench with Machin just behind. Two men, he assumed police officers, sat close by. He couldn't tell who was more pleased to see him, Salibi or Machin.

'Mr Salibi, I'm glad you got here at last. Are you under arrest?'

'I'm not sure, sir,' Salibi said.

'We've not been able to ascertain that, my Lord,' Machin said, rising.

Deed glanced at the men on the third bench as one of them got up. 'He's not under arrest at this stage, sir.'

'You are?'

'Inspector Teal, Counter Terrorism, sir.'

'Thank you for delivering Mr Salibi. You can go now.'

'We need to question him further, sir. Our instructions are to return him to Paddington Green Police Station – with your leave, sir.'

Deed shook his head. 'I'm not giving it, Inspector. If you have evidence that indicates questioning this gentleman further is necessary, then present it to me and I'll consider it.'

'With the utmost respect, sir,' the inspector said in a way Deed had heard a thousand times in court from people offering no such thing, 'Mr Salibi is a substantial flight risk and might disappear abroad meanwhile.'

'Where to, do you suggest, Saudi Arabia?' They didn't get the joke. 'If that were his intention he would have been long gone. Off you go.' He watched them shuffle out of the court, dejected.

'You have a court appearance here with Mr Machin in two days' time, Mr Salibi,' Deed said. 'I'm certain you will show up, even though I can't guarantee the outcome. Do you feel confident of remaining free and safe until then, or do you require to be placed somewhere secure? Like Paddington Green?'

'I believe I can secure my own safety, sir. Thank you. I will be here for the hearing on the 27th.'

'Do you think the police will try to collar him again, Judge?' Coop asked on their way back to his room.

'I always try to think the best of the police. They'll think twice with Supt Hamblyn languishing in Brixton, especially when realising I haven't resigned.'

'Are you going to let her out tonight, Judge?'

'Has she made a request for me to hear her apology?'

The same question he put to Sir Ian Rochester when he telephoned him at home later that evening, pointing out the Counter Terrorism unit had released Salibi. Deed told him he was missing the point.

'It is terribly dangerous for a police officer in counter terrorism to be held in prison, even for one night,' Rochester said.

'At this juncture there is no telling how many nights she might be there. As for danger, you think she might hang herself?' There was a long silence on the phone. 'There does seem to be an epidemic, Ian. She could go into isolation for her own protection.'

After an even longer pause, the senior civil servant said, 'Are you tendering your resignation, my Lord?'

'If I've second-guessed this situation aright that may not be necessary.'

'Then let us pray you do have it right, my Lord.'

When the conversation ended, he sat and looked around the sitting room, feeling even less secure here. If it was the Saudi secret police who planted the explosive in his TV and were in his room at the Law Courts earlier there was a possibility they would try again. Having upset the Counter Terrorism police how hard might any of them try for him? That was stupid, he told himself, but the anxiety didn't recede. He telephoned Jo to see how she was feeling, but got a cool response.

'Are you asking if I'm all right, John,' she said in a subdued tone, 'or if I'm on my own?'

'This is one occasion I hope you might not be.'

'It does feel a bit weird here after what happened,' Jo told him.

'There are police officers in a car outside, I hope?' he said.

'Are they staying all night?'

'Unless I come across there and stay with you,' Deed suggested.

'Not a good idea.'

He wondered if in fact she had the judge there who seemed to be replacing him in her life. He didn't feel better when he shut the phone off, and didn't manage to sleep much. Jessie Rogers entered his thoughts; still he didn't know how she died, much less why. In his waking hours he determined to stop his obsessive pursuit of women and commit to the one woman he loved above all others. He just hoped it wasn't too late.

CHAPTER TWENTY-SIX

ENTERING THE OFFICE OF THE Home Secretary on the first floor of Marsham Street, Rochester at once felt the electric atmosphere with Haughton in a high state of excitement and Percy Thrower looking almost as pleased.

'Is it possible, Ian? Is it remotely possible it could have been Deed who actually murdered this poor young woman?' Haughton asked, glancing at Sir Percy as though he had the answer. Rochester certainly didn't.

'I have no more information than that which Percy gave me.'

'Either way this is certainly the end for Deed, embroiled as he now is in a murder investigation. There can be no question of his continuing as a High Court judge. This is so, Ian? Tell me it is.'

'The only thing would be for him to resign with immediate effect.'

'I knew it!' Haughton punched the air triumphantly. 'What's the Lord Chief Justice saying?'

'I've yet to brief him, Home Secretary, or the current Justice Secretary,' Rochester said, catching Percy's eye again. 'I needed the fullest report from the police before doing so.'

'Colemore is on his way here to brief us,' Percy Thrower said.

'We'll need an urgent damage-limitation strategy…'

'To hell with that,' Haughton said, cutting Rochester off, 'Deed can roast in the hottest fire of adverse publicity.'

'I was thinking more of the bench than Mr Justice Deed,' Rochester said. 'This could do the judiciary a lot of harm unless managed carefully.'

'I don't care how it's managed as long as the result is the same: Deed out of office, better still in the dock. That'll teach him to keep his lust under control. I can so easily imagine him taking advantage of that young woman and losing it, forcing himself on her when she didn't allow him into her bed, and then killing her to save his precious position. Yes, that's what happened.'

Even with no liking of Deed, Rochester at least contained his feelings so they didn't distort his judgement. Again he glanced at his Home

Office counterpart, wondering how he had suffered Haughton for so long.

'The media will rip him to shreds, and rightly so after the way he always claims the moral high ground. Oh, I'm going to enjoy this.'

'We must give Deed an opportunity to explain himself, Home Secretary.'

'Of course, Ian, then we'll hang him out to dry.'

The phone on the large mahogany desk rang once and Percy Thrower picked it up. It was one of the secretaries.

'Deputy Assistant Commissioner Colemore is here.'

'Wheel him in, Percy,' Haughton beamed, 'let's hear the good news.'

The DAC wore the expression of a man bringing only bad news. Perhaps that was understandable, as Rochester knew the policeman was a friend of the soon to be ex-judge. Even so, he winced when Haughton said, 'Don't keep us in suspense, man, is there enough evidence to arrest Deed?'

'I wouldn't go that far at this stage, sir. There's enough to interview him under caution,' Colemore said, 'if anyone's brave enough.'

'Oh we're brave enough, Assistant Commissioner.'

'Deputy, sir – Deputy Assistant Commissioner. Mr Justice Deed was in the deceased woman's bedroom around the time of her death. He was caught on the CCTV cameras going into the hotel. There was also a call from his phone to her, we assume just prior to his arriving. We are making a search of all phone data via GCHQ to hear the content of that conversation.'

'Excellent! I knew there was a valid reason for collecting all that phone traffic. We don't just catch Muslim extremists with it. Anything else?'

'Rape was attempted but not achieved. Her attacker must have worn gloves as there were no third-party DNA samples on the dead woman or her clothes. The investigating officers did find two shirt buttons at the scene of the murder, from an expensive shirt made by Peter Werth with the initials JD on them.'

'Hah, John Deed.' The Home Secretary's shouted excitement was met with silence. 'Were there prints on it, DNA samples?'

'There was a partial print on the button and enough DNA – when we have someone to match to. A search of the police databases didn't reveal a single possible.'

'Have you tried Deed?' Haughton asked.

That caused DAC Colemore to hesitate and look to Sir Percy for guidance. 'Mr Justice Deed has neither his finger prints nor his DNA on record, sir.'

'I'm sure we could arrange to lift them from his room. That can be arranged, Ian?' Haughton enquired like he was ready to send someone in to do it.

'I would caution against that, Home Secretary,' Rochester said. 'It might prejudice any subsequent trial and make a conviction unsafe.'

'Oh God, I can smell success here, but you're right, let's not risk the quarry escaping through wrong procedure. That's just the sort of tricky move Deed would make.' Haughton smacked his hands together and for a moment Rochester thought he might dance a jig.

'What's our next move, Assistant Commissioner?' Haughton said, wrongly elevating his title again. 'Do you haul him for questioning?'

'First I should speak with the Chief Justice,' Rochester said.

'Yes, that's a courtesy, of course. I don't want it to impede justice in any way, Ian. Let's get this investigation underway and show that no one here is above the law. How ironic as Deed often says as much.'

Deed was late getting to his room and found Sergeant Bridges there with Coop drinking coffee and chatting in a familiar way as if they'd spent the night together – he gave too much time to contemplating such things. Soon he learned that Jake Bridges had been using his initiative, something many police officers were lacking in the current bureaucratic climate, having taken it upon himself to investigate Kozlowski further in the light of finding what was almost certain to prove the murder weapon at his flat. From enquiries to the police in Krakow he'd discovered the dead man carried a conviction for blackmail.

'Fascinating, Mr Bridges,' Deed said, not wishing to discourage him, 'but where does it lead us?'

'Well, if this politician at the flat was involved in the murder of Peter Bartlett, Kozlowski may have been blackmailing him – the politician, if you follow me.'

'Oh, I do,' he told him, seeing where this was going. 'We've got Mr Kozlowski's bank statements that DAC Colemore provided. They show no large payments going into his account. None of this takes us to the politician.'

'If we could get the original hard drive records of the account, they might tell a different story, sir.'

'Why, do you suspect these aren't accurate records?'

Jake Bridges looked at Coop, uncertain. She helped him out. 'Well, Judge, strange things have happened around this case.'

'How do we get the hard drives, sergeant?'

'The police conducting the murder enquiry could get them.'

'They'd want to know why, presumably?'

'It might have been a motive for killing him,' the policeman said.

'If I issued a court order could you get them?'

'And anything else you ordered them to release.'

'Such as?' Deed wanted to know.

'Ms Ortega had an account at the same branch of Barclays Bank, sir.'

Deed signed the order and the sergeant went off like a man on a mission and was back before court was sitting. Then it was Deed's turn to get both excited and alarmed when he saw the bank-issued statements from their computerised deposit records: they differed significantly from those Colemore had supplied. They showed three lots of two thousand pounds being deposited in Kozlowski's account a month apart and three separate thousand pounds going into Ortega's account the next day, whereas the statements the DAC supplied showed the deposits of two thousand pounds which stayed in Mr Kozlowski' account.

'It seems both may have been involved in blackmail,' he said.

'Mrs Cooper says you have copies of the politician's bank statements, sir.'

'From the same source I got Mr Kozlowski's, which seem not to be accurate.'

'I'd say the ones from the bank today are genuine, sir,' Bridges said. 'I saw the account manager get them from the computer.' He waited a moment, and then added, 'Could we get the politician's bank statements in the same way?'

'Not without a great deal of risk, sergeant. Someone at the bank would be certain to contact the gentleman in question.'

'If he's got nothing to hide, sir, there's no harm done.'

Deed laughed, but didn't comment further. It was a typical police response that assumed the man was guilty. The statements he received on James Pollock's account which Row Colemore supplied showed three two-thousand-pound withdrawals, each being one day after Kozlowski's deposits. This meant he either had no connection with their money which possibly didn't derive from blackmail or the statements had been altered with such subtlety as to throw him off, giving Pollock the benefit of the doubt. Would Colemore do that? Or was he a party to it without knowing? He may never know without forensically examining both the senior policeman and Pollock. This was the proverbial Rubicon, and he hesitated with no one to advise him. Perhaps his hesitation was his answer. But was his uncertainty out of concern for his own career, or for James Pollock? The moment he posed the question he got the answer.

Shortly following the notice for James Pollock MP to appear again at Southwark Crown Court, Deed received what amounted to summary refusal. The message was that the Minister was too busy with affairs of state to attend court. 'This arrogant bastard will appear,' he told Coop and sent her to get two court police officers to arrest him if he wouldn't come voluntarily. Another surprise awaited Deed when Coop returned and told him the officers were under instruction not to respond to such requests.

'Who gave such an instruction? Does everyone believe I've actually resigned? You're sure you didn't hand them a copy of my letter, Coop?'

'No, of course not, Judge.'

A third shock then hit him when a few moments later Rochester arrived with Joe Channing and two men who Deed guessed were detectives. They all looked as sombre as undertakers and he soon understood why: both he and his career were under threat.

'This is quite preposterous, John,' Joe Channing said at once, 'it's the reason why I insisted on being present.'

'I'm sure it is, Joe, but I don't know what "it" is.'

A surprised Joe Channing said, 'You haven't heard? These police officers think you're mixed up in the death of that pretty young marshal you had here.'

'Well, I am,' Deed said, 'in as much as I had a relationship with her.'

'What sort of relationship, Sir John?' one of the detectives asked.

'You are?' he said, outwardly hoping he was appearing calm, which wasn't what he was feeling, seeing himself being sucked into something he might not be able to control.

'I'm Detective Superintendent Maheson, from C1 at Scotland Yard, sir.'

'C1 is what these days?' he asked, trying to gain a little time.

'We're a specialist crime unit working to the Assistant Commissioner, sir.'

Deed nodded as if it meant nothing. 'Jessie worked on a case I was putting together – in my room in the Strand. She was a very smart lawyer. We grew very fond of her in a short space of time.'

'Yes, she was so full of life,' Channing said, 'it was hard not to let her affect one.'

'We understand she liked to party a lot, sir.'

'I didn't get invited to any, did you, John?'

Deed laughed, seeing where the detective was heading without Joe Channing's help. 'I daresay most young lawyers do – I did – a means of relieving stress from some of the traumatic situations they must deal with.'

'Did you meet Ms Rogers socially at all, Sir John?'

They knew he was at her hotel, and thought about telling them he went there to discuss the case they were working on. He didn't as it seemed a such stretch.

'Socially, no, that hardly describes it.' He hesitated. The lead detective waited along with everyone else in the room.

'I believe Mr Justice Witham had a go with her,' Joe Channing said, clearly still attempting to help him. 'I'm not sure he got far.'

The detective didn't follow that direction, instead said, 'What do you mean, Sir John, "socially hardly describes it?".'

After a moment Deed confessed, 'I felt attracted to this young woman, despite the difference in our age and rank. I got the impression she felt the same about me.' He noticed Rochester avert his gaze like the guilty party he was. Jessie had told him about the pressure put on her to try to entrap him.

'Did you go to her hotel room late the night before last, Sir John?'

Working on the assumption that this detective wouldn't ask unless he knew the answer, he said sharply, 'You know I did. What you can't know is that I felt I was taking advantage of her, notwithstanding her feelings, so I left soon after.'

'What time would that have been, sir?'

'Am I a suspect in this case, Superintendent?'

'That's utter nonsense, John, how could you be?'

'I was at the scene of the crime, Joe, with clear designs on the victim.'

'She practically threw herself at you, Judge,' Coop put in from behind the two detectives. They turned and gave her a blank stare.

'Perhaps, Coop, only I was too vain to see it. Was that her instruction,

Ian?' He felt in control when he was asking questions. 'Was the plan for her to have a relationship with me and entrap me?'

'I'm uncertain what you're implying, my Lord.' Rochester's use of his title seemed to isolate him more than protect him.

He didn't wish to fight this battle in front of these detectives, but was satisfied with sowing the seeds of what he was sure had been Rochester's plan.

'You didn't tell us what time you left the dead woman's hotel room,' Detective Supt Maheson pointed out. Deed noted his tone was less polite now and he dropped the 'sir'.

'Oh, around 11.30, give or take a few minutes.'

'Where did you go after that?'

'I went to Balham to meet someone involved in a High Court case, then to Tooting police station to free a woman being held there against her will – then to my room here – I had an intruder who I managed to wound in the leg. Any progress on that investigation?'

'We are working on trying to identify him, sir.' The detective waited, then returned to his interrogation. 'You arrived at the flat in Balham at approximately 1.00 A.M. according to the police officer there. He said you were in an agitated state.'

'I was. There'd been an attempt on my life earlier, and on Mrs Mills' life – a barrister in a case before me.'

Superintendent Maheson skated over that. 'Between leaving the Pestana Hotel and going to Balham do you recall what you did?'

'I got lost – going to Balham. I shouldn't really have been driving.'

'Had you been drinking, sir?'

'Earlier, after the bomb was discovered at my apartment – a couple of brandies. This wasn't the cause of my confusion.'

'Did you speak to anyone, or anyone speak to you during that period?'

'No, I don't think so,' he said, meeting the detective's look. He hesitated, remembering the phone call from Jessie and what she had said, how someone who she thought was him returning knocked on the hotel room door. To tell them would implicate him further, while not telling them would make him appear guilty when they eventually discovered it – assuming they didn't already know.

'Jessie called me on my phone. I listened to the message, but didn't speak,' he found himself saying, knowing this was the truth.

'Do you have a tracking device on your phone, sir?'

Deed laughed, one hollow note. 'My phone is very basic. It has none of the modern app features.'

'Is the message you received still on your phone?' the detective asked.

The whole room listened to Jessie's seductive tones and heard her saying in response to the knock at the door that it was him. Had he been hearing this before a jury he would have put much emphasis on that statement. The lead detective did. At the end of this interview he said, 'Would you come to Holborn Police Station and make a statement, Sir John?'

'Sir John Deed is a senior High Court judge,' Joe Channing said with force, 'you must accept his word in this matter.'

The detective stepped back and began to apologise and possibly would have conceded but for Deed saying, 'That's all right, Joe, I can't be seen to be above the law. I'm in the middle of a murder trial, and can't delay it further.'

'You can't contemplate going on in the circumstances, my Lord?' Rochester put in. 'I understand it's all but collapsed. There can only be a retrial at best.'

Turning a cold gaze on him, Deed said firmly, 'Not so. We will see this through with the Defence Minister appearing here to answer more questions. Make an appointment with my clerk, superintendent, and I'll pop along to the police station – doubtless with the media alerted.'

'I wouldn't do that, sir,' the detective stammered.

'Not personally,' he said, and again noticed Rochester glance away. 'Now if you'll excuse me, having summoned this witness to appear, either he attends immediately of his own volition or he'll be brought here.' This was said for Rochester's benefit, knowing it would go straight back.

After everyone had departed Deed sat at his desk feeling very alone, unable to see a clear strategy to his defence. It was ironic that as a barrister he always found a way through in even apparent hopeless cases; as a judge he quickly identified schemes and smoke screens offered in court, but now he felt lost and knew what this course could do to him, and that truth alone might not protect him.

Another surprise was Row Colemore, who caught him as he awaited word of Pollock's arrival, saying he was there to argue for Supt Hamblyn's release from prison, while in his body language Deed read a different agenda.

'Don't you think she may have learned her lesson, Judge?'

'Quite possibly, but I haven't received any signal indicating that. She'll know the form for getting out. She has to purge her contempt.'

'I'll make sure she does, and does it with gilt-edged sincerity.' The senior policeman waited, on the brink of saying something else, when he stopped.

'Row?' he invited, and got a dismissive shake of the head.

'Could I just have a word with Mrs Cooper?' Without waiting for his permission he dived out of the room. A few minutes later Coop came in and handed him a note inviting him outside.

Colemore was in the corridor and apologised for his strange behaviour. 'I'm not sure if your room is bugged, John. There's so much at stake for these people there's no telling what they might do.'

'You'd better start explaining yourself. What are you caught up in here?'

'The fact is I'm not sure. Some kind of conspiracy, but to do what, I don't know. Some sort of cover-up, but what's being hidden I don't know either. What I do know, or suspect, is the bank statement I gave you from Pollock's account I believe has been doctored.'

'Why do you think so?' he asked without revealing what he believed.

'The way it came to me – via a civil servant in the Home Office,' Colemore said. 'I think you were supposed to run at Pollock in court and shoot yourself in the foot. He would have trumped you with his daughter's bank statements showing that those fairly large cash payments went to her.'

Even knowing it was a pointless question, he felt obliged to enquire about the civil servant, only to be told he would deny the conversation. 'Do you have any idea about what it is Pollock might be involved in?'

'No, but he's a Government Minister running Defence, so it's bound to be something murky.'

'I was thinking about the murder trial I'm hearing.'

The DAC shook his head and confessed, 'We've been less than diligent over the deaths of Kozlowski and Ms Ortega. There's been a lot of pressure from the Home Office steering us off things.' He met Deed's eye and quickly looked away. 'Again, no one will put their hands up to that. It would just be my word against theirs. You can guess who'd be believed. Whistle-blowers aren't much in favour these days.'

'Are the police being any more diligent in investigating Jessie Rogers's death?' he asked. 'Or are they going to let rumours about my involvement swirl around until either I'm forced to recuse myself from the case or resign?'

'We are being thorough, but I don't know if there is a hidden agenda concerning you in this investigation.'

Colemore didn't offer to find out as he departed. Coop came and informed him that the witness had answered his summons. Now he wondered if Colemore was still part of some hidden agenda, if his visit was warning him to step back from trying to nail Pollock.

CHAPTER TWENTY-SEVEN

WALKING INTO COURT, he found James Pollock back to the witness box without the jury present, and every other seat in the room occupied with as many people standing in the aisles and at the side. Who were they here for, him or Pollock? The Attorney General, although not involved in this case, was on the front bench alongside Newman Mason Allen, with Jo Mills and Heathcote Machin at the opposite end. The benches behind them were more crowded, many being lawyers from the Attorney's office.

'Thank you for attending so promptly, Mr Pollock,' Deed said with strained politeness. 'You are not a participant in this trial, neither as a material witness nor a suspect...'

'Well, I'm very pleased to hear it.' Pollock glanced towards the empty jury box as if forgetting his constituency wasn't present. 'There was a window in my schedule and I'm glad to oblige as I do recognise the supremacy of the courts, my Lord,' – said like he had rehearsed this speech.

Even without a jury to influence Deed could see what this politician was endeavouring to do: own the ground. He was happy to allow this if it lulled him into a false sense of security. 'I wish to ask you some questions about the case, so I would like you to take the oath.'

'I don't know what I can tell you that has any bearing, but I'm happy to swear on the Good Book.' With a glance at the Attorney, who gave a slight nod, Pollock took the oath and then turned to the bench, as if challenging him.

'You do fully understand the significance of the oath, Mr Pollock?' he asked, as if dealing with someone of limited intelligence.

'Of course,' the Minister replied and laughed, again glancing at the Attorney, who seemed on edge as he waited, as if anticipating something unpleasant.

'I wish to ask you again about your relationship with the now deceased defendant, Mariana Ortega.'

'I told you before,' Pollock snapped, 'I don't know this woman.'

'I remind you of the oath you've just taken,' Deed said, 'and ask you to consider carefully before you answer. Perjury is a serious crime. The Romans used to throw people off the Tarpeian Rock for perjury. A term of imprisonment is enough to deter citizens today.'

This angered the witness, as Deed knew it would. Pollock glowered up at the bench. 'You do seem determined to ruin my reputation, Sir John. How many times have I got to tell you? If you've got some evidence, bring it on.'

'My Lord,' the Attorney said, rising and adjusting his robes, 'the usual procedure, should there be any evidence against Mr Pollock, is for it to be presented to the police and tested by the Crown Prosecution Service.'

'I am aware of the procedure, Sir Alan,' Deed replied in an even tone. 'I can assure you I've no intention of straying beyond my authority. Mr Pollock, I ask you again, what was your relationship with Ms Ortega?'

'I'll go on telling you until I'm blue in the face, I didn't have one.'

'Then would you care to look at this recording from a CCTV camera and tell the court if this in fact you?' he said, galvanising everyone present. 'Mr Usher?'

The usher dragged the television monitor forward and took the disc from Deed, inserting it into the player. There wasn't a murmur in the room as the machine whirred and an image appeared of the entrance to the block of flats in Wimbledon. An unknown person passed under the camera and disappeared, then about thirty seconds elapsed which seemed like a lifetime and made Deed anxious: what if the image wasn't there, if it had somehow been wiped? He could only imagine what Pollock was feeling right then, knowing how he felt when Detective Supt Maheson implied he was involved in Jessie Rogers' death. This man, being a consummate politician, showed no emotion. When at last the image of Pollock appeared showing him coming into Brunswick House with Mariana Ortega, anger exploded from him.

'This is a fucking outrage,' he said, appealing to the press gallery before turning his invective on Deed. 'It's the worst abuse of power. That's doctored, a complete construct for your own political agenda, to save you having to resign. It's an abuse of power. I won't tolerate it a moment longer.' Pollock flew out of the witness box and headed for the exit and might have made it but for the crowd impeding him.

'Officer, lock the doors!' Deed instructed. 'No one leaves this court until I say they can.'

'More abuse of your unbridled power,' the Defence Minister shouted to those around him as if expecting them to assail the bench and pull Deed down.

Throughout this the Attorney was on his feet demanding to know the provenance of the recording, but Deed ignored him. This was between Pollock and himself. 'Please return to the witness box, Mr Pollock.'

'I won't be subjected to your political agenda, sir. I will not.'

'I have no agenda other than to uncover the truth,' Deed said, finding difficulty in staying on course in the face of such provocation. 'You will either return to the witness box and I will resume this examination, or you'll be conveyed forthwith to the cells for contempt.'

'More abuse of power! Why do we put up with this rubbish from wretched left-wing judges?' Again appealing to those in court, but getting no response.

'I would ask you to consider who you are dealing with,' the Attorney said. 'Mr Pollock is a senior minister in Her Majesty's Government, a politician of unimpeachable integrity, not some common-or-garden criminal.'

'In this court, Sir Alan, everyone is equal under the law and is treated with equal respect, provided they show the court respect. No one is above or below anyone else until a jury deems otherwise. Mr Pollock has a simple choice. He can return to the witness box and answer my questions or be taken to the cells and from there in the van to Brixton Prison.'

'It is an abuse of power,' Pollock said again, returning to the witness box.

Deed waited and considered ignoring him but knew he must disabuse him of his misconception or the Attorney would press the point. 'It is not an abuse of power, Mr Pollock. The judge in a criminal trial does have the authority to call and examine a witness. The Court of Appeal in R. v. Roberts in 1984, 80 Criminal Appeal Reports at page 89, is my guide, a power to be used sparingly. Where it is exercised, it should be for achieving the ends of justice and fairness, which is what I am doing.'

'Before we proceed further with viewing this CCTV evidence which Mr Pollock says must be doctored,' the Attorney said, waving his juniors back to their seats, 'can we know its provenance?'

'It was among the possessions of Mr Kozlowski, the porter murdered within the precincts of the court centre. He was a witness in a murder trial I am hearing,' he explained for the record.

'Then possibly, my Lord, it has, as Mr Pollock suggests, been fabricated to incriminate him.'

'I've examined it in detail, so have police officers,' he said. 'We found no evidence of tampering. After Mr Pollock answers my questions, we can have it examined by both a Home Office and an independent expert.' He smiled at the Attorney and waved him back to his seat before turning to Pollock. 'As uncomfortable as this may be, please watch the rest of the tape. Mr Usher?'

They watched in silence save for exaggerated sighs from the man in the witness box as the usher fast-forwarded to a point where the Defence Minister appeared again with Ms Ortega, smiling like a man who had had a good time. It was then Deed realised Pollock was wearing the suit Kozlowski had been wearing when he gave his evidence. He hadn't noticed this before.

'Do you still claim this is not you with Ms Ortega?' Deed asked.

'Well, of course it's me,' Pollock snapped. 'Any biased fool can see that. What's clear is that it's not me in relation to that woman. The image has been manipulated to put me there with your connivance.'

Patience now wearing thin, Deed struggled not to go where Pollock clearly wished him to go. 'I hoped it wouldn't be necessary, but we will have the tape forensically examined.' He switched lanes without any signal and said, 'Did you give Mr Kozlowski one of your suits, Mr Pollock, the one you were wearing in that captured footage?'

'No, of course not. I didn't know this man. I've said that, how many times must I repeat it? I wear suits from Marks and Spencer.'

'I see.' He struggled to keep irritation out of his voice. 'Mr Usher, wind back to the image of Mr Pollock so we can get a closer look at his suit?' He waited as the machine whirred and stopped on Pollock. By chance he chose a frame showing a clear image of this. 'Perhaps you could tell me the branch of M&S you shop at. I'd like to get one of their suits if they look that good.'

'My Lord, is it necessary to humiliate the Defence Minister in this way?'

'I'm doing no such thing, Sir Alan. I'm trying to establish the truth.' He turned to the witness. 'Mr Pollock, was Mr Kozlowski blackmailing you?'

If Pollock wasn't such an egotist who had to spout off the whole while his ministerial colleague might have beaten him to the punch. 'That's ridiculous, of course not,' Pollock insisted before the Attorney was up saying, 'He shouldn't answer that in case it later incriminates him.'

'No, of course he shouldn't, Sir Alan, but he has,' Deed said and turned back to Pollock. 'Are you sure this wasn't the circumstance? A sexual encounter which possibly led you to Brunswick House and led to some form of blackmail isn't an indictable offence, however inconvenient for a politician who happens to be married.'

There was a long pause from the man in the witness box and Deed could almost see Pollock's brain calculating his response. Whether he could think of nothing plausible or considered the odds not favourable, he stuck to his position. 'No, I didn't know this damned Kozlowski and he wasn't blackmailing me.'

Deed gave him look, thinking he was a fool. So many men were fools for women, himself included – Jessie jumped into his thoughts; what might await him at Holborn Police Station. Snapping back to the present he saw Pollock watching him, unflinching. Covering his microphone, he turned to Coop to ask for the parcel she'd brought into court. Opening the bag she placed the onyx Buddha on the bench where Pollock could see it. This momentarily broke his stare and his eyes flicked away from it and a nerve by his left eye twitched.

'Do you recognise this, Mr Pollock?' he asked.

'What kind of cunting stroke is this?' Pollock demanded. 'What the fuck are you trying to do to me?'

The Attorney was back on his feet looking for damage-limitation. 'Again, my Lord, I must ask what sort of trial you're conducting? The minister has not been charged with anything.'

'Sir Alan, truth is my only driver...'

'Your perverted fucking truth,' Pollock cut in with great vehemence and again he turned to the gallery looking for support.

'I've given you a lot of leeway, Mr Pollock,' he said, 'not because of who you are, but in order to be fair. You stand in contempt and the court would like an apology from you.'

'It's me who wants a fucking apology,' Pollock batted back. 'putting up with all your snide behaviour. You're deeply embroiled in the murder of that girl at the hotel so you try to pull me into another murder trial to direct attention away from you. Either put up or shut up.'

The buzz flying around the court was like the rasp of a chainsaw and he found as much difficulty ignoring it as he did Pollock's statement. It was obvious he was privy to the police investigation and Deed wondered what else he'd been told. The Attorney buried his attention in his papers, wanting no part of this. Somehow Deed knew he needed to restore order; adjourning wouldn't do it. Reaching for the onyx Buddha in its exhibits bag, he lifted it in his palm and the court quietened, expectantly. 'This we believe is the missing murder weapon in the trial I'm currently hearing. It is likely to have the murderer's finger-prints, as well as the victim's and those of the deceased defendant. These we can eliminate. Would you voluntarily agree to being finger-printed and giving a saliva sample for a DNA test, Mr Pollock?' As soon the words were out Deed knew this was a mistake; he might be asked the same in relation to the murder of Jessie Rogers and was creating a precedent for not refusing.

'The bollocks I would,' Pollock said. 'I've just about had enough of this shit.' With that he crashed out of the witness box and charged for the exit, which was still locked. He rattled the heavy door. 'Are you going to let me out, or are you just going to throw your weight around like some Stasi bully? Make the most of it because I guarantee this time tomorrow you won't be in post.'

That started the chainsaw buzz again. Speaking above it, Deed said, 'Mr Pollock, you're going to be taken to the cells, and then to Brixton Prison. There you will stay until you purge your contempt. I will ask the police to obtain your fingerprints and a DNA sample.'

'I'll be there about five minutes before a more senior Judge lets me out,' Pollock said. 'That I guarantee.'

'Yes, of course,' Deed conceded and waved on the police officers. 'If he gives you any trouble, handcuff him.'

The Defence Minister was taken out protesting and, issuing more threats against Deed, who he said was being charged with murder. He almost got crushed in the rush of journalists scrambling to file their story. There was nowhere to go then. Deed adjourned and would resume the trial if and when he got Pollock's DNA sample and fingerprints to compared with those on the Buddha. This of course would be dependent upon whether or not he was still a High Court judge.

Jo came to see him in his room, very distraught. 'John, the whole building is awash with rumours about you being charged with the murder of your marshal. It's causing more excitement than what happened to Pollock.'

'Yes, who'll care about his possible involvement in a murder case when the judge becomes a suspect in another?'

'That's nonsense, it won't run, it can't.'

The note of uncertainty in her voice caused him to hesitate, unsure how much to tell her. When finally he told her everything her long silence unsettled him.

'What a bloody fool you are,' she said at last, her despairing tone suggesting she had reached the end with him. 'It beggars belief that someone as intelligent as you could behave so stupidly. You know they will have you out of office, even if they don't actually manage to send you to prison.'

'Nothing in all of this wounds me as much as you not believing me.'

Shaking her head, Jo said, 'I don't know what to believe anymore – oh, not your sexual shenanigans, we've seen plenty of those, but the way you handled this. Did it never occur to you that your sexual obsession might one day destroy you?'

'Obsession doesn't work like that, Jo,' Deed told her. 'You don't reason it out and weigh it in the balance; it so often takes you over.'

Her anger rose as she said, 'Then you're not fit to be a judge and the sooner you resign the better.' With that she slammed out of the room.

Not often was he given to shaking but her hostility tore through him. She was right, but what hurt him more was his good friend and on-off lover not dismissing the idea of his involvement out of hand. A few moments later Coop came into the room with some tea for him.

'Is Mrs Mills all right, Judge? She flew past me without a word.'

'No, Coop, all is not well in her world, or mine. Perhaps it's time I thought about delivering that resignation letter.'

Coop became subdued and he thought she might cry. Instead, quietly setting the tray down and straightening her back she looked him directly in the eye.

'Forgive me for saying so, but that's stupid, Judge. I know you had absolutely nothing to do with that young woman's death. Anyone who thinks so is either barmy or malicious. There are plenty of both who want to pay you back, but we won't let them, Judge.' With that she poured some tea, taking the cup she had brought in for Jo Mills.

With a slow nod, he said, 'Thank you, Coop,' – feeling humble and grateful. As much as he appreciated her support it didn't change his predicament one jot.

Sir Ian Rochester was his next visitor and he wondered what had taken him so long. Perhaps he was waiting for Jo to leave. He came, he said, to ask if Supt Hamblyn could now be released – as if having a

Government minister in custody meant a lesser hostage could be freed. Having these in prison would have been as serious a worry to the Permanent Secretary. Sending Government ministers to gaol for contempt wasn't something that happened every day, though should have more frequently for the contempt they so often showed the electorate.

Deed said he'd heard nothing from the detective superintendent that suggested she wanted to apologise and purge her contempt. 'She can stay in another night, Ian. If I'm approached tomorrow, I'll hear her apology.'

'Will there be a tomorrow for any of us, John?' Rochester said in his most solicitous fashion, showing a sly smile. 'Setting the judiciary in direct conflict with the Executive can do none of us any good. I daresay you will have a stream of important people queuing in the corridor waiting to advise you to release Mr Pollock forthwith.'

'They will all receive the same response, Ian,' – more determined than ever to follow through with this. 'He'll stay banged-up until he purges his contempt.'

'He won't do that, John,' Rochester said, changing his tone. 'I beg you for the sake of good governance, step back, show that the greater good is prized above personality.'

'It's the greater good I'm pursuing. I imagined you of all people would have appreciated that. However important James Pollock is to Government, however great for British business, he's not above the law. Without the rule of law, without the supremacy of the courts, we'd have something little better than the so-called Islamic State, no values, no principles, just a depraved rabble ripping at one another's throats for ascendancy.'

There was a long silence before Rochester pulled himself to his full height and said, 'I take it you do not intend to allow a retrial to take place in view of the current circumstance concerning yourself?' Deed let his look stand as his answer. 'Then I think it only fair to tell you, my Lord, the Attorney General is approaching the Lord Chief Justice on behalf of the Government to have the Defence Minister released.'

'The Chief might even release him,' Deed said with a resigned smile.

Were that to happen he believed it would be a significant body-blow to the independence of the judiciary and a tentative step on a downward path towards corporate governance. This thought depressed him, but they'd be no better off if he acceded to the Government's wishes – he might considerably improve his own position. Pausing, he reflected how far he had fallen from his possible elevation to the Appellate Bench. That was unlikely to happen now no matter how well his interview at Holborn Police Station came out.

Later, back at his room at the Law Courts, Joe Channing came to see him in an animated state and told him the Lord Chief Justice didn't make a knee-jerk response, but insisted on reading the court transcripts before giving his decision. 'He said there was clear contempt, John, and refused to release Pollock.'

'Did he refuse leave for them to apply elsewhere?' Deed asked.

'This may cause our brethren to unite as never before. The Defence Minister stays in Brixton Prison until he purges his contempt. A good day for justice, I'd say. Now you must deal with this despicable attempt to undermine your authority as a judge.'

That was the rock upon which Deed knew he might yet perish. His authority was undermined, his reputation damaged and couldn't be fully restored whatever the outcome of the police investigation.

CHAPTER TWENTY-EIGHT

❦

HAUGHTON WAITED AS HIS number-two secretary, whose name he wasn't sure of, poured coffee for everyone and withdrew. He could barely contain his excitement. 'It might have been precipitous of me to have ordered champagne – Dom Perignon, rather than Waitrose coffee.'

'It's just turned eight A.M., Neil,' James Pollock replied, spooning three heaps of sugar into his cup. 'Deed could turn us all into dipsos.'

Some of those present laughed, including Rochester and Detective Supt Maheson, but neither Sir Percy, DAC Colemore nor his note-taking secretary did so. Colemore he understood, being a former friend of Deed's, and perhaps his Permanant Secretary, who would doubtless miss the excitement when he slipped off to Justice without him. 'We're absolutely certain about the evidence standing up?'

'Well, sir,' the detective started, glancing at Colemore, 'nothing's ever absolute in police work. The CPS think there's enough to charge him.'

'I talked to the senior lawyer there, Neil,' Sir Alan Peasmarsh said, combing his long hair. 'They'll wait to see the transcript after the police interview Deed.'

'He had both motive and opportunity to kill that girl,' Pollock put in, 'the hypocritical bastard. That's what you're saying superintendent, and no alibi?'

'In a nutshell, sir. The message on the dead girl's phone is unequivocal. He returned to see her.'

'We don't have any CCTV footage of him returning,' DAC Colemore pointed out.

'Well, I think you'd make a point of avoiding the cameras sneaking back for what he planned,' Pollock said and swallowed some coffee. It was a done deal for him, and Haughton was on board.

'As attractive as the prospect of bringing Deed down is, Neil,' the Attorney said, 'I wouldn't counsel arrest at this point. Have someone talk to him and get him to resign first. It would be less damaging to the judiciary and the Government were it to go wrong. But at least you'd be rid of an irksome judge.'

'What could go wrong?' Pollock wanted to know.

'Many things in my experience, Minister,' Rochester said. 'I think Sir Alan's approach would be the most sensible.'

'Would you advise Deed on his honourable course, Ian?'

'He's unlikely to heed my advice, Home Secretary. Perhaps I might brief Joe Channing for this one. If we showed him the evidence, he might persuade Deed to do the decent thing. When he learns of the Defence Minister's release from prison, he'll realise there's no support for him anywhere.'

'Excellent, give it a try. After all, we're not vindictive,' Haughton said, smacking his hands together. Turning to Colemore, 'Your lot should go on with their investigation, but hold off approaching Deed until the Lord Chief Justice has accepted his resignation. Excellent.'

There was another surprise for Deed when he arrived at court and Coop said, 'You haven't heard, Judge? James Pollock was released from Brixton late last night after an appeal to the President of the Supreme Court.'

Deed stared at her in disbelief at the audacity of whoever had bypassed the Chief's refusal. This meant he had but two choices, to go quietly or dig in for a fight, even though he might be less and less effective in the latter approach. Worse, he knew he'd be even less effective if he was off the bench. He felt slightly nauseous as he tried to think through his next move. Perhaps he had been arrogant and headstrong in sending the minister to gaol, but the contempt was profound and confirmed by the Lord Chief Justice. What had happened to change that, he wondered, as anger now began pushing away the sick feeling?

'It was on the news this morning,' Coop was saying, 'and about the police needing to interview you about Jessie.'

'Do we have any further details?' he asked. He eschewed news broadcasts during a trial, especially one with potential for controversy.

Coop knew only what was on the *Today Programme* this morning. Joe Channing wasn't available when he rang him, nor was the Lord Chief Justice, whose secretary told him as far as she knew the application to release the minister was from the Home Office. He might have guessed Haughton was involved.

Trying and failing to reach Rochester in the Justice Department, Deed's feeling of paranoia expanded, along with his sense of isolation. Next, he tried his ex-wife, who answered her cell phone in her familiar brusque manner as she headed into chambers. She was surprised to hear him.

'John! Are you still free? I thought you'd be in clink by now.'

'Is it that bad, George? I only put a Government minister in a cell for contempt.'

'Along with half the Met, is what I hear. If I was advising you it would be to tell you to pack a bag and run,' she said like she was enjoying herself.

'What would I be running from?'

'Powerful people with long knives and longer memories.'

'Lover boy prominent among them, I'd guess?' Deed speculated.

'Well, you have thwarted him on a number of occasions. You must have known Neil would eventually get even.'

'Pollock showed the court blatant contempt, even the Chief agreed.'

'That's the least of your problems. Neil says the police have evidence enough to charge you with the murder of your young researcher. I don't believe for a moment you'd kill a beautiful young woman to cover your sexual indiscretion. Why would you bother?'

'There was no sexual indiscretion. I made my excuses and left.'

'That must be a first. It won't matter one bit to them. By the time they've finished dragging you through the mill you wouldn't even be able to get a job driving for Deliveroo,' she said. 'Gotta go, got a con starting. Just watch your back, chum.'

Before he had time to absorb this information the door was rapped and Joe Channing pushed in past Coop and gave her a look that suggested she should leave. Coop took the hint.

Without prelusive niceties Joe Channing said, 'You must resign forthwith.'

'For putting a contemptuous Government minister in gaol?' Deed tried.

'Rochester came to see me to discuss your untenable position and the damage your staying on will almost certainly do to the bench.'

'You know me, Joe, I'm likely to go down fighting,' he said, putting on a bold face while inside he was wailing.

'I wouldn't advise it, John. Rochester showed me the evidence the police have connecting you to the killing of that beautiful young woman.'

'You believed it?' Deed said.

'What I may or may not believe has no relevance, it's what a jury might be inclined to believe. The police have been thorough and intend to charge you. Only the Attorney's intervention has stopped them thus far. You must do the decent thing and deal with this away from the bench.' He slid a manila folder onto the desk and distractedly lit a cigarette. 'That's the main thrust of their evidence. Rochester gave me a copy. You might like to take a view when you've read it and consider instructing someone to defend you.' It was then he noticed his lighted cigarette and squeezed it out in the waste paper bin.

His departure left Deed feeling betrayed. Here was a colleague, a senior judge, who less than twenty-four hours ago was prepared to defend him. Just below betrayal was a deep, gnawing fear that clutched at his intestines and cramped his stomach. Despite what he knew to be the truth he feared the system would fail him as it failed many before who were innocent of that with which they'd been charged. He realised what a sorry admission this was having both supported the institution and fought it all his working life.

Jo Mills was someone to defend him, only he wasn't sanguine about that in view of their history and the manner of her departure. Trying her number anyway, he got her voicemail and hesitated before saying, 'Jo, I need to talk to you urgently.' He realised she may be in court awaiting his arrival.

'Judge, are you all right?' Coop asked coming into the room. 'You look dreadful. Should I call a doctor?'

'An undertaker might be more appropriate. It seems I might be moments away from being arrested, unless I resign first.'

'That's ridiculous.'

'Coop, don't stay out of misplaced loyalty. You've got a career at the MoJ to think about.'

'If anyone there believes this about you, I wouldn't want to be associated with them. You've got to fight them, Judge. You must.'

'Yes, Coop, but how long I can hold out..?'

'Long enough to deal with an urgent request from Supt Hamblyn,' she told him. 'She wants to apologise.'

'I wonder why,' he said vacantly; then it hit him. 'Get her in as soon as you can.'

Coop started out, and then turned back with, 'Judge, would you like me to ask Jake – Sergeant Bridges – to review the police evidence?'

'I'm not sure what he'd find that would help. His senior colleagues have been pretty thorough. It could bring career risks for him.'

'He wouldn't worry about that.'

'I would, Coop.'

'He'd do it for me like a shot.'

He paused to study this woman, wondering what he'd done to deserve such loyalty, other than on occasion make the dry law a little more interesting. 'Thank you, Coop,' he said again.

As she went out Sir Ian Rochester pushed in unbidden. If ever there was an indication of his demise it was reflected in this man's present attitude.

'Thanks to your legal arrogance, my Lord,' Rochester said with great emphasis on his title, 'it seems we shall lose a champion for British arms manufacturing. Your hounding Pollock has all but ruined him and caused such stress it will almost certainly result in our losing a massive arms sale to Saudi Arabia. I'm to inform you that when Haughton comes to the MoJ his number one priority will be to curtail the unfettered and much abused power of judges.'

'Until he pulls off that particular trick, and there's no guarantee he will,' Deed responded in the same calm tone Salibi employed in dangerous situations, 'you will show my office the respect it's due or you too will be in a cell for contempt.'

'Yes, of course, my Lord,' – using the same emphasis and stepping back, as if fearing he might seize him and throw him into gaol personally. 'That curtailment of powers is likely to happen despite your anticipated resignation.'

'You might have a long wait for that,' Deed informed him.

'The alternative is certain to be your arrest, in which case the Chief would be obliged to advise the Queen to sack you from the bench.'

'What happened to the presumption of innocence, or is that going out the window along with judges' unfettered powers?' In his anger Deed began to see a strategy to outmanoeuvre these people. 'You might go and tell your soon-to-be new minister that in the event I would talk openly to the media about the shenanigans of this dishonest cabal at the heart of Government.'

'Who would believe someone facing a murder charge?'

'It's likely that I'd be believed over corrupt Government ministers. There would be a great weight of provable facts to back my statement,' Deed said. 'Be assured, it's not an idle threat. Would they survive? Could they survive such an onslaught, Ian? I doubt it, or you for that matter.'

'I'm entirely impartial in this matter.'

'The shoe rather pinches on that foot. I suggest you leave and inform

Haughton that his trusted colleague has a prima facie case to answer over the death of Peter Bartlett. This will be something for another judge and jury to determine. Meanwhile, I have a trial I am conducting.'

'I would strongly advise you not to proceed a step further, Sir John.'

'You know my answer. And I want Pollock back in court to apologise.'

The Mandarin waited a moment, but thought better of arguing further.

'God, I've never seen that side of Sir Ian,' Coop said after Rochester's departure, and stepped forward off the wall where she had been making herself all but invisible. 'He was very rude, Judge. You should've banged him up. Can Mr Haughton change the power of judges when he goes to the MoJ?'

'They will make life very difficult for him if he tries.' He noticed his clerk's worried expression. She had been through a lot of his fights with the Executive, none greater than the one he now faced. He didn't want to worry her more, but wouldn't exclude her. 'This could be the start of open warfare. As the great constitutional lawyer Dicey said at the beginning of the last century, although legislation is manifestly the work of Parliament, over 50 per cent of what the Acts mean is delivered in court judgments. Now more than ever we must ensure an independent judiciary is strong enough to protect justice from political malfeasance. There's not much we can do about what they send to us, especially with senior law officers being part of the Government, and most of those being partial.' It was a bleak prospect and he wasn't optimistic about his brethren being united. He may yet be surprised as he had been with the Lord Chief Justice initially agreeing with him banging up Pollock. The ground was still shifting and 'they' controlled all the mechanisms of justice, and with higher ranked judges trumping him by releasing the minister from gaol.

CHAPTER TWENTY-NINE

❧

The urgent meeting with Deed requested by Supt Hamblyn wasn't just to apologise for her behaviour in court. This she did with appropriate humility, which surprised Deed, who at once released her from the contempt. It was then she revealed the reason for the urgency. She had been in the cell next to the one the Defence Minister occupied on the segregation wing in Brixton Prison and heard him speaking on his phone.

'I'd have been surprised if they had deprived a Government minister of his phone,' Deed said cautiously, wondering where was she going with this.

'Mr Pollock was speaking in Arabic. I'm not fluent, sir, but I understand enough to know I was hearing threats to your person,' she said, galvanizing him. 'I'm certain he said, they should make a better job of things if they had to go after you again.'

A cold chill washed over Deed as he thought about the bomb threats and the man who almost suffocated him with a plastic bag. 'Apart from speaking Arabic, were there any other clues to the person's identity?' This was a day for shocks and he had an uneasy feeling about the person issuing threats somehow being involved in the other murders.

'No, sir. If I started to investigate the minister's contacts it might cause the suspect to run. Certainly alarm bells would start ringing if we get GCHQ to run checks of his phone.'

'Then what do you suggest should be done, Superintendent?'

'Increase your personal protection, sir. I will make the discreetest of inquiries without alerting anyone, hopefully.'

The paranoid world he was penetrating more deeply left him uncertain about trusting this policewoman. He hoped he was wrong about her, but unease was causing tension to bunch in the back of his neck.

'Tell me, is this Judge complete fucking loon, Neil?' James Pollock demanded as he stamped around the room.

Haughton didn't have a simple answer, not to the question he suspected the Defence Minister was really asking. He glanced over at Sir

Ian Rochester, hoping he would offer a solution. None was forthcoming.

'You know what I think?' Pollock continued, turning to Sir Alan Peasmarsh who was dropping dead hair from his comb onto the rug, 'we should forget what it might do to the judiciary, Alan, and simply arrest the fucker and haul him in. We will just have to live with the scandal.'

'I fear he's right, Alan,' Haughton ventured, without insisting. 'We don't want Deed to be seen to be getting away with it.'

'Well, you're the Home Secretary, Neil,' Peasmarsh responded. 'The police are yours to direct as you will. As Attorney I only advise on law.'

'Any thoughts, Ian?'

'Nothing much else will bring Deed to heel, Home Secretary,' Rochester said. 'The evidence seems to be sound.'

'Of course it's sound.' Pollock was red in the face and looked like he was about to burst blood vessels in his head.

'I fear it's the only course left open to us.'

There was no effective alternative to this dangerous course, yet still Haughton was reluctant to give his assent. Everyone in the room was waiting for his lead. His throat suddenly went dry as he hesitated and was afraid to speak. Finally he nodded at Sir Percy Thrower. 'Get it done, will you, Percy?'

The Permanent Secretary jerked out of his torpor like a knife had been thrust between his shoulder blades and Haughton thought he heard a distressed squawk, but it may have been Jim Pollock chortling.

Deed knew the bluffing was over when Coop informed him that Sir Ian Rochester was on his way to see him with Detective Superintendent Maheson from Scotland Yard. It was clear what that meant.

'Coop, see if Mrs Mills is in court.'

'She is, Judge, with Mr Machin. I'll get her.' She went out quickly, knowing what was about to happen.

Perhaps Heathcote Machin might have been a better person to advise him over what would be his defence. It would be meaningless anyway, for once the charge was laid it was game over.

'They wouldn't dare, John,' Jo said after he briefed her, 'would they?' She sounded incredulous and this worried him. 'Have you got something to counter their so-called evidence?'

'That's not the point, is it?'

'Do you want me here when the fuzz arrives?'

'Unless you go out through the window you won't be able to avoid them. Coop informed me the detective is in the building with Rochester.'

'Oh, I bet he's enjoying this.'

'Along with other members of the Executive, I dare say.'

'I'm finding it difficult to take seriously.'

'I wish I could.' Outwardly he appeared in control, but was nothing of the sort.

Rochester was surprised to find Jo present, but he seemed to have grown in stature from the five-foot-six, his thinning grey hair springier, his complexion less sallow. Maybe Deed hadn't noticed these things before, only his suits. They were always immaculate. That took him right back to the immaculately-tailored suit the dead porter had been wearing in court. His questioning the provenance of that had set this whole chain of events in train, and he remained convinced it had been made for James Pollock.

'Ah, Mrs Mills,' Rochester said and shifted awkwardly, 'how nice.'

'I've asked her to stay. You stay too, please, Coop.'

Rochester glanced round at his clerk where she stood in front of the door as to stop anyone leaving. 'It falls upon me, sadly, to inform you, Sir John, that the police are going to charge you with the murder of Jessie Rogers.'

Both Jo Mills and Coop let out a derisive 'Humph!' which caused Rochester to look round to the policeman accompanying him. 'Superintendent?'

'Yes, sir. In order to avoid publicity, I'm going to ask you to attend Holborn Police Station at 6 P.M. this evening, Sir John, where the charge will be read, if that's all right, sir? You will be able to have your legal representative present. That might seem strange in view of who you are, sir, but in the circumstances, I would advise you have someone there.'

'I'll be there, with my lawyer,' Deed said, then as an afterthought, added, 'and my publicist.'

'I'm sure that won't be necessary, Sir John,' Rochester said.

'I'm sure it will. I warned you the gloves would come off. Now if you'll excuse me, I have a trial to conduct.'

'No, that's not possible,' Rochester said, losing composure, 'the Attorney is stopping the trial.'

'He does so at his peril,' Deed warned. 'I am a High Court judge; the only way I can be stopped is by impeachment. Good luck with that, if your boss wants to take me on. Under the Judges (Enquiry) Act of 1968 he needs a Parliamentary Committee to examine the issue, and then a vote by two-thirds of either House to approve it. If the Lord Chancellor can do that before day's end I'd be amazed.'

'The decent thing would have been for you to resign, Sir John, and spare any embarrassment and scandal,' Rochester said.

'That might spare you and this craven Government, but then it's not either of you fighting for your life. This audience is over, gentlemen.'

'Wow, I love your casual bravado, John,' Jo said when Coop showed Rochester and the detective out. 'Are you seriously intending to continue with the murder trial today?'

Deed laughed louder and longer than the situation called for, feeling relieved that he hadn't been hauled off to the police station. 'I doubt the trial would have my undivided attention, and doubt Pollock would answer my summons. No, I shall try to work on my defence.'

'Perhaps I should too,' Jo said. 'I'll check with you after lunch.'

'Jo,' he began, but didn't know how to go on. There was so much he wanted to tell her, but wasn't sure here and now was appropriate. He watched her go with a grim smile.

Perhaps now was time to abandon John Deed, to walk away and forget he was ever part of her life. Jo felt despair and desolation at the prospect but knew it was for her own salvation to do so. She had been through many emotional highs and lows with Deed, none with the potential to destroy him like this could. Most ups and downs were personal, matters of the heart, almost all related to his sexual waywardness, and despite them she had come close to marrying him on two separate occasions. Perhaps if they had married he wouldn't be in this fix, only she doubted it. She thought long and hard about walking away and not helping him, and each time she tried to go in that direction she found she couldn't move forward.

Nothing she had faced with him in the past had alarmed her as much as this situation, and nothing about it improved for hearing Row Colemore lay out the evidence as he paced in his stark, partitioned room that reflected nothing of the elegant '30s façade to New Scotland Yard. As she listened something niggled at her about what he was telling her. The DAC's apparent sympathy and frequent sighs like he was suffering too weren't helping her to bring whatever it was to the fore to analyse.

She assumed her emotional involvement was blocking her and for that reason decided maybe she wasn't the person to defend Deed.

'The very best advice I can give, Jo, is for him to get a good lawyer,' the DAC said. 'But John's smart enough to know that faced with all this evidence.'

'Something's wrong here, Row. You're a good detective – come on, what is it?'

'It's a long while since I was a detective. All I can see are reams of evidence going from A-to-B-to-C-to-D-to-E. I could go right through the alphabet; it doesn't help him.'

It was then she got what was wrong and feared she may have somehow revealed her hand when Colemore gave her a quizzical look with, 'Jo?'

'Oh, nothing,' she responded, staring him straight in the eye. 'Too emotionally involved. I don't want to believe it.'

'Exactly my sentiments. I'm a policeman, and evidence as neat as this is pretty damning.'

There, he said it. The neatness of the evidence was what troubled her. 'Have you interrogated the evidence, Row?'

'I have – as much as I dare. My bosses know I'm friends with John. The only conclusion I can come to is what stares at me from these pages.'

'I've got to go,' Jo said, quickly getting from the armchair in his office that looked onto the side of the adjacent Norman Shaw building. Grabbing her briefcase, she started away. 'I might come back to you, if I may.'

'Any time,' he said. 'I'll show you out.'

'That's all right, Row, I'll follow the line of breadcrumbs I left on my way in.'

She fled along the recently partitioned corridor with its look of impermanence and found herself on a similar corridor that didn't lead her to the lifts. Jo felt desperate to get out of the oppressive, dissembling atmosphere of the building and wasn't convinced she could even believe the young woman pushing a file trolley who directed her. Outside on the Embankment she was able to breathe again and hailed a black cab to take her back to Southwark and Deed.

There she was as uncomfortable as she had felt with Row Colemore. It was like a cloud of depression had enfolded Deed and he was no longer reachable. Jo could understand that, faced with what he now faced.

'John!' she said firmly to get his attention, 'I can see what an uphill battle this is, but for what it's worth, I know you didn't kill that young barrister, despite all the police evidence.'

'Then you're a fool,' he told her bluntly. 'You know no such thing. All you have is my word.'

'Your word should be enough for anyone,' she argued with more emotion than logic, realising how much she still loved this man, despite his faults and probably because of them. They made him human and vulnerable and there weren't many High Court judges who allowed that, and none like him. 'I've been examining the evidence Row showed me. I'm a criminal barrister and I've seen lots of police evidence, but this is all too neat and placed to be a random collection. In the words of an old lag, it's a fit-up.'

'Maybe,' Deed said, 'but it doesn't change my current predicament.'

'It would if we can bust through this arrangement of police evidence.'

'Before 6 P.M. this evening? Fat chance.'

'We could show a vindictive motive for such a move,' Jo said. 'If your instincts are right the papers belonging to Anita Plant I gave you for safe-keeping, which you gave to Joe Channing, could help.'

'What might they reveal that would stop this? Once I walk into that police station this evening, it's over.'

'We'll stop it. There must be recordings of you leaving the hotel, showing times that put you elsewhere while Jessie Rogers was ringing you when her door was knocked. The thrust of the police evidence is it was you returning. Their case collapses if we can show you were elsewhere. If the police are withholding those tapes they will be in serious trouble.'

'All they need do is 'discover' them after my arrest. It happens all the while. They'll apologise, but by then the damage is done.'

'Row Colemore must know if recordings exist and where they are,' Jo said.

Not once did the DAC meet her eye when she went back to his office to challenge him about the evidence. He argued the neatness of evidence was due to police being ultra-thorough in view of who the suspect was. Hearing the word 'suspect' had a strangely disturbing effect on Jo, yet at the same time energised her to push harder.

'The CCTV cameras at the hotel must show John leaving and the time in relation to the time of her call to him.'

'I wish it were that easy, Jo. There is no CCTV footage, the lobby cameras were down,' Colemore said, again not meeting her look.

Growing more sceptical by the moment, she said, 'There must be other cameras showing his whereabouts. London is full of cameras. We're more watched than the citizens of Pyongyang.'

'Why would the police look for those? It's not their job to show he's innocent.'

With her jaw almost hitting her chest in surprise at this, Jo took a moment to recover. 'You ought to be deeply ashamed, Row. John was once your friend. You should be moving heaven and earth to help him.' Without bothering to hear his pathetic justification she got up and left, easily finding her way out of the labyrinthine building this time.

CHAPTER THIRTY

THE PAPERS DEED PASSED TO Joe Channing for safe-keeping related to a massive bribe organised by the Defence Minister. The British Government paid an arms dealer to facilitate the sale of £40 billion's worth of planes and tanks to the Qataris, one that was likely to badly piss-off the Saudis, with whom Pollock was trying to foment another huge arms deal. The Oxfam field worker, Anita Plant, readily gave Jo Mills permission to use the contents of the contentious document against the Government in Deed's defence. The man who received the payment was Mansour Salibi's boss.

'This might deepen both Pollock's predicament and the Government's, Jo,' Deed said, intrigued but not surprised, 'but it still doesn't improve my situation.'

'It might if we show Government ministers desperate to keep this closed up,' Jo argued. 'Maybe the Lebanese man can help.'

'It would all go towards my defence but won't stop my reputation and career ending up in ruins. And Salibi would get booted to Saudi.'

Forgetting formality, Coop burst into his room in a state of excitement with, 'Judge, Judge, Jake Bridges made some enquiries at the Shell garage on the roundabout from Chelsea Bridge where you stopped that night. When he tried to get the recordings from their CCTV cameras the manager told him he couldn't give them up without a warrant.'

'Quite right, Coop.'

'Jake tried to get one, but his superiors must have alerted someone in the Home Office. When he went back to the garage…'

'No recordings,' Jo said. 'It's getting to be a habit!'

'He was told the police already collected them,' Coop informed him. 'Can't you make the police show you what's on the tapes?'

'I can request that, and they would certainly have to disclose them in evidence.'

'That could take weeks,' Jo said.

'It's certainly not going to happen before six o'clock today.'

'There must be some way to get them,' Coop said, growing more agitated with her frustration. 'Wouldn't Deputy Assistant Commissioner Colemore get them for you? He's a friend, after all.'

'That begs the question, Coop,' Deed said.

'Another High Court judge could order sight of them.'

'Who do you suggest, Jo? Mr Justice Channing? At our last meeting he made in clear he thought the police evidence sound and that I should resign.'

'He might change his mind if we show him some of what you think is evidence for the defence,' she said.

'Let's see if Mr Salibi can confirm any of this,' Deed said, seeing a glimmer on his bleak horizon. 'Would you see if you can locate him, Coop, and ask him to come to my room at the Strand. Perhaps you'd better ask Superintendent Hamblyn to come there too.'

'Is that wise, John? Will Salibi talk freely in front of her – she thought he planted the bombs in our apartments?'

'If he doesn't I'm no worse off; if he does then he might improve his chances of not being packed off to Saudi Arabia. He will be if I'm not around.'

'I still don't know if you should trust this policewoman.'

'I'm not sure of her, Jo, but at this moment the only three people I trust in the world are in this room. I have to reach out to others. While we're at it we'll have a party. Get Machin along as well, Coop, and Sergeant Bridges, if he'll come.'

'Oh, he'll come all right.' His clerk flew out with renewed energy.

Jo departed with less enthusiasm for his plan; where she was going, she didn't say, he assumed back to her seedy set of chambers to check her mailbox. When he left for the Strand he met a phalanx of reporters camped at the back entrance. There was no way to avoid them other than climbing over walls and he wasn't about to do that. It was hard to ignore their questions and was tempted to give the fullest of explanations, but resisted as he escaped into a taxi.

There was an uneasy hiatus as the various parties gathered in Deed's room, with awkward glances from Salibi and Hamblyn ricocheting off each other to the amusement of Heathcote Machin. Perhaps Jo was right, mistrust preventing Salibi saying anything useful, or the detective believing it anyway. In order to break the tension as they waited for Jo to arrive, Deed brought them up to date about what had been happening, the difficulty in getting hold of evidence and the clock ticking on his career. Was this wise, as Salibi might realise with no office he might not be able to give him immunity? The excellent tea Coop served seemed little appreciated.

'Did Mrs Mills say how long she would be, Coop?'

'No, Judge, only that she was in the building and would be along directly.'

'That was fifteen minutes ago,' he pointed out, more acutely aware of time before his appointment with the police. When she arrived a short while later Tom Witham was with her and it soon became clear another High Court judge added another layer of suspicion.

'Mrs Mills persuaded me to come along here to listen to what a potential witness had to say. If I'd realised it was Mr Salibi,' Witham said with a nervousness to his manner, 'I would not have agreed to be present. You might conduct yourself in this way, Sir John, but I don't. Mr Salibi's in a case before me.'

'I haven't got time for your holier-than-thou attitude, Tom. Why don't you shut up and sit down,' he said brutally, 'or shall we rehearse your recent peccadillos?'

That did it. The younger judge sat on an upright chair and took a cup of tea from Coop without protest. 'Thank you. Mr Salibi, we believe you have some information that, while not bearing directly on who killed Jessie Rogers, might indicate who did. Would you mind if Mrs Mills asks you some questions?'

The Lebanese man hesitated and shifted uncomfortably in his chair, glancing first at Witham, then Superintendent Hamblyn. 'She can ask, sir. I don't know if I'll have the answers you want or if I'd answer assuming I do.'

'Let's try, shall we? Jo?'

From habit Jo got to her feet to question him. He felt it would have been better had she stayed seated, but resisted directing this.

'Mr Salibi, did you know that your employer, Mr Ali bin Talib, was named in the papers that came into Anita Plant's possession?'

Without a moment's hesitation Salibi said, 'Yes, of course.' He glanced towards Hamblyn who didn't move a muscle.

'You also know also that British Government ministers are named in those papers as being involved in paying bribes to Mr bin Talib?' Jo continued.

'I do know that.'

'Do you know which minister is named as the organiser?'

'It's Defence Minister Pollock. He and bin Talib have a mutually beneficial relationship, they've done a lot of business together,' Salibi said without hesitation.

'Yes, of course, he's the Defence Minister,' Witham put in, 'Mr bin Talib is a leading arms dealer.'

'I would prefer it, my Lord, if you didn't comment,' Jo said, 'and allow me to explore the relationship through Mr Salibi.'

'I apologise, Mrs Mills. Carry on.'

'Has any of this business involved bribery?'

'On several occasions. They've become close friends.'

'Could this friendship extend to one helping the other out of a tight corner?'

'My boss would do anything to help Secretary of State Pollock.'

'Could that extend to murder?' Jo asked.

Salibi glanced at Deed and hesitated. 'Ordinarily I would caution a witness about answering in case he incriminated himself, but as I said at the start, this entire conversation is off the record. It cannot subsequently be used.'

'Is this quite proper, Judge?' Witham asked.

'This is a quest for the truth, nothing more.'

'It was bin Talib who organised the explosives in your apartment and the judge's apartment – to stop him pursuing information about bribery.'

Deed could see Supt Hamblyn itching to ask a question and guessed what, so gave his assent. 'Mr Justice Deed said you warned him about the explosives in the television at each of the apartments,' Hamblyn said. 'Why do that if your boss had them placed there?'

'I no longer worked for him, following a big disagreement.'

'Would you tell us what about?'

Salibi hesitated and again glanced at Deed, who nodded. 'He'd been supplying arms to Middle Eastern terror groups.'

Witham was unable to stay silent and Deed took this to be a good sign. 'Is that with the knowledge of the British Government?' he asked.

'I can't tell you it was signed off by the Cabinet, but Ali bin Talib told me that Mr Pollock knew who some of the arms were destined for.'

'Is that credible, Mr Salibi? – a Government minister who has been at the forefront of the fight against these terrorists,' Witham said.

'A sale is a sale, sir.'

'Hard as this is to swallow, Tom, we mustn't lose sight of the fact these people are dealing in armaments; there's no morality here,' Deed said.

'In this relationship you describe,' Jo said, 'suggesting your ex-boss would do anything to help his friend, might this include the murder of Ms Rogers in the hotel room?'

Salibi smiled. 'From your own experience you know such things can be arranged. It's a small matter for Ali bin Talib to arrange to prevent Mr Deed drawing the Defence Minister into the murder trial he was hearing by implicating him in one of his own.'

'I cannot hear this,' Witham said, getting up. 'I'm sorry, John, any more must be heard in a formal setting.' He put his cup down and left before any further argument could be made.

Supt Hamblyn followed in just as much of a hurry and without explanation. He wondered if she was chasing after Witham to discuss the feasibility of dismissing all this – more paranoia? 'Do you need to make your excuses and leave, Mr Machin?'

'I do need to get back to chambers.' He got up, but stopped. 'If any of this comes to trial, I would like to be counsel for the defence. I can't see it happening in view of what Mansour's told you – with treachery afoot and the other side's hands on most of the controls.'

That thought depressed Deed. As plausible as Salibi was, they were in possession of no hard evidence that he could see to pull him clear, and not before 6 P.M.

'What do you say, Baba?' he asked his little dog who was looking at him quizzically when they were alone. His gaze moved on to equally familiar objects in his room, as if he were looking at them for the last time.

If he had possessed the power to instantly sack a police officer, and he believed he ought to be able to do that as Home Secretary, he would have sacked Supt Hamblyn for thwarting him. Percy Thrower cautioned against such a move, saying they would have the police Superintendents' Association up in arms. Let them, was Haughton's view, he'd happily sack the entire police union, but most especially he wanted to punish the policewoman standing before him. 'I understood you're part of the Counter Terrorism unit,' Haughton said. 'I would have thought you had plenty to contend with chasing the terrorist. Just what do you imagine you were doing interfering in the murder investigation being conducted by Superintendent Maheson?'

'Trying to help show a man is innocent, sir.'

Haughton turned his gaze to his Permanent Secretary as if he might explain the sense of this, then back to the police officer. 'That's not your job. Supposing the police attempted that with every suspect – can you imagine the cost of policing? Hand over the computer files from each of those CCTV cameras forthwith or face the consequences.'

'I no longer have them, sir,' Supt Hamblyn said. 'I passed them to a police officer to be handed to Mr Justice Deed.'

This caused anger to explode in Haughton so that he felt he might hit this idiot before him. When he spoke he could barely get his words out. 'Unbelievable, I'm incredulous. The murder suspect could destroy them.'

'But he won't, Home Secretary, as they almost certainly show how Sir John couldn't possibly be the murderer.'

'That's for a jury to decide, Superintendent, not you. Handing vital evidence to a murder suspect, however high his standing, is likely to cost you your job.'

'With respect, sir, the way this information was being held suggested it wasn't to be shared with Sir John or anyone on his team. I would say those responsible for that might need to be held to account. From my assessment of this situation what's gone on in relation to Sir John Deed is likely to end the careers of one, possibly two senior Cabinet ministers.'

'Out, get out,' Haughton shouted and the policewoman fled his office.

Paradoxically, time hung heavily yet seemed to slip away so fast he found himself glancing between his inexpensive Swatch and the electric clock on the wall, hearing the seconds go by, taking him ever nearer to his appointment. Anxiety was put on hold by a very animated Coop arriving with Sergeant Jake Bridges. At first Deed assumed his presence was the cause of her excitement; it was, but not in the way he imagined.

'Judge, Jake's got some good news.'

'Well, some physical evidence, sir,' Bridges said coming forward and putting a package on his desk. 'The recordings from the CCTV cameras in the hotel lobby and lift landings, and the one from the Shell garage.'

'They show you sitting in your car on the forecourt at the time Jessie phoned you, Judge – for over an hour afterwards! Coop bubbled with excitement and he found himself affected by it. Relief swept through him and he couldn't respond immediately.

'How on earth did you get them?' he asked finally.

'From Superintendent Hamblyn, sir. She asked why I was making enquiries about the CCTV footage,' Bridges explained. 'I wasn't sure I should tell her so I tried to avoid her questions. That seemed to do it for the Superintendent. She asked me if I could make sure these discs were put in your hands. Well, I knew I could get them to Mrs Cooper all right.

'Why didn't she come herself? I misjudged her, I need to apologize and thank her,' he said, feeling humbled.

'She was summoned to the Home Office. I got the feeling she's in trouble, sir.'

'She may well be, but shouldn't be, if these prove useful to me.' He felt more humbled watching himself at the garage when Jessie phoned him. The time on the digital clock in the corner of the recording corresponded to the time on her phone when she speculated that the visitor arriving at her bedroom door was him. The recordings from the hotel showed him leaving twenty-one minutes before her call, but more interesting was the image of a short, squat woman wearing a dense niqab with a narrow slit showing her eyes as she got out of the lift just prior to the time of Jessie's lethal visitor. The angle was such that the door to Jessie's room wasn't visible, but the time was unmistakeable. This woman must have seen whoever approached the door. A lot of Arabs stayed at this hotel, the register would show who was on that floor and would be able to identify her. There was something odd about the image and they played it again. On the third run Sergeant Bridges got it.

'That's a man,' he said, almost shouting. 'Look, the shoes he's wearing – go back, Rita. Stop,' he ordered. There it was, seen briefly under the hem of the long black garment that was being lifted by someone unused to wearing it, an expensive-looking men's brown leather shoe. Then they noticed other things, the way his eyes darted about on leaving the lift, unlike demure, fully-covered Arab women, and the walk was mannish. This person wasn't a potential witness; it was likely he was the murderer. Deed began to shake, remembering the man on the Law Courts corridor who tried to kill him. Were they the same?

Summoning Jo back to his room they viewed the CCTV footage yet again, checking and re-checking the time frame. He felt a weight lift off him when she said she would go to Holborn Police Station one minute before the appointed hour and tell them he wouldn't be attending, show them the recordings and leave them with Supt Maheson.

That cause Coop some alarm. 'Might they try to conceal them?'

'They'd have a problem now, Coop. They wouldn't dare,' Jo said. 'I think you should try and get Mr Salibi here. If he's right about his ex-boss, he might know who the man in the niqab is.'

'We should invite Supt Hamblyn as well, Coop.'

The young Lebanese man and the detective arrived within minutes of one another, and he almost suspected one was watching the other. Salibi looked at the recording only once before announcing it was almost certainly Atif Saad Al-Daran from the Saudi security staff at the embassy.

'Could he now have a limp?' Deed asked.

'Whether he does or not, sir, this is a big headache for the Home Office as he'll have diplomatic status,' Supt Hamblyn said. 'They'd have to go through the Foreign Office to approach him for an interview.'

'Are you sure that's who it is, Mr Salibi?'

'I can't be absolute, but I have seen him many times.'

'Then we won't risk him escaping a possible murder charge because of his so-called status. I'm going to issue a bench warrant for his arrest.'

'It'll cause an almighty row, John,' Jo warned.

He laughed out loud, more with relief than humour in the situation. 'After what I've been through, Jo, I'll hardly notice. If he proves to be the suspect, we won't worry. Perhaps tomorrow we can get our murder trial back. Can you alert everyone, Coop? And I want Mr Pollock here, too.'

CHAPTER THIRTY-ONE

On resuming the murder trial at Southwark Crown Court, Deed wasn't surprised to see every seat taken. He assumed the interest was the anticipated appearance of the Defence Minister with the trial itself an anti-climax as it wound to closing skirmishes, no one paying much attention to witnesses, waiting instead for him to summon James Pollock from the witness room. A further wait was in store after Coop handed him a note. Supt Hamblyn was in his room.

'An urgent matter has arisen,' he informed the court. 'I'm going to adjourn for a short while. The jury can return to the jury room for some coffee.' He rose and went out briskly, stirring further the interest of those in court.

'Atif Saad Al-Daran has fled the country, Sir John,' Supt Hamblyn told him. 'When we approached the Saudi embassy, we were told he'd returned to Riyadh. We confirmed he left Heathrow on a flight for Riyadh the morning following Jessie Rogers's death, sir.'

'Have you examined the images from the hotel landing again?' He was growing impatient to lock down the identity of the person who entered Jessie's room so he could take action if the Government proved reluctant. 'Can we get a clear enough image of the eyes of the person wearing that niqab for a positive identification?'

'We're working on it, sir. Then it's a question of how we get him back here.'

'You worry about collecting enough evidence to satisfy the CPS, Superintendent. If you do, I'll pressure the Foreign Office to demand he comes back here to face charges. I'll embarrass the Foreign Secretary and the PM, if necessary. This young woman's murder won't go unpunished,' he said and started out, but turned as questions began to assail him related to the current trial and he hesitated, fearing he was once again straying into that familiar paranoid mind-set. Too many things reached back to Pollock and he questioned if his seeing these connections wasn't more extreme prejudice on his part. 'Could this man be involved in the deaths of Mr Kozlowski and the defendant, Mariana Ortega?' He was referring to the Defence Minister, while Supt Hamblyn thought he meant Atif Saad Al-Daran.

'He'd have a very long reach, sir. With the sort of money the Saudi security service has to spend they could get almost anything done.'

'First you would need to establish motive. Why would they do this? What's their interest?'

'If Mr Salibi's information is correct, protecting the bribe money might be it. From the way they died it's reasonable to assume the same person killed all three of them. If Pollock was pulled further into this murder trial, it would also be reasonable to assume his corrupt connections with Ali bin Talib and the Saudis would come out.'

'They're only alleged corrupt connections, Superintendent,' Deed reminded her; something he mustn't forget. 'That begs the question, was there a directing mind organising these murders? What danger did they represent to someone who would want them killed?'

'And frame you along the way, Sir John.'

'Damn near succeeding!' Deed shivered at the thought of what might have resulted; then anger flooded through him. For the whole of his career he had abhorred the death penalty for capital murder, but would willingly make an exception and have it re-introduced for the guilty party who killed Jessie Rogers. He was hoping to draw Pollock further in to the murder trial so that he might get nearer to the truth, but again stopped himself as questions swirled around the politician. He saw Hamblyn wanted to say more, so gave her space.

'This is mostly speculation, sir, but we might assume the Saudis realized Pollock wasn't as powerful as he made out when he couldn't stop you pushing forward with the bribery allegations, then dragging him into the murder trial.'

'Why would Mr Salibi reveal documents to Ms Plant showing the extent of the bribery which implicated both the Crown Prince and bin Talib, as well as the Defence Secretary?' Deed wanted to know.

'We don't think it works against the Saudis; we believe Salibi changed sides. The Crown Prince's been trying to get out of an earlier deal made with the British Government for fighter planes.' Superintendent Hamblyn waited, as if unsure about going on. Deed waited too. 'From what we've picked up, sir, the new regime in Riyadh thought they were overpaying. With oil no one's favourite commodity now they wanted to renegotiate. They could cry foul and blame the previous lot – even though they're the same family. Ali bin Talib and the prince's brother-in-law, Sheik Muhammed bin Faisel, were having none of it.'

'This is speculation on your part?'

'Some of it's been patched together from information obtained through monitoring of phone and email conversations.'

'Then what was your original role in trying to obtain those papers from Mrs Mills?' he wanted to know. 'Was it to reveal a malfeasance or to assist with a Government cover-up?'

'The fact is, I don't know, sir. I'm only a cog in this particular machine.'

This gave him pause, suspecting this detective was too shrewd not to have worked things out. 'None of that explains the bombs planted at my apartment and Jo Mills' flat, or Salibi subsequently saving us.'

'We're almost certain it was instigated by Ali bin Talib for the benefit of Pollock who you were bringing near to meltdown,' Hamblyn said.

'Killing innocent people? Are you saying Salibi was part of that?'

She shrugged. 'Until recently it was in his interests you went on doing what you were doing, either ruining Pollock or dragging him in for the murder of Peter Bartlett during their sex escapade.'

'And now?' – surprise in his voice, even though he'd guessed the answer.

'He seems to be back working to Crown Prince Ayad's ground rules,' she said.

'And perfectly happy to be extradited to Saudi Arabia.'

The inter-woven layers here would require a lot of unpicking, and then he couldn't be sure they would get anywhere close to the truth. Recalling his feelings when approaching Jo's flat with Salibi he saw in his mind's eye him step straight to the right door without being told. Now he questioned his judgment for having trusted him, but there was consolation in the fact he had saved both his and Jo Mills' life, notwithstanding his possible involvement in first endangering them.

Such was the nature of politics where intrigue and deception were all-pervasive. He suspected not even a judicial enquiry would reveal who was double-crossing whom with so many vested interests colluding. How much of what Supt Hamblyn revealed was true or who he might trust to give him the facts was open to doubt and something he would have to live with.

'It would be sensible to invite Mr Salibi here for further questioning.'

The Counter Terrorism detective slowly shook her head and he knew what she was going to say. 'He's gone, sir. He gave our people the slip. We think possibly he departed soon after he identified Atif Saad Al-Daran. We're checking all passport images of males departing for the Middle East in the last forty-eight hours.'

Deed gave a hollow laugh. 'Presumably he identified Al-Daran either to deflect us from him or impress his new boss?'

He welcomed going back to the relatively straightforward task of hearing a murder trial.

'Mr Pollock,' Deed said evenly from the bench, 'thank you for returning to court and interrupting your schedule.'

'It's pretty hectic, but we're obliged to accede to the diktats of the court,' Pollock responded in a similarly even manner.

'I'm sure the ground is familiar by now, but I hope you've somehow found time to reflect on your answers about both Mr Kozlowski and Ms Ortega…'

'I already told you. How many times must I repeat myself,' Pollock said vehemently. 'I don't know either of those fucking people. Those recordings you showed in court were doctored.'

'Mr Pollock, I understand you're angry, but you will respect the court when making any reply,' he said. Better than any judge sitting he knew what being accused felt like: slipping into a deep pit with no means of stopping your descent. Despite suspecting this man lay behind what had happened to him, Deed tried not to let it affect his own responses. 'The CCTV images you refer to have been forensically examined and were found to be intact. I'm going to give you the opportunity to consult with a solicitor, should you wish to do so, before I question you further…'

'I don't need to do any such thing,' Pollock said, 'this is all political bollocking on your part.'

'Then I'm directing the police to obtain both your fingerprints and DNA samples and see if they match any of the evidence to hand…'

'You can't do, it's fucking outrageous,' Pollock said, turning to his court room audience, which was now very audible; no one came to his aid. Through the general noise Rupert Fish wasn't at first heard until Jo's strong voice cut through the babble and drew his attention to the defendant.

'I'd like to say something, sir,' Fish announced as the room fell silent.

'Is it pertinent to this trial, Mr Fish?'

'Yes, sir, something Mari told me – Mariana Ortega.'

'Then perhaps you should consult with your legal team first in case it in any way incriminates you. Mrs Mills?'

'If I could have a few minutes, my Lord?' She moved out of her place and around to the door of the glassed-in dock.

'What is this?' Pollock said. 'Am I free to leave now?'

'I'm afraid not. You may sit down for the duration.'

Pollock hesitated and looked around as if considering bolting, but seemed to think better of it and dropped onto a chair, dejected. Curiously, Deed found himself feeling sorry for this man who was trapped in a similar way to himself by sexual desires. They may have taken a different form but the root was familiar enough. He had taken a long while to recognise his own problem and even longer to identify the root: his inability to commit to one woman was the result of fear of being left as he was left by his blood parents at the age of eight. Such recognition was only the first step to resolving the problem.

When she returned to her place on the front bench Jo said, 'Mr Fish would like to make a statement to help clarify the situation regarding his involvement in this case. I've advised him of the possible consequences but he wants to make the statement anyway.' She turned and nodded to her client who stood up slowly and placed his palms against the glass of the dock.

'I remind you that you're still under oath, Mr Fish.'

First glancing down at Pollock, then directly the jury, Rupert Fish spoke in a strong voice that hadn't been heard before in court, telling how Mariana Ortega had been involved in the death of Peter Bartlett in as much as she helped Pollock dispose of the body in the wood in Surrey after Pollock had bludgeoned him with the onyx Buddha in the bedroom where they had been making love.

'This is bollocks, total bollocks,' Pollock shouted as if the stop the flow.

'Mr Pollock, you will be silent or removed from court to a custody suite. The choice is yours,' Deed told him.

'But it is,' the politician insisted.

'Then we'll hear from you after Mr Fish. For now he will continue.'

'Mari told me he was very angry about her love-making with Mr Bartlett. After the attack they wrapped him in my duvet and took him down in the service lift to the back of the building and put him in the boot of Mr Pollock's car. Later she asked me to help cover this up. I loved her and couldn't refuse. She said we'd go away together and that she could do anything now because she'd have money and Mr Pollock would do anything she asked.'

'No, no, no!' Pollock screamed, 'he's a total fucking fantasist.'

'Possibly you're right, Mr Pollock. I'm going to stop this and suspend the trial until the court has obtained your fingerprints and DNA sample. It would be sensible if the police forensically examined your ministerial car.'

There was such a rush for the door the reporters couldn't immediately get through and then it was over, bar a few details.

Soon it was confirmed that James Pollock's fingerprints were on the onyx Buddha, while matching DNA was found in the wardrobe with the two-way mirror and on the suit Rudi Kozlowski had worn to court. Pollock became the prime suspect in the killing of Peter Bartlett – possibly in a fit of jealous rage, but that was for a jury. Deed could understand the emotions that caused someone to lose control and might have reflected it in any sentence were the case to have come before him, which it couldn't in the circumstances. He instructed the CPS to drop the murder charge against Rupert Fish and Jo persuaded her client to plead guilty to perverting the course of justice, whereby he deferred sentencing until after reports. He didn't anticipate giving Fish a custodial sentence, or if there was one, it would be time already served. Depending on the reports, perhaps the young man would make a life for himself now without the obsessive influence of Ms Ortega. With obsession came pathology, whether through sex or any other object of excessive desire. Sometimes it was better to deny oneself, but at times that was almost impossible, even though it often let in disaster. Deed realised he couldn't help himself any more than the heroin addict could and that depressed him.

EPILOGUE

THE STREAM OF VISITORS TO his room at the Strand seemed endless, mostly judges saying what a splendid job he'd done in exposing the Defence Minister. Some thought it the tip of the iceberg, suggesting the whole of Government needed examining for just such practices now that James Pollock had been charged and was held without bail. All expressed faith in the judicial system and said they hadn't for a moment believed the rumours flying around about his involvement in the death of Jessie Rogers. How nice it might have been to have found such support in his darkest hour.

Joe Channing had difficulty meeting his eye when he came to see him and shifted about like a man much in need of a cigarette. 'I owe you an apology, John,' he said finally, lifting his gaze. 'I'll have to take a more sceptical view of so-called police evidence in future. Perhaps I should resign. I must be losing my marbles in ever thinking for a moment you could be culpable.'

'I should apologise to you, Joe, and Tom Witham. Salibi slipped away from the security people who were watching him and fled the country.'

'Yes, Rochester told me – rather too gleefully, I thought. Perhaps he imagines that absolves him of any blame for the tawdry behaviour of the Justice Department throughout. The irony is that both Tom and I came to the conclusion that we should allow his appeal against extradition.'

Deed laughed. 'Perhaps we should contrive the means of letting him know – he might even decide to return. Meanwhile, I suppose we'd better rule on that case and return Ms Plant's property to her.'

'I'm not sure the Government would appreciate our doing so, John. Tom Witham is against returning the papers.'

'She wasn't in touch with terrorist factions, Joe.'

'Perhaps we should give the Government agencies a little leeway here.'

'If we do, they'll drive a tank through the gap,' Deed argued.

'You're right, of course. The courts can't do the Government's bidding, no matter how convenient it might be. Let's go and advise Tom.'

Once more Deed felt proud to be associated with this judge, even though he knew neither of them would get to that promised land of the Supreme Court. 'Perhaps we could persuade him to join us in pressing the Justice Department for a judicial enquiry into the workings of the Defence Department over the allegations of bribery,' Deed suggested as they went down the stone steps to Tom Witham's dungeon-like basement room.

'I can't, I'm afraid, John,' was Witham's casual response, 'I've got a date.'

At once Deed suspected it was with Jo Mills and felt an aching sense of loss, as if the centre of him opened up to nothingness. Could he make a life for himself without her influence? He didn't know, and wasn't sure he wanted to try, and thought about racing his younger rival to her side. That old jest rose again in his throat: irrational jealousy.

When Deed tried to slip out of the rear entrance of the High Court to find a taxi, making a point of taking Ms Plant's property to Jo's chambers to give it to her in person, journalists were waiting for him on the pavement, their questions raining down on him with the stinging force of hail about how involved James Pollock was in the murder. Most he ignored but one jumped out at him. Did he feel any responsibility over the death of the Oxfam worker, Anita Plant? He stopped and pressed in on the questioner. 'How is she dead?' He hadn't heard anything. 'She can't be dead.' At once he realised it was a naïve question.

'The news just broke. She was found hanging in her flat by her sister,' the reporter told him.

The information hit Deed like blow from a hammer, knocking the air out of him; his mind reeled. There was no answer to satisfy them or him as he made his way into the taxi, pursued by photographers. Was he culpable? The question haunted him and he suspected the reason for her death might have been connected to the MP who was in Belmarsh Prison on remand – if true his reach remained dangerously long. Deed remained strangely affected by this woman's death even though he barely knew her. He should have insisted she went into police protection and promised himself there would be nothing left out of the investigation into her death. He would make such trouble for the Home Office if the result wasn't to his satisfaction.

A young clerk at Jo's chambers in King's Cross with no idea who he was told him Jo was in conference with a client and didn't know how long they would be. Without further comment Deed said he'd wait, looking round the dowdy basement reception area. He still found it strange that Jo chose to place herself in such circumstances, but knew the quality of law practised here had nothing to do with the surroundings. Some lawyers with the smart W1 or EC4 addresses offered less than good advice that was too often related to billable hours.

'Sir John,' a young barrister said in surprise as he came through. 'Does Jo know you're here?'

'She's in a con. I didn't want to interrupt.'

'I'll put my head around the door and tell her,' he said and disappeared.

Ten minutes later several people came from a room along the narrow corridor connecting the adjacent basement, some with the familiar look of criminal solicitors. Someone said he was to go through. He found Jo at her small desk making notes.

'I'm devastated about Anita's death – murder, of course,' she managed to say before she started to sob; then wailed and began beating him hard on the chest until he caught hold of her and held her close, neither speaking for a long, long while. At last she sniffed and glanced up at him. 'Are we safe now, John?' she asked with a slight tremor in her voice.

He thought about that for a while, wanting badly to reassure her, but couldn't so deflected the question. 'Are we ever safe in what we do, Jo – from half-crazed clients, vindictive businessmen, treacherous apparatchiks of State?'

'It had to somehow be the work of that wretched Cabinet minister,' Jo said.

'Ex-Cabinet minister,' Deed pointed out. 'If it proves to be the case, I will endeavour to make sure he stays in prison for the rest of his life.' He doubted he could achieve that and Jo probably knew it. 'The job doesn't get any easier.'

'You sound as though you need a holiday.' She turned away and reached for a tissue and blew her nose, before putting the file she was working on in a steel cupboard and locking it.

'A holiday, yes, but I don't want to go away on my own,' Deed said.

'You can't think of anyone to ask? You surprise me.'

'I'm not sure the person I want to go with will go with me,' he replied.

'Have you tried asking her? I assume it is her, and not a trip to Thailand?'

Without responding, he looked at her and she looked back, and then they were in each other's arms where he wanted to be and kissing like it meant something to both of them. 'I think we're safe for a little while, Jo.'

Later, in bed with her, his hand cupped over her familiar breast, she asked what was troubling him. Why he couldn't sleep as it was gone 2 o'clock. 'I ought to be able to, Jo, having earlier made love to the woman I love.'

'Twice,' she reminded him.

'I had the opportunity of a seat on the Supreme Court bench. I wonder now why I pushed so hard to expose what was going on, to what effect.'

'All you had to do was keep your mouth shut, and your eyes closed, and maybe abandon your conscience,' Jo told him, craning around to give him a challenging look.

'It was pure delusion, of course.' Deed sighed. 'But for a moment I was thinking I could help change the way our sleazebag politicians work the system for their own benefit and that of their friends.'

'I wouldn't worry about it. You're doing more than most people.'

'When I negotiated that move with Haughton and he so readily agreed to it I realised just how grubby his world is. Nothing's likely to change there.'

'It was what you wanted, John. It's what all Judges want.'

'It's what Haughton and his cronies like to think we want. That's the power they have over the bench. They will come after us.'

'Not with a bomb wired to the TV,' Jo said.

'That still nags at me – why Salibi ducked out like he did.'

'What will you do about it now?'

'Go on asking questions; not get elevated to the Appellate Bench; marry the woman I love; make love to her again. Not necessarily in that order.'

'Will this woman marry you?' Jo said.

'That's my fervent hope. I could even kneel and ask her.'

'Perhaps after you've made love to her again,' she said.

'I have so missed you,' Deed said and kissed her hard on the mouth.